THE SILVER FLAME

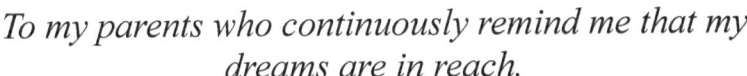

To my parents who continuously remind me that my dreams are in reach.

To anyone who thinks they do not belong, let this book inspire you to find where you do.

There exists a place for every person.

THE SILVER FLAME

Book One in the Argentum Series

Paige Nicole

CHAPTER ONE

THE SNOW NEVER FELL in flakes here.

It came in thick, heavy veils. Endless clouds blurred the world into soft gray shapes until nothing felt real. Not the jagged cliffs of The Ridge beneath my boots. Not the aching cold seeping through layers of fur and wool. Not even me.

I walked alone, as I always did. The Ridge was where ancient glaciers had once met and clashed, their frozen bodies splintering into jagged walls of ice and snow that now loomed around me like sleeping beasts. Wind howled through them, whistling mournful songs I sometimes imagined only I could hear. As if they were singing just for me.

My breath misted in the air, curling like smoke from a dying fire. I buried my gloved hands deeper into my cloak pockets, fingers already numb. The braid I'd woven into my hair that morning had unraveled in the wind. White strands now whipped across my cheeks, stinging like they were angry at me for believing I could tame them.

Behind me, the village glowed faintly. Tiny flickers of candlelight in a sea of snow, barely visible from here. Home, if it could be called that. Greyhold was the capital of Virellia, yet you would never be able to tell. The cobblestone cottages spread vastly, but there were no towers or castles here. There were no riches or jewels or gold.

Ahead, the silver-frosted hills stretched forever, still and quiet. They shimmered faintly under the weight of snow and moonlight, from the frost that had gathered the night before. Beyond them lay the Vedan River. If I followed that river far enough, I could reach all seven regions of the kingdom. I'd memorized their names. Mirun, Hestel, Delva, Calem, Seren... and Aurea. The golden heart. The capital of the entire kingdom of Valerieth.

Where the King lived. Where the palace shimmered like the ending of a fairy tale. Beautiful, golden, and built to make you forget. Where warmth wrapped the marble halls like silk, and yet, where Virellia was nothing but a shadow, left to rot at the edge of history.

I'd imagined it so many times that I could have drawn it from memory. Endless gardens, green and flowering even in winter. Golden towers that caught the sunlight. Courtyards filled with music and laughter. Maybe even animals, or people, that weren't half-starved. A place where I could wear silk instead of wool, where I could feel my toes without needing tripled-layered socks. Where no one would whisper when I walked by.

I glanced down at my hands. The gloves were the same ones I'd worn for years. I rubbed at the soft leather, stitched tight at the wrists. I couldn't remember the last time I'd taken them off outside of bathing or sleeping, or maybe I'd just stopped counting.

They called me *witch-born* when they thought I wasn't listening, and sometimes even when they knew I was.

When I walked into the apothecary beside my father, the whispers followed like ghosts. I was used to it by now, the alienation. The glances, and the way people stepped aside just slightly, just enough to say, *"Don't touch me."* The children who flinched when I passed, held back by mothers hissing warnings. I wondered what they told them. That I'd hex them with a glance. That my skin carried curses.

It was utterly ridiculous, and yet, I wondered if they were right. Because the truth was, I'd never touched anyone. Not really. Not skin to skin.

My father, *Master Healer* Dalen Seravell as Greyhold knew him, made sure it stayed that way. He was a man of precision, discipline, and distance. His hands were always clean. His words careful, controlled. I had never once seen him angry, but I'd never seen him laugh either. The man was comparable to a stone sculpted statue.

The gloves had been his idea. *"To keep the medicines sterile and safe,"* he always said. *"To keep distance. For your sake and theirs."*

All this said and yet, I had never treated a patient. I'd only watched and attempted to learn. I ground herbs into powder, stirred poultices, arranged bottles in neat rows. It wasn't training though, not really, not without the actual treatment part.

I wondered if he was trying to make me a healer at all or trying to make me invisible.

After eighteen years, I thought I knew the answer.

I sighed and turned back towards Greyhold. The snow had piled high around every home, leaving only the narrow doorways clear. The square was empty. No one lingered long outside in the freeze, especially not after dusk. The only people who remained were the royal guards who had appeared a few weeks ago. They wore armor coated in glinting polished gold, but I could tell it did little to fend off the cold. Their chattering teeth echoed in the square if the evening air was still enough to hear it.

I had asked my father why they had come, and more importantly, why they had stayed. He always answered with the same lone word.

Protection.

I wasn't so naive.

Hunger was a powerful thing. Famines had attacked the southern regions for nearly a decade, and it didn't take long after the first year of scarcity for the trade routes that brought crops and grain to run dry. There's no soil in Virellia. No way to grow our own wheat or corn. Part of me considered the possibility that the south was purposefully starving us out. Part of me hated that I believed I could be right.

I tried to assume the King was a right and just man, and that the Prince followed obediently in his father's footsteps, but even I could not force that lie upon myself.

The bloodline that ruled over this kingdom was anything but selfless. Prince Cassian was reared in a palace built upon avarice and conceit. The Vaelros family cared about one thing and one thing only.

Power.

In Aurea, power came from golden reputations and wealth. Here, power came from warm fires and food.

Our cottage was small, built from thick gray stone, and colder inside than out on some nights. Flickering firelight spilled from the hearth and the scent of dried juniper curled in the air as I pulled the door open. Lounging fireside was my one and only friend, Selene.

She was sprawled across the wool rug, her auburn red hair spilling in tight coils around her like a halo. She held a book open and dangling above her head, her laugh sharp and bright as she read its pages.

Selene was the only one who treated me like I was whole. I threw the door closed and flopped down beside her. Holding in my laughter, I tossed my disheveled braid over her face.

"Your hair is a disaster," she teased without breaking eye contact with whatever book held her attention. Some old fairy tales it seemed. She tugged at the loose braid, and I squealed in response, pushing myself up onto my elbows before I quipped back at her.

"Want me to stitch you a gown of thorns to match your personality?"

I snatched the book from her hands and held it out of her reach. She threw me a mockingly dirty look before grabbing at my hostage.

I pulled back before she could reach for my gloves, the reaction automatic. She flicked her eyes to me, in question. I set the book down gently beside her, closing the moment and praying she let it end. My hands vanished behind me, safe again. She rolled her eyes but didn't say a word. Relief flooded me. This is why I loved Selene.

One day, maybe I wouldn't flinch. Maybe I wouldn't feel like something broken and harmful, but until then, at least Selene could handle a little danger.

She stood and turned toward the mirror just right of the hearth, beginning to braid her own hair. "Come to the winter festival this year," she said, securing the end of the plait in a faded pink ribbon. Her voice was light, but I heard the plea beneath it. "Don't hide like last time. I'll even dance with you."

Her reflection in the mirror met my eyes, her smile small and hopeful.

I wanted to say yes. My stars, I wanted to say yes.

There was nothing more that I wanted than to be seen and to dance. To belong, even just for a moment, but I could already hear my father's voice in my head, a cold and final thing.

"Selene, you know my father would never allow it."

She started to argue, of course. She always did. Something about asking him, about this year being different, but I ignored her, moving my eyes to the flames that swirled in the stone fireplace. I watched as the orange and yellows rose and broke off, dying out towards the top. I reached my hand out to feel its warmth as a book hit the wall above the fire and came clattering down. I whipped around to Selene who faced me, hands planted on her hips.

"Hello, I'm talking here." She waved her hands wilding in the air. "Lyra, you aren't even listening."

I sat with my mouth hung open as I glanced between her and the book. Selene huffed a breath and dropped down onto the rug, grabbing the book and placing it in her lap.

"I just hate telling you all the stories about it the next day when you could have been with me."

My eyes were glued to the floor as I ground specks of ash into the rug. I drug my face up to hers as she cocked her head at me, her mouth contorting into the widest, fakest smile I had ever seen. I sighed as I tried to keep my voice steady.

"You're pleading with the wrong person."

Her smile faded into something softer. Sadder. "Just ask. For me, okay?"

All I could do was nod my head, eyes falling back to the ash speckled floor. Selene sat with me for a moment, neither of us talking.

Eventually, she grabbed her cloak and headed for the door. "My mother's waiting for me. Supper and all." Her words came quickly, like she was trying to leave before I could say something that might hurt more.

The door shut behind her as the goodbye left my lips.

I closed my eyes and let my head hang back. I hated being put into that position, and Selene knew that. She knew I wasn't able to go, so she shouldn't have even bothered asking.

I sat up and ran angry hands down my braid. I pulled at the leather string bounding the end of my hair as I raked fingers through the plait, effectively destroying it. I stood and moved to look out the thick glass window. The storm outside had grown wilder. Wind screamed through the eaves, rattling the shutters like it wanted in.

The back door creaked open, and in the window's glare I saw my father return home carrying his brown leather satchel. He emptied its contents, his hands careful and sure as he set the vials and jars onto the kitchen table. White leather gloves were clasped tight. They were clean, sterile, and free from any stains or specks of dirt. He made sure to keep his gloves perfect, so if any medicine got on the leather, he would be able to identify it based on the color. It was a rite of passage for healers. To receive their white gloves. I wondered if I would ever receive a pair, or if brown was a color I would become overly familiar with.

Through the window's reflection I could see the various colors of different powders and liquids and sludges, each substance carrying medicinal purposes of their own. My father's image shifted in the glass as he stirred something thick and dark in a clay pot, a sleeping draught probably. He hadn't spoken a word. He rarely did when we were alone.

My focus returned to the storm surging outside. I watched the snow spiral down and asked, before I could stop myself, "Do you ever wish I was normal?"

I looked back, truly turning this time to face him. There was a pause.

Then, without looking up, he said, "You are what the stars made you. That is enough. Put out the fire before bed."

I waited for something more, something human, but those were the only words to leave his mouth. He returned to his vials as if the question was never asked.

So, I did what I was told. I grabbed the pail and doused the fire but hesitated with a bit of water still slouching in the metal. I watched as the flames vanished in a hiss. The ashes still glowed faintly, curling gray smoke into the air like ghosts, but one stubborn ember flickered in the center, clinging to life. Its yellow and white glow flickered, as if deciding whether to die out, or fight back.

For a heartbeat, I didn't move. I wanted to leave it there. Let it burn. Let it know someone saw it, but it was just a fire.

I tipped the rest of the water over it, and the ember died with a final, desperate sizzle.

I trudged up the narrow stairs, the chill of winter settling deeper into my bones. My father's rhythmic movements echoing from the kitchen. I trailed a gloved hand along the cold stone wall, the same way I had since I was little, tapping each block that passed under my fingers.

Then I passed her.

The only picture in the house. A painting, no larger than a square foot, hung crookedly on the wall. The wooden frame had been warped by time and cold, the carved initials cracked and worn.

T.S.

I ran my fingers across the letters. She stared down at me with *my* face. White hair, silver eyes, and snow-like skin.

The town called her a curse, the stars' only mistake. My father called her my mother.

He never spoke of her directly, only that she was "*beautiful*" and "*brave*" and that "*she died in childbirth.*" He kept the painting up like a monument, like it made me something other than what I was, or at least explained it.

It did neither.

I'd always told myself it was a lie. I convinced myself that she was a myth he invented so I wouldn't feel like a burden, but the longer I stared into that painted reflection, the harder it was to believe it was just fiction. The woman in the portrait wasn't a goddess. She wasn't someone fantastical. She was someone like me, and maybe that was the cruelest part of all.

I continued walking, running my hand along the last of the stones before I reached my bedroom door. I turned the metal handle, the cold biting into my palm. It closed softly behind me. The light from my father working below poured in where the door didn't quite meet its frame. I ripped my hands free from their leather prison and laid the gloves on my small nightstand. I shed my boots, furs, coats. I undressed all the way down to my beige tunic and pants before letting gravity pull me down into bed.

The furs smelled of smoke and moss, but I didn't care. I rolled my body up in their soft warmth and stared out at the storm.

CHAPTER TWO

THE WIND THAT HAD battered Virellia through the night had vanished without a trace, leaving behind a blue so deep I wondered if the open ocean reflected the same. The sky shone crisp and cloudless, stretching endlessly across the pale horizon.

I threw the thick furs off my cot and swung my legs down, toes brushing the cold wooden floor. My gloves waited for me on the nightstand. I snatched them up and bolted from my room, barely noticing the bite of the floor underfoot. The sky was calling.

The door groaned as I yanked it open, and the air hit me like ice water. I gasped, lungs burning, eyes wide. The snow hadn't really deepened, just danced through the night and rearranged itself, sparkling now beneath the first light of dawn. The sun had only just begun its rise, scattering streaks of orange and rose across the drifts. I liked to imagine them as flowers. The splays of colors as rows and rows of petals blooming across a frozen field. Virellia never thawed, never truly softened, but sometimes it pretended to.

The streets below were already stirring. People moved quickly, bundled and brisk, but they weren't going about their usual routes. Everyone seemed to be headed the same direction. Confused, I leaned out, scanning the motion, until the sound came.

A horn. Deep. Clear. Royal.

My heart plummeted.

I tugged my gloves on with numb fingers, and I pushed my bare feet into my boots. I rushed down the narrow back stairwell, out into the snow-packed alley. I wasn't dressed for this at all. I had no coat, no layers. Nothing but the tunic and pants I'd slept in and boots without socks. My breath fogged the air in ragged clouds as I pushed toward the town square.

By the time I reached it, the cold had burrowed into the marrow of my bones. My teeth chattered, my fingers went stiff, and my legs ached like they'd been carved from ice. The stone buildings around the square echoed with whispers and footsteps, a hollow kind of cheer.

"Stars, Lyra—"

Selene found me instantly, yawning but still somehow glowing even with sleep still clinging to her like a fog. She wrapped an arm holding a blanket around me before I could even blink, her furs thick and warm and smelling faintly of lavender oil.

"You look whiter than normal," she said, tugging me closer. "You're practically ice."

I hesitated, but eventually leaned in, accepting the heat of her body and the comfort of her presence. Cloth divided us, yet the weight of my gloved hands sat heavy against my chest. The wind cut through the crowd like a blade, but it wasn't the cold that made me shiver. Something in the air thrummed, sharp and anticipatory. A tension I couldn't name.

Then, the horn blared again.

The sound was swallowed quickly by cheers. All around us, people clapped and chattered and reached onto their tiptoes for a greater view. I followed Selene as she weaved through the masses, laughing like this was nothing more than a spring fair.

Duke Viremont, her father, stood to the side of a royal servant who had taken the stage. The platform itself looked pitiful. The wood was splintered and sagging, barely standing against the frost. But the man atop it gleamed in gold and violet, a stark smear of wealth against the dull gray square.

"Ladies and gentlemen of Virellia," the servant boomed, voice cutting through the noise like thunder. "By command of Prince Cassian Vaelros, heir to King Malik Vaelros and crown of Aurea, I hereby decree that each region shall present a representative daughter to participate in the Prince's marriage selection. A bride must be chosen..."

His voice faded, words lost beneath the sudden rush of blood in my ears.

Beside me, Selene squealed with delight, her smile so wide it would normally be infectious, but there was no joy in the one I forced in return. Girls around me gasped, screamed, clung to each other like lovers reunited. One fainted outright, and someone caught her just in time.

Others broke out in fits of rage. Parents held back their daughters, and one older gentleman in particular was screaming, spit flying, mere inches away from a golden-suited guard.

Everyone seemed to understand what this decree meant, except for the girls who were about to thrust into its declaration.

The Prince didn't want a bride, he wanted unity. He wanted to pretend like the northern regions mattered, pretend like Virellia mattered, all while turning a blind eye to the starving citizens he supposedly cared for.

This wasn't romance. This was politics. This was control, and I despised every part of it. The clapping rang in my ears, but my heart sank lower with every beat.

Selene glanced at me, her smile faltering just a bit at the far-off stare I undoubtedly had plastered on. The furs slipped from my arms. Maybe I dropped them. Maybe they dropped me.

Then —

A rough tug yanked down on my sleeve.

I barely turned before laughter broke against me. A group of boys, local ones, chuckled as mischievous smirks grew on their faces. I recognized them even if I didn't know their names. Cold wind found my shoulder and bit at my skin. I looked down to see thread and fabric moving with the breeze. One of them had ripped my tunic.

"Nice clothes, witch!" one spat as he walked backward into the crowd. The others howled with laughter, like it was the cleverest thing anyone had ever said.

I stumbled back, breath stolen. My bare skin prickled. The chill should have been unbearable, but it wasn't the cold that made my vision blur. It was the heat of humiliation. I was too scared to look up. I imagined myself turning, looking around, and only getting judging stares in return. Shame crawled up my throat. I squeezed my eyes shut as if I could forget the moment. As if I could will the memory to be erased.

No one noticed. No one cared. Everyone was too busy either dreaming of gold and glory, or dreading it, but that fact didn't stop my mind from spiraling. This village had enough to talk about when it came to me.

Selene stepped between me and the crowd the boys had vanished in. Her voice rang, sharp as sleet. "Say that again and I'll have my father send you to shovel sewer frost!"

The boys scattered further in the crowd, laughter still ringing over the mingling voices, but my body refused to stop shaking. I wrapped my arms around myself, trying to hold everything in.

"Let's go, Lyra," Selene said, tugging me gently, but I couldn't stop glancing around. My thoughts swirled as I wondered if they'd come back. Wondering if anyone had seen.

As we moved away, her fingers reached for my sleeve. A casual thing, meant to be nothing.

"They didn't even tear it at the seam, how rude—"

The moment her skin touched mine, it happened.

A flicker. A shimmer. A breath of light. Warmth that wasn't just heat. It *hummed*, like a note struck beneath the skin. My heart stopped. My skin seemed electric, burning yet glacial. Energy sprinted through my veins, my bones, my being, and connected with Selene.

She froze. A solid figure, yet not from the frigid air. Her eyes, for just a moment, weren't green. They were silver.

She pulled her hand back like she'd touched fire, fingers pressing to her temple. She glanced around, as if to gain her bearings back. The color in her eyes gradually returned, as if whatever had been taken was returned just as quick.

I moved my head towards hers, trying to find her gaze as they seemed to scan the mob.

"What is everyone doing in the square?" she murmured. Her brows furrowed, confusion etched into her features, but something was missing behind it, like the memory of the past few minutes had been scooped clean out of her.

She turned back to me, and her eyes went wide all over again when she noticed what I was wearing. Her gaze was focused on my torn sleeve, her hand reaching out towards me.

"Stars, Lyra! You're going to freeze to death! And you need a new tunic, Lyra. This one is ripped, and not even on the seam."

She tried to pull the furs around me, but I backed away.

"Selene," I whispered. "What—"

Her eyes landed on the man still atop the stage.

"What is a royal messenger doing here?"

I didn't move. My hands hovered at my sides, gloved fingers brushing the edge of the torn fabric. It still burned where the cold had touched me.

Where she had touched me.

"Selene, there's going to be a marriage selection. For Prince Cassian."

She shrieked with joy just as she had moments ago, elated all over again at the prospect of traveling to Aurea. She smiled then, bright and easy like none of it had happened. Like she hadn't forgotten, because she never knew.

What was happening?

The meeting ended not long after. The Duke called out his closing words, riling the crowd with promises of splendor and royal favor. Selene flitted away to find her father, giddy with possibility.

She told me she wanted to ask how Virellia would choose its representative. I already knew what she hoped the answer would be. She would be perfect. Bold, beautiful, someone people would love and someone the royal court would want.

I lingered behind, in the shadows cast by snow and stone. I stood watching as the families finally left to go home, holding their daughters tighter than normal. I listened as they shuffled past, whispering both promises of a crown, and promises of safety.

Selene stood beside her father, laughing with some other girls, the morning sun catching in her hair. She didn't remember, but I did.

With every breath, something in me stirred, slow and sharp and burning at the edges, something that hadn't been there before. Or maybe it had.

Maybe it had just been waiting.

CHAPTER THREE

SELENE SHOWED UP AT my door mere hours later.

The sun had just slipped past its highest point, and I opened the front door to her cheeks flushed with cold and excitement, a thick wool scarf wrapped like a halo around her red curls.

"Come on," she said, eyes sparkling. "We're going to the seamstress. Tomorrow my father is selecting the representative for Virellia, and I refuse to look anything less than stunning, even if I'm not the one chosen."

I hesitated in the doorway, then bundled up in my thickest cloak and gloves. I peered through the window at Selene, and somehow felt underdressed next to her, even if style was not necessarily a priority in Virellia.

I always did think Selene looked like she'd been born for a different world. One where people were made of sunlight and celebration.

We walked through the streets of Greyhold together, boots crunching across packed snow, skirts lifted from the slush. The air was crisp, biting at the skin of my cheeks, but Selene didn't seem to notice. She waved at nearly everyone we passed. Merchants called her name. Children darted out from behind market stalls to greet her. One elderly woman clasped Selene's hands in hers and said, "You'll be a vision, my dear. A real Aurean rose."

Selene laughed, a soft, bubbly sound that made the whole street seem brighter.

When they looked at me, their smiles faltered. No one dared to be hostile with Selene at my side. They weren't rude. Just tight, uncertain. Eyes dropped quickly. A few stepped aside as we passed, muttering half-greetings that caught in their throats.

I pulled my gloves tighter and kept my head low, suddenly too aware of every layer I wore.

I didn't belong here, and they knew it. I could feel it in the way their gazes slid off me like I was something dangerous, or fragile, or both.

Selene didn't seem to notice. She was already tugging me toward the seamstresses' shops, chattering about silks and satin, lace and lining.

"They're doing it by draw, you know? Every eligible girl gets their name on a slip of parchment. My father said it'll be totally random. Can you imagine? A real chance."

I could imagine. I imagined my name pulled, slow and deliberate. The crowd going silent. Selene clapping, beaming. The others staring.

I imagined Virellia watching me walk to the front and feeling the chill of one hundred unspoken thoughts.

"I'm thinking pale green," she said as we entered the one and only seamstress in town, shaking snow from her cloak. "Maybe with a sheer sleeve. Elegant, right? And I want my hair up, something regal. With the little jeweled combs my mother gave me. And I'm using the rouge this time. Not too much, just enough to make my cheeks look kissed."

The shop was warm, filled with the scent of wool and dried lavender. Dresses hung like phantoms across the walls, soft and shimmering. Fabrics in all sorts of colors adorned the space, but I couldn't look away from all the pale blues, the icy grays, and the glints of frost-colored embroidery. One in particular caught my eye, tucked in the far corner. Deep navy blue, bordering black, with silver thread woven through the hem like starlight on water.

The cool tones were a part of the northern regions, woven into our cultures and customs. Virellia had always been paired with white, for its snow, but the other northern regions wore an abundance of blues and grays. I seemed to float over to the gown without even noticing. My hand grazed down the front of the dress, watching as the silver thread caught different bits of light with every sway. It looked like the night sky. The people of Mirun likely spun this fabric. I turned, building up the courage to possibly ask to try it on, but the seamstress didn't even look at me.

She swooped toward Selene instead, all smiles and compliments, already rifling through bolts of fabric to find something that would match her *radiant energy*.

Selene turned back to me, arms full of fabric, her smile wide. "You should try some fabric colors too. We both are fair toned, but you're definitely more blue undertones, and I'm more rosy."

I didn't have the heart to tell her I hadn't even thought about dress shopping or color palettes or how the idea of being chosen in any gown filled me with a kind of crawling dread I couldn't name.

Still, I nodded and turned back to the dress hanging in front of me. I let out a breath as I passed by the navy gown and wandered through the rows, letting my gloved fingers brush velvet and silk, trying to feel like one of the girls who giggled in the dressing rooms.

Selene exited, revealing a beautiful pale pink gown that flowed down body as she was the muse it was draped upon. The sleeves draped long past her wrists, making her seem like the human embodiment of a springtime flower.

She kept talking, to herself or me I couldn't tell, her voice singing like birdsong.

I walked over to the small pedestal Selene stood on as she spun the fabric bunched in her hands. In the mirror, I caught my own reflection. Ghastly skin, shadowed eyes, too-sharp collarbones. The glove on my left hand had slipped slightly, revealing a glimpse of the pale skin beneath. I yanked it back into place.

Selene caught my eyes in the mirror. She jumped off the small, raised circle and marched over to a dress hanging on the near wall.

"You'd be stunning in this," she said, holding up the gown of royal blue chiffon. "The color would bring out your eyes." The dress was gorgeous. Every inch was covered in delicate beading. Pearls cascaded down in rivers of white, with small blue gems following their path. It was beautiful. It was regal. It was something I could never imagine even wanting to try on.

I tried to smile. "I don't think it's really… me."

She grinned. "That's the point. Maybe it should be."

There was so much hope in her voice it hurt. I wanted to tell her that I hoped she was chosen, that she deserved the gowns and the crown and every petal of adoration this kingdom had to offer. I wanted to tell her that I didn't know what would happen if I went to

Aurea, but only that something inside me whispered it wouldn't end well.

But I said none of it.

I let her pick two dresses for me and stood in the back of the shop while the seamstress half-heartedly measured my shoulders over my clothes. I let Selene twirl in front of the mirrors, radiant in every color she touched. I listened as she imagined her name being drawn, her future opening up like a flower in bloom. I played along as she acted it out every single time, and I tried not to think about how the moment she touched my skin in the square, she forgot everything.

How everyone seemed to forget or pretend. How maybe, even if my name wasn't drawn, something else had already been set in motion.

My head snapped back to the mirror in front of me as Selene let out a gasp of delight. She had chosen a gown the color of soft lilacs in spring, with sheer sleeves and pearl embroidery like morning dew frozen in lace. She looked every bit the princess Virellia saw her as. No, more than that. A queen if the world would let her.

The navy blue dress had been too intimidating to even try.

I picked something quieter. A simple dress in the color of the Ridge's ice pale blue with a white underskirt that peeked out like frost when I walked. The fabric shimmered just slightly when the light caught it, but there were no pearls sewn into the bodice, no crystals at the waist. No jewels or gemstones.

And yet I looked like a child playing dress-up beside her.

Selene grabbed my gloved hand as we stepped out of the shop, twirling me in the snow-dusted street. Our other hands each held our dresses. The bundles of fabric were wrapped in brown paper and tied with a bow of twine.

"You looked beautiful," she said, sincere. "Like winter came alive."

I gave her a crooked smile. "Then you must be summer."

A sharp cry cut through the dusty air, and I turned just in time to see a scuffle break out near the edge of the square.

Two men grappled over a sack of grain, their arms thin, their faces hollow. Desperation was carved into each line of their bodies, into each visible rib that pressed through the layers they wore. A young girl shrieked nearby, trying to tug the older and bigger of the two men back. She had to be younger than ten. The man shoved the other to the ground and bolted. With one arm, he clutched the sack of grain tight against his chest like treasure. In the other, he held the girl.

He didn't make it far.

The royal guard who stood in the square like always surged forward from the edge of the market, metal gleaming in the evening light. His armor was pristine, unscathed, and his body was untouched by the pains of hunger.

He stalked forward, hand on the hilt of the sword that didn't own a single scratch. It didn't seem like he had ever used it. Not once.

The man hugged the grain tighter, pulling what must be his daughter behind him as she sobbed. His own eyes flew open so wide I could see the whites from where I stood.

"No, please! My family...my little girl hasn't eaten in three days and—" the man gasped, still clutching the grain.

The guard didn't hesitate.

Steel flashed.

The man crumpled to the ground with a gurgled cry, the sack splitting open and revealing a river of red. The guard pulled his sword back and held a small towel in his hands. He ran the blade along the towel, paying no mind to the man whose blood had dirtied it.

Grain spilled into the snow, dark and scattered like seeds of violence. The little girl screamed, dropping down to her father's side. She tried to pull the grain off of his body, but it was no use. The sack seemed to weight more than her.

She dug through the slash and pressed her hands against her father's wound, but her hands were too small to stop the blood that soaked the earth. Her panicked breaths were warm clouds in the frigid air.

Everything froze. The air itself seemed to recoil. Around us, people turned away. Not out of indifference, but helplessness. Hunger was a dangerous thing, but power, power was much worse.

The guard finished cleaning his blade and tossed the cloth to the side, walking back to his post without a word.

I didn't even realize I was holding my breath until a hand landed between my shoulder blades. Steam curled from my nostrils at the impact. I turned to see Selene's father, his hands resting on me and Selene, but his eyes were on the scene before us. I began to look back at the man who I knew would never get up again, but the Duke held my body towards him and simply shook his head. Tears rolled down Selene's face, and she quickly wiped them off as they came, but she couldn't bury the sobs that escaped her. I wanted to cry, not out of sadness, but anger.

The tears just never fell.

"Why did he do that? Why are those men even here, Father?" Selene's questions had no answers. I could tell by the way Duke

Viremont's face turned into one that resembled guilt. Yes, he was a Duke, but that's no match for a King, or any royal for that matter.

"Let's get you two somewhere warm. Your mother will want to see the dress you chose dear." His eyes flicked to me with sadness flooding his face. "And Lyra's of course." His swallow seemed thick in his throat.

Viremont's hand pressed against my back, and we began towards his home, Selene's home, but I couldn't push the man from my mind. He wasn't the only man killed for wanting to survive, yet no one would ever know in two hours time. The guards would likely come and drag the girl away from her father. He wouldn't get a funeral or a service. He would get thrown into a fire, burned, and forgotten. The blood would be covered by snow when another windy day comes, and no one would remember the man who was killed for a sack of grain.

But I would.

We arrived at her home just as the sky began to blush into dusk, pale pink streaking across the cold horizon. Virellian guards opened the metal gate in front of the two wooden doors of the Duke's mansion. The rusted hinges rang in the still air. The wood of the front doors was long worn, weathered down on the outside from the constant snow and ice, but as the set swung open, ornate carvings swirled on the inner panels. Pictures of snowflakes and trees, curling air and clouds. A sweeping staircase curled down both walls of the main chamber, wrapping upwards towards the bedrooms and tearoom. The downstairs consisted of the sitting room, Duke Viremont's office, and the delightful smelling kitchen. Selene and I made our way up to her bedroom, where we hurriedly tried on our dresses. I carefully unwrapped the brown paper, careful to not rip the parchment while Selene torn it clean in half. Her mother gushed over the dresses as we floated down the stairs, and I thought that would be the end of it. Gowns chosen, nerves braced for the drawing tomorrow, but Selene had other ideas.

"You have to come to the Winter Festival tonight," she said, tossing her new gown over the edge of her bed. It was as if the man never existed to her, like the man she had cried over had been a dream. "There's a masquerade. No one will even know it's you."

I raised a skeptical brow. "Right. Because everyone in Virellia has white hair." I grabbed a fistful of frozen strands and dragged them forward like proof.

Selene just laughed, sweet and melodic. "Then we hide it." Her eyes sparkled with something between mischief and desperation. She flung a wool cap at my feet. "Come on. Just for one night. Stop worrying so much and get dressed. Please?"

Her voice cracked just slightly at the end, and when I looked at her, I didn't see the confident girl from the square. I saw someone who needed this, someone who needed a night of pretending, a night of joy. Maybe she hadn't forgotten, just chose to ignore.

Compartmentalize.

So, I sighed and pulled the hat over my hair, tucking the ends up into the fold by my neck. "Fine."

She squealed and tossed a mask at me. I caught it just before it hit my chest, flipping it over in my hands. It was beautiful. The paper mâché was molded into a cat-eye shape, elegant and slim and painted with silver edges. It had curled points at each side and delicate carvings and patterns I hadn't noticed until I held it close. A silk string was meant to tie behind my head. It wasn't flashy. It didn't glitter. But somehow, it still felt like a little bit of magic.

I pulled it on and turned to the mirror.

It was still me. Same pale skin, same bone-sharp features, but there was something veiled about the reflection, like a stranger I almost recognized. Maybe, just maybe, I could get away with being invisible tonight.

Selene got ready in a flash, slipping into a plum-colored cloak and brushing glitter over her cheekbones like it was war paint. We snuck out the back where her handmaiden waited, eyes warm and smiling, and silently opened the door.

I thanked her with a nod, and she winked.

Then we were off, half-walking, half-running through the snow like schoolgirls escaping lecture. The wind kissed our cheeks and tangled our breath, but our laughter cut through it like candlelight in a storm.

The festival square was breathtaking.

Lanterns strung overhead flickered gold and crimson, casting pools of light across the snow. Sculptures of ice lined the walkway. Horses rearing on their hind legs, palaces sparkling with crystal windows, crowns raging with spikes and icy jewels, carved like something divine. Children ran through the maze of light, masks fluttering. Couples twirled on the snow-packed dance floor, music swelling from a small group of fiddlers and flutists standing near a roaring bonfire. I tried to look for the man and the fallen grain. I tried to keep his memory alive, but the atmosphere vibrated with energy. Joy pulsed in the air, thick as the smoke curling into the stars.

And for a moment, I was part of it.

No one stared when my coat brushed theirs. No one flinched when I passed. No one whispered. I was just a girl with a silver mask and a wool hat tugged low, my hair tucked away and hidden. And in the sea of colors and laughter, I was normal.

I was free.

Selene pulled me into the dance, and I followed, awkward at first, but loosening with each step. Her grin never faded. I spun with strangers, laughed when I stumbled, clapped when a little girl showed off a twirl of her own. The warmth inside me was so foreign it made my chest ache.

Why had my father kept me from this?

The question came suddenly, unbidden. He had kept me in the dark, tucked away from all of this. From life, from light, from joy.

Selene caught my hand mid-turn and squeezed it, pressing a seam of the leather into my palm. I looked at her, breathless and flushed, and something unspoken passed between us. I didn't say thank you, but I didn't have to.

She saw it in my eyes. But suddenly, her smile broke.

Her gaze snapped over my shoulder, and her whole body stilled. Her fingers slackened in mine. Her eyes went wide.

I turned.

My heart dropped. There, standing just at the edge of the square, was my father, Dalen Seravell himself. His face was carved from stone, mouth set in a hard line. He didn't yell. He didn't move toward us. Just stood there, snow curling around the edges of his boots, steam smoking from his nostrils with each breath.

"We're leaving. Now," he said, and turned on his heels.

Selene's hand flew to her mouth. "I'm so sorry, Lyra. I didn't mean to— I didn't think— I didn't want to—"

I cut her off with a hug, careful to keep only our cloaks touching. Then I slipped the mask from my face and pressed it into her hand.

"Keep it," I whispered.

Then I ran.

The snow was deeper now, sticking and sucking at my boots, slowing me down. I stumbled twice, my gloves scraping across the ice, but I caught up to him eventually. He didn't look back. He didn't wait. He said nothing.

When I tried to speak, tried to apologize, to explain, he raised one hand, not in a gesture of comfort, but a command for quiet.

So, I obeyed.

The walk home was long and bitter and filled with silence so loud it rang in my ears.

When we arrived, he opened the door without a word, stepped aside, and pointed toward my room.

"Go to sleep," he said.

I didn't answer. I walked up the stairs and shuffled to my room.

I didn't cry. At least not until the door was closed.

Inside, I peeled off my coat and yanked at my gloves, not bothering to place them neatly like I always did. I threw them across the room. They hit the stone wall and dropped like dead birds, soft and useless. I wished they'd left a mark.

I pulled the wool cap from my head and let my white hair fall loose, tumbling down my shoulders in tangled waves.

Tears burned hot behind my eyes.

And this time, I didn't stop them.

CHAPTER FOUR

THE AIR BUZZED LIKE a struck chord, sharp and endless, as the crowd gathered in the town square. Bright banners danced in the wind above us, flickering like fire against the pale gray sky. Snow spiraled through the air in lazy drifts, catching on cloaks and eyelashes. The scent of spiced cider curled from merchant carts, warm and sweet and completely at odds with the tight coil of dread in my stomach. I tried to find the spot where the man's blood had likely frozen to the stone, but thick rugs and carpeting was laid out over the entirety of the town square. I huffed a breath of frustration. I should have known.

He was as good as forgotten.

I looked around at the golden embellishments that had found their way onto the wooden stage. It was still splitting where the nails had kept the wood together, but now it glimmered in the bits of sunlight that made its way through the clouds.

It seemed as though almost every girl in Virellia used this as an excuse to get a new dress. Flashes of color danced across the square as friends found friends. The only girls who didn't wear vibrant gowns stood in the far corners, seemingly willing themselves to disappear. Deep down, I yearned to join them. To wish myself away just the same.

Parents and families gathered around, pulling their daughters close and enveloping them in tight hugs that looked to break ribs. Mothers shed tears, while fathers stood tall, their faces what I imagined the stoic demeanor of a soldier would be as they faced defeat on a battlefield.

For some girls, this moment was a dream come true, a moment of pure joy and happiness. For everyone else, it was a nightmare.

This morning had been chaos.

Duke Viremont had sent his carriage to deliver my dress. He had attempted to re-wrap the fabric in its brown paper, but it was crinkled and folded with clumsy seams. The twine bow sat in a misshapen knot on the top. Even so, I forced a rigid smile and thanked the driver as I took it from his outstretched hand, careful to avoid any touch.

My father had fussed over me with a strange, frantic energy. His hands were wrapped in their usual white leather, and they trembled slightly as he helped me into the ice-blue dress, throwing the paper and twine in the fire. I hadn't expected him to care so much.

He hadn't mentioned the festival or my and Selene's attendance. Only the drawing as if nothing else mattered at all.

"You must look presentable, Lyra," he had muttered, more to himself than to me, as he stepped back to assess the fit of the dress.

I tugged at the sleeves, suddenly hyperaware of how delicate and exposed the fabric made me feel. "But it's just a town meeting," I protested, though my voice had sounded weak, even to me.

"No, *no!* This is more than a meeting." He was already digging through the old wooden box on the dresser for the few hair pins we owned. "It's an announcement. You're representing our family. Our region."

The weight of it all settled on my shoulders like snowfall, soft at first, but accumulating faster than I could brush it away.

He shoved the pins into my hand, and I swept my hair back without protest, twisting the top half into a swirl behind my head. I left the rest down, pale strands tumbling over my shoulders like wisps of moonlight. One of the pins had a tiny pearl on the end. It was barely noticeable, but it caught the light like a small bit of hope.

I had ditched my boots in favor of old gray flats lined with silver thread along the seams. My feet were already numb, and I hadn't even left. My father was still tugging at my hair, arranging rogue strands with the intensity of a battlefield surgeon.

"You'll be standing in front of all of Virellia," he murmured. "A bit of dignity goes a long way."

His voice was warm with pride, but there was worry underneath it, deep and thrumming. Something unspoken that made the gloves on my hands feel like shackles. The silver-threaded leather gloves made my fingers ache to be free.

When he was finally satisfied, he stepped back, smiling faintly. "You look lovely, my dear. Remember—confidence is key."

I nodded, but any words stayed caught somewhere in my throat. I barely had enough time to eat a small bit of bread as my breakfast. It was a bit stale, but in my haste I hardly noticed.

Now, standing among the gathered townsfolk, I could still hear his words echoing in my head.

Confidence is key.

My father had stayed home. He had forced some excuse of patients and medicines that needed his attention, but we both knew the truth. He simply hadn't wanted to attend. He couldn't bother himself with the embarrassment that was his daughter.

I wrapped my arms tighter around myself as the sun continued to rise. I stood at the edge of the square, pressed into the shadows beside the bakery's frost-covered window. From here, I could see everything and everyone, especially the obsidian chest perched atop the platform. Its carved surface caught the weak reflection off of the snow like it was watching me back.

The Duke stepped onto the raised stage, his voice booming above the wind. "Today, we honor our regions and our daughters who will compete for the Prince's favor! It's a time of celebration!"

The crowd roared. With cheers or growls I wasn't sure.

Against the vibrant cloaks and flushed cheeks around me, I looked ghastly. The dress only made it worse. I felt like a ghost, pale and out of place. A smear of frost among the living.

"Can you believe it?" Selene's voice broke through the haze, and I turned to find her beside me, cheeks red with excitement and curls bouncing with each breath. "This is our chance to be queen!"

I hadn't even realized she'd found me.

"I'm not sure I even want that," I said quietly, my voice lost in the cry of the crowd.

Selene didn't hear me, or maybe she chose not to. Her gaze was fixed on the platform. On the obsidian chest at its center.

The royal servant stepped forward and began reading from the parchment, naming the other girls from each region. I barely registered the names—Rhea Damaris, Clara Montgomery, Naelle Zarathos, Elena Morwyn—my mind was locked on the chest.

It sat like a sentinel, unmoving, but heavy with something more than parchment slips. At the top was a small circular hole, slightly wider than a closed fist and carved just enough for a hand to slip inside. Selene's father stood behind it, trying and failing to appear calm. A bead of sweat slid down his temple, absurd in this cold.

The servant finished his decree and turned to the Duke with a stiff nod. Slowly, ceremoniously, the Duke reached into the chest, his hand stirring unseen names inside.

I held my breath. Not out of hope, but out of instinct, or maybe even fear.

He cleared his throat. "From the Northern region, our representative is... Lyra Seravell."

Silence.

I didn't move. My spine went rigid, but not from the frigidity.

The world held its breath. Then came the murmurs. Sharp-edged whispers slicing through the air, and worse, the laughter. Familiar, echoing laughter I had learned to brace against. My eyes immediately went to the ground. I didn't want to look up. I didn't want to see everyone staring.

I kept my head down at my gloved hands and wrung them hard, as if I could rub away the silver thread, the truth, the eyes.

"Lyra?" Selene nudged me. "That's you."

My name sounded foreign on her tongue.

I stepped forward, barely aware of my feet moving. Everything felt distant and unreal, like I'd stepped into someone else's dream.

Me? Why me?

I scanned the crowd. Some faces were lit with envy, others with disbelief. Selene's expression was a strange tangle of joy and concern and slight disappointment.

As I climbed the platform, dread tightened around my ribs. This didn't feel like luck. It didn't feel like fate. It felt like a march to my own death.

The Duke extended his hand. I took it. The moment our palms met, something passed between us, something heavy and sharp, like the crackle of lightning before a storm.

"Congratulations, my dear," he said, smiling, but the smile didn't reach his eyes.

The crowd blurred in front of me, my breaths coming in short, sharp bursts. I couldn't shake the feeling that something, someone, was watching. Not from the square though, from beyond.

"What's wrong?" Selene called, her voice laced with worry. She'd pushed through to the front of the crowd, craning up at me. "You look pale."

I forced a smile. "I just... I didn't expect this."

"Maybe that's why it happened." She shrugged, and her focus went elsewhere for all but a second before she gently shook her head. She tried to force a smile, but her eyes betrayed her. "Besides, you probably know the most about Aurea, so you'll do the best anyway. You have to. Virellia needs you to win."

Her words landed like a stone in my chest.

I nodded again, stepping to the back of the platform to brush off some of the attention. My legs shook with every step.

Deep down, I knew. This wasn't about winning. This was about survival, and I had just been thrust into a game I didn't understand, with stakes I couldn't even begin to fathom.

The crowd cheered as streamers flew. Cider spilled and music began to play. I looked back at Selene, uncertain and trembling and trying to pretend I hadn't felt the ground shift beneath me. Trying to pretend I didn't feel like a pawn carved from ice, placed on a board long before I ever learned the rules.

The celebration in the square faded into a dull hum, like a song slipping underwater. Everything narrowed into a single, unbearable moment. My breath caught. My heart felt caged in ice.

The Duke stepped forward, cutting through the noise like a blade. His face was a mask of composure, untouched by the remnants of the celebration still clinging to the air like smoke. His hand found my shoulder—firm, not unkind, but final.

"Come with me, dear," he said, his tone clipped and absolute.

"What? Where?" I stammered. My voice cracked under the weight of rising panic. I looked for Selene again, her face, her eyes, some kind of anchor in the blur of this unraveling moment.

"You're leaving now, Lyra. We must make haste to my estate."

His words crashed over me like icy water.

"But I haven't said goodbye! I—"

"*Lyra!*" he snapped, and I flinched. His gaze held no patience. "There is no time. You'll understand soon enough."

Before I could argue, two guards appeared at either side of me. The crowd shifted like a parting sea, faces blending into a smear of confusion, envy, awe. My heart beat so fast it might have bruised my ribs. I wanted to scream, to run back to Selene, to my house, to before.

But instead, I let them guide me forward. The tide was already dragging me out, and I didn't know how to swim against it.

They led me into Selene's home, a place that was once a haven but now felt cold as The Ridge under my feet. The walls that had once rung with laughter and childhood secrets seemed to close in. More guards followed behind, carrying folded banners, rich tapestries, and the obsidian box.

I stopped.

It pulsed within their arms, not with light but presence. My attention fixed on it like a magnet. Something deep inside me stirred.

They weren't royal guards. Their uniforms bore the insignia of Virellia. They were the Duke's men.

I fell behind, steps slowing, and slipped away around the side hallway before they could notice. The corridor was dim and still smelled faintly of lavender and ash from the hearth. Around the corner, I crouched low, peeking.

One of the men placed the box in the Duke's office and locked the door before disappearing down the hall toward the kitchen, following the same route Selene and I had once used to sneak pastries. Carefully, I approached the door and knelt beside it. The lock stared back, familiar. We had picked it once before.

We were seven or eight, caught in a summer obsession. Selene's father had joked that summer was "locked in his office," and so we, fearless explorers of warmth and wonder, sought to free it. Selene had plucked a pin from her perfectly styled hair—her mother had a thing for adornments—and fiddled with the lock until it released. We burst in expecting sunbeams and petals.

There had been only dust and ledgers.

We cried on the floor for hours, swearing summer would never come again. Her father had been furious.

I pulled my own hairpin free, the tiny pearl reminding me of only a few hours ago, with my own father. My hair spilled down my back like a white waterfall as I separated the prongs and eased one into the lock. I nudged the mechanisms up and down until I heard a satisfying click.

The door creaked open. The obsidian box waited on the desk like something ancient and alive. The room hadn't changed. Books spilled from shelves, parchment curled in loose stacks, ink blotting the desk. The air smelled like memory and old paper.

I shut the door behind me softly and stepped closer, one foot soundlessly in front of the other. The box hummed against the silence. I reached the desk, and I hovered my hand over the opening, blocking the contents from view. I braced myself, moved my hand, and then, relief.

Inside, the black void was stuffed with parchment slips that seemed to be stacked in no particular order. I exhaled shakily.

So, it was chance, I thought.

Something about that calmed the storm inside me. I even laughed a little.

What if someone else had been chosen? Who would be in my place at this very moment?

I imagined myself in the middle of the square as Duke Viremont. I looked out to my imaginary crowd and gestured dramatically to the black box.

Still smiling, I plucked a slip free and unfolded it.

Lyra Seravell

My breath caught. I stared at the name. Anxiety threatened to bring bile up my throat.

Of course. Viremont just put my slip back on top. That made sense.

I pulled another.

Lyra Seravell

My fingers turned numb. I threw the obsidian lid off the top and reached deeper, faster now, the parchment crackling beneath my trembling hands.

Lyra Seravell   Lyra Seravell   Lyra Seravell

I kept digging. Slip after slip, name after name. Finally, I held one more. I didn't want to unfold it. I already knew. I held my breath and closed my eyes as the parchment fell open.

Lyra Seravell

They all said *my name*.

Each one. All mine.

The tears came without permission, burning my eyes. Viremont had only ever meant to send me.

This wasn't fate. It wasn't a lottery. It was a setup. A trap.

I shoved the slips back into the box and slammed the top shut just as voices echoed in the hall. Panic flared. I bolted for the door and closed it quietly behind me, slipping to the opposite side of the hallway just as the Duke rounded the corner.

"Lyra." His brow lifted slightly. "We were looking for you."

I met his eyes, forcing myself to breathe evenly, forcing my heart to stop screaming. He had no idea what I'd seen, what I knew.

"I—I just needed a minute." My head spun so fast the hallway seemed to narrow.

He looked at me for a moment, his gaze equivalent to one you would give a dead animal as you pass it. Helpless and useless sympathy. He stepped closer, voice softening. "You can't hide forever. There's someone we'd like you to meet." He held out his arm.

I hesitated. Then I took it, carefully masking every trace of fear from my face. We stepped out into the square. It was empty. The tapestries, banners, carpets were all gone. The music, the dancing, the cheers, even the people had all vanished like a dream. Only a single carriage remained.

It was small and elegant, bone-white with curling marble vines gilded in gold along its edges. It looked like something pulled from a bedtime story. It looked like it belonged anywhere but here, and leaning beside it, waiting, was *him*.

He was tall and not at all a boy. There was nothing boyish about him. Sun-browned skin ran over lean muscle, like he'd been carved from golden light, not Virellia's gray. His suit was a deep, dangerous purple with gold embroidery burning along the cuffs and collar. His boots gleamed. Chestnut waves tumbled across his brow.

And then he smiled. Too bright. Too perfect. But it was his eyes that caught me. Green that was too vivid and clean, but behind them was something else. Control, maybe kindness, but definitely power.

He was the most beautiful man I had ever seen.

He pushed himself off the carriage and sauntered over, as if the slick ice beneath his feet melted on command.

"You must be Lyra," he said, his voice smooth as velvet.

I stared. He wasn't from here. He was from Aurea. There was no doubt in my mind. The thought made my head spin. Were Aurean girls just as gorgeous? Did they all have little gorgeous families with little gorgeous children?

Misty breaths curled like smoke from his nose. He tucked his hands in the pockets of his coat and ran his eyes down the length of me before connecting with my own.

"Name's Kaden. I'll be your guard."

I looked at the fantasy of a man in front of me. My voice barely found its way out. "Guard?"

"At your service." He flashed a grin while giving a mock bow, both somehow impossibly charming. Viremont was still at my back and gave me a gentle nudge towards the carriage. I followed the Aurean man, Kaden, towards the door as he spoke and unlatched the handle.

"Someone's got to make sure you survive this mess in one piece. Don't worry." He swung out towards me, landing close to my ear, and whispered, "I'm not as scary as I look."

My stars. This cannot be happening to me right now.

He pulled open the carriage door. Inside, plush seats and a carpeted floor gleamed. It was royal, undeniably, and yet, I wanted nothing more than to bolt under it and hide forever. The driver waited by the other side of the door. He was an older gentleman with wind-worn skin and careful eyes. The driver held out a hand to help me up, but as I stepped forward, he flinched.

Just barely, but I saw it. The sting hit deep. That old look.

Witch-born.

"Are you alright?" I asked, softer than I meant to.

He hesitated. "Just surprised, is all." Then, his eyes steadied, and he reached for my hand again. Our fingers touched, and even through my gloves a sharp jolt snapped between us like lightning, or like memory.

My heart jumped. It was nothing, maybe nerves or an expected reputation. I forced it away. The exchange only made me miss Selene. Made me miss the ease of her.

The driver looked away, throat clearing. "Right. Let's get moving." Kaden jumped into the carriage behind me, latching the door closed and giving two knocks to the roof above us.

The carriage lurched forward. Kaden leaned back, arms spread across the back of the seat he sunk into.

"You'll be fine," he said almost too casually. "Johnson's a good coachman. Fast, efficient."

I barely heard him. I was facing the rear window, my eyes locked on the village shrinking behind me. The life I never got to say goodbye to. The one I was unsure I would ever live again.

"What's going to happen?" I asked, barely above a whisper. I turned and faced Kaden. "With the selection."

"Not what you think." His tone shifted. It was slight but just enough for him to pull his arms from their comfort and into his lap.

"The selection is based off of trials. Five of them. Representatives eliminated after each. They test more than poise or charm. It's not just gowns and the ease at which you flutter a fan."

I swallowed. "I thought it would at least be polite."

"Brutal is the more fitting word." He leaned in slightly, his voice low. "The last representative standing will be crowned, but let's be honest, it's not exactly a victory. This isn't a game. It's a strategic maneuver, a political one."

A chill slipped down my spine. "What do you mean?"

Kaden hesitated. "What better way to test the regions' fealty than a marriage selection?" He leaned back into the seat, pulling at his cufflinks as if they were chains. "My advice—don't say what everyone can't know. Secrets are more than simply words."

There was fog creeping up the windows as the carriage warmed, but I felt cold.

"What about you? Can I trust you?"

He smiled faintly, but a distance lingered. "I'll keep you safe. But trust? That's not something you give away freely. Not there."

I turned back to the window, my reflection dim in the glass. The sky outside was beginning to darken into twilight, and with it, so did the road ahead.

And I had no idea what awaited me.

CHAPTER FIVE

THE SOUNDS OF THE carriage wheels shifted from the crackling of ice to the crunching of gravel. We rode into the neighboring region of Mirun, crossing the Hiems Bridge which connected us to the south.

When the carriage hit the wooden structure, I couldn't help but stare as The Ridge came into view in the mix of water and glacier below. Virellia has no technical land borders, as glaciers and ice have slowly begun to heave an ever-growing gap. I used to have nightmares about the glaciers pushing us so far away from the rest of Valerieth that the entire region became nothing more than legend. Now, I quite enjoyed that fact. In a way, it made Virellia something that seemed untouchable. Something that would stay the same. Frozen and separated from the rest of the world.

We continued to travel for several more hours, and sleep took me more than once. Eventually, we entered a town near the southern edge of Mirun called Colpus. The snow here didn't coat everything in an impermeable layer of white. Banks were driven high on either side of the road, but beyond that, sprigs of grass fought through to break the surface above. I pressed my hand to the glass window and felt the cold seep into my palm. Still not the warm Aurean summer, but also not the arctic of Virellia.

I felt Kaden's eyes on me as I studied the town, but I didn't care. As a child, this would have felt like a dream come true. The possibility of being a queen. The chance to wear a ballgown and attend royal feasts. But now, it felt like nothing more than a snare set in secret.

I couldn't stop thinking about the box in the Viremont's office. Of how each slip said my name and my name only. If he had wanted me to go, why hadn't he simply asked me? The only answer I could think of was as simple as this.

He didn't want any way for me to refuse.

I couldn't bring myself to say it aloud.

The two horses pulling the carriage were as black as night and as silky as velvet. I could hear them huff and whinny as the sky fell to dusk, but a part of me always thought that animals didn't fear the darkness as we did. I felt sorry for them. We had both been forced into situations we didn't agree upon.

The carriage rolled to a halt outside of a dimly lit building that had a swinging wooden sign hanging above the entrance.

It read,

Mabel's Tavern & Inn

I stared the sign and turned to Kaden, my face most definitely a portrait of horror. I knew I would have to learn the art of small talk, but I wasn't expecting to converse with anyone until we reached Aurea.

Kaden smirked as he moved to the carriage door and undid the latch.

"After you, Miss Seravell."

He swung the door open and stretched his hand out to me, palm up.

I sat up in my seat, my elbows resting against my knees. "Why are we stopping? I thought we had to '*Leave immediately?*'" I threw quotes in the air with my hands as I spoke.

"Well, hate to break it to you, but horses don't always go with the timeline we humans have planned." He glanced at the horses who whined and scuffed at the ground with their hooves. He nodded down towards his hand, offering once more.

I hesitated, overwhelmingly conscious of the gloves that adorned my hands and the bare skin of his own. I took his hand, and stood, shuffling over to the carriage door. Kaden leapt down, releasing my hand to unfold the narrow staircase tucked under the carriage. He gave a dramatic hand wave as if to usher me down, but I froze, stuck in the doorway. I wrung my hands in front of me, eyes sweeping from left to right. Even as the moon climbed and night began, people still bustled through the streets. I wasn't sure if I was ready for a new array of stares. I didn't know if I ever would be.

I let my hands fall to my sides with a sigh. "You know what, I think I'll just sleep in the carriage. I'm used to the cold, and then I won't be a bother to you or—"

"My *stars*." Kaden's hands grabbed hold on my waist as he lifted me from the carriage, cutting off my thin excuses. He let out an exasperated breath, and I froze in his grip as my feet landed on the stone road. He let go and stared at me, hands resting on his hips as he quipped, "Now, do I need to throw you over my shoulder and cause a scene to go inside, or can you walk yourself?"

I stood motionless with my mouth hanging slightly open. My eyes were wide as saucers, and my arms stayed halfway up in the air, like a child who wasn't sure where to put them.

"I'll walk."

Kaden nodded once and stepped away, strolling into the tavern as if it had been nothing. I crossed my arms, letting a huff of breath create a cloud in front of me before following, begrudgingly.

He led me into the tavern, and immediately the smell of bread and bitter alcohol filled the air. Patrons sang a song plunked from a musician's fiddle. Girls poured pints from barrels resting on the counter. Burly men clashed their steins together, sloshing golden ale on each other and laughing.

It was entirely overwhelming.

I kept my head down as we walked past the tavern entrance and made our way into the inn portion of the building. Seated at a quaint front desk was an elderly woman. Her hair was wiry and gray, but long and braided intricately. Silver thread was woven into the strands, and it shimmered when she raised her head to smile at us.

Kaden approached the woman and leaned over the desk to wrap her in a gentle embrace. "Hello Ms. Mabel."

"Kaden, darling, oh how wonderful to see you." She turned and met my stare. She smiled even wider, and I swore I saw tears make her eyes go glassy.

"And even more wonderful to see *you*."

The woman walked around the desk and hobbled over to me. She grabbed my hands from my sides.

"Oh, I'm sorry but I—" I tried to pull my hands back, but Mabel had an iron grip.

"Don't worry darling." She looked down at the gloves. "You'll warm up." She gave me a wink before she walked back over to Kaden.

"I'm guessing you'll be needing two rooms tonight? Or should I make it one?" A mischievous smirk grew on her lips.

My cheeks reddened. I opened my mouth to respond, but Kaden beat me to it.

"Two beds tonight, Mabel. Sorry to disappoint." Kaden threw a look over his shoulder, shaking his head and chuckling.

"Alright, alright. If you insist." Mabel reached behind her and pulled two keys off of the rack.

"Room numbers are on the key. You lose your key, you buy me another one, but you know that rule well, don't you Kaden."

"You are never going to let that go are you, Mabel?" Kaden sighed with a laugh. Mabel only shook her head. Her eyes were still glassy, and her smile hadn't faded a bit.

Kaden and I walked up the spiral stairs to the third floor. The hallway was narrow, so narrow Kaden's shoulders almost brushed both sides. We were the first two doors. His room was closest to the stairs while mine was one door down and across the hall. Kaden passed me my key, and I slid it into the lock.

The door opened, and I stepped inside of a small room with a slanted roof running towards the back. A bed was tucked under the lowest portion of the ceiling with a window by the foot. Outside the night had completely overtaken the sky, clouds swirling in to cover the moon and stars. A wooden nightstand sat near the bed on the left wall while a small circular table with two chairs was tucked into the right corner closest to me. I wandered further, setting the key down on the nightstand as I heard footsteps behind me.

"Lavish, I know."

Kaden leaned against the doorframe of my room. His coat was gone revealing a crisp white button up. The cotton of his shirt was tight over his biceps and shoulders. His cufflinks were gone, allowing his wrists to be unbuttoned along with his collar.

"What is this place?" The question slipped before I could contain it. It wasn't the only question swirling in my head, but the others were stuck in my throat, on my tongue, between my teeth.

"The woman downstairs is named Mabel. She owns this humble establishment."

"You didn't answer my question."

Kaden grinned, running a hand along his jaw as he pushed himself off of the frame and closed the door as he walked inside.

"Touché." His neck was bent slightly to the side under the low ceiling. "This is an inn with a tavern downstairs. A tavern, I might add, that has very good ale. Mabel likes it strong."

I wrinkled my nose. I had never really drank before besides wine with supper. The only time I had, it had been this horrid liquid called rum. I don't think I had ever vomited so much in my life.

"I'll pass on the tavern, but please, go enjoy yourself." I waved my hands at him, mockingly shooing him out. "I'm sure the ladies would love if you drank enough to lose those royal manners."

Kaden's eyebrows shot to the top of his forehead. "If you think this is royal, you're going to have quite the rude awakening when we reach Aurea." Kaden shoved his hands in his pockets, rocking back and forth on his heels. "Besides, I'm not going to the tavern." He pointed to one of the chairs tucked under the small round table. "May I sit?"

I walked over to the other chair, holding the backrest with my hands and leaning against it.

"By all means."

Kaden pulled the chair out and flopped down, leaning back and somewhat slouching into the seat that was far too small for him. It even looked a little small for me.

"I'm sure you have questions about—"

"What did Mabel mean about buying the key?"

He shook his head, letting out a low laugh.

"You really want to ask about that right now? What about the trials? What about the other representatives? What about Aurea?" He raised a finger for each question I should have asked, but at the moment, my sole focus was on uncovering Kaden.

I simply shrugged, pushing off the back of the chair and strutting over to rest my hand on the doorknob.

"If it's super embarrassing and you won't tell it, I'm sure Mabel would."

I jokingly turned the knob, the metal clanking under my hand. Kaden's eyes narrowed, but humor rested in the grin he fought to hide.

"You wouldn't dare."

I smiled wickedly, showing my teeth.

"Oh, but I would."

I pulled the door from its frame, just enough for the torchlight in the hallways to flood over Kaden's face. His eyes seemed to swallow the glow whole as they shone that irradiant green. As if even in their slitted state they seemed to observe everything about this world. I could only stare back in return, the smile on my face no doubt lost in the thoughts that seemed to cloud my head.

Kaden broke the stare, dropping his head into his hands and surrendering to his inevitable defeat.

"Alright, if you insist. But only if I get to ask you a question after." He pointed a finger, wagging it at my chest. I only laughed quietly and nodded in response as I moved to settle into my own seat.

Kaden smiled, leaning forward to rest his elbows on the table. "So, about four years ago when I was seventeen, I came here. I had just been knighted and therefore was able to join the royal guard, but when you join the guard, you can never marry. It's a lifetime commitment to the crown, so a lifetime commitment to a wife…"

He trialed off, his grin fading into something sorrow. Almost like he was reminiscing on what could have been. He took a deep breath, fixing his face as he continued.

"And you see, I grew up training for knighthood. Which sounds impressive, until you realize all I knew was fighting invisible enemies in a dusty painted circle."

He wrung the back of his neck nervously.

"I guess I just—I just wanted to have some sort of experience before I swore off women forever."

Now it was my eyebrows that shot up.

"Sir Kaden. My goodness, you rascal," I joked sarcastically as I threw my hand over my chest, mouth wide.

Kaden waved a hand at me as he sat back in his chair, folding his arms over his chest.

"You truly are terrible, you know that?" He shook his head even as the corner of his mouth rose in a smirk. "Anyway, I came here hoping to find a girl and ended up being so nervous I drank myself dry and still to this day cannot remember a bit of it."

Kaden shrugged and pursed his lips into a thin line, eyes meeting mine. I wasn't sure how Kaden, out of everyone, could be nervous to talk to women. There was no doubt that he was handsome. He was charismatic even. Maybe in a slightly awkward and humorous way, but he was, nevertheless. He was kind, and that should have been enough for any girl he fancied.

"So, wait. Big bad Aurean knight got scared of women, drank all the ale Mabel had, and then lost his room key?"

Kaden huffed a laugh as he stood and wandered over to the window, having to bend down to fit under the slanted ceiling. Outside the clouds seemed to run across the sky as wind whipped at everything in its path.

"Stars gave you a wicked sense of humor didn't they. Or did the Virellian cold just seep into your bones?" He turned back to me, a faint grin on his lips.

I peered down at the gloves on my hands. I flexed them in front of me, turning them over and studying the leather fitted with white seams. I laid my hands on the table, palms up, as if it was some form of sacrifice.

Everyone seems to think so, I thought.

I tucked my hands back onto my lap under the table, like a child who closes their eyes to hide. If I couldn't see them, they didn't exist. I forced a smile, but my eyes didn't match it.

"Just one of my many talents, I guess."

Kaden pointed a finger at me, and my face turned from fake levity to confusion. He walked back over, pulling the chair out to sit down

"*Many* talents?"

I pinched my eyebrows together as I opened and closed my mouth soundlessly. Like a fish out of water.

"Well, I— I was really just joking."

"I'm sure you have some talent or skill."

I wasn't sure I truly had anything to offer at all, but Kaden's eyes were so hopeful it felt like butchering a snow white lamb.

"There's not many trades or crafts in Virellia."

Kaden waved his hands as if to shake off the words. "Doesn't have to be any profession or occupation." He put his palms together, pressing his hands towards me. "You gave me one question in return for answering yours. So, what are you good at Miss Seravell?"

Nothing.

That's what I had wanted to say.

"I can blend in."

That's what I went with instead.

Kaden nodded, his eyes trailing around the room as he thought before his gaze landed back on me.

"That's a start, but not good enough. Blending can only get you so far." He brought a hand over his mouth. His fingers moved up and down his cheek until his palm turned skyward. Whatever grand idea just came upon him was visible on his face.

"Can you fight? Do you have any experience with self-defense or a sword. Maybe knives?"

What in the stars.

"Uh, no."

"Okay then. What about education? Did you have any form of schooling?"

No. They wouldn't let me attend school. My father tried, but he was never much of a teacher.

I didn't say that either.

"My father taught me about healing."

Kaden snapped his fingers, his smile brightening. "That's it. Perfect. So, you may not know about fighting, but you know anatomy then?"

My eyes dropped to my fingers as I picked at the wood splintering off the table.

"Well, I didn't really ever heal anyone. I only know how to make the ointments and salves..."

Kaden looked at me as if he was waiting for me to reveal some joke. When he realized I was in fact not joking and truly had nothing to offer, he sighed, running a hand through his hair.

"So, let me get this straight. You trained as a healer under your father, but you never healed anyone, you didn't have a formal education, you don't know a thing about fighting, and you have no note-worthy skills."

All I could do was nod.

"Stars have mercy." Kaden hung his head off the back of the chair, his eyes closing as he simply breathed for what felt like forever.

I wanted to apologize. I felt like I should. Kaden was just like me and the horses. He hadn't chosen this for himself. He had been given orders, not a choice, and now he was suffering because of my inadequacies.

Kaden brought his head back up, opened his eyes, and sucked in a breath. He clapped his hands and rubbed them together, as if his disappointment was tangible.

"When did you begin to work under your father?"

I wasn't really sure. I had always watched and observed him, so when I began, it wasn't as if he had to train me in anything. More just give me the responsibilities he no longer deemed necessary of his time.

"About a year ago, maybe?"

Kaden nodded his head. His hands snaked back up again to cover his mouth.

"And how many ointments, salves, or medicines do you know?"

Stars. I knew more than I could count. There was sleeping draughts, infection aids, pain relievers, stress relief, poison antidotes, poisons themselves, and so much more. I wasn't sure how he expected me to respond.

"Do you truly want me to count?"

Kaden nodded his head once, a singular sharp movement.

I began to count, holding a finger up for each medicine, salve, draught, anything I knew. I quickly reached ten and restarted, hitting twenty just as easily. I continued, counting until I hit fifty before pausing and peering up at Kaden.

His eyes were wide, and his low spirits had seemed to heighten.

"Should I keep going?"

He waved his hands as he shook his head, effectively stopping my count.

"You're telling me you memorized over fifty medicines in a year?"

"It may have been like a year and a few months, I'm not exactly sure the exact timeline. I'm just— "

"No, Miss Seravell, this is what we needed."

It was?

"If you can learn all of those as quickly as you did, we just need to make sure you are adequately trained for each trial. You're a fast learner. That's your skill. That we can work with."

We can?

I had never given my ability for observation nearly the title of *skill*. It had been more survival than anything.

"So, what does that mean?"

Kaden leaned towards me, his smile reappearing in all of its genuine, charming beauty. "That means all we need to do is figure out the trials before they happen." His voice dropped to a hushed whisper. "And luckily for us, I just so happen to have an inside source."

I should have protested. It was cheating, clear as day, but to be blatantly honest, I didn't care. The crown had cheated their way into royalty. The Aureans cheated their way into wealth. Viremont had cheated his way into shipping me off. Everyone else had taken the liberty of bending the rules, so why should I hold myself to any higher standard?

I was just a Virellian girl anyway. There was nothing that I could do that would cause something cataclysmic.

"Then let's do it."

He beamed as if for the first time, he thought I might have a chance.

CHAPTER SIX

KADEN HAD STAYED IN my room discussing the trials until the sun had begun to rise on the horizon. He left only when his own eyes began to droop, each sentence punctuated with a yawn. Or two. Now, I laid in my bed, alone with my thoughts that seemed to flash faster than the lightening of the storm brewing outside. On my nightstand sat my leather gloves and a piece of thick parchment covered in sprawling notes. Kaden had given me any and all of the information he had.

"Find the girl from Mirun. Her name is Elena Morwyn, and she is going to be your best bet at an ally. If they're wearing northern colors, assume they're wearing it for a reason. They might not like you, but any northerner would rather one of their own on the throne when it truly matters. If they're wearing gold, assume the opposite. Assume the absolute worst."

The words still sang in my head like a solemn song. Like one you play only at funerals. It felt like receiving orders to go into a battle you knew would end in nothing but bloodshed.

"There're two girls, Rhea Damaris and Naelle Zarathos who come from very powerful families. Rhea is from Aurea and Naelle from Calem. The two regions have been in an alliance since the Vaelros

family ascended to power. Naelle will be a quieter terror, but Rhea, she'll make herself known. Very, very known."

I had nodded along when Kaden spoke. I had scribbled half-legible names and notes. I tried everything to look like I was contemplating what information he was providing me. And yet, for some reason, I felt more unprepared with each bit I gained.

"One girl seems very similar to you. Quiet, but with hidden knowledge. Clara Montgomery. Seren's representative. Her father is an admiral in the harbor patrol unit. A born and raised military child. She's experienced and intelligent, both dangerously so."

I shook off the memory as I turned over in bed to face the wall, listening as sleet pattered down. The mix of rain and snow was thick and loud against the windowpane. At home, I would have slept peacefully to the storm, as if it were a lullaby. Here, it felt more like a threat.

I hadn't had much time to even miss home. To think that just yesterday I was getting ready with my father for the drawing seemed entirely impossible. I had never expected to need my father. I always thought that we would only be separated in death, and while I would mourn, I never saw myself *needing* him. It seemed I had gotten that one wrong.

I flipped over in the thick covers, my head now resting at the foot of the bed where the window opened towards the storm. Lightening flashed, and thunder rumbled high. The walls and streets were entirely soaked with that mixture of both water and ice. I was suddenly grateful for Mabel. If we hadn't stopped, I wasn't sure the carriage would have survived. I couldn't see the sun, but I knew it had to be at least early morning, if not later. I exhaled, letting the breath deep in my lungs fog the window glass. I wasn't going to sleep tonight.

I sat up, pulling the covers off and slipping out of bed. I had taken off my dress to attempt to sleep, standing now in only my undershirt and a pair of tight cotton pants. I grabbed the icy blue gown from the back of one of the chairs and threw it over my head. I pulled at the laces of the corset behind me, tying it off with little to no grace. I didn't have much of any belongings to gather, so I folded the notes I had taken with Kaden and tucked them up into my sleeve. I grabbed my gloves and pulled them over my hands, hiding the remaining bit of parchment. I left the key in the center of the nightstand.

I grabbed the covers that were now lopsided on the bed and piled them onto the floor. I smoothed the sheets and thick furs back on the mattress, recreating it to be exactly as it was before I ever got here. When I finished, it would look as if I had never even visited.

I was fixing the last of the wrinkles from my pillow when a knock rattled my door. I walked over, but my hand paused and hovered over the handle before a familiar voice rang through the cracks in the wood.

"Seravell, you awake in there? To make it to Aurea on time we need to leave within the—"

I opened the door, cutting off Kaden mid sentence. His mouth froze open as his eyes ran down my dress. I peered down at it myself, each and every wrinkle screaming. I hadn't even noticed. I tried to smooth the imperfections out with my hands, pulling the fabric taunt, but every time I let go, they reappeared. I looked up at Kaden, expecting to get scolded. He only smiled, holding a closed hand up to his mouth to stifle his laughter.

"Always a lady, Miss Seravell."

I scoffed at him. "It's not like I had time to bring other gowns."

His hand dropped from his face, but laughter still bubbled. My face burned with embarrassment.

"Oh, we have dresses for you. Don't you worry your pretty little head about that. I'm more enjoying the fact that you even put that back on."

I gave him a puzzled look. "Are dresses *one-time use* in Aurea?"

Kaden sucked in a breath through his teeth, his shoulders raising to his ears. "No one there would be caught dead wearing a dress twice. Especially not one so…disheveled." His head turned towards the fireplace and the flames that rippled against the stone. "Most of them burn their gowns after wearing them."

I grabbed at the fabric. It was smooth and cool in my hands, but more than that, it was a piece of home. "I rather like this dress, thank you very much." I went to shut the door, but Kaden's palm hit the center and pinned it open. My heart seemed to skip a beat.

"Johnson is bringing the carriage to the front. There is a plethora of dresses stowed in its storage that I can get for you, along with space to bring this one to the palace." His eyes raked over me once more, and his lips curled up into a smirk on one side of his face.

"I'm thinking yellow."

And with that, Kaden was gone. He seemed to dash down the stairs at light speed, skipping down steps two at a time. I let my head fall back, my eyes closing. Dread crept into me from every angle. I paced the room and pretended I was in Aurea. I pretended to walk into the palace and meet both the King and the Prince. I imagined our conversation, acting it out as if I were on a playwright's stage.

"Well, hello there Prince Cassian. You look absolutely repulsive this evening." I sunk into a low curtsy, making the words high pitched and sing-songy. Then, I turned and became the Prince, dropping my voice low.

"Miss Seravell. How lovely to at last have someone who isn't a pompous spoiled Aurean brat." I spat the last word in my own voice. I spun again, becoming the lady once more.

"Oh Prince Cassian, save me from these northern ruffians!" I threw the back of my hand to my forehead, leaning back as if I was fainting. My voice lowered once more, as I adopted my princely persona. I threw my hands up in mock dramatics.

"I must rescue my perfect and beautiful Miss Seravell at once! I will make her my queen, and we can rule all of wretched Valerieth togeth—" The door swung open. Kaden stood there holding a perfectly folded flaxen gown. I froze with my hands still thrown above my head. My mouth paused, halfway forming the end of my sentence. I let my arms fall as I cleared my throat.

"I don't suppose you heard any of that? Did you?"

Kaden cringed, his nose and mouth scrunching up. "Unfortunately, I heard every word." He walked in and laid the dress on the table as my head fell into my hands, my cheeks burning hotter than the fireplace behind me. "I'll leave you to your actress training, but I'll let you know, Prince Cassian would never fall for a damsel in distress."

He winked, and then he was gone, shutting the door behind him. I moved to the table to grab the gown when his voice cut through the wooden walls.

"Change m'lady and then it would be my pleasure if you would accompany me to break our fasts!"

I rolled my eyes but couldn't help as a grin broke out on my lips. I pulled my gloves off, the parchment in my sleeve falling with them. I untied the laces of the wrinkled gown I currently wore and pulled the new one on. This one laced up the front with thick embroidered ribbon. I tied the ends together in a large bow and pulled the small puff sleeves over my shoulders. The gown was tiered with layers of butter yellow chiffon. The center of the skirt was paneled with the same embroidery patterns of the ribbons, and as much as I hated to admit it, the dress was beautiful.

I laid my notes in the center of my blue gown, folding the fabric and tucking it under my arm. I pulled my gloves on and grabbed my key before leaving the room. I walked down the spiral stairs and expected to hear the clamor of the tavern below, but as I landed on the ground floor, I noticed the once teeming space had calmed into a gentle morning café.

Kaden sat at a table in the far corner, and his eyes found mine immediately. I stepped out from behind the wall and gave him a small curtsy, showing the gown he had selected. He flashed me a smile in return as he waved me over. He had changed into a suit of full white. It seemed to shimmer, just faintly, like snow in morning sun. I weaved between the tables dotted with customers and sat down with him. On the table sat two large blueberry muffins that smelled downright heavenly. I hadn't realized how hungry I was.

"Mabel made those this morning. They're for you."

I looked up at him. Kaden must have realized my stare. I pushed one towards him and took the other. He hesitated for a second before grabbing the still-warm muffin and peeling the paper wrapper. We ate in near silence. I knew I hadn't had anything to eat since a rushed breakfast while preparing for the drawing, and if Kaden was traveling to Virellia during that time, I can't imagine he's had much either.

When we finished, Kaden stood, dusted the crumbs from his hands, and grabbed the wrappers in one hand and my folded dress in the other. I followed suit, standing and pushing in my chair. We walked back towards the front lobby where Mabel's desk was. She sat behind the counter and talked animatedly with the girl I saw behind the bar on the night previous. The girl noticed us and hurried off. Mabel then turned towards us and clasped her hands together.

"Lose any keys?"

I held mine up, the brassy metal shining in the light. Kaden fished his out from his pants pocket and plucked mine from between my fingers. He set both down on the desk and shot Mabel a look, all while a smirk grew on his lips. This was a happy place for him. That much I had gathered.

"It was nice to see you too, Ms. Mabel."

Kaden was speaking, but Mabel's eyes stayed glued on me. They hovered over my face, catching on my hair and landing on my gloved hands folded against my stomach. It wasn't an uncomfortable stare, but there was something deeper there. She looked like she found something she has been searching for, but I couldn't imagine what.

Kaden grabbed Mabel's hand, pressing a kiss to the back of it, before turning and nodding his head toward the door in a signal of our departure. I turned, fully aware of the eyes burning into my back. Kaden trailed out behind me but still beat me to the carriage door. He pulled open the latch, swinging the door open and offering a hand to help me up. I didn't hesitate to take it.

CHAPTER SEVEN

SOMEWHERE ALONG THE ROAD, the rhythmic clacking of the carriage finally lulled me into some sleep. The clatter of wheels against uneven stone, the low groan of wood under weight. It all blended into a sweet melody, and for the first time since this whole process began, the relentless buzz of worry drifted from my mind. As if swept away like clouds on a summer breeze.

When I woke, the world had changed. The shadows outside had thinned into pale light, and the hum of voices, distant at first, grew clearer as we approached the heart of the capital. I blinked slowly, rubbing my eyes as I sat up. The window beside me framed a blur of color and motion from the markets just beginning to stir, elegant buildings sculpted from ivory stone, and people moving like waves in a tide. Sunlight spilled into the carriage, heating up the glass. The air smelled faintly floral, tinged with heat and spice and something sweet.

Across from me, Kaden sat still and silent, his posture alert despite the smudges of exhaustion under his green eyes. The soft morning light caught on the loose strands of his hair and the gleam of his white suit. I sat up and stretched, feeling the constraints of my dress on my arms.

"Have you gotten any sleep at all?" I asked, my voice drowsy.

He hesitated. Just long enough for me to catch the flicker of weariness he tried to hide.

"No," he said finally, dragging a hand through his hair. "Can't guard while you're sleeping. And it's not like anyone else is taking shifts in here."

There was something oddly sweet about his concern. Before I could say anything more, the carriage lurched slightly, slowing as the city of Aurea unfurled before us.

The driver didn't speak as he climbed down. He didn't offer his hand as he opened the door, just stood back with the stiff movements of someone who had already decided what kind of person I was.

The heat of the air rushed in and immediately, my palms went clammy under my leather gloves. The layers I had grown accustomed to in Virellia would be *torture* here.

I leaned out, and my breath caught in my throat.

The palace of Aurea stood like something out of a dream. No, something beyond that. White marble gleamed in the morning sun, so bright it seemed to glow. Veins of gold were woven into its surface like thread through silk, catching the light and scattering it in shimmering patterns. Balconies stretched out like the wings of birds, and curling columns lifted the weight of the structure like it was nothing at all. Flowers spilled from every ledge and urn in bursts of riotous color. Crimson, violet, soft yellow, and blue as deep as the sea. This was not a palace built for war or functionality, no. It was built only for glamour and beauty.

It was stunning. Perfect. Otherworldly.

And somehow, that made me angry.

This was the kingdom's beating heart, where abundance poured from fountains, and gold gleamed from every edge. They had everything they could possibly dream of at their fingertips, and now so did I, but I could not stop thinking of home. My mind circled the hungry faces and thin bodies I had grown so accustomed too. The man who'd been killed for a sack of grain was a dark stain in my memory. Did the people here know of the famine in the northern regions? Were they even aware of the work-cracked hands and empty bellies?

Kaden stepped down behind me and gently linked his arm through mine. I stiffened. The contact was so casual, so natural that it startled me more than it should've. Even with layers of fabric between us, I felt his presence. A heat pressed close to my skin.

"Welcome to Aurea," he said softly. There wasn't arrogance in his voice. I wasn't even sure there was pride. "The heart of our kingdom."

The city pulsed around us like a living thing. Children's laughter echoed through curved streets. Merchants opened their stalls with lazy grace. The buildings were open-air, clearly made for Aurea's gentle weather. Every wall and column were adorned with mosaics or carvings. I saw scenes of winged beings dancing in fields, of queens robed in fire, of stars falling from the sky.

The opulence was dizzying.

We passed through the palace gates, the guards allowing our entry without a word. Inside, the air cooled instantly. I caught the scent of blooming jasmine and something warm, like honey or sun-drenched stone.

We wove through hallways that twisted like vines, each one more labyrinthine than the last. No wonder they didn't need guards posted at every corner. The palace was a maze designed to disorient and awe. My fingers brushed against the smooth walls, occasionally passing tapestries so fine they looked painted. I trailed my hand across one with blue fabric kissed with golden flames.

Silver flames, I realized. Hidden beneath the gold.

"Touching the tapestries won't help you win any trials," Kaden said behind me, tone dry but with the edge of a smirk. "Might impress the nobles if you have good taste."

I turned just enough to glance at him, letting a smile tug at my lips. "Maybe I'll just enchant the Prince with my good looks."

His already feeble smirk faded quickly.

"You need to play your cards right, Seravell. The trials are more than a game. More than a crown."

I nodded, but nerves twisted again in my gut.

Kaden gave me a look before he turned, stepping sideways and revealing the space beyond.

We stepped into the throne room, and everything else fell away. Light poured through towering stained-glass windows, casting molten colors across the floor. Every window was different, but they all depicted the same thing. Eyes. Eyes that watched. Eyes that followed. Blue and gold, some with flame around them, others lined in gold lashes that glimmered. I shivered, despite the warmth.

The throne room was vast, yet intimate. Grand arches framed a ceiling of gold leaf and pearl, and thick silk banners hung down like tongues of fire. At the far end atop a grand staircase stood the throne itself, golden barbed with rays shooting out in every direction. They said it was made to look like the sun. I thought it looked like a crown of fire, an eternal halo meant to blind, and sitting atop it was the King.

King Malik Vaelros was as grand as the room, and just as grotesque. Rotund, draped in velvet the color of ripe grapes, his solid gold crown heavy with sapphires and rubies. The gems caught the light and scattered it into little shards of blood and sea.

Two girls wandered around the stage, one holding a water pitcher while the other held a platter the King ate from. They both were clothed in strips of silk that wound around them to form dresses, if it could even be called that. The fabric was sheer and draped over each shoulder to be left free flowing down their front and back. A golden chain was clasped at their waist, the only anchor for the so-called gowns.

The King didn't even glance up when my name was announced for my arrival. No fanfare. No regard. Just another representative among the regions. And the representatives below happened to be fully clothed. Something far less interesting for him.

My earlier joke about *enchanting good looks* tasted sour now.

The other six regions' representatives were already in the room, scattered like chess pieces across the marble. I was the last girl to arrive. I scanned their faces, searching for kindness, for danger. I'd grown up learning how to read people, how to hide behind my gloves and my quiet smile. I wasn't about to stop now when it truly mattered.

As I scanned the room, one girl caught my eye. She wore deep navy, the dress reminding me of the one I had wanted in the shop, her long black hair gleaming like spilled oil. She looked delicate, but not frail. Nervous, but kind. She caught me staring and glanced behind her, as if checking I really was looking at her, and gave a timid wave.

"Mirun," Kaden murmured at my side. "I told you about her back at Mabel's. Her name's—"

"Elena." I finished for him. "And her?" I tilted my chin toward the girl standing closest to the throne, gorgeous, bold, and glowing like the palace itself.

"Rhea," he said darkly.

"From Aurea." I had remembered his warning, and I didn't need to hear it again. Rhea's gaze found mine like a blade. She smiled, but it didn't hold any warmth.

Her beauty was undeniable. Golden skin that shimmered with sun, eyes the piercing blue of the skies overhead. Half of her blonde hair was down and cropped to her collarbones, the rest swept up into a swirl of pinwork. I touched the back of my head without thinking, remembering the similar style that I once wore. The hairstyle that I had undone hastily to pick a lock in a Duke's office.

That cursed memory still stung. I had so many questions that were forever going to be left unanswered, but I couldn't linger on it. I pulled my head back to the task at hand. These girls were my competition, but also my only chance at allies.

I crossed the room, stepping out of Kaden's shadow.

"Lyra—" he hissed under his breath. He reached to grab at my wrist, but I had lived years avoiding people's touch. I continued forward.

Elena saw me approach and straightened, a hopeful glint in her eyes.

"Hi," I said, offering a nervous smile. "I'm Lyra. From Virellia. I'm guessing you're from Mirun? The navy kind of gave it away."

Her face lit up. "Yes! Oh my stars, I'm so glad the southern girls didn't notice." Then she blushed. "Not that noticing is bad. I just—I appreciate you noticing. With you being from Virellia and all. I didn't mean—I just—I'm Elena."

She thrust out her hand, and I couldn't help but laugh. A real, soft laugh. She was nervous too. I looked at her bare hand. I rubbed at the leather on my hands and hesitated but then reached out and shook hers.

A throat cleared behind me. I turned to see Kaden's scolding look that he didn't even try to hide. I broke the handshake with a smile before walking back, stopping a few steps in front of Kaden.

"You said to make allies."

He huffed a breath, and I stepped back beside him, facing forward once again, but I didn't miss the tension in his jaw.

I don't think he realized what he was getting himself into.

Then again, neither did I.

The throne room buzzed with anticipation, the air thick with a mixture of excitement and apprehension as we stood waiting for our formal introduction to the King and his son. I stood among the other girls, each a representative of their region, collected like ornaments against the sheer splendor of the palace. Everything about the room felt like something plucked from a dream. Marble walls etched with swirling patterns of gold, towering windows that bathed the space in molten light, and banners of blue and gold cascading down from the arched ceilings like flowing rivers of royalty. I looked down and saw my own face staring back, a thorn in a rose bush.

Then the horns blared, sharp and commanding. The girls stiffened. A hush fell like a curtain.

Kaden leaned closer, his presence grounding in the sudden stillness. "Line up in order of region, starting from the south," he murmured, his voice low but firm. His posture straightened, shifting into that of a guard rather than a friend. "Just follow suit, and stay calm."

I gave a small nod, trying to still the pounding in my chest. I watched the others file into place with a mix of poise and fear, each girl holding her chin a little higher than the last. None of them wore gloves. Their hands were bared like weapons, proud and exposed. I felt the fabric of mine itch against my palms, but I didn't dare remove them.

Elena stood beside me and flashed me a look, her eyebrows raised, lips tugging upward in a small smile. I gave her a weak one in return, my mind racing ahead to whatever would come next.

The grand doors swung open.

He entered like he owned the sun.

Prince Cassian Vaelros strode into the room, cloaked in a suit of deep royal blue trimmed with gold. His skin was bronzed, kissed by their seemingly endless summer, with tousled warm blonde hair that fell in perfect curls down to his sharp cheekbones. A dusting of freckles traced his nose, catching the sunlight like scattered gold. His eyes were a light brown containing flecks of something brighter, almost amber in the right light. He was the physical embodiment of gold, and for that, I hated him.

When he smiled, it was with the ease of someone who knew the effect he had. He was someone who didn't know what hunger even felt like. Someone who had never heard the word 'No.' Effortless charm clung to him like a second skin, and every girl around me instinctively straightened, drawn to the warmth he radiated. Standing there, I felt utterly different from them.

My white-blond hair and pale skin marked me as something foreign. A glare in the soft golden light. My silver eyes caught in the polished surfaces, ghost-like and strange. The contrast was stark, and I hated that I felt it.

Then again, I hated a lot of things. I hated the prince who ignored the suffering of my region, who lived in warmth while Virellia froze. I hated the perfectly tailored suit he wore. I hated the boisterous air of confidence he had. I hated that my pulse quickened anyway.

I shook off the charm and the smiles and the obscenely practiced poise, and I told myself that I would never fall for Cassian Vaelros.

I refused to be one of the reasons Virellia starved.

The Prince moved to the sit beside the throne with the grace of someone raised in power. The girls immediately strolled over, putting extra sway into their hips and moving the fabric to the side of themselves. One perched herself on the armrest of the chair. She placed her hand on his chest as she pressed a kiss to his neck. The Prince's hand wound around her waist just as the other sat in his lap facing him, no doubt giving him a view through the translucent silk. Prince Cassian licked his bottom lip, clearly enthralled in whatever the girls had planned for him.

The King rose, tall and sharp in his golden regalia. His voice echoed through the chamber, commanding and cold.

"Welcome." His tone left little room for anything but obedience. Even the half-naked girls paused their plan with the Prince, turning their heads to face the King. "I am delighted to see you all gathered here for this historic occasion. Each of you have been given a wonderful opportunity. If you so choose to remove yourself, or if you are chosen to be removed, you shall be sent home to your region. Though I cannot think your people will be overjoyed with their representative coming home empty-handed." The King gave a devilish grin as a chuckle escaped his lips. The others in the room followed suit, but the laughter was tense and utterly fake. "Nevertheless, these trials are more than a measly competition; they are a chance for our kingdom to choose a bride for my son and heir, Prince Cassian Vaelros."

At the mention of his name, the Prince whispered to the girls who giggled and scurried off, peeling themselves from his grasp. He stood and bowed, the picture of desirability, before prancing down the grand staircase. His expression shifted into something downright mischievous as he reached the first girl in line. One by one, he greeted each representative, lifting their hands to his lips and offering them a soft, practiced kiss. Gasps and giggles followed him like shadows.

He reached me too quickly. I felt the weight of his gaze before I saw it. His eyes filled with something heavy and curious, something I couldn't name. He stopped in front of me, all glowing skin and dangerous confidence, and offered a smile that looked like it could topple empires.

"Welcome to Aurea, Miss..." His voice trailed, expectant.

"Seravell," I blurted out, too fast and too loud. My insides shriveled, but I kept my expression neutral.

"Miss Seravell," he repeated, a smirk curling his lips. "I'm Prince Vaelros, but please, call me Cassian."

He reached gently for my gloved hand but paused as his eyes flicked down to them. He crooked his head to the side, biting the inside of his cheek. Those golden eyes snapped back to my own.

"Hiding something, Miss Seravell?"

I wasn't sure what to say. I peered over my shoulder, hoping to find Kaden.

"Take them off."

The command pulled my attention back. My head spun, meeting the Prince's eyes as he smiled heinously.

"Excuse me?"

"We don't wear leather in Aurea." He yawned, his chin lifting as if this entire conversation was below him. Down the line, girls snickered. The Prince moved to stand by my side, his eyes gliding back up to the two girls atop the raised platform. "We like our clothing a bit more...flitty." His smirk told me everything he had in mind after the throne room had cleared.

I had never met someone so absolutely rotten.

His attention came back to me, pointedly at my gloves.

"Go on now. Take them off."

I blinked rapidly. Kaden hadn't lied when he said the Prince would never fall for a damsel in distress. In fact, he seemed to prey on them.

I gritted my teeth as I hissed back, "As you wish, Prince Vaelros." I half expected him to slap me right then and there for my intonation alone, but his smirk only grew into a toothy grin.

I peeled off the first glove, the air hitting my skin like pins and needles. I took the second off and held them in my hands as my eyes stayed on the floor. I felt the burn as blood rushed to fill my cheeks.

Prince Vaelros snapped his fingers and suddenly, a servant rushed over.

"Bramwell, take her gloves and burn them, would you?"

The servant, Bramwell, bowed in response. He shifted to face me and reached his hand out to take the gloves away. I laid them into his palm. I watched as Bramwell walked away holding the one thing I had of my father.

The Prince grabbed my hand, his skin connecting directly with mine. I gasped at my contact, my eyes snapping to the skin touching my own. My chest rose and fell rapidly as I braced for something, anything.

But nothing came. No confusion filled his gaze. No silver flooded his eyes. I waited for him to flinch back, to pull away like I was poison itself, but he didn't. It was like a wall blocked me from him, like our hands were on opposite sides of a glass pane.

Every nerve in my body was alight with panic, and the Prince knew. He kept his eyes on mine as he lifted my hand, brushing a soft kiss to the back of my knuckles with a devilish smile.

What a sadist.

The touch was featherlight, but it sent shocks through my entire body. I wasn't sure if the electricity was my fault or not. And then, he pulled back, still holding my gaze, and something flickered behind his eyes. Something more than charm. Interest.

My breath felt stuck in my throat, but I forced it steady. I refused to give him any more than he had just taken.

Kaden, standing nearby, released a quiet breath I hadn't realized he'd been holding. Prince Cassian spun on his heels, smirking as he ambled back up the grand stairs. He returned to his seat beside the King, lounging in the miniature throne. He reminded me of a child once they become bored of their toys.

The tension slowly unspooling as the King raised his voice once again.

"Now, you will each be assigned quarters," he announced. "I expect you to prepare yourselves for the trials ahead. May the best region win!"

Music began to play as the space filled with laughter and song. The girls erupted into soft chatter, the pressure of the room loosening now that the worst was over.

Kaden appeared beside me again, his mouth set in a grim line, and gestured for me to follow him. I fell into step beside him as the crowd began to thin. My eyes stayed stuck to the floor as humiliation burned into my face. I looked at my hands and the pale skin that covered them. I looked at my nails and the thin line of dirt underneath them. I looked at my weaknesses, and all that stared back was myself.

"He's awful," I whispered, the words escaping despite my better judgment.

Kaden glanced at me over his shoulder. "Yet you survived." His eyebrows were pinched together in something that almost resembled sympathy.

We wove through the palace's winding corridors, each one more stunning than the last. The walls glittered with gold-leaf flourishes, and intricate mosaics told stories of Aurea's ancient rulers. Sunlight streamed in from arched windows framed by blooming vines, their petals spilling onto the white stone floors like scattered paint. Everything smelled of honeyed air and garden roses. To think that such beauty was wasted on such cruel individuals.

When we reached the door to my quarters, I paused. The room beyond was tasteful. Not overly frilly or luxurious, but nothing in this palace could ever be described as quaint.

Sunlight spilled across a velvet settee, soft and inviting. A four-poster bed stood against the far wall, draped in pale silks that shimmered like water. A copper bathing tub was tucked into the far right corner, and next to it, an armoire bunched full of fabrics that seemed to create its own rainbow. A desk stood against the rightmost wall. Its chair was tucked neatly beneath with stacks of loose parchment sitting on the wood. Quills and pots of ink laid perfectly organized along the desk's panels. Warm wood floors and rich golden tapestries gave it an elegant comfort, and to my left, a pair of glass doors opened onto a balcony. I moved to them like I was in a trance.

Beyond lay the palace gardens. Rows upon rows of vibrant flowers, their colors blazing in the dying sun. Towering willows swayed gently beside ponds that mirrored the sky. In the distance, a greenhouse gleamed like crystal, tucked between hedgerows and stone paths.

"Home sweet home," Kaden said behind me, dry sarcasm in his voice.

I huffed a quiet laugh. "I suppose it will do."

I stepped out onto the balcony as the sun dipped lower, casting the sky in hues of orange and rose. The breeze was warm against my skin. For the first time since arriving in Aurea, I let myself breathe.

Virellia had no sunsets like this. There, the sky turned gray and cold by dusk, and the wind always bit. The trees in Aurea might shed their leaves in autumn, but nothing here would ever resemble winter.

I stared out across the expanse of color, feeling something bloom in my chest that I couldn't quite name.

Behind me, the soft click of the door told me Kaden had left. I didn't turn. I kept my eyes on the sun as it dipped lower, gold melting into blood-orange, into violet. I wouldn't sleep until it disappeared completely.

These colors were too beautiful to miss.

CHAPTER EIGHT

I WATCHED THE SUN sink all the way beneath the earth, its final sliver melting into the horizon like gold poured into deep water. I imagined it sizzling as it touched the sea, the water ending the day and ushering in the night. Eventually, darkness arrived, and the stars began to appear, but not like the stars of Virellia.

Back home, the stars were woven thick into the night, threaded so intricately the sky itself looked stitched by divine hands. They danced in spirals and blooming arcs, forming constellations that shimmered with life. But here in Aurea, only a few of the boldest dared shine through the haze. The light from the city below roared too loud, drowning them out. It made me ache. Not just for home, but for the careless freedom I hadn't realized I'd lost. Something about this emptier sky, this one simple absence, made me feel small and far away. It made me angry, too, in a way I couldn't describe. Virellia wasn't just distant from Aurea, it was absent.

Reluctantly, I pulled myself away from the window and drifted back inside. The bed, a towering four-poster draped in delicate fabric, felt too pristine, too foreign. The covers were not fur-lined like I was used to, but woven from something light and shimmery, cool against the heat of Aurea's nights. I slipped beneath them, sinking into the plush mattress, though comfort didn't follow.

The moonlight streamed through the open windows in quiet beams, casting the shadows of the windowpanes in long rectangles across the wooden floor and pale walls. The grandeur of the palace surrounded me. Carved pillars, silk hangings, the faint scent of incense still lingered in the air, but all I could feel was the weight pressing on my chest. The expectation. The danger. The watching.

Yet you survived.

Kaden's words echoed inside me like a bell tolling low and final. Surviving felt less like a goal and more like a cliff's edge I was clinging to by my fingertips.

I turned on my side, trying to will sleep into being, but my mind wouldn't quiet. Images spiraled beneath my eyelids. Memories floated to the surface, and I relived the eerie calm of the throne room, the Prince's cruel behavior, Rhea's sharp-edged presence that felt like a blade pressed to my back.

I couldn't take it. I kicked the covers aside and sat up. The bed was warm, but a cold had crept inside me, and no blanket could push it out. I thought about going to the balcony again, but I already knew that sky would only make things worse. Instead, I needed something solid, or maybe someone. Maybe Kaden's room was close to mine, like at Mabel's. Just knowing he was there might steady the storm in my chest.

As I approached my door, I paused at the faint glow leaking through the frame. The heavy wood didn't quite meet its frame, leaving a thin gap just wide enough to see the flicker of torchlight and the edge of Kaden's boots where he stood, but then, I heard a voice. And not Kaden's.

It was low and warm, inviting in the way fire draws you closer on a cold night, yet threaded with urgency. Smooth as golden honey, but something in it made my skin prickle.

"—she must win. Or at the very least survive," the voice said, hushed and intense.

I held my breath. My hand froze on the doorframe. The voice was unfamiliar, but it carried weight, authority, like someone used to being obeyed.

"She's the Silver Flame," the man continued, the words heavy with meaning. "Just like we've waited for. These trials are structured very specifically. They're designed to be unfair, and there's nothing I can do if this goes badly. I have to keep face."

What in the stars was *a Silver Flame*?

I leaned closer, pressing my ear to the wood, heart thundering in my chest.

"I know," Kaden snapped, his voice taut like a bowstring. "But if your father is watching her, we can't just parade her around. We have to be cautious. She's stronger than she realizes. I don't even think she knows who she is..." His voice trailed off. Kaden mumbled to the figure standing before him, "...or what she is."

My stomach twisted, dread curling through me like smoke. I stepped back, trying to retreat quietly, but my foot hit the leg of the desk chair, and it scraped sharply across the floor.

Silence.

The conversation halted like a cut thread. I could hear the shuffle of movement, a breath drawn in too quickly, then nothing. Whoever had been speaking was gone. Or hiding. A moment later, the door flung open.

"Miss Seravell?" Kaden's face was pale, his eyes wide with alarm as he stepped into the room. "Are you okay?"

"I—yes," I stammered, caught somewhere between shame and fear. "I'm fine. I just... Who was that? What's going on?"

He hesitated, nearly reaching for me before his hands hovered, uncertain. "You're tired," he said finally, his tone gentle but unyielding. "You should sleep."

"I heard you," I insisted. "You were talking about me."

"We were talking about the trials," he said, avoiding my eyes. But the flicker in his expression, the twitch of unease, told me more than his words. "It doesn't matter right now. What matters is that you're safe. You *are* safe, Seravell."

I swallowed hard. "You promise?"

"Of course." This time he did touch me, a hand on my shoulder meant to be steady and grounding, but his careful fingers only dared to touch the fabric of my gown. "Just rest. You have a long day ahead."

I stared down at the floor, then admitted in a whisper, "I can't sleep."

His face shifted, his features tensing with something between concern and exasperation. "Do you want me to get you something from the apothecary? Or food? Or—"

"No!" I whipped my head up. "I've made hundreds of those disgusting sleep draughts. I'd rather stay up all night."

Kaden blinked, caught off guard. "Then what is it?"

I bit down on my lower lip, embarrassed by how small it felt. "The stars," I said.

"The stars?" he repeated, baffled. "The *stars* are keeping you awake?"

"Well—no. Not exactly. It's just... Virellia had stars for miles. A sky so full you couldn't see the darkness between them. And here, there are so few I could count them all. It just—it made me homesick, that's all."

To my surprise, Kaden didn't mock me or scoff. He stepped closer and gently guided me toward the balcony with a warm hand at my back. I followed him into the night air. The wind was cooler now, rustling my hair, brushing against my cheeks. I looked up again. The sky had darkened fully, and more stars had emerged, timid but present, though nowhere near the canvas I longed for.

"We don't have as many stars," Kaden said quietly. "But we do have this."

He nudged me to the left, toward the edge of the balcony where the palace wall curved away, and suddenly, the city opened before me like a glowing tapestry. I couldn't see it all, but I could see enough.

Aurea pulsed with life even at this hour. The streets shimmered, golden with torchlight, and laughter rose on the breeze. Music, too. Faint but bright. The buildings twisted like the palace itself, narrow and tall and full of strange grace. It was chaotic. Luminous. A world apart from Virellia's soft snow-covered charm. I could pretend to hate it, but I'd be lying if I said it wasn't marvelous.

"Aurea is nothing like Virellia," Kaden said. "But take that as an opportunity. One that works best if you *sleep*." He said the last part with the same tone a parent would a child. I scoffed at him lightly, but the view of the city kept any rising irritation at bay.

And just like that, he turned and left me standing there. I stayed on the balcony a moment longer, watching the city breathe. Then I turned back to the bed and sighed. My body was exhausted, but my mind refused to still. Still, I crawled beneath the covers, letting them wrap around me like a cocoon.

Doubt clung to me like a second skin, whispers of secrets and silver and crowns circling through my thoughts. My dreams came in flickers when sleep finally pulled me under. Swirling visions showed fragments of power, memories that didn't feel like mine, and voices I didn't recognize whispering truths I wasn't ready to hear.

I saw freckle-faced princes and twirling ballgowns. I saw dancing couples and guards hidden in shadows.

I saw visions of gilded crowns melting away to reveal silver underneath.

CHAPTER NINE

I WOKE WITH A GROAN, sunlight already pouring through the soft white curtains like liquid gold. My head ached from restless sleep, dreams full of whispers clinging to the corners of my thoughts like cobwebs. That smooth honey-sweet voice was stuck in my head. His whispers of secrets laced in urgency ran on repeat in my mind. My heart thrummed with unease, and even after the terrible sleep, I was wide awake.

A sharp knock rattled the door.

"Seravell," came Kaden's voice through the wood, bright and sing-songy. "Rise and shine. Trial number one's been announced."

My jaw nearly dropped. One day. I'd been here for one day and they'd already thrown down the gauntlet. The Prince clearly didn't waste time.

I dragged myself to the door, cracked it open, and blinked at the explosion of pale blue fabric in Kaden's arms. It shimmered like a cloudless sky. The layers of tulle and satin and delicate embroidery glinted in the light. I swung the door wide open as I tried, and failed, to hold in my laughter. The amount of fluff and sparkle nearly swallowed him whole.

I peered around the edge, chuckling. "What... is that?"

Kaden grinned like a cat. "A dress. A weapon. A prison. Take your pick."

"I'm not wearing that."

"Oh, but you are," he said, dumping it into my arms before I could protest. The weight of it surprised me. The dress was heavier than I expected, like it carried some kind of burden.

I trudged back toward the desk, letting the dress tumble across its surface in a whisper of satin and sequins. Kaden followed, adjusting his collar where the dress had wrinkled it. "The first trial is a ball," he said, as if that were normal. "Tonight. Dancing, charm, composure. All the things I suspect you've had zero experience with." He grimaced and held up his hands. "No offense."

I shot him a flat look. "Excuse you. I am very composed by Virellian standards. I'm sure no Aurean girl would be particularly composed while being chased by wild dogs."

Kaden raised a brow but said nothing. His silence gave me time to process what he'd said.

"Wait—*tonight?*"

He didn't even blink. "Into the gown, wild dog." He pointed with exaggerated flair at the dress.

With a groan, I scooped it up and disappeared behind the folding screen. Slipping into it was an ordeal. It hugged my torso like it had been sewn to my ribs, the bodice structured with tiny silver-threaded boning. The layered satin skirt rippled like moonlight over water when I moved, embroidered with frost-kissed blossoms and patterns that shimmered in the light. I caught my reflection briefly in the mirror. The pale blue reminded me of the dress Selene and I had picked out together. The one I'd arrived in. There was something sacred in that memory.

When I stepped out, Kaden's silence told me everything.

He blinked once. Then again. Cleared his throat far too quickly. "Not bad, Seravell. You almost look like you belong here."

"Almost?" I lifted a brow.

"Well, you're a little pale, missing a tiara, and need about ten pounds of ego, but otherwise," He waved a vague hand. "You'll do."

He held out a pair of white long gloves that were embroidered with careful silver thread.

"From the Prince."

I rolled my eyes, but I pulled them on. The fabric reached past my elbows, almost connecting with the cap sleeve of the gown.

A reluctant smirk tugged at my lips. "So, what now?"

"Do you know how to dance?"

I gave him a suspicious glance as he mimed twirling a partner through the room like he was performing for a crowd. He ended with a dramatic spin, throwing his hands up in the air and grinning at me ear to ear.

"I don't dance."

Kaden dropped his arms with a sigh that could've wilted flowers. "Well, Seravell, you're going to have to. Come on, I know a place."

I groaned again, and honestly, I'd have rather taken my chances with wild dogs.

He led me through the palace, its white marble halls glowing with the rising sun. The arched ceilings were kissed with gold, the delicate mosaics glimmering, as sunlight dripped through open windows like honey. The air smelled faintly of citrus and stone. I tried to track our path—left at the lion statue, right at a hallway blooming with stained-glass—but everything blurred together in a dreamlike haze.

Then we stepped into the gardens, and I forgot how to breathe.

It was like walking into a storybook. Golden blossoms curled over ivy-draped archways, their petals glowing as if lit from within. Paths wound like ribbon through whispering willows and glassy fountains. The air was sweet with jasmine and honey. Orange trees hung heavy with fruit, casting dappled shadows on the marble benches tucked beneath them. Ponds dotted the ground, each one swirling with brightly colored koi fish. The whole place shimmered, a world apart from anything I'd ever known. I slowed, fingers brushing a golden bell-shaped flower.

Kaden led us along a narrow trail until a domed structure came into view. It gleamed like a cut jewel half-sunken into the greenery, glass walls catching the sunlight.

"The greenhouse," he announced, pushing open the door.

Inside, the air was warm and alive and rich with the scent of soil, sweet leaves, and blooming foliage. Plants climbed the glass walls, vines hung from the rafters, and flowers of every imaginable shape bloomed from polished stone beds. The morning sun poured in from above, lighting the floor in scattered light.

Kaden moved to the center of the room and turned toward me. He paused, his eyes running down the length of me, then, he extended his hand.

"Dance with me."

I paused. "But there's no music."

"Doesn't mean we can't pretend"

I stepped closer and took his hand. It was warm and rough and familiar. He pulled me close, one hand at my waist, the other clasping mine. He only touched the fabric of my dress and gloves, his hands careful and measured.

"You're not touching me," I said flatly.

"I wouldn't dare," he said with a wink. "I am a gentleman, believe it or not."

I snorted. Still, I stepped into position.

He guided me clumsily at first, gripping the heavy fabric like reins. I tripped twice, once nearly dragging us both into a bed of blood-red snapdragons.

"Wow," he muttered, catching my elbow just in time. "You really can't dance."

"Yeah, well, we don't tend to have balls in Virellia," I snapped, cheeks burning, but after a few more rotations and a healthy amount of grumbling, I started to get it. Kaden taught me a million steps. Waltzes, something called a foxtrot, a maddening thing called the quickstep. My feet stopped stumbling. My limbs remembered how to move. Eventually, I was gliding instead of tripping.

"So, you're not hopeless. Or maybe you were, but I'm an amazing teacher," Kaden said, grinning.

"Thank you, gracious dance master," I said as I stepped back with a theatrical bow. Kaden let out a low chuckle as he wiped a bead of sweat from his brow. He leaned back against a wooden arch bound by flowering vines.

He raised his arms above his head to hold the top of the frame. The motion was almost too easy, and I hadn't realized how tall he was. The light hit his dark hair and lit the edges as if they were on fire.

We locked eyes, and suddenly the silence wasn't so unnoticeable. He didn't move, didn't blink. Just stood there and looked, like he'd caught a star falling where it didn't belong.

I hadn't even taken the time to really look at *him*. He was dressed in court finery, pale yellow and ivory silk that shimmered faintly in the light, tailored to his broad shoulders and every band of muscle. He really was beautiful. I wasn't sure how every girl in Aurea wasn't fawning over him.

Kaden tensed under my gaze, just slightly, but I noticed. As if he wasn't sure what this moment meant either.

He let out a huffed breath as he broke the stare, and with it the trance we seemed to have been put under. He cleared his throat and pushed himself off the arch.

"Should we keep practicing?" he said, voice low and smooth, but edged with uncertainty.

I swallowed. "Yeah. Yeah, we probably should."

He studied me for a beat longer. Then his lips curved. Not a smile, not quite. More like a dare.

"Want to learn another?"

I threw my head back with an exasperated sigh. "Another? There's more?" I lifted my head back and cocked it dramatically to the side.

"There's hundreds," he murmured, eyes drifting down to drink me in—my dress, my flushed cheeks, the loose strands of hair framing my face. He stepped closer. "But this one is my favorite."

His hand extended politely, but his stare meant something else entirely.

My gloved fingers slid into his.

Kaden guided me forward, his other hand resting low against the small of my back, fingers splayed. We began to move.

It was slow, smooth, effortless. It seemed to come naturally. He didn't bark orders of steps, didn't drag me around the space. We simply moved in tandem like we'd danced this way a hundred times in another life. His hand tightened slightly at my waist, drawing me closer, and my skirts swirled against his legs as we turned. Blue mixed with yellow. Ice mixed with gold.

The greenhouse spun gently around us, all glittering glass and bursts of crimson and violet blossoms. The soft sound of rustling leaves was stirred by our motion.

His gaze never left mine.

His eyes were so green they made the sprawling plants look dull.

"You're not bad," he murmured, amusement curling in his voice. "For someone from Virellia."

I raised a brow with a scoff. "Oh? And how do I compare to a girl from Aurea, then?"

He smiled, sharp and wicked.

Then, before I could realize what he was doing, he swept his foot behind mine, hooked my ankle gently, and I tripped backward with a startled gasp.

But he caught me.

His arm circled my waist in a flash, steady and strong, dipping me low with a flourish. My breath caught. My hand clutched his shoulders so hard the fabric bunched in my grip. His face hovered inches above mine, green eyes gleaming.

"That," he said, voice low and smug, "is good for someone from Aurea."

I blinked up at him, heart pounding. "You almost *dropped* me."

"Ah, but I didn't." He looked at my hands white-knuckling his shoulders. "And you seem to have a pretty good hold on me anyway."

I hadn't noticed I was still holding on. I loosened my grip, and as I sunk down, he held me tighter.

I let him pull me upright, and for a moment, just one, I didn't think about trials or crowns or anything at all.

It was just Kaden. And me.

He turned us beneath a growth of flowering vines, and light filtered through the petals, casting rose-gold shadows across his face. His hand pressed a little firmer at my back, the touch making me look back up at him.

"Are you nervous for tonight?"

I didn't answer.

My body moved with his, chest brushing chest, breath mingling in the air between us.

"I would be nervous too," he said, barely audible.

He leaned closer, so close my face was practically in his neck. He smelled of smoke and leather and nothing like the cologne that plagued the other men. Kaden paused, holding me there for just a moment before he spun me out, graceful and devastating. My hand slipped free, and my skirts flared like petals in bloom. When I came to a stop, I hesitated, looking out the windows of the greenhouse to the gardens before turning back to face him.

"What was that dance called?"

Kaden stared in response. He opened his mouth, then closed it as he let his head fall forward. He ran a hand across his neck before finding my eyes once more.

"I just followed you."

My pulse skipped. Stars help me.

I forced a laugh. "Smooth, Kaden. Real smooth."

"Honest."

I folded my arms, pretending I wasn't flustered. I took a step towards him. "Then I guess I get to name it."

He nodded solemnly as he also stepped forward, closing the space between us even further. "Seems only fair. I need something to tell people when they ask what my new favorite dance is called."

I narrowed my eyes. "You expect people to ask that?"

"Oh, they will," he said, flashing that rare, crooked grin. "It'll be a sensation. I just need to know what to write in the history books. You don't want to miss your chance."

I laughed under my breath as I moved even closer. "Alright. How about… 'The Stumble and Smirk'?"

He gave a mock gasp. "Blasphemy. That dip was flawless."

"Because you tripped me!"

"I guided you."

"Into the floor?"

"Into glory."

I bit back a smile, shaking my head. "You're impossible."

"You seem to handle me just fine," he said, stepping so close that any other movement would have us touching. His voice dropped just enough to make me forget I had to breathe. "So, clearly not impossible, just… particular."

I didn't know what to say, and Kaden, ever unreadable, just stared. He looked at me for a beat too long, like he was memorizing something he didn't quite understand.

Then he stepped back, the air cooling instantly in his absence.

"Well then," he said softly, "thank you for the dance, Lady Seravell." He pulled at his cuffs, adjusting them as he spoke. "But we better start heading back. I'm sure your handmaidens are already fuming that I don't have you right on schedule."

"Handmaidens?"

Kaden bit back a laugh, looking back up at me. "Welcome to the palace."

We walked back side by side, but every once in a while, our hands would brush. I thought about what that might feel like without the gloves. Without the fabric that so clearly divided us. That divided me from everyone.

He opened the door to my room, and sure enough, four girls around my age, one slightly younger even, were waiting. They fidgeted with the fabric of a silver silk dress, and one held a box of pins and bobbles. I turned back to Kaden to find him already looking at me.

"Thank you. For your help today."

He gave me a smile and grabbed the frame of my door, just like he had done earlier in the greenhouse.

"Just doing my job."

We both knew that was a lie.

He pushed himself back and let his arms fall. "Let me know when you think of a better name. I'm not dancing it with anyone else." And then he turned and left. I watched as he walked down the hall, and part of me hoped he would look back to check if I was watching too, but he didn't.

"Lady Seravell?"

I spun to see the oldest of the four standing behind me, head down and hands holding the glittering silk gown.

Right. The ball.

CHAPTER TEN

I SAT AT THE VANITY, hands folded tightly in my lap. The scent of rose oil and candle wax lingered in the air as the handmaidens pinned the final coils of my hair into place. They wore gloves the entire time. I wasn't sure if it was out of kindness or caution. I wasn't sure which one hurt more.

My hair had been swept up into an intricate updo, the pale strands curling like drifting clouds. Each twist was anchored by gleaming pearl pins and slivers of silver that caught the candlelight. A few soft ringlets framed my face and cascaded down my back in deliberate spirals, the kind of detail only reserved for someone important. Someone who belonged here.

The dress they'd given me was similar in shape to the one I wore this morning, but the fabric was something else entirely. The silver silk clung to my shoulders and arms, high on the neck and shaped like it had been poured over me. The dress was tailored so precisely it seemed to be sewn directly onto my bones. The back was completely open, and the fabric shimmered with each breath I took. Embroidery glittered subtly along the hem and neckline—moons and stars in the shape of constellations, if one looked closely enough. Not frilly or gaudy, but convenient. Regal. Dangerous.

This one was me.

I slipped on the same gloves as this morning and flexed my fingers in the silk as I peered up to look in the mirror.

I barely recognized the girl who stared back, but maybe that was the point.

The handmaidens didn't say a word as they finished. They just bowed quickly and slipped through the door, murmuring to someone outside. I already knew who it was before I heard the knock.

I opened the door to find Kaden standing there, dressed in fully royal regalia—a dark midnight coat embroidered with golden thread. His sleeves were tailored sharply to his frame, his hair slicked back like the perfection he was meant to be. He looked more than handsome. He was maddening.

The memory of the dance swirled in my mind. It echoed and ached, and part of me would be lying if I said I was completely dreading tonight. His gaze flicked over me, lingering for a second too long before he masked whatever shift had just crossed his face. A sardonic smile replaced it.

"Well," he said with a low whistle, taking my gloved hand and spinning me once with exaggerated flair. "You clean up."

I rolled my eyes, chuckling under my breath, but the heat crept into my cheeks anyway. "Is that a compliment?"

"Don't get used to it," he muttered, offering his arm.

We walked in silence through the corridors, the torchlight dancing along the polished walls of gold-veined marble. With each turn, the distant murmur of string instruments and laughter grew louder. We passed through open-air walkways draped in vines, the night wind lifting the scent of jasmine and something else. Something old and sweet, like a forgotten memory. It clung to my chest.

By the time we reached the corridor leading to the ballroom, my breath had all but left me. Golden lanterns floated above our heads like tiny suns, casting a warm, romantic glow that dripped across the moss-dappled floor and trailing ivy. It was magical. If this was just the entrance, my stars.

I allowed myself to pretend for a heartbeat. Pretend this was a fairy tale and a dream come true, but only for a heartbeat. Because this wasn't a dream, it was a trial, and the ballroom was waiting.

The doors loomed ahead, carved from dark wood inlaid with golden rivers flowing where the wood had cracked. A pair of guards pushed them open as we approached, and the sound hit me like a wave. Strings and laughter and clinking glasses filled the space, and the low hum of power and performance was woven into every breath.

I stepped inside, and it was like falling into a dream. The ballroom was enormous. It's ceiling was lost in shadows and glittering chandeliers that floated weightlessly above the dance floor like constellations. Silk draped from the rafters, soft ivory and gold, moving ever so slightly as if stirred by invisible hands.

The walls were mirrored in places, tall enough to reflect the entire room. I caught sight of myself, a figure of pure silver, alien and glittering. My throat tightened. I didn't know her, but she looked like she belonged here.

Nobles spun across the marble in sweeping arcs. While their gowns shifted like ships on a turbulent sea, their laughter came soft and effortless. Already the other competitors were making their rounds of curtsies, handshakes, and measured smiles that danced just short of sincerity.

I stayed back, hovering at the edge of it all. Kaden continued walking as he talked to other guards and men who wore the royal colors, no doubt some of the King's men. He hadn't noticed I'd stopped.

Elena was radiant in coral silk, drifting across the dance floor like a breeze. Another girl wore something sharp and tailored, almost androgynous, but still stunning. But Rhea, Rhea glided down the staircase like it had been built for her, all violet velvet and cold fire. She didn't look nervous. She looked like the stars themselves had dressed her for war.

I tugged my gloves higher.

The King's voice rang out like a bell, cutting through the murmuring crowd. "This evening marks the beginning of your first trial. Poise. Grace. The art of observation. To rule is to see and be seen."

I shrank to the edge of the room, barely breathing, trying to melt into the shadows. The enormous space suddenly didn't seem big enough. Music swelled, and couples danced with practiced ease. I wasn't like them. I didn't know how to move like that, didn't know how to smile like it cost nothing.

Kaden continued his conversation with one of the guards as I finally reached the end of the stairs and hit the marble floor. I took the moment and disappeared along the edge of the room.

"Elena," I whispered when I saw her skirting the edge of the chaos.

She turned, her eyes lighting up. She squealed as she jumped up and down slightly, her curled hair bouncing with her.

"This is everything I've ever dreamed of," she said, her voice quiet. She slid in closer to me as her eyes scanned out towards the couples twirling across the floor. "But why do I feel like we're about to be fed to wolves?"

"Because we are," I muttered. "Except they're wearing crowns."

Kaden appeared like a ghost at my side, bowing with dramatics. "Let's make you look like you know what you're doing." Before I could refuse, he pulled me onto the floor.

He led me through the opening steps of the Viennese waltz with unexpected grace. The dance was formal, rooted in tradition—one foot forward, right, close, then back, left, close. Kaden moved like he'd been trained in it from birth. He probably had.

"Don't think," he murmured. "Feel."

I did. For a few precious heartbeats, I let my body follow the rhythm, let myself forget where I was. The music carried me, Kaden's hand firm at my back, the chandeliers spinning above. For a few precious heartbeats I felt like I could have a place here.

Then the partners shifted.

I turned and was caught by another noble, a man with a forgettable face and unkind fingers. His hand clamped down on my waist too tightly, pulling me forward into the next step before I was ready. I stumbled. He smirked.

Embarrassment burned hot in my chest.

Kaden was back before I could unravel further, his voice low against my ear. "You're fine. Breathe."

I exhaled, and then I felt eyes.

Eyes on me.

I looked up, and there he was.

Prince Cassian Vaelros stood near the far wall, barely lit, half-lost in the shadows cast by a towering pillar, but the chandeliers betrayed him. Gold light clung to him like it knew better. Of course it did. It loved him like everyone else in this forsaken city.

He wore royal blue, a high collar, and a silver pin at his throat. Understated, devastating. His tousled hair, his perfectly unbothered posture, his crooked smile. His arms were crossed, and he looked— stars—amused. No, *enthralled*. Like he'd been waiting for me to notice him.

I shook my head slightly, as if I could shake off his eyes.

The music ended. Applause scattered across the room like coins.

Kaden spun me in a theatrical flourish, for show, no doubt. My vision blurred for a second, and when it cleared, I fled. I slipped between nobles and out of the crowd, stumbling toward the refreshments.

The wine burned as I gulped it down. I welcomed the sensation. Another glass followed.

It dulled the sting in my chest. Dulled everything. My thoughts turned loose and fizzy. The world began to shimmer at the edges, like it, too, was wearing a mask.

I danced again, barely. Kaden swept me into one, then another. I couldn't remember the steps, didn't care. When I stepped on his foot and giggled, he hissed a soft 'Ow' and shot me a look, but I just laughed harder. I didn't care anymore. None of it mattered.

Eventually, when another guard pulled Kaden aside, I slipped away for good from the nauseating ballroom.

I snuck out of the large wooden doors and into the corridor, the laughter and strings fading behind me like the end of a dream. My heels clicked against marble as I wandered, one hand skimming the stone paneling. The air out here was cooler, quieter. Still thick with the scent of lilies and smoke drifting in from the ballroom but touched now with the cold hush of night. The palace halls felt endless as they glowed with candlelight and dusted shadows. My dress swished like a living thing, silver rippling like water beneath moonlight.

I leaned against a column and pressed my fingers to my temple, the silk of my gloves a welcome cool against the heated air. Everything felt a little too bright. A little too loud. The music had become something warped in my ears, like it belonged to another realm entirely.

Stars. I'd had too much wine. The wine was strong, or maybe I was weak. Either way, I was floating.

A glass was held lazily in my other hand, the deep red liquid sloshing dangerously close to the edge, but I didn't care.

I took a drink from the glass. And another. And another, setting the now empty cup on a table full of royal artifacts I didn't know or care about.

I wandered.

I wasn't sure what I was looking for. Air maybe, or freedom.

When I turned the corner too fast, my head spun. The walls of the palace stretched and curved like they were made of spun glass. I giggled. Why did I giggle?

Then, I tripped as the silver fabric of my dress tangled with my slow-moving feet.

Two strong hands caught me before I could hit the floor.

"Stars, you're a menace."

The man steadied me, arms warm around my waist, and suddenly, my back was pressed against him. He smelled like something expensive and terrible for you. Cologne mixed with cedar and the last drop of stolen wine. Maybe the wine was me.

I craned my neck back to see Prince Cassian Vaelros in all his splendor.

"You," I said stupidly.

"Me," he replied, clearly amused.

I clawed at the arms around me. "Let me go," I whispered.

"You'll fall."

"I don't care."

"I do."

I blinked up at him. His face was too close. His eyes seemed to swallow me whole, devouring me in all my drunken glory.

"You disappeared from my ball," he said, borderline snidely. "And I was so enjoying watching you dance."

His suit was so rich of a blue that it was almost iridescent in the dim light. The silver pin up by his neck glinted.

He noticed me looking and offered a quiet smile. "Wore it for you." His grin was soft and unlike the cat-like smirk from the throne room. "I see you received my gift."

I looked at the gloves on my hands. The wine made the silver thread seem alive, swirling and spiraling across my fingers and wrists.

"Only because you burned my leather ones."

Prince Vaelros only shrugged, raising his shoulders with complete indifference. "I tend to do as I please."

My lip curled as I scoffed. I pushed at his hands that still held my waist.

"Then go back to your idiotic ball."

That granted a low chuckle.

"Idiotic doesn't sound particularly pleasing now does it, Miss Seravell?"

I looked away, out the tall windows where the night bled over the horizon in deep bruised blue. "I can't breathe in there," I whispered.

The Prince nodded once. "Then don't go back. Stay with me."

I let my head fall back against his chest, my eyes finding his as they looked down at me.

He would've been devastatingly beautiful if it wasn't for his horrid personality.

"Well did you at least bring more wine?" My voice slurred.

He let out a deep rumbling laugh and leaned down, the edge of his jaw brushing my hair. He was so close to my bare skin, it crawled.

"You're already drunk," he whispered close, his breath warm against my ear.

I blew out a breathy laugh dramatically. "Not nearly enough for this conversation."

He pulled his head back, eyes wide with mock disbelief. "Never thought we would agree, yet here we are."

I huffed a breath, letting my head hang back onto his chest with the pull of gravity suddenly much heavier. His words were sharp, but his face spoke another language entirely. He looked down at me like I had the same effect on him as the wine did me. His eyes drank me in fully.

"At least I know the wine's good," he said. "Shame it was gone before I got any. Wouldn't happen to know who drank it all, would you, Miss Seravell?"

I met his gaze or tried to. "No idea, Prince Vaelros. But I'll keep an eye out. Just for you."

He laughed, low and warm. "Just for me? How kind." He began to guide me slowly with a hand on my waist through the palace halls, as if time itself would yield for him. For us.

"This place is so stupid," I mumbled. "This dress is so stupid. This ball is so stupid."

I tried to kick a lion statue as we passed it.

The Prince raised an eyebrow. "What'd the lion do to you?"

"Looked at me funny."

"You're out of your mind." He released his grip slightly and immediately, gravity took full advantage of my drunken balance, or lack there of. I swayed like grass in the breeze as I walked forward, the halls warping and moving like waves of water. He caught me again as I stumbled, but this time, instead of steadying me, he lifted me off the ground. Into his arms.

I squeaked. "What are you—"

"Shh." His tone was teasing, but his arms were gentle. His gaze flicked down to my mouth and back again. "You're lucky it's me."

"At least you're attractive," I slurred, then immediately winced. "Wait. That wasn't—"

His smile was slow. "No, no, I liked that one."

I buried my face in his chest. "This never happened."

"Whatever you say, little flame."

He carried me through the palace like a prince in a fairy tale, and for a moment, I forgot the terror he was.

The Prince took me to my room in silence, and I didn't protest. He opened the door, carried me inside, and set me down gently on the edge of the bed. He pulled back the covers with slow, careful hands, then lifted me again. I let out a yelp at the sudden movement, but he just chuckled. He laid me down and tucked the blankets around me. I melted into the silken sheets.

"Thank you, Prince Cassian Vaelros, son of King Malik Vaelros, heir to the awful, hideous crown of Aurea," I muttered sarcastically as he turned to leave.

He looked back at me with that same crooked smirk. "Anything for you, Miss Seravell." My name on his lips hit like a spark.

The last thing I saw was his silhouette in the doorway, facing me, not the exit.

CHAPTER ELEVEN

I WOKE WITH A MOUTH like ash and a headache pounding behind my eyes like war drums.

Sunlight speared through the curtains, cruel and golden and far too bright. I groaned, rolling over and burying my face in the pillow, but it did nothing to stop the slow roll of nausea in my stomach or the flood of memories beginning to resurface, one blurred moment at a time.

The ballroom. Wine that tasted like cherries and heat. Laughter. The Prince catching me in the hallway. My legs refusing to cooperate.

And then—

I froze, eyes flying open.

Prince Vaelros's arm around my waist. The warmth of his body steadying me. The brush of his fingers near, but never touching, my bare skin as he guided me through the halls, saying things I couldn't quite remember. My face burning against his chest. The feel of him settling me onto the bed like I was made of thin glass.

Stars, I'd let him *tuck me in*.

I let out a long, strangled groan and buried my face again. I had made a complete fool of myself in front of the one person I couldn't afford to be vulnerable with—the one person I had vowed to hate.

A sharp knock jolted me from my spiral.

"Don't," I rasped, but it opened anyway.

Kaden stood framed in the doorway, arms crossed, his silhouette cutting a clean line through the brightness. His coat was buttoned high, as always, but there was a softness to the way he leaned on the doorframe.

"You're alive," he said flatly.

"Unfortunately."

He stepped in, the scent of leather and cold air trailing behind him. "You drank yourself stupid."

I curled farther into the pillows. "I'm aware."

He raised a brow. "The girl from Hestel tried to sneak into the guards' wing last night. Rejected. Sent home this morning."

I peeked up at him, wincing. "Is that supposed to scare me?"

"No," he said simply. "It's supposed to remind you that you're lucky. The King is watching all of us. You, included. Keep this up, and I'll start locking you in before dusk."

I gave a dramatic groan and rolled onto my back. "I'm never drinking again."

He huffed, turning for the door. "Everyone says that, and they never mean it."

"Well, I mean it this time."

Kaden paused with one hand on the handle.

"Try not to get caught doing anything you're not supposed to be doing. I have a meeting."

"Have fun in your golden dungeon."

He disappeared with a soft click of the door, and I dragged myself upright, limbs aching. My dress from last night lay crumpled on the floor, the hem stained with spilled wine. I must have peeled it off sometime in the night, but I didn't quite remember when. My skin smelled like roses and sweat and faint smoke, a combination of perfume and poor decisions.

I shuffled toward the bathtub in the far corner of my room, the floor cool beneath my bare feet. I ran the water as hot as it would go, throwing in whatever herb was in the jar that sat at the edge. Steam billowed from the tub, and I sank into it like a corpse returning to the earth. The water smelled of crushed mint leaves and lavender, and I let the heat undo the knots in my shoulders and the dull pounding behind my eyes. By the time I emerged, pruned and soothed, I felt somewhat human again.

I dressed in a soft, pale linen gown and left my hair damp, braided loosely down one side. I didn't know what I was looking for, only that the walls of my room were closing in.

The halls of the palace glinted gold and glass. Every footstep echoed. Servants passed with arms full of pressed fabrics, polished silver, or pitchers of rosewater. I kept my head down, drawn by the faint memory of a breeze and eventually, it led me back to the gardens.

They were still breathtaking. Wisteria dangled in sheets of lilac from trellises overhead, and bees murmured among the bright clusters of blossoms. I followed the winding stone path until I found one of the many koi ponds. It glittered with gold-flecked fish and a familiar figure perched at its edge. Elena.

She wore a pale pink gown that complimented the dark black of her hair, and she was tearing crusts from a heel of bread, tossing them into the water with a meditative air. The fish darted and swirled, their mouths opening and closing as they nibbled at the offering.

"You're feeding your breakfast to the fish?" I asked, my voice hoarse.

She grinned as the threw another chunk in the pond. "They deserve good things." She turned to face me, her hand flying to her face as she tried to muffle the giggle and growing smile. "Forgive me, but you look like death."

"I feel worse than death. Death would be merciful."

She giggled and scooped up her dress as she stood. "Follow me. I have a cure."

"A fairy tale resurrection spell?"

"Better. Come on."

We slipped back inside the palace, and Elena took the lead, winding us down through the narrow servant halls. The air down here smelled of baked sugar and polished wood. Servants brushed past us with murmured apologies, some casting Elena brief glances of familiarity and amusement. She clearly had come here before.

"Elena," I asked, trailing her through a tight corridor toward the kitchens, "how exactly do you know where you're going?"

"I used to sneak into the kitchens back home in Mirun," she said, peering around a corner. "The staff there adored me. I'd sneak pastries off the trays and then listen to the gossip. I've always preferred the servants' company to the nobles'." She paused and glanced back at me, her face growing almost somber. "I needed to feel a piece of home, you know?"

I gave her a soft smile and nodded. I understood that completely.

The scent of fresh bread hit me like a wall, the air filling with the smell of yeast and toasted crust and melted butter. It made my mouth water instantly.

We ducked into a pantry tucked beside the main kitchen. It was warm and dimly lit by a single hanging lantern. The shelves were stacked to the ceiling with fresh loaves, glossy fruit tarts, clay jars of honey, and blocks of salted cheese wrapped in linen.

I blinked. "This is heaven."

"Careful," Elena whispered, reaching for a loaf of sourdough with golden bubbles crusted on top. "Don't speak too loud."

She handed me a chunk and broke off her own piece, both of us chewing in silence. The bread was still warm.

As we turned to sneak out, someone yelped.

"Lady Elena?"

A boy stood frozen in the doorway. He was gangly, with flour dusting his dark curls and a smudge of jam across one cheek. His tunic was half-untucked, and he held a copper pot like he'd just retrieved it.

He gaped at her like she'd descended from the heavens.

Elena froze, blood rushing to her cheeks. "Hi, Will."

He blinked rapidly. "You—you're not supposed to—well, I mean —hello—hi—"

His red face matched Elena's as he yanked off his cap, stumbling to the side like her presence physically startled him.

"Shhh," she said with a finger to her lips. "We're just leaving."

Will nodded so vigorously his curls bounced. "Right. Leaving. Of course. I didn't see anything."

We slipped out, and as soon as we were out of earshot, I laughed. "So, who's Will?"

Elena groaned. "He's just sweet. That's all."

"Sweet enough to let you rob the pantry."

We made our way back out to the gardens, settling under the wide limbs of a willow tree. Its branches fell around us like green silk curtains, dappled light playing over our skin. The grass was cool, the air thick with jasmine and heat.

Elena lay back on her elbows. "Want to know something scandalous?"

"Always."

She leaned closer. "Last week, one of the guards was caught kissing a laundress in the stairwell near the observatory. The girl's skirt was inside out."

I cackled. "Please tell me you saw it."

"I only heard about it. But I did also see Cassian smirk at you during the introductions. You noticed too, right?"

"Oh, I noticed," I said, smirking back. "But I'm not the only one he smirks at."

Elena sighed dramatically. "I've always thought of him as the *golden boy* of Valerieth. He's pretty, and he knows it."

"Agreed."

We lay in the dappled shade, the sun slowly dipping lower in the sky. Our bread was nearly gone, our stomachs full, and for the first time in days, I felt calm. Not hunted. Not haunted.

"I used to climb trees back in Mirun," Elena said softly. "I'd tear my dresses. Get sap in my hair. My father would shake his head and say, 'Elena, you're not a boy.' But my mother would just laugh."

"I miss the stars," I said. "We used to chart constellations. My father said if you could name something, it meant you were never truly lost."

She smiled, and for a moment, we just watched the leaves move.

Then—

"Seravell!"

I sat up, blinking against the glare. Kaden stood near the path, arms crossed, the late sunlight painting golden fire along the sharp lines of his uniform. He didn't look angry, just tired. Watching.

I turned back to Elena with a reluctant smile. "Duty calls."

She reached her hand out to lay it near my dress skirt, close but not touching. "You ever need to disappear again, or need to be revived, find me."

"Thank you," I said, meaning it.

I rose to my feet, brushing stray grass from my skirts, and made my way toward Kaden. The heat of the day clung to the stones beneath my feet, and the willow's shade lingered cool on my back. As I reached him, he looked me over, his eyes briefly flicking to my flushed cheeks, the chunk of bread still cradled under my arm.

"Are you cured?" he asked.

"Barely."

His mouth twitched upward, fighting a smile. "So, you want wine with dinner tonight?"

I cringed at the thought. "Don't even say that word."

Kaden just chuckled as we walked beside each other, wandering slowly back through the labyrinthine palace path. The shadows were growing longer now, stretching like ink across the marble floor. Birds chirped from the rooftop gardens, and the soft rush of distant fountains filled the quiet.

Kaden didn't speak for a while, and I let the silence settle between us. It wasn't uncomfortable, but more like an old coat you could wear without thinking.

"You seemed lighter," he said eventually. "Out there with her."

"I needed to breathe," I admitted. "And Elena—she's good at reminding me what that feels like."

He nodded, but his eyes didn't meet mine. "Mirun girls are steady. Strong roots."

"And what are girls from Virellia?" I joked, halfway expecting him to not even respond, but that comment made him glance at me.

"Unpredictable. Dangerous." His voice softened just slightly. "And necessary."

I swallowed, unsure how to respond.

We reached my room, and I paused in front of the door, fingers brushing the edge of the carved wood. The scent of lavender and dust lingered faintly in the hallway, mingled with whatever incense the servants had lit earlier.

"I assume your meetings weren't exciting?" I asked, offering a small smile.

Kaden rolled his eyes. "I listened to a dozen men argue about new uniforms for guards of my rank." He held up his arms, and I realized the stitching on the seams had turned golden. It reflected the light like bits and pieces of sun. "You had more fun, and more sense," he mumbled, clearly unamused by the change.

His gaze shifted to the loaf in my hand. "Bread thievery though?"

"Not technically theft. It was for medicinal purposes."

He shook his head, but the corners of his mouth curved. "Should never have expected you to actually listen to me. Try not to get thrown in a cell before the next trial."

"I'll do my best."

For a moment, neither of us moved. The world felt quieter in that corridor, like time had given grace just to us. Kaden's expression shifted, a flicker of something softer, less guarded.

"I know I've been..." He trailed off. "Tense. It won't always be like this."

I didn't know what he meant, not really, but something in his voice told me he was being genuine. Whatever storm brewed inside him was beginning to pass, or maybe he was simply tired of pretending it didn't exist. I nodded but stayed silent. His eyes met mine, and for once, there was no mask there.

He stepped back. "Rest, Seravell. Tomorrow will be harder."

Then he turned and walked away, boots quiet against the stone.

Inside, I shut the door gently behind me and leaned against it, heart still ticking a little too fast.

The room was warm and still. My bed was made. A fresh pitcher of water waited beside a tray of dried fruit. I set the bread down, unbraided my hair, and crossed to the window, letting the wind brush against my face.

In the reflection of the glass though, I saw a paper wrapped package lying on my nightstand. Brown parchment was carefully folded and tied with golden ribbon, the bow precisely and perfectly centered. I crossed the room, hovering my hands over the gift. It looked so beautiful as it was, I wasn't sure I even wanted to open it.

Eventually, I pulled at the shimmering yellow ribbon, the bow pulling away and fluttering to the sides around the paper-wrapped package. The parchment crinkled as I peeled it away, careful to only pick at the creased lines already made. Fabric peeked out from between the brown folds. Icy blue fabric.

My heart lurched as I pulled a pale, ice blue gown from the remaining brown parchment. The dress I had picked out with Selene. It had been washed, pressed, and smelled undoubtedly of expensive herbal soap, but it was the same. The same silken fabric. The same white under-skirt that reminded me of caught snow. The same subtle iridescence. I laid the dress carefully on my bed, as if the sun streaming into my room might set it ablaze. I turned back to the paper, only to see a small piece of stark white parchment at the very bottom.

Careful script wrote just five words.

Saved this from the fire.

I set the note down on my nightstand as I gathered the brown wrapping and yellow ribbon. I carefully folded the parchment and bow and set them on my desk as I hung my dress carefully in my armoire.

And for the first time in what felt like days, I didn't feel like I was sinking. Like maybe, just maybe, this could be survivable.

I spun to look out my windows at the sunset before me.

Somewhere in Aurea, a pale blue dress was hanging.

Somewhere in the palace, a guard was at his post.

Somewhere down in the gardens, the willow swayed.

And somewhere, somehow, that had become enough.

CHAPTER TWELVE

THE SUNRISE WAS FULL OF BIRDSONG. It whispered through the sheer curtains like it was meant for someone gentler than me.

For the first time since arriving at the palace, I felt steady. Not safe, not free, but grounded, as if the day had finally started on my terms.

I sat up slowly, sunlight cresting over the marble balcony to flood my room in gold. The light touched everything. The carved bedposts, the pale linen sheets, the tray of untouched fruit on my desk. There was a strange sense of calm in me.

I pulled the sheets off and swung my legs out of bed. I walked quietly over to the vanity that was home to a small mirror. Long white strands, soft and cloud-colored, slipped between my fingers as I wove them into a braid that coiled over one shoulder. I opened my armoire to my Virellian dress and slipped the blue fabric over my head, letting the layers fall where they pleased. It was a bit too thick of a fabric for Aurea, but I didn't care. I finished just as the quiet knock sounded at my door.

Kaden. Right on time.

I had been wanting to ask him about the dress. Wanting to thank him for giving me a piece of home. For protecting every part of me he could. But when I opened the door, he looked less than open to conversation. Kaden was standing like a statue carved in stone and shadows, a folded parchment in hand. Wax sealed it shut, glossy and golden, pressed with the royal emblem. The circle stamp depicted a phoenix with a crown perched atop its head like it had always belonged there.

He didn't speak, only flicked his chin toward it in a silent gesture for me to open it.

I reached out, grabbing the parchment and running my finger along its edge. I slid my finger beneath the wax, the seal cracking like brittle ice. The paper was thick, heavy with importance.

Second Trial: Maze.
Training with Lieutenant Corvallis will commence for the next three days, starting today at noon.

I stared at the words, brows furrowing.

"A maze?" I said flatly. "Really? I thought these were trials for a queen. Not some children's riddle."

Kaden let out a sharp breath, half amusement, half frustration. "This maze simulates the inner city alleyways. You've never been through them. Never even seen them. I wouldn't be so cocky just yet." Kaden looked me up and down, staring at my pale blue gown.

"You need to change, and not into another dress." He turned his nose up at the dress. It was a seemingly jokingly gesture, and I tried to laugh, but it turned sour on my tongue. He didn't recognize the dress.

Kaden continued, brushing past his unintentional insult. "Thane isn't exactly known for his kindness." He turned in the doorway, pivoting on his heels to leave.

"Who's Thane?"

"Lieutenant Corvallis." He glanced down the hall, already moving. "You'll see."

The dread was instant. I sighed, rolled my shoulders back, and dressed in a fitted tunic and slim-cut trousers, both dark and made for movement. I carefully folded and tucked the pale blue fabric into the bottom drawer of my armoire. I slid on the long silken gloves, immediately longing for my leather ones. The one thing *not* saved from the fire.

I pulled at the white silk, but with my sleeveless tunic, a band of skin stayed perpetually vulnerable to the air. I didn't have the time to care.

When I stepped into the corridor, Kaden was waiting, arms crossed, gaze already sweeping over me like a checklist. I raised my hands, as if to say, *satisfied?*

He gave a curt nod and led me through the maze of palace halls until the scent of polished wood and stone gave way to morning air.

The training grounds sprawled before us—a wide, shaded open-air pavilion that smelled faintly of sand and sweat and old blood. The yard was ringed with marble columns and tangled with creeping vines.

A narrow spiral staircase wound up the interior column of the pavilion, carved from ancient stone. The steps were uneven. Ridges and valleys were carved into the stone from years of rain trickling down. A few of the girls stumbled, catching themselves on the central rail, and by the time we reached the top, we were all breathless.

And then we stepped onto the platform.

The wind hit us first, a sharp thing that tugged at our cloaks. The soft morning had given way to a quite breezy day. The trees flowed in the current, the leaves resembling a green sea.

The platform itself was circular, with no rails to keep us from the sheer drop to the training mats under us. From here, the entire world looked smaller, but what truly stole our breath was what lay in front.

The maze.

And stars, the thing was a monster.

Walls twice my height, made of wood painted to resemble stone, towered above the training yard. The color was off, gray and ash-toned, but close enough to mimic the rocky city walls I'd seen from my balcony. It wasn't just a maze, it was a maze that breathed, that waited. Narrow corridors twisted into blind corners. Wooden crates and broken carts were stacked against some walls to mimic debris. Ropes and laundry lines crisscrossed over tight corridors. There were even shadows cast by suspended canopies, making it impossible to see the turns beyond them. It wasn't just large. It was endless. And yet somewhere, at the far side, was an opening.

In front of it all stood Lieutenant Corvallis.

Thane.

He was enormous. Not just tall but built. His deep brown skin was taunt over rippling muscle. Thick arms scarred from blade and battle, shoulders like stone. His eyes were dark, unreadable. He looked at us like a man studying insects he was trying not to crush beneath his boots. Unimpressed, unmoved.

I didn't like him. Mostly because he reminded me the King's guards. He reminded me of the guard who killed the man back home.

Girls started filing in behind me, following my gaze. One I barely recognized. The rest I did. Elena, of course. The girl I didn't recognize at the ball I now knew was named Naelle. Then Rhea. Then Clara, the girl from Seren. The small platform grew smaller as the space filled. The groups formed naturally, alliances drawn in invisible ink. I stepped closer to Elena, grateful when she offered a soft smile. Her hair, normally free flowing, was woven into a makeshift braid. Hair jutted out in awkward places, and the plait seemed to twist awkwardly, too tight in one place, too loose in other. But before I could ask, or say anything for that matter, Thane's voice sliced through the murmuring.

"The queen must survive," he said, loud and grim.

Silence fell like heavy fog over the platform.

"If separated from her guard. If cornered. If attacked. She must survive."

He gestured toward the maze behind him with a sweeping arm. "This is your test. A simulation of Aurea's lower city. There are no rules. No second chances." Another man entered the platform from the same narrow staircase. He had a cloth tied around his head that covered his nose and mouth, flowing down to the nape of his neck. I could only see his eyes, and when they found mine, I swear they narrowed. "You will be chased by a palace guard who will not hurt you but won't make it a pleasant experience. This is not a race. You must escape without being caught. And if you are caught—"

His pause was slow, heavy, and a sickening smirk grew on his face.

"You're out."

Rhea scoffed, loud enough for those nearby to hear. "Ridiculous," she muttered. "Like I didn't play in this city as a *child*."

Thane's expression didn't shift.

"We've mapped it to match the real maze used in the trial. Memorize it. Practice it. I don't care. If you get caught here, you will not survive there." He jabbed a finger towards the city that seemed to sprawl around the entirety of the palace, the hum of day in full swing.

With the same stomach-twisting smile, Thane looked directly at the girl from Delva. "Let's begin."

One by one, the girls went in.

The Delvan girl, who I learned was named Jamie, went first. From above, we watched as she stepped into the mouth the maze, shoulders squared, fists clenched at her sides. She took off sprinting, but it was clear she had never been in the city. While our knowledge was alike, our reactions were anything but the same. Jamie didn't panic. Instead, she dropped low, crawling beneath an arch of thorns that I didn't even see with the movements of a street-born girl who knew how to survive in tight places. She made it out, but the guard grabbed hold of the back of her shirt just as she broke through the opening. Thane declared her caught.

Clara was second. She didn't even make it halfway. I heard her scream before I saw her. The guard had tackled her from behind, yanking her by the ankle. She sobbed, fighting him off, but he dragged her through the sand and dumped her at the edge like trash.

Naelle barely broke a sweat. She walked the first part. Walked. Her hair was pulled up, tight coils spilling down. Not a curl out of place when she emerged two minutes later. She smirked at Clara, at all of us, like this had been a game.

Elena went after. She hesitated at the opening, her shoulders pulled back like she was bracing for war. When the horn sounded, she took off, her steps light but sure. I watched her disappear around a corner, staying low, then reappear three minutes later at the exit, panting, scraped, dirt smudging her pale cheek. She was clutching her arm where debris must have snagged her, but her smile was triumphant.

Rhea didn't just win. She attacked. When the guard tried to grab her, she spun and took him down, knocking him flat and sprinting for the exit. Thane didn't stop her. No one did. When she emerged, she raised both arms like she'd won something far more important than survival.

Then it was me.

I stepped to the edge of the maze. My heart thundered so loudly I thought everyone could hear it.

I hadn't been in the city, or any city for that matter. Ever.

Panic crept in. My vision wavered. My legs felt numb. My breathing was erratic. My lungs seemed to not even register the oxygen I was giving them.

Thane said something beside me, but I couldn't hear it. His voice was muted, like sound underwater.

Then, his hands were on my arms.

Rough. Real. And right where my gloves were not.

Skin on skin.

Heat and energy poured into my veins. My head was flung back by the force of its entry into my body.

A jolt, lightening. My vision flickered, but not out of panic. It flickered with— memories?

No, not memories. Not quite. But images, impressions. Paths. Corners. Uneven bricks. Market stalls. Alley shortcuts. Ladders bolted to crumbling walls. I blinked hard, suddenly dizzy. I knew the maze. Not logically. Not by study.

But my body knew it.

Thane again yelled in my face, but he quickly gave up, letting his hands fall away back to his sides.

The moment his skin left mine, I gasped back to life as if I had been revived. I blinked away the visions still sitting on the edges of my mind.

The horn blew, and I ran.

My feet launched forward before my thoughts could catch up. I veered left without knowing why, the scent of dust and old wood thick in my nose. The gravel crunched underfoot as I skirted a wall painted to mimic crumbling stone, the edge broken just enough to allow me to duck behind it. I didn't question the move. I just did it like I knew something would be waiting on the other side if I hadn't.

Right. Sharp turn. Another instinct. My fingers scraped brick as I swung around the corner, nearly losing my balance on a patch of uneven cobblestone. My feet found solid ground at the last second, adjusting before I could fall. There, up ahead, a low crate blocked the path. I didn't hesitate. I launched over it, landing in a crouch that sent a jolt up my knees.

Left again. Narrow alley. A slatted fence. I dropped to the ground and slid beneath it, my shoulder brushing a splintered beam that tore the fabric of my tunic. My braid caught for a moment but ripped free when I pushed off the dirt and ran again. Another turn. This one tighter, hidden behind a rack of market stall props meant to resemble crates of fruit. The smell of citrus and rot lingered faintly in the stifling air.

I dodged a hanging tarp, blue and sun-bleached, and sprinted through a cluttered corridor, ducking beneath a sagging laundry line with someone's ghost-white shirt fluttering like a specter in my face. My vision tunneled. My breath came in ragged bursts. But I didn't stop. Didn't slow.

There was a stair, half-collapsed. I didn't think, didn't calculate, just jumped. My hand caught the ledge. My foot slammed against the wood, and I vaulted up and over, landing hard on the other side with a grunt. Right again. No, wait—left. The light shifted just so, and I knew. I knew the shadows curled deeper that way. I followed them.

It was like I'd lived in this maze, like I'd run it in another life. Like it was built from my own memories except I had none.

I passed a crooked sign overhead. A detail. A landmark. Turn right. I could hear footsteps behind me. Not close. But there. Tracking. A breath. A scrape. My heart seized. I darted through an open passage I shouldn't have noticed, tucked behind a leaning doorframe, and the noise vanished. I lost them.

I sprinted harder. Past a mural of painted vines. Past an arch of stone. My lungs screamed. My thighs burned. The pulse behind my eyes pounded.

And then light.

I burst from the final turn with a cry, the sun flashing off the sand ahead of me. I stumbled, nearly collapsed, my knees wobbling under the weight of adrenaline and disbelief. My braid clung to my spine, soaked and heavy with sweat. My chest heaved, but I'd done it. I'd made it, even if I didn't understand how.

A minute or so later, the guard chased out behind me and ripped the cloth from his face. He gasped, red-faced, as he was unable to hide the shock that I'd outrun him.

I turned and began my walk back to the platform. My arms hugged my stomach, pressing and willing the cramps tearing at my sides to lessen. Each breath leaving my lungs rattled, shaking and running high on adrenaline. When I finally looked up, I scanned the courtyard. Everyone was staring directly at me.

Kaden stood with the other guards, mouth slightly open, eyes wide. There was something like pride on his face, though I wasn't sure he knew it, but it was Thane I looked to next.

His arms were crossed. His mouth flat. His eyes *furious*.

But *why*?

I'd passed. No, excelled.

Then I heard a voice like a thread of silk woven into flame.

"Well, that was impressive."

I didn't have to look to know it was him. The way the air shifted was enough. The scent of cedar and smoke floated toward me on the breeze like a whispered memory, but I turned anyway and there he was.

Prince Cassian moved through the courtyard and up the spiral stairs like it was his stage. His golden suit caught the sunlight that managed to break through the clouds and his boots didn't make a sound on the stone platform. People noticed him. They always did. Guards, servants, even the other girls. Every head seemed to tilt, every conversation faltered for half a beat as he passed, but he didn't see them. His eyes were on Thane. He walked right up the man, standing less than a yard away. The Prince had to tip his chin up to meet Thane's eyes.

"You're not cleared for this section of trials," Thane said, his voice quiet, cold. "Especially not during an official training."

The Prince didn't flinch. In fact, he stepped closer, lowering his voice just enough that his usual arrogant tone dropped. "I'm cleared for every sector. You know that." He pulled at his suit jacket, seemingly disinterested in the entire conversation. "Unless something changed while I was sleeping."

"Not everything is yours to stroll into, Cass."

"I don't need everything, bud." His lips formed into a sly grin. "Just the parts that matter."

For one wild second, I thought he was going to deck the Prince right there in front of everyone.

Then, Thane, man made of stone and war, smiled.

Not a smirk. Not a twitch.

A smile.

Thane laughed. One short, rough sound. He clapped Prince Cassian on the back, hard enough that I swore I heard the breath leave his lungs.

"Still a smug brat," Thane grumbled, the grin still hovering on his lips.

"Still terrifying," the Prince returned.

Prince Cassian called him *"bud."*

And Thane let him.

Thane called him *"Cass."*

And the Prince let him.

I stared, my pulse suddenly louder in my ears than it had been inside the maze. The people, the heat, the scrape of boots and rustle of breath all faded into the background.

Prince Vaelros's eyes found mine, just for a moment. Just a flicker of something I didn't have the words for. Recognition, maybe, or realization. Then, it was gone as Thane whispered something to his ear. He turned to Thane and murmured something low, something too quiet to hear, but it made his jaw tense and flex.

I looked back at the maze, my heart still thudding against my ribs. The air felt too thin. The world just a little off-balance, like the ground beneath me had shifted when I wasn't looking.

Something wasn't right. Something was beneath all of this, and I had no idea what I'd just tapped into.

The rest of the girls were already beginning to descend the stairs from the pavilion's platform, muttering about their times, their bruises, their next breaths. Elena walked off with her guard, arm already bandaged and cleaned. She gave me a shy wave as she left, but I just smiled, my limbs still buzzing from my own run. Kaden was waiting at the base of the stairs by the path back to the palace, eyes locked on me. He looked pale. Off. His hand twitched like he meant to reach for me but didn't.

Prince Cassian got to me first, exiting the narrow staircase just as I passed.

"Go ahead, I'll walk her back," he said smoothly to Kaden, already falling into step beside me.

"Cassian, she's still shaking." Kaden tried to object, raising his arm towards me as if it the twitching wasn't noticeable enough. He simply cocked his head and gave Kaden a smile that said *please* without words.

Kaden stared at him for a moment, expression tight and unreadable, then rolled his eyes and gave a small nod, stepped out of the way.

"Do I not get a say in this?" I threw a hand to my chest, trying to keep the trembling at bay.

The Prince looked at me like I had three heads. "No. You don't."

I put my hands on my hips, concreting my feet to the floor. "Now where are those royal manners, Prince?"

His eyes ran from mine down to my hips. "Wouldn't you like to know."

My lip curled with disgust as I began walking back to the palace, with or without either of them. Cassian trailed behind me, his low laugh audible. He didn't say anything for a while as he fell into step beside me. I half-expected him to make some sort of joke about my previous drunk endeavor, but he never did. I was at least grateful for that.

We walked side by side along the cobble path back toward the palace, and I forced my legs to keep moving, even though I could still feel the maze under my skin. Still feel the pull of whatever had guided me.

"So," Cassian said at last, casually, almost like he was speaking to the wind. "What was that?"

I blinked. "What was what?"

He looked over at me, one brow raised. "That run."

I shook my head. "I don't know. I just—I didn't think. I kept moving. I guessed."

"Guessed," he echoed softly. "Interesting word choice."

My mouth was dry. "Well, you asked. And that's what it felt like."

"Felt like?" His tone was light, but there was something underneath it. He was watching me too closely, listening not just to what I said but how I said it.

"I didn't know where I was going," I blurted. "I just reacted."

He didn't respond, just simply nodded, keeping his eyes glued forward.

We crossed under the tall archway toward the inner palace. Torchlight bathed the walls in gold. I kept my eyes on the flagstones, the pounding in my chest refusing to settle.

The Prince stopped a few paces from the main doors and turned to face me. "You know you had the fastest time today."

I looked up sharply. "What?"

"By far," he said. "No one came close. Not Miss Morwyn. Not Miss Damaris." His voice dipped lower, quieter. "The only person who has run a time close to that was Lieutenant Corvallis. He does have you beat, but it's slim."

My mouth opened. Closed. "I didn't even realize. I wasn't trying to be fast. I wasn't trying to win."

"Strange, then, how you did."

He didn't say it unkindly. There was no accusation in his voice, just something else that made my stomach twist. I couldn't name it.

"I don't know how," I admitted, barely a whisper.

Prince Cassian tilted his head, eyes never leaving mine. "Perhaps you should begin trying to figure that out."

He stepped back, letting the space stretch between us, his expression unreadable once more. And before I could ask what he meant, he turned and disappeared into the halls.

I stood there, breath trembling, the palace looming behind me.

My bones felt heavy. My braid was snagged, rouge wisps of white flowing with the breeze that drifted in. The sweat that once made me feel like I was burning alive had dried into an icy sheen on my skin. I was exhausted. I walked in the doors and immediately up to my room, where for once, the silken sheets didn't feel like chains, but heaven.

Today had been enough for me. I didn't care what dinner I was missing, or what dress I wasn't able to wear. All I wanted was for this day to be over.

So, in the horrible, sweat covered clothes I wore, I closed my eyes and let today melt away.

CHAPTER THIRTEEN

THE NEXT TWO DAYS passed in a blur.

Everything melded together until I couldn't decipher which day was which. Time felt suspended, as though the palace itself was waiting, watching.

Each day at noon exactly we had training in the courtyard. Thane ran us harder than before, pacing like a predator as we trained.

Everything was slowing down. The trees in the gardens had begun to blush gold and rust, the fountains sputtered quieter, and the sky stayed dim longer in the mornings, but we were only going faster. The tension inside me wound tighter with every passing hour, until even silence felt like it might shatter me.

Thane's voice cracked like a whip. He stalked between us, calling out instructions, barking corrections. His mood was volatile, snapping one moment, strangely quiet the next. I wondered if he even feared the maze. In his own way.

Each girl moved differently now, with purpose and maybe even desperation. Though we were all meant to be preparing for the same trial, it became clear we each envisioned something different at its core.

Naelle trained with icy precision. While the rest of us sweated through drills, she knelt beside the columns and drew chalk symbols onto the stone. She was always counting, measuring, mapping. I watched her eyes track invisible routes like a navigator following stars no one else could see. Once, I caught her murmuring in a language that curled against my ears like smoke. It was heavy with something old, forgotten, or forbidden. I didn't ask. I wasn't sure I wanted to know.

She would do well in the maze. Her mind was built for it. She was cold, but methodical. Dangerous.

Rhea was the opposite. Pure brute strength and feral pride. She turned every exercise into a fight, every obstacle into an enemy. Hay-filled dummies crumbled beneath her fists. She roared when she struck. Her rage was volcanic, unrestrained. I didn't think she planned to solve the maze. I think she planned to desolate it.

If someone else got in her way, well, I'd seen the look in her eyes. She wouldn't hesitate.

Elena moved like a shadow, soft and quiet. She was still healing from our pervious session, with a bandage wrapped tight around her arm, but she trained anyway. Her braided hair was still a tangle of woven strands. She focused on agility, slipping through Thane's drills like water around rock. I found her once in the middle of the night, barefoot in the gardens, darting from stone to stone, climbing walls, disappearing into the hedges like a whisper. She grinned when I caught her. "I'm practicing how to vanish," she said.

And then there was me. I tried to train like them. I traced Naelle's chalk lines. I followed Elena into the trees. I fought alongside Rhea until my shoulders burned, and my hands bled. But none of it felt right. It felt like reaching into someone else's skin.

The memories of the city stirred too often now, slipping through me like mist. When I reached for them, they thrummed in my bones, all bright and silver visions that were barely contained. I couldn't always tell if I was moving through them, or if they were moving through me.

I didn't tell a soul. I didn't dare.

On the final night, training stopped. The halls were quieter than usual, as if they too were waiting for morning.

We were served a silent meal in the mess hall, surrounded by shadows and the faint drip of distant water. Roasted root vegetables, thick herbed bread, slabs of tender meat, slices of fruit glazed in honey and cinnamon.

No one spoke much. Even Rhea was quiet. She ate with her eyes fixed on the fire, jaw tight. Naelle barely touched her food, fingers twitching over invisible lines in the air. Elena sat beside me and took my gloved hand under the table. Her skin was cold even through the silk, but her grip was firm.

Later that night, I stood alone in an open-air hallway that overlooked the hills. The moon hung low, thin as a blade, casting faint silver light over the rooftops and trees.

Beyond the garden, just past the marble pavilion, I could still see it. The maze.

It sat in the dark like something waiting to wake. Like it already knew our names. Twisting shadows, high walls, narrow turns, and something deeper behind it all. A pulse I could feel under my skin. I wrapped my arms around myself as the wind curled past, lifting strands of hair from my face. It whispered through the columns, tugged at my cloak like it had something to say. A warning. A dare. I tore my eyes away and slowly made my way up to my room. I traced the walls with my fingers, remembering how I used to count the stones at home. My heart squeezed at the memory.

I made it to my door, where Kaden stood outside. His eyes seemed tired, hollowness crept under his eyes and cheeks. We didn't speak as he opened the door, and I walked in. It was late, and I needed rest before tomorrow, but not one part of me was ready to sleep. I continued walking onto the balcony, where the city still pulsed with life on the far left side. I sat there and watched. I imagined the streets that filled my head, even though I had never seen them. I wandered the alleyways and the street vendors. Toured the grand center fountain and looked up through the city lights. I imagined a life where I was anywhere but here.

Would I have grown old, finishing my training as a healer and carrying out my days in Virellia? What if I moved to Colpus and worked for Mabel? Would a handsome knight who was scared of women find me there? Bring me up to his room?

Would I have married for love? A frail piece of me always thought there had to be someone created just for me. Someone who was my balance. I never so much believed anyone to be equal, but balance seemed possible enough.

That possibility seemed to be decreasing exponentially. Though I had never felt love, I had read once that it felt eerily similar to fear.

For that reason, and that reason alone, I vowed to never be afraid. Not here.

Just before midnight, the bell tolled once, low and haunting.

I turned from the balcony, the humid night air still clinging to my skin, when a knock struck my door. Not tentative. Not polite. It was sharp. Certain.

I opened it to find Kaden still standing in the hall. He wore the King's colors, royal blue and gold, and the pin clasped on his shoulders was in the shape of a phoenix, the royal crest. I wasn't sure he had worn that earlier. I wondered if he changed. The flickering torchlight cast long shadows over his face, and for the briefest moment, I saw something different behind his eyes.

"The King wants to see you," he said.

My heart dropped to my feet. "Me?" I asked, breath catching.

He hesitated, just a heartbeat, but then shook his head. "Not only you. Everyone. Now." He didn't wait for me to respond. Just turned and walked down the hall without another word.

I dressed quickly out of my sheer nightgown, yanked on my gloves, and followed. My heart ticked faster with every step. I found the others already waiting near the obnoxious wooden doors. Elena glanced at me as I joined them, her brows tight with worry even while her eyes hung heavy with sleep. Naelle stood stone-still, arms folded, eyes cold.

We moved together in silence, winding through narrow corridors and up the marble stair that gleamed like bone in the candlelight. Our footsteps echoed too loud, too long, swallowed by the hush of the hour. Cold air slipped beneath our cloaks and pressed against our spines.

The golden doors to the throne room loomed ahead. Two guards pushed them open, and the groan of ancient hinges spread through the palace like a warning bell.

The room beyond was more cavernous than I remembered, domed high above with a mural of stars etched into obsidian and gold. The air smelled faintly of smoke and old myrrh. Shadows clung to the stone like cobwebs, and the tall stained-glass windows lining the walls lit the floor with an eerie moon-light glow. The eyes that filled the glass seemed like they had been stained onto the marble.

At the far end, in front of the raised dais of golden-threaded quartz, the King waited. He stood like a statue carved from dusk itself. His throne rose behind him like a mountain of molten gold sharpened into points, every edge catching the light and reflecting back almost silver in the night. He wore a crown like always. This one was a ring of bright gold wreathed in golden thorns, resting heavy on his brow. A mantle of black velvet swept down from his shoulders, fastened by a metallic clasp in the shape of a flame.

He didn't speak right away. He just looked at us. Not cruelly. Not kindly. He stared as if we were a question he already knew the answer to.

We stood in a crescent before him, barely breathing.

"I remember when the maze was first carved," he said at last, his voice smooth and low, curling into the corners of the hall. "It was meant to teach, not test, but things change."

The torchlight flickered. A girl shifted beside me. The sound of a swallow, a footstep, the whisper of fabric brushing skin. It all felt too loud. Then his eyes landed on me. It wasn't overt. Just a flicker of focus. A pause too long, but I felt it like pressure behind my ribs.

"For some of you, this will be your making," the King continued, his words measured, even. "For others, there is no shame in returning home." He smiled, just barely. "Being here is a privilege, not a prison. You may leave whenever you would like."

The words hung in the air like a lifeline wrapped in barbed wire. No one reached for it. No one moved. He ran his gaze over me again, as if extending the offer personally.

"You will not watch each other run," the King continued. "Each of you will be taken to a separate chamber. Alone. You will not know who came before you. You will not know who failed."

Elena's fingers twitched at her side. Rhea shifted her weight. Naelle didn't so much as blink.

Then the King's eyes landed on me again. "And everyone will be watching."

It shouldn't have meant anything. It should've been a warning to all of us, but the way he said it, quiet, heavy, like he knew something I didn't, sent a chill down my spine. He rose from the throne in a slow, fluid movement, descending the dais with the grace of something ancient and patient. His crown caught the light and shimmered like oil on water, an unnatural gleam.

He stopped a few paces from us, hands clasped behind his back.

"That is all," he said. Then, his eyes locked with mine. "Good luck."

The silence that followed was absolute. The girls turned, slowly, one by one, but I stood still for half a breath longer, the words clanging in my head like a warning bell only I could hear.

The King did not look away.

Not until I did.

Not until I turned and followed the others back into the shadowed hall, pulse hammering in my throat.

CHAPTER FOURTEEN

I STOOD IN THE HALL like a ghost.

It wasn't the King's words that had struck, but his seemingly undivided attention towards me.

Kaden must have noticed my blank stare. He came up beside me and brushed my arm with his own, the long sleeve of his uniform acting as a barrier between us.

"This changes nothing, okay Seravell?" he whispered into my ear. I wanted to believe him. I wanted to act like everything truly was okay, but deep down, I knew something was different. The King knew too, and he was worried enough to call a midnight meeting over it.

I shifted towards him. He searched my eyes with his own as if to make sure I was convinced. I forced light into them, making the corners of my lips curl into what appeared to be a smile.

"Yeah. Yeah, no. You're right."

He didn't believe a word of it. His frown gave that away instantly. He sighed as he wrung the back of his neck with his hand.

"Come on."

He began walking backwards down the hall, eyes still on me.

I stood still as I tiled my head, confused. "Where?"

"You eye that garden from your balcony every day. I don't think you'll ever get enough of it."

I wrapped my arms around my torso. I hadn't realized he's ever noticed.

I slowly followed, receiving a grin from Kaden before he turned around. I trailed behind like a shadow as we wound our way down into the gardens. We walked through an open hallway with no torches. The moonlight lit our steps, and I had never seen something so alluring.

We reached a wooden door, and Kaden swung it open to the quiet gardens.

The golden hue that seemed to coat every part of the palace had melted away to a cool silver. The night sky reflected and flickered in the koi ponds, and the flowers that once bloomed in every color all seemed to take on shades of blue and gray.

It should have looked lifeless, dull even, yet it was anything but that.

I stepped off the stone and wandered aimlessly through the swirling gardens. My fingers reached down to brush the flowers. The petals were soft to the touch. Delicate. Fragile.

I looked up to the hills that rolled beyond the bush hedges at the far end of the garden. I wondered what laid beyond them. I wondered if anybody knew.

Kaden joined my side and stared out in the same direction. His hands were shoved into his pockets, and in the light of the moon, the skin under his eyes looked dark and tired. It could have been the light, but I doubt it.

I moved over to a larger koi pond and watched as the white and gold fish swam lazily just below the surface. The larger koi inhabited the edges, causing swirling water to hit the rocks that created the pond's border. The smaller ones though, stayed in the center, as if they were preparing to dive down at a moments notice. Each of the smaller fish were white. The larger gold. There was only one koi, the largest of the pond, that was a mix of both.

The stars that danced on the water stole my attention next, dragging my eyes up to the sky.

I couldn't see all of the constellations like in Virellia, that was true, but the moon never changed. This was the same moon I watched at home, the same one Selene and my father were watching now, and the same one I would watch forever.

And that was enough.

Kaden was silent behind me, just watching as I let the calm of the gardens ease in.

I waited there until every bit of tension, every thought, every doubt left my mind, or as close to leaving as they would get. I filled my lungs repeatedly with the cool night air, as if I would never get the chance to breathe it in again.

Slowly, I turned and simply absorbed all that surrounded me. I hated this city and its abundance. I loathed the King and his greed. I despised the Prince and his charm.

But some part of me, some childish and girly part of me, would truly die for these gardens.

I stared at the moon, watching as a faint shooting star streaked the sky just below it.

I took that as a sign.

I turned back to Kaden whose eyes only watched me. He had moved, now leaning back against the trunk of a willow tree. The branches and leaves curled down, creating a curtain between us. It waved and flowed in the breeze, making Kaden look like a mirage in the heat of the night.

I looked from him, to the palace, and back to him.

He nodded and pushed himself from the tree with his foot, falling into step beside me as we walked back.

He opened the wooden door, gesturing for me to enter the palace and the twisting halls that always seemed to engulf me entirely. I stepped inside, Kaden following closely at my heel.

I glanced back, watching the silver of the gardens slowly fade as the door closed.

CHAPTER FIFTEEN

I WOKE TO THE heavy silence of the palace.

No knocking. No summons yet. Just the knowledge of the day's guaranteed cruelties.

The air felt sharp against my skin. I had awoken hours earlier, but I couldn't bring myself to dress and put on the deep brown boots set on my desk. They had thick laces with heavy tread on the bottom. They were built for running, and that fact alone made my stomach churn.

I had curled up on the balcony instead, letting the morning sun warm my skin. Time seemed to condense, the sun rising to land above my head before I had even moved. I could have stayed in that gentle silence forever, but the palace didn't stay quiet for long. The hallways were bustling with movement now, and I heard nearby doors as they swung open and closed, one girl after the next. The footsteps weren't light and lady-like. They were heavy. They all had their boots on.

I sighed, letting my head fall back against the glass door behind me. Eventually, I dragged myself over to my vanity, grabbing a brush and running it through the tangles in my hair. I wove the strands into tight, intricate braids. Each movement was steady, practiced. I pulled at the plaits, wrapping them around my head into a crown.

I opened my armoire and shuffled through, finding a dark tunic and pants. I pulled them on and grabbed the boots from the desk. Something slipped out from between the pair, falling with a soft thud.

Gloves. Leather gloves.

Something welled in my chest, but I wasn't sure it was gratitude. I loosened the laces of the boots and slid them on, tying them as tight as they would go. My hands shook, and my lungs seemed to rattle with each breath. I pulled on the gloves, wrapping the attached strap around my wrist and buttoning the end. My tunic was short sleeved, leaving my arms open to the heated air.

The knock at my door came just as I finished dressing. I opened it to find Kaden waiting, his face unreadable.

I hadn't even eaten breakfast.

Wordlessly, he turned and led me down the corridor. My boots thudded softly on the worn stone floors. My heart felt louder, pounding against my ribs.

He led me down into the lower levels of the palace, down into mossy damp stone. The corridors twisted and turned, like a second maze meant to distract and blind. We reached the chamber door, and a royal guard stood at each side. They both wore golden armor dotted with outrageous gemstones. One guard had sapphires embedded into his armor while the other wore emeralds, but they both seemed dull in the low light. The sapphire guard stepped forward with his hand raised.

Was he shaking my hand?

I reached out to meet his handshake, but his hand clamped down on my arm instead. He pulled me forward, yanking me by the wrist into the chamber.

The touch was rough, impersonal, and skin to skin.

In that moment, the world itself tilted on its axis.

Power and energy seemed to rush into my body like a river current, pulling and tugging at whatever was in its path. Flickers filled my mind. Visions, but not visions of a memory. This wasn't like before. I wasn't seeing the past. I was seeing a plan.

A plan for me.

I saw myself broken, bloodied, and sprawled across the stone ground of the chamber. My legs bent at unnatural angles on the floor, and blood pooled in a red circle around me. It soaked my hair and seeped into the braid, red infecting white. Tears streamed down my face, and I was begging for mercy. I gasped and jerked back instinctively, but the guards grip held. My chest heaved. My arms trembled. My vision seemed to blur around the edges, knees on the verge of caving in.

My eyes snapped to Kaden's, wide and pleading. My mouth opened, but no sound came out. My entire body buzzed as if electricity itself was flowing through my veins. I only managed a whisper, so faint I could barely even hear myself.

"Don't leave me."

He hesitated only a fraction before stepping forward, shoving the guard's hand off me with a sharp snap of his wrist.

"She is not to leave my side," he said, his voice a low and dangerous growl. His hand slid around my back and waist, supporting me as my knees rebounded. "By Prince Vaelros's orders."

The guards exchanged looks but didn't push it further. Kaden stayed close, his hand hovering near his sword as we waited. His other arm stayed wrapped around my torso, holding up more of my weight than I'd like to admit. My skin crawled and itched, the guard's touch a vivid memory.

A horn shattered the heavy silence.

I flinched, and before us the enormous stone gate groaned and rose, revealing glaring sunlight.

I blinked against the brightness, stepping out of Kaden's hold and into an outdoor arena. Stone seating curved around the space, towering and ancient. People filled every seat. Nobles, servants, guards, everyone. The monstrous maze sprawled before me, its walls no longer flimsy painted wood but real, brutal stone. Weathered. Unforgiving. A labyrinth carved to swallow the weak.

A figure stood at the mouth of the maze dressed entirely in black, cloaked from head to toe with his face hidden behind a dark veil. Only the faint glint of armor peeked beneath the folds of cloth. My stomach twisted.

That's who I had to outrun.

I heard Kaden shift behind me. He stepped to follow, to stay by my side as he had said earlier, but the two guards were on him in an instant. They seized his arms roughly, yanking him back. Kaden snarled, thrashing like a cornered wolf. The emerald guard caught a fist to the jaw and staggered, blood blooming at the corner of his mouth. But the sapphire guard twisted Kaden's arm behind his back, forcing him to his knees with a brutal shove. He leaned down, so close his breath stirred Kaden's hair, but his cold, gleaming eyes were fixed on me.

"I take orders from a different Vaelros, bastard," he snarled.

A low growl rumbled deep in Kaden's chest. His elbow drove into the guard's throat with a sickening crack. The man crumpled, gasping for air. The other grabbed at Kaden's clothes only to be hurled aside with brutal strength, crashing into the arena wall with a thud that rattled the stones.

"Kaden!" I gasped, reaching for him, but more guards flooded in.

Three.

Four.

Five.

They swarmed him, trying to drag him down, but Kaden fought like a demon. He twisted out of their grasp, striking and kicking, every movement raw and lethal.

One guard went down screaming, blood spraying from a broken nose. Another reeled back, clutching a dislocated shoulder.

For one heartbeat, Kaden was free.

He dragged himself half to his feet, teeth bared in a furious snarl. He staggered toward me, bloodied and wild, arm outstretched. His eyes locked on mine for a split second, desperation clouding them, before another blow struck him across the back.

A guard had lunged at him from behind, but Kaden spun and slammed the man's head into the stone with a crack. Kaden sagged and dragged himself along the stone wall, panting, muscles trembling from the effort of staying upright. Blood trickled down the center of his face from a cut that must have been somewhere on the top his head.

"Lyra!" he shouted, raw and desperate.

I took a step toward him, my hand out. The ground shuddered beneath us.

The massive stone gate groaned and then slammed down between us with deafening finality, sending a tremor up my legs. Dust billowed in the air, stinging my eyes.

"Kaden!" I cried, slamming my palms against the wall. I could barely hear him pounding on the other side, roaring my name, but it was too late.

I was alone.

I stared at the stone, anger and fear both working in tandem to make my entire body twitch and shake. I turned to face the arena behind me once more.

The sun glared mercilessly overhead, heat already sinking into my tunic. I squinted, hand raised to shade my eyes, as I looked toward the royal platform, spotting two figures.

The King lounged in his throne, wearing that same wicked, knowing smile from the night before. His eyes found me instantly, a glitter of cruelty sparking in their depths. He smiled wider and lifted his goblet no doubt full of the same wine that had gotten the best of me only a week before. He had wanted this. He had planned this, and beside him, his son.

The Prince sat in a wooden chair, nothing even comparable to his father's golden throne. He wore the Vaelros family blue, and his golden skin seemed even brighter against the fabric. He looked regal, pure royalty, and yet his composure said otherwise. His face was a mask of perfect indifference at a glance, but something about the set of his shoulders betrayed him.

Tension.

Tight and contained like he hated every second of this. Like he knew more than he should.

The horn blew again, sharp and final. I turned, and the guard was already sprinting toward me, black robes flaring, closing the distance with terrifying speed.

I didn't think. I ran.

The entrance to the maze yawned open before me like a beast's mouth, and I hurled myself into its shadows. The stone walls rose high, rough and cracked, twisting in ways that made no logical sense.

I sprinted forward, boots slapping hard against the uneven ground. Dust kicked up around me. Every few strides, sharp jutting stones broke from the walls. No doubt traps, meant to trip or slice if I misstepped.

A low, rhythmic thudding echoed behind me. The guard. Gaining.

I swerved left, dodging a crumbling ledge, then right, leaping over a low wall that had collapsed inward. My lungs burned, each breath a jagged knife in my chest.

Ahead in the alley, a narrow gap, almost too narrow, opened between two towering slabs. I hurled myself sideways, scraping through, and pain sliced along my arm where the stone snagged me.

Keep moving, keep moving.

The maze twisted again, doubling back, tricking me. I skidded to a halt just before I would have run into a pit hidden by shadow. Barely visible, barely wide enough to catch me if I fell. Behind me the heavy pounding of the guard's boots. Closer.

Too close.

I spotted another path and took it, feet slipping on loose gravel. My muscles screamed in protest as I vaulted over a stone barrier, heart hammering so loud it filled my ears, and then—

I saw the end. Sunlight. Open sky.

I sprinted for it, every step raw and desperate. The guard roared behind me, a harsh, guttural sound, and I felt the air stir as he reached out, fingers brushing the hem of my tunic.

With a final gasp of effort, I lunged. I tumbled forward, staggering out into the open just as a black-gloved hand swiped through the empty air behind me. I fell to my knees, dust clinging to the sweat beading on my skin.

The crowd was silent. Utterly, unnervingly silent.

I staggered upright, breaths sputtering, perspiration dripping down the line of my back.

The King was no longer smiling. His face was a mask of irritation, his lips pressed into a thin line as his knuckles grew white from the force of his grip on his throne. He didn't look at me. He refused.

But the Prince looked at me like I was the sun itself, fierce and bright and untouchable.

I only wish I knew why.

I spun slowly, taking in the silent crowd. Hundreds of faces, watching and judging.

A royal guard approached, his armor gleaming in the broad sunlight. His face was unreadable. His movements brisk.

He reached for my arm, then hesitated. His hand fell back to his side. Instead, he gave a sharp jerk of his chin toward the exit.

Dismissed.

I gave a stiff nod, though every fiber of me screamed to collapse. Somehow, I forced my legs to move, each step jarring through my aching body. My heart was still hammering against my ribs, wild and uneven, the thud of it echoing in my ears. Adrenaline surged uselessly through my veins, leaving me cold and shaking.

I stumbled into the hallway beyond, and the noise hit me like a crashing wave.

Guards barked orders over the thud of hurried boots. Servants darted between nobles, balancing trays, documents, bandages. Noblemen and women shoved past, their jeweled slippers and sweeping cloaks flashing in the torchlight, their perfumes cloying and thick in the already stifling air.

Then, I saw Jamie. Stars, she was practically unrecognizable, and in that moment, I knew she had failed. And the guard had been anything but kind.

She laid on a cot with two women in healers white scrambling around her. Her knee was twisted, and her face was covered in streams of blood that poured from the crown of her head. Silent tears left clean skin in their wake. She opened her eyes as best she could and looked directly at me. She lifted her arm that was beginning to bruise, angry inflamed scrapes running from her shoulder to elbow. She raised her arm and pointed. She pointed at me.

I staggered back. It was too much. Too loud. Too bright.

The walls seemed to close in around me, the shouts and clatter ricocheting off the stone and hammering into my skull. I brought my hands up to my temples and pressed my palms into my head. I panted, chest rising and falling rapidly as the weight of everything threatened to swallow me whole.

I needed air. I needed space.

Without thinking, I turned down the first side corridor I saw, then another, and another. I followed the familiar path from only a night ago.

The world narrowed to the slap of my boots on ancient stone and the racing beat in my chest. Shadows stretched along the halls, cool and empty. I clung to them, slipping deeper into the quiet parts of the palace where few dared to tread.

Finally, the stone walls gave way to green.

I stumbled through an archway into the gardens, and it was like plunging into another world.

The gardens seemed different in the sunset light. Warm air kissed my skin, heavy with the scent of jasmine and blooming citrus. The evening sun, which had moments ago blazed like a merciless brand over the arena, now spilled molten gold across the marble pathways. Every leaf and petal in sight seemed gilded with the low sun.

The chaos behind me dulled, fading into a distant hum.

Here, the world moved slower, softer, and I gulped down the calm air like a drowned man.

I wandered down a path lined with flowering vines, their blossoms drooping lazily in the heat. The rustle of leaves overhead was a lullaby, a whisper against my frayed nerves.

I passed trellises heavy with roses. Their petals seemed to glow like embers as the sunlight filtered through the delicate colors. Stone fountains burbled gently, their cool spray misting the air. A butterfly flitted past as a flash of cobalt blue in the honeyed light. I didn't know where I was going. I simply knew I needed to keep moving until the tightness in my chest eased. Part of that tightness was Kaden. Wondering where he was. Worrying if he was alive at all.

At last, tucked away in a shaded corner of the gardens, I found a hidden bench half-swallowed by ivy and framed by a canopy of lilacs.

I sat heavily, and then I laid back against the cool stone, heedless of the scratches from the creeping vines. My eyes slipped closed, and my body finally, finally began to let go. The tension in my muscles blurred into the background, replaced by a gentle, aching sort of tiredness.

The roar in my blood faded to a whisper.

The terrible pounding of my heart slowed.

For a sliver of time, there was no arena, no King, no future clawing at my heels. Just the sun, warm against my skin, and the heady, floral perfume spinning around me.

Five girls remained.

The thought sliced through the calm like a blade. Another dream shattered. Another life stolen.

I hated it. I hated all of it. I wasn't ready to be alone again. I wasn't ready to lose more.

I only prayed Kaden was waiting when I returned. I didn't know what I would do if he wasn't.

A shadow crossed over my face.

I blinked, disoriented for a breath, and found myself staring up into blue eyes sharp as broken glass.

Rhea.

Her perfectly curled hair framed her face like a golden crown, but her expression was anything but regal. It was twisted into something cruel and hungry, her lips curling at the corners in a smile that didn't reach her eyes.

"You should really learn your place, northern," she said, her voice smooth as silk, a queen addressing a peasant. Every syllable dripped with venom. "You're not going to win this. So, either go back to your frozen scum, or I'll send you somewhere else." She hissed the last sentence through barred teeth.

A cold shiver slid down my spine.

Slowly, I sat up, keeping my movements measured even as every instinct in me screamed caution, screamed danger.

"If I'm not going to win, why bother with me at all?" I asked, my voice steadier than I felt.

Rhea's smile deepened, a glint of vicious satisfaction lighting her gaze. Dust from the maze lingered on her otherwise pristine clothes. "Can't a girl just have some fun?" she purred. And then, movement.

A flash of silver.

I caught the glint of the knife a second too late.

My heart lurched into my throat as I surged to my feet. Rhea lunged, fast and low, the blade aimed for my ribs.

My vision tunneled to the gleam of steel and the whip of her hair in the wind. Without thinking, I lashed out, grabbing her wrist just as the tip of the knife kissed the fabric of my tunic, tearing the fabric but fortunately nothing deeper.

Her hand closed around my arm, moving to tear it away, but she froze. The moment her skin touched mine, energy exploded through my veins. Wild. Raw. Uncontrolled.

It cracked down my spine like a whip, searing through every vein, every nerve. My vision went white. Sparks danced across my skin, and the world trembled at the edges.

Rhea's body locked up, frozen mid-lunge, her eyes going wide, and then silver. A pure, unnatural silver. The color of a raging storm.

The knife clattered from her numb fingers, falling to the garden path with a hollow clang. I gasped, yanking my hand back like I'd been burned. The instant the contact broke, Rhea stumbled back, her breath coming in short, ragged gasps.

For a single, shattering heartbeat, her mask cracked, and I saw it.

Not hatred, not anger, but fear. Real, raw, terrifying fear, painted plain across her pale face.

She recovered quickly, straightening with jerky, panicked movements. Without a word, she spun on her heels and strode back toward the palace. Her spine was ramrod straight, her fists clenched tight at her sides, but she couldn't quite hide the way her hands shook.

Or the way she kept glancing over her shoulder, as if she was terrified the monster she'd awakened might be just behind.

I stood frozen among the lilacs, chest heaving, the crackle of some power still humming faintly beneath my skin.

The knife gleamed in the dirt at my feet, forgotten. I threw the blade in a nearby pond, watching as the metal gleam grew dull from the depth of the water. The fish continued swimming as if the metal meant nothing more than the pebbles it sat among.

The evening air smelled too sweet, too heavy, like it might choke me.

Perhaps it should.

CHAPTER SIXTEEN

THE EVENING SUN SLIPPED beneath the horizon in soft bands of gold and pink, painting the palace walls in a glow that warmed the stone but did nothing to soothe the storm swirling in my mind.

I had wandered back to my room somehow, but the travel itself was lost from my memory. I seemed to have floated here on instinct, relying on my feet to take me wherever they saw fit. I sat curled on the edge of my balcony, my legs drawn tight to my chest, the breeze tugging at the loose braid falling over my shoulder. I had taken the braids down from their crown, but left their woven patterns intact, like I couldn't quite let them go. My dust-covered clothes sat crumpled in a heap on the floor. A navy dress flowed down my body and arms, the light fabric much more comfortable in the heat.

From here, the gardens stretched out in shimmering green as it caught the last breath of daylight. I hadn't stayed there long after Rhea had found me. I couldn't shake her golden hair from my mind. The fear that seemed to boil under my skin at her touch. I looked down at my arms, at the pale skin still tingling faintly. I remembered the flash of silver in her eyes. The way some kind of power had roared through me like a second heartbeat, wild and sure.

Selene flooded my every thought. The memory of that morning in the square ran rampant in my mind. My memory and her lack-there-of.

My mind seemed to burn. The past four days had been unexplainable.

I wanted to interrogate Kaden. I wanted to demand answers about the conversation outside my door few odd nights ago. About the *Silver Flame*, the mysterious figure, the secrets and the lies. About why Kaden had stayed with me in the chamber this morning. About what he had done. About what I had done.

About what I was.

Every question, every half-formed thought I had, turned back to that moment outside my door. The memory of the voice like golden honey. Warm but threaded with something urgent and desperate, speaking to me through the darkness.

A knock hit the door, its sound brief and sharp. It cracked open before I could answer as Kaden leaned in the doorframe.

I gasped and stumbled to my feet, my hand flying to my mouth.

He was a mess. A split lip, bruised and bloodied. A thin cut sliced across the bridge of his nose. His sleeves were rolled to his elbows, and white bandages wrapped both forearms, the centers stained pink with fresh blood. His hair, usually combed and neat, was tousled and tangled. Kaden caught my stare and, with a crooked, lopsided smile, said lightly, "You should see the other guy. Well... *guys*, technically." He gave a breath of laughter but winced slightly, his hand brushing along his ribs.

"Kaden..." I breathed, feeling my heart crack a little at the sight of him. I reached a hand out, beckoning him inside. He crossed the room in a few easy strides and bent down to catch my gaze. His eyes, usually hard with calculation, were soft now. "Hey, Seravell. It's okay. This isn't the first time I've been a little scraped up, and it sure won't be the last."

Tears burned the backs of my eyes, but I nodded, pressing my lips together.

"You made it," Kaden said, his voice lowering, "even after what you saw." His eyes scoured my face, as if *he* was worried *I* was injured. Once satisfied, he straightened, looking out the open balcony doors. "Cassian's already... handling it."

Of course he was. Of course Prince Vaelros was already fixing everything, smoothing it over like an artist erasing a mistaken brushstroke.

I rolled my eyes, not at Kaden, not exactly. I followed his eyes out to the night sky unfurling in velvet blue.

"Jamie didn't make it, did she?" I asked quietly.

He hesitated, just long enough to confirm what I already knew.

"No. She didn't."

Jamie. The quiet girl from Delva. She wouldn't even have her name spoken now. My chest tightened. The grief was too raw. Too sharp.

"She was kind," I murmured.

"She was," Kaden agreed, but his voice turned careful, guarded, like he didn't want to stay in this place of sadness any longer. He turned, facing the edge of the sprawling city just in view. I kept my eyes on the night sky. On the few stars that dared to shine.

"But we don't have time to waste mourning. I know it's harsh, but the trials won't stop because you lost a friend."

I whipped around to face him, anger beginning to boil.

"Kaden, I thought they had killed you," I snapped. "And after my trial, I walk out to find Jamie blood-soaked with a broken knee. Why would they *break her knee?* They didn't even—" My voice broke. "They didn't even clean the blood. They left her there for everyone to see, and they did nothing."

My voice fell into a sharp whisper by the end. My hands trembled. Kaden's eyes spun to find mine and glowed like leaves reaching for sunlight. There was sympathy there, but Kaden was built as a solider. His version of sympathy was pity, and that wasn't what I needed. Not now.

He ran a hand through his hair, a nervous tick I've come to realize. "I know. I know, and I'm sorry. I never said this was fair," he said quietly, his voice roughened by something he didn't name. "But hey, at least we're not easy to kill." He said it with a small, almost broken smile. A joke that didn't quite land.

He stood with his head cocked, waiting for a response. When I didn't give him one, he huffed a breath and pinched the top of his nose in his fingers, brushing the bandage just under. He lifted his head and let his palm fall face up towards me.

"Listen, Seravell. There's a reason you survived, and she didn't."

I drew in breath after breath, shaking from head to toe. I was so angry, but it wasn't at him. I refused to let the King's twisted games turn me against the one person who was still here.

Who always would be here.

I turned away, stalking to my vanity. My fingers shook as I grabbed my brush, yanking through the tangles of my braids. Anything to cool off. Anything to think about something else.

"Why did you really come here, Kaden?" I asked, my voice tighter than I meant it to be. In the mirror, I saw him exhale, grateful for the change in subject even though the tension in the air remained.

"The next trial is different," he said, stepping forward. "One of wit. Stately judgment. Battle strategy, actually."

Well, the King was surely not wasting time. I paused, brush halfway through my hair. "Battle strategy?"

He nodded, folding his arms. His bandages were pulled tight over muscle. "If the King is away, or dead, the queen has to know how to make decisions. Strategic decisions. Lives-on-the-line decisions."

"Oh," I said, dropping the brush into my lap. "That sounds... riveting."

Kaden huffed a dry laugh. "It can be. Once you learn the patterns."

"And if I don't?"

"You will," he said, his voice full of certainty. He smiled at me then, small and a little crooked, but real. "I'll help you."

He jerked his head towards the door. "Come on. The palace has a library that makes most kingdoms weep with jealousy."

A small, unwilling smile pulled at my mouth. The thick air loosened its grip. I tossed the brush aside and threw a shawl over my navy gown, following him out.

The library was even more magnificent than I could have imagined. Vaulted ceilings soared into shadow. Spiraling staircases laced up the walls like ivy as rolling ladders filled the spaces where the steps didn't reach. Endless rows of shelves stretched into infinity, packed with old tomes and crumbling scrolls. Spines of every color book filled the walls, all varying in height and width. Some seemed to be thousands of pages while others were no bigger than a page or two bound with string. Massive, arched windows poured silver moonlight across the floors, and the smell of old parchment, candle wax, and cold marble filled the air like incense. I stopped in the entryway, wide-eyed.

"The palace gem," Kaden said with a smirk.

He led me to a tucked-away alcove between two windows. Plush armchairs waited by a low table already stacked with a few neglected books. I tucked my legs under me on a chair as Kaden began pulling volumes from the shelves. His arms were piled high with books on old wars, ancient sieges, naval battles, rebellions fought and lost and won.

We settled in, shoulder to shoulder, heads bent over pages. Sometimes our arms brushed when we leaned too close to the same diagram, the fabric of my nightgown hitting his skin. Sometimes his voice dipped into a low rumble when explaining a tactic, and I found myself clinging to each word like it was something solid in a world that had gone terrifyingly fluid.

I asked questions. So many questions.

"Why had the western flank collapsed in the Siege of Mirun?"

"Why hadn't they reinforced the harbor at Seren?"

He answered patiently, smiling when I interrupted him, guiding me when I stumbled. Hours slipped through our fingers like sand. At some point, I slumped deeper into the chair, the weight of the day pressing down.

My eyes blurred over the diagram in front of me, some forgotten fortress with its walls breached by treachery. Kaden's voice kept talking, low and soothing, but the words turned to soft hums in my ears. The world faded into parchment and candlelight.

When I stirred again, it was to the sound of gentle whispers and a soft hand shaking my shoulder. I blinked once, drowsy, and forced my eyes open. I yawned off a bit of the sleep that had pulled me under as Kaden wrapped the shawl I must have dropped back around my shoulders. He carefully handed me the edges and grabbed a stack of books from the table as I stretched and found my feet. I looked out a window to find the dead of night stretching outside. A dark navy night sky dotted with stars that while few and far between, still managed to look gorgeous with the sprawling city below.

Part of me had wished the memories of the city had never invaded me. I think I would have enjoyed exploring the labyrinths that laid below. The music that drifted on the wind, and the laughter that crawled with it. I heard Kaden's footsteps as he returned and spun away from the window. I hadn't even realized I was shivering until he peeled his guards' coat off and laid it gently over the thin shawl. He paused in front of me, close enough for me to realize he has a few freckles too, before he cleared his throat and nodded to the door. Heat rose in my cheeks, and I walked hurriedly down the hall. I pulled the coat tighter, the scent of oak and worn leather surrounding me. As different as Kaden was to the Prince, they smelled shockingly similar. Must be some expensive royal cologne.

Kaden opened the door to my room with a soft click. I walked in and expected to hear the same sound signaling the door had closed, but he entered after me, only closing the door once he was also in the room. I paused, turning to look back at him.

Why did he follow me into my room?

The question must have been visible because his face turned a red so bright he seemed to be on fire.

"Uh—sorry. My coat?"

Embarrassment spread in my veins like ice.

"Of course, yeah. Sorry." I nodded as I slid the coat off my shoulders and folded it in half. I walked over and handed it back, feeling the blush on my cheeks parallel his. He gave me a flat smile and turned to flee whatever awkwardness had plagued us. He blew out a candle on my desk as he reached for the door.

I blurted into the dark, "Thank you."

Kaden froze for a beat too long, like he hadn't expected it. I felt the weight of his gaze lingering on me, heavy with something I didn't have the strength to name. He gave me a real smile this time.

Then, he was gone.

CHAPTER SEVENTEEN

THE SUNLIGHT WOKE ME GENTLY, soft and aureate, crawling across the stone floor like a slow-moving river. I stretched, feeling the warmth on my skin as I rolled out of bed. For once, there was no alarm, no rush, no scheduled training for a trial or danger hanging over me. Just the promise of a quiet morning. I smiled to myself. The pressure and awkwardness that haunted the air yesterday had calmed, and I let myself bask in it until the very last minute.

I hurried through my morning routine, pulling on a simple dress and cloth flats, the fabrics warm from the sunlight that spilled on them. My hair fell in loose waves around my shoulders as I braided it quickly, not bothering with any fancy twists today. My fingers trembled slightly as I pulled on my gloves, but I tried to ignore it. I was in a rush. A rush to make sure Elena was still here. That she had made it out.

The palace dining hall was quieter than usual. Only a handful of servants setting up the tables. The air was fragrant with the scent of fresh bread and honeyed fruit, and for the first time in days, I allowed myself to relax.

I saw her, and my shoulders released every remaining bit of tension.

Elena sat at a smaller table near the windows, her face still pale but glowing with a softness that made my heart swell. Her eyes caught mine immediately, and her lips lifted in a smile that spread from ear to ear, making the room feel warmer.

I rushed to her side without thinking, my feet nearly stumbling over themselves. I didn't even say anything before I cautiously wrapped my arms around her, making sure fabric stayed as a barrier between us. She froze for a moment, then laughed, a soft, relieved sound.

"Lyra…" Her voice shook slightly, and she pulled back, just enough for her eyes to roam my own. "You're alive."

"Of course I am," I teased. "Did you really think I'd let them catch me that easily?"

She smirked, though her eyes softened when she looked at me more closely. "I didn't think they ever could. Us Northerners are tougher than we look."

The warmth of the sun spilling through the windows seemed to wrap around us. It was so easy to forget the burden of everything else when I was with Elena. We became freed of the regalia and the trials. Freed of the crown that seemed to bear more weight than simply gold.

"You've got that look," I teased, lowering my voice dramatically. "The one where you're about to tell me something."

Elena raised an eyebrow, bringing her elbow to the table to lean her head on her palm. "Do I?" she said, a mischievous glint flashing in her eyes. "Perhaps I'm just trying to figure out how to say you look lovely this morning. New dress?"

I laughed. "You're a terrible liar. I look like I got around in a rush this morning." Mostly because I did.

"You do not," she said, her voice full of humor. "I've seen Prince Vaelros seek a glance every now and then"

I shoved a bite of bread in my mouth, eyes widening as a smile grew with each chew. "Oh really? Well, he's not the only one looking over here."

She raised her eyebrows. "Oh?"

I leaned forward, my voice dropping to a whisper. "Will. He can't seem to get enough of you. Not to mention I saw you looking at him earlier."

Her face flushed pink instantly, and I couldn't help but laugh. "Elena. It's obvious. You might as well be wearing a banner that says, 'I'm in love with Will.'"

Her hand flew to her chest, her face the picture of mock surprise. "*In love with him?* What are you talking about? You're crazy."

"Right," I said, grinning widely. "You can't fool me."

She swatted at me, but the smile was still tugging at her lips. "You're ridiculous."

"I'm serious!" I protested, though I was laughing. "I'm here for you, though. Whatever you need to win him over. I'll wing-woman you."

Elena shook her head, her shoulders shaking with silent laughter. "Lyra, you don't know what you're talking about." But she was grinning now too. Ear to ear.

I leaned back in my chair, folding my arms across my chest, watching her with a grin. "Will probably knows."

Her eyes widened at the suggestion. "Don't say that. I don't think he—"

"Elena," I interrupted, laughing. "Trust me. He knows."

She opened her mouth to retort, but then a shadow passed by the door. Both our eyes flicked to the figure, and I knew instantly who it was.

Will glanced over to us, waving shyly at Elena. I let my head drop towards her dramatically, as if to say *"I told you so…"*

"Stop!" Elena burst out laughing, but her voice was full of affection. "You're terrible."

"I'm just calling it as I see it," I said, grinning. "But seriously, you're blushing. It's cute."

Her cheeks flushed deeper, laughing all the while. "I'm not admitting anything," she said firmly, but I could see the way her eyes hovered when she glimpsed back at Will. The way her gaze lingered on him before she quickly turned away.

"Of course not," I replied with a wink, feeling a rush of fondness for my friend.

There was a long, comfortable silence as we both relaxed into our food, the easy rhythm of friendship settling around us. It was moments like this, small and quiet, that made me feel completely human again. I didn't have to be the girl in the trials, or anyone for that matter. I could just be Lyra, sitting at a table with a friend, laughing about nothing but boys.

It felt nice, or at least it did.

That peace lasted approximately three bites before someone slid smoothly into the seat beside me.

"Morning," came a voice like golden honey.

I nearly choked on my bread. My head snapped up to find Prince Cassian lounging casually at my side, one arm draped along the back of the bench behind me, his body so effortlessly at ease it made me stiffen in response. A slight smirk tugged at his lips, like he knew exactly what he was doing to me.

I swallowed hard, my heart racing. "Prince Vaelros sitting with a peasant?" I managed, trying to recover quickly. "Bold of you."

Cassian chuckled, low and rich, the sound wrapping around me like a velvet rope. "And good morning to you, Miss Seravell. Always so polite, aren't you?"

My cheeks flushed despite myself. I forced myself to look away for a moment, focusing on the bread in my hands, but I could feel the weight of his gaze on me, like it was pressing against my skin.

He stood and offered his arm, his eyes never leaving mine. "Well, if we're being so cordial, I would most enjoy your presence." The Prince gave a dramatic bow, keeping eye contact with me as he bent down.

My pulse quickened, and I stared at the arm he offered, the sleeve of his shirt stretched taut across his bicep. It wasn't a question. It was an invitation, and I couldn't quite bring myself to decline, though my mind screamed that I should.

"My presence for what?" I asked, my voice portraying more curiosity than I intended. My gaze flicked back to Elena, who was watching the two of us, her eyes fixed and the corners of her mouth raised in a small smile.

Prince Cassian's own smirk deepened, though there was a flicker of something else in his eyes. Something harder, more intense than usual.

"You'll see."

I hesitated, my eyes lingering on him for a moment longer than necessary. Something about the way he stood there, waiting for me, made my heart thud painfully in my chest. He was so casual, so easy in his own skin, and I was anything but. His presence, so very close, made everything around me feel charged, as though the air coating my lungs was thick with tension.

"Don't keep me waiting, Miss Seravell," he said, his voice just a little too smooth, a little too sure.

I opened my mouth to protest, to tell him 'No,' but the word caught in my throat. Instead, I stood slowly, avoiding his gaze as I moved to follow him. I took the arm he offered, slipping my hand into the crook of his elbow. I could feel the weight of his attention on me, like a pull, tugging at the very center of me. When I reached his side, he didn't immediately move. For a moment, we simply stood there. Too close with too much electricity crackling between us.

"You're not going to have me carry you again I presume?" His tone was light, teasing, but there was something sharper beneath it.

I took a deep breath, forcing my voice to stay steady. "I don't need you to carry me anywhere, Prince."

He laughed, a sound that was so effortlessly charming it sent a ripple of something uncertain through me. "Good. Then let's go."

He led the way, and I followed, unable to stop myself from stealing quick glances at him as we walked. His presence filled the space around us, drawing all my attention in a way I couldn't explain. The slight tension in his shoulders, the way his hand rested so casually at his side, the quiet confidence that radiated from him. It was all so distracting.

On the surface, I forgot I hated him. I forgot about the *golden boy of Valerieth* and the *flitty clothing* he so adores. I forgot about his bloodline, his father, his crown. I forgot about his guards stationed in Virellia. The one who murdered a man who's only crime was hunger.

I forgot that this man was a prince, that he was *the* Prince, but only for a second. Only a second, and nothing longer.

"Where are we going?" I asked again, my curiosity once more winning over the knots in my stomach.

Prince Cassian glanced down at me, his eyes flickering with something that looked like amusement, though there was a sharper edge to it. "You wouldn't dare question your Prince, now would you?"

The words felt like a joke, a casual statement, but my heart picked up its pace. I couldn't shake the nagging feeling. This unspoken thing between us, this magnetic pull that seemed to hang in the air whenever he was near.

Prince Vaelros was the kind of person who made everything around him feel more intense, more intimate. And I wasn't sure what I was, or what I was supposed to feel in this strange, charged space between us.

I wasn't sure if I was supposed to feel anything at all.

CHAPTER EIGHTEEN

THE HALLS TWISTED LIKE a maze. My flats brushed over the marble in near silence, every step echoing faintly in the endless corridors. The golden light slanting through the high windows set everything aglow, but it did nothing to ease the knot of unease growing in my stomach.

"So, Miss Seravell. Tell me your first name."

I stiffened, a prickle running down my spine. "I thought royals didn't bother themselves with such things," I said tightly. "Wouldn't want the court to assume you truly *enjoy my presence*, as you said."

A sharp smile ghosted across his mouth. Something borderline predatory. "Denying your prince and assuming rumors." He clicked his tongue. Mock gravity dripped from every word, but when his eyes connected with mine, they were anything but humorous.

"Tell me."

I hesitated, heart pounding in my throat. Every instinct screamed at me not to give him anything. Not a word, not an ounce of trust, not any secrets, just as Kaden had said, and yet...

"...Lyra," I whispered.

Cassian smiled then. Not the mocking smile he wore for the court. Not the lazy smirk he wore for the world, but something different.

Slow. Devastating. Real.

"Lyra," he repeated, like he was testing the sound of it on his tongue. Like he was savoring it. "I quite like that."

He said it once more, muttering a word after so quietly that I couldn't hear what he had said. "If I call you by yours, it's only fair you call me by mine. I am Cassian to you, and nothing more."

I wasn't sure how to respond, so I gave him a sharp nod before fixing my eyes on the hall before us. We continued walking in a comfortable silence. The space seemed to bend to Cassian's will, the halls ebbing and flowing as he desired. He sauntered around the twists and turns as if he himself had designed this maze.

When we rounded the final bend, realization hit me a second before Cassian countered, "Yes, we're going to the throne room. No, no one's there. That I made sure of."

The massive doors swung open with a whisper, and my breath caught.

It was just as beautiful as I remembered. Maybe even more so. The air was warm, and sun kissed. The room was coating in gold and white, in endless sun and gleaming surfaces. Towering windows behind the throne bathed the chamber in sunlight, so blinding it felt almost unearthly. The eyes arranged into the glass didn't seem to steal glances at this time of day. Their colors melded with the swirling floors in a mosaic of light. At the top of the steps sat the throne itself, sharp and majestic, a thing born from both dreams and nightmares.

Cassian spoke to me as he strode forward without hesitation.

"You took the liberty of the wine to its fullness at the ball." He smoothed out his suit coat before he looked back, extending a hand. "I thoroughly enjoyed the aftermath, but I never got to see those courtly manners you're constantly nagging me about." He jutted his chin up the stairs. "Climb the steps. Act like you're one of us. See what it feels like."

"I never meant to—" I started, but the words dried up.

"Go on," he said, his voice low, coaxing. "Sit on my father's throne and pretend that you're my queen."

The air left my lungs before I could even exhale.

I ignored his offered hand, but reluctantly, I climbed the steps. I felt the heat of his gaze all the way up. He followed, but he didn't walk to the throne. He stood beside it.

I stood before the golden obstruction, turning to face the endless room. I couldn't bring myself to actually sit, but it didn't matter. From here, the palace didn't feel so menacing. From here, it felt conquerable.

A strange hum sung down my spine. Thrill. Awe. Something older, deeper. Something that wasn't mine alone.

I turned to look at Cassian, but he stood simply looking out to the room, as if he himself was also imagining being a ruler. Being a king. For some reason, the moment felt private, so I looked away, refocusing my gaze on the windows behind the throne.

Though I hated what the throne stood for, the actual structure was marvelous. It looked as if the gold had been plucked and pulled upward by hands far more skilled than my own. It shot up in spikes that ran so sharp they seemed to disappear into the sun-lit air.

I ran my hand down the seat of the throne, hovering an inch above the surface. As it traveled down, I caught a flash of light. I moved my hand back up, and right at the center of the backrest, where a person's heart would rest, were words.

Light-formed script sat on my hand, and as I looked around, trying to find where they came from, I saw nothing. Nothing above reflected down as the only light came from behind the throne. It was faint, barely there, and I had never noticed it when the King sat smugly on this seat. I tried to read the sentences glowing on my hand, but it was twisted and layered with riddles.

When golden flesh is split and bled,

And crimson stains the seat of dread,

The silent flame shall rise once more,

To shatter crown and gilded lore.

Sanguis regis, Aurum fractum.

A shiver seemed to run up my spine, bringing a chill to the once warm space. My head swiveled over to Cassian once more. As I shifted, my hand brushed against one of the jagged golden points of the massive structure.

A sudden sting made me flinch.

I looked down and blood welled at my silk of my gloves. I pulled the red-stained fabric from my hand, seeing a small pin prick on the tip of my finger. I watched as a drop of blood ran down my hand and fell to the throne. The blood seemed to soak into the metal, sizzling and humming as if alive.

And then, the world *shattered*.

Not physically. Not like glass. It broke with sound. A scream without a mouth, a pressure that ripped through the air and detonated inside my skull.

My head split open like a dam undone, and everything, *everything*, poured in. I became like a broken mirror, each jagged shard reflecting someone else's mind, someone else's entire being.

Thoughts ravaged my skull. Thoughts that weren't mine. Memories I'd never lived. Faces, voices, centuries of emotion crashing into me like a tidal wave of other people's lives. I was still standing, or maybe I wasn't. I couldn't tell. Couldn't breathe. Couldn't hold onto myself. I reached for something solid, something mine, but it all slipped through like water.

I gasped. Choked. Stumbled back as invisible forces slammed into my chest, each one heavier than the last. I finally dropped down to my knees on the marble steps, the cold biting through me like a blade, but I barely comprehended it. Voices filled the space around me. Whispers, cries, laughter, screams. They all overlapped, tangled, tore at my mind like a twisted melody.

They clawed at my thoughts, dragged nails down the walls of my mind. Some begged. Some raged. Some simply watched. I didn't know who I was anymore, only that I was no longer the same person who had walked into this room.

I had become someone vast. Someone terrified.

Something terrifying.

"Lyra!" Cassian shouted, but his voice was distant, muffled by the storm roaring inside me.

He caught me before I could crumble further, his body now sitting behind mine. His arms locked around my body as he pulled me into his lap. My legs and arms felt limp, but his body was solid and warm, though trembling slightly. Through the chaos, I felt him—a bright, pulsing presence—desperately reaching for me.

Stay with me.

Please, stay.

We need you.

His thoughts poured into me like a tether. Calm and fierce all at once. I wasn't sure how, or why, but I clung to them like a lifeline.

Does she know?

Oh Stars, don't let her fall.

She's meant for so much more.

She's meant for everything.

I heard the servants that whispered in the halls. I heard the guards that marched in patrol. I felt their emotions as they came and went. I felt the handmaidens and their aching backs. I heard the thoughts of the kitchen servants and their longing to try the food they had prepared.

Tears blurred my vision. Not from pain, but from the overwhelming force of knowing everything, everyone.

Cassian's fingers slipped beneath my chin, tilting my face up to his.

Skin to skin.

The touch felt electric, sending rippling energy through me as everything that made up Cassian Vaelros poured into my mind.

Fear and bravery.

Love and hate.

Devotion and desperation.

Love and longing.

And then there was me.

I flickered through each wave that trailed from his hand that now slid to cup my jaw.

"Come back to me," he breathed.

His thumb stroked across my cheekbone, and the contact was like a lighthouse in a raging sea. Steady. Warm. Unmoving.

His emotions wrapped around me, not overwhelming, but anchoring. Worry, yes, but also trust. Belief. An almost painful tenderness that felt entirely too foreign to be his.

But it was. It all was.

I clung to his jacket, fisting the fabric. His scent, clean, smoky cedar, wrapped around me like a cloak.

I blinked, trying to focus, but images still flickered behind my eyes. Visions that weren't mine. Dreams and memories I had no right to. A girl with silver eyes. A battlefield soaked in moonlight. A crown, broken in two.

Cassian leaned closer, held me tighter. His head rested atop of mine as he gently rocked both of us back and forth.

"Breathe with me. Just breathe."

I followed his voice.

In. Out. Again.

Slowly, painfully, the storm began to ebb. The voices dulled, the pressure lightened, but not enough.

I leaned back slightly to meet his eyes, and there it was again, the flood but softer now. More controlled. I didn't just feel him. I saw into him.

This begins and ends with her.
She's all I ever need.
My heart lurched.
"Prince..." I whispered.
"I'm Cassian to you. Only Cassian."

He watched me with eyes that held too much. His hand slid down to take mine gently, like he wasn't sure I'd let him. Our fingers laced. The sensation sent a chill through me. Some connection or bond, whatever it was, was there. It was real. It seemed to glimmer and glow, a golden thread. Not physically, but I could feel the bridge between us. Something ancient, old, sacred.

I looked down at the throne. The blood was gone. No, not gone. It had been wiped away. I found the smeared stain on Cassian's sleeve, and my gaze returned to the throne. I found the spot where my blood had been, and beneath where it had fallen, I swore I saw it.

A faint silver circle. I blinked, and it was gone.

My bloodied and torn glove was tucked in the top pocket of his jacket, the red forefinger peeking out.

"Can you stand?"

I hadn't even realized he has asked me a question.

"Lyra—" He moved his hand back to my face, but I evaded the touch. I didn't know if I could handle any more. The rejection flashed over his eyes, clear and evident, or maybe I had simply felt it myself.

I nodded slowly, and Cassian helped me to my feet. His hand wrapped firmly around my waist, hauling me upright. His other never left my own.

"Are you alright?" he asked, voice hoarse, eyes searching my own.

No. Yes. I didn't know anymore.

"Fine," I said, though it was a lie neither of us believed. As I went to take a step down from the front of the throne room, my knees wobbled, and Cassian was already back at my side.

We walked down the wide steps and through the looming palace doors. I felt like I was dragging him behind me, though in truth, it was the other way around. My legs moved, but each step felt like wading through deep water. My heart thundered in my chest, my breath coming in sharp bursts as I stumbled forward, half-aware of where I was going. The echo of what had just happened crashed over me in relentless waves.

What had just happened?

Cassian didn't falter beside me. He was steady, calm. His arm stayed wrapped around my waist as if holding me upright cost him no effort, as if I wasn't dead weight. The halls blurred past us, tapestries and golden sconces melting together like a fever dream. I barely noticed them. I barely noticed anything except the rising tide in my mind.

We were going back to my room. I knew that much. Part of me prayed Kaden wouldn't be there. I couldn't handle hearing his thoughts. I couldn't risk catching a glimpse of what he truly felt, especially not after we had our strangely tense night. Some part of me already knew it wouldn't be anything I wanted to see.

The palace wasn't empty. Courtiers and staff passed us, and their thoughts spilled into me, leaking through like water through cracked stone. Their minds were loud, messy, and bursts of color and emotion that didn't belong to me. I couldn't separate mine from theirs anymore. Everything swirled together. Confusion wrapped tight around my chest like a chain, squeezing until my throat threatened to close.

Then we turned a corner and collided head-on with Clara Montgomery, the representative from Seren.

I reached out instinctively, grabbing her by the arms to steady her.

Skin to skin.

The moment we touched, her eyes flashed silver, almost white. For a heartbeat, it was as if she reflected something buried deep inside me. A spark jumped between us, a jolt of energy so powerful I gasped. It surged through my veins like lightning, breath-stealing and bright.

I let go immediately, staggering back a step.

Clara blinked, her eyes dazed. "Lyra? Prince Vaelros?" she said, voice thin and confused. Her body swayed slightly as she tried to bow, clearly off-balance.

Cassian offered her a warm smile. He placed a light hand on her shoulder. "Thank you, Ms. Montgomery."

The silver in her eyes slowly vanished. The deep brown returned, but they stayed uncertain. "What are you doing here? What am I doing here?"

"I—I don't know," I stammered. The words felt useless, slipping out of me without meaning. Cassian's hand at my waist tugged tighter, silencing me.

Cassian caught her gaze with his usual effortless charm. "Ms. Montgomery," he said smoothly, "I've heard the garden willows are beautiful this time of year."

Clara hesitated, then gave a wobbly smile. "Okay... I'll go take a look. Thank you, my Prince." She glanced at me once more, a weak smile spreading on her lips before she continued down the corridor, still unsteady. Every step seemed unsure.

I didn't linger, couldn't. I looked up at Cassian, and he gave me a small nod before guiding me even faster through the hall. Kaden wasn't at his post, thank the stars. When we reached my door, he opened it for me, and I stumbled inside, pulling myself from his hold the moment we were through. I slammed the door behind me and leaned hard against it, my breaths ragged, my chest tight.

Cassian wandered to the center of the room, turning back to face me. I barely registered him. My mind was still full of noise, stray thoughts from passing strangers, fear from Clara, that jolt of silver energy, the sharp twist of my own panic, but when I finally saw the situation around me, I couldn't help but laugh incredulously.

Prince Cassian Vaelros was in my room.

Oh my stars.

I pushed myself off the door, but when he took a single step toward me, I held up my hand to stop him. I refused to meet his gaze. I didn't want to know what he was thinking. Not now. I already knew too much.

"Lyra, please," he said softly. "I can help you."

I stared at the wooden floorboards beneath my feet, focusing on the ridges between them, my hand still up even while my arm shook. "You can help by leaving."

His head fell to the side, hurt flooding me even while he wasn't touching me. I wasn't even looking at him. I felt him move closer, sensed it in the air, and I stepped back further.

He stopped. Ran a hand through his hair. "Of course."

And then he left.

The door clicked shut. I exhaled, long and slow, realizing I'd been holding my breath nearly the entire time. I let my arm fall and my head hang back, my eyes fluttering closed towards the ceiling. Even with him gone, the whispers didn't stop. They were quieter, more distant, but still there, like a draft slipping through in the dead of winter, impossible to ignore.

I now knew far too much about the handmaiden and her lover next door.

I dragged myself to bed and collapsed, my limbs heavy, my mind thrumming with fatigue. Sleep took me quickly, but my bed was no haven.

In my dreams, shadows danced and shifted, forming places I didn't recognize yet knew with eerie certainty. Vast, open lands I'd never visited. Cities I'd never walked through. Memory after memory flickered through me like candlelight in wind.

And then I stood in a grand hall, open and echoing, thick with unspoken tension. At the top of a wide marble staircase sat a golden throne, and before it knelt a woman.

Her hair was the soft brown of an autumn forest, her posture proud despite the weight that hung off her like a chain. I knew her face. Not from portraits, not from stories, but from something else. Someone else.

Cassian's mother. The late Queen of Aurea.

She looked older, worn with grief, her eyes storm-dark with sorrow. She was pleading on her knees. Her voice was a whisper, barely audible. "Please, you must listen to me! You can't do this—"

Who was she begging?

The vision began to fade, its edges blurring like paint left in the rain. I reached out for it, desperate, but it dissolved in my hands like smoke.

I woke with a jolt, heart pounding. The remnants of the dream clung to me like a second skin as I peeled the sweat-soaked sheets from my skin.

A sharp knock did little to ease the tension in my chest. Kaden entered carrying a stack of books, his dark hair falling into his eyes and his chest moving fast with deep breaths. His expression shifted the moment he saw me, concern giving way to confusion. "Lyra," he said, stepping closer. "Are you alright? I heard you shouting."

I sat up slowly, still tangled in blankets. "I'm fine," I said, though my voice didn't sound like mine. "Just another day in paradise," I muttered, more to myself than to him.

His brow furrowed. He set the books down on the desk and watched me like I might shatter. "Is something bothering you?"

I hesitated. I wanted to say yes. I wanted to scream that everything was bothering me. That nothing felt right anymore, but he interrupted my train of thought, blurting, "Because I had no intention of...well...I didn't mean to make you uncomfortable last night. I wasn't trying to do anything like that, I swear—"

Stars. He was still trying to untangle one awkward night, and I could barely hear him over the roar in my head. I wasn't angry. I just couldn't reach far enough to care. Not right now. Not when everything inside me was still splintering.

"Kaden, it's fine." His shoulders visibly fell with relief. "Just... had a weird dream."

Kaden nodded slowly, though I could see the doubt behind his eyes. "You need to be careful," he said gently. "I know the last trial rattled you."

"I'm fine," I whispered, rubbing my eyes. "I just need to get my head straight."

He lingered, like he wanted to say more. Then finally, he nodded and turned toward the door.

"I'm here if you need to talk." He whispered the words so gently. Kaden was an overwhelmingly soft soul, and I refused to tamper with that kindness.

The door shut behind him, and I slumped back against the pillows.

The silence was thick.

I stared up at the ceiling. Something had changed. I didn't know how to name it, but it was there, settling inside me like a second heartbeat.

Whatever it was, it wasn't going away, and for now, I just wanted quiet.

CHAPTER NINETEEN

I TOOK THE DAY SLOWLY and didn't leave my room. The last thing I wanted was to be back in those halls.

Even here, voices and whispers echoed in. They seemed to drift on a phantom breeze that was downright relentless. I pulled on my gloves, trying to create some cage for whatever I had released, but it was no use. I ripped them off. Besides, with my silk pair destroyed I only had leather. The dust reminded me too much of the maze. Too much of Jamie.

I need a distraction.

So, I went through and organized every dress the palace had given me in my armoire. I did color order, then fabric type, then length, then my own personal ranking, and landed on functionality. The ones that allowed for the most movement on the left, down to one that was downright hideous on the right. The last one was so obnoxiously tight I don't even think it would have fit over my shoulders. I shoved the gowns I never would wear into the back, saving room for whatever else I decided should be stored there.

I kept my dress from home, the one I purchased with Selene, in my drawer. Carefully folded and tucked away as if the wooden armoire could protect the fabric from the palace's vile nature.

I sat out on the balcony and tried to name every flower in the garden. I saw roses, lilies, daisies, lilacs, and then realized I had little to no knowledge on flowers whatsoever. I guess living in Virellia would do that to a person.

I sighed as I flopped back down on the stone. I turned so my back rested against the railing and let my head do the same. I closed my eyes and just breathed, trying to quiet my mind. I focused on the black of my shut eyelids, on the sound of the wind, on the heat of the sun and the shade of the occasional cloud.

Nothing worked.

I let out a frustrated sigh, and as the air left, golden warmth slithered in. A little string laced up my spine like a corset and even though I chose to stand, I could have sworn it pulled me towards my door.

I opened it to find Cassian lounging against the wall opposite my room, one foot up so his heel rested against the stone. His hands were tucked in his pockets, and his eyes were fixed on my door. He hadn't even knocked.

"May I help you, Prince Vaelros?" I spoke with false nicety coating the words.

He pushed himself off the wall, walking toward me with long slow steps.

"I could have sworn I told you to call me Cassian, *Lyra*." He smirked something wicked. "But what else should I expect from a Virellian if not disobedience?"

I scoffed, bunching my eyebrows in clear annoyance. I folded my arms over the nightgown that was undoubtedly a bit too sheer for this conversation.

"Well then, *Cassian*, to what do I owe the pleasure?"

"Normally girls are overjoyed when I come to their rooms." He stared down at the arms folded over my chest, making it no point to hide his gaze. "They rush me inside, push me onto their beds."

"I would have assumed you to be the one pushing. Not them."

Cassian only shrugged, his lip curling with amusement. "I have my days." He had walked across the entire hall, now standing under my door frame. "The real question is, will today be one of them?"

I scoffed, recoiling back with disgust. "You are foul."

"And you are no fun at all." He laid a new pair of silk gloves onto my shoulder, the white fabric shimmering faintly. With that, he let himself inside, turning sideways to slide around me.

I bit the inside of my cheek to fight my grin as I pulled the gifted gloves onto my hands, flexing my fingers in the cool silk. No fancy embroidering or beading laced the fabric except two small flames on my palms, stitched in silver thread.

I turned back, shutting the door as I went. His head snapped back, his eyebrows raised at the sound of the door hitting its frame. A teasing smile spread across his lips, showing teeth.

I threw up a finger at him. "Don't get any ideas."

He sucked a breath through his teeth, his smile holding on for dear life. "Too late. Perhaps I'll just make a list for later."

I exhaled sharply, a laugh escaping at his absolute arrogance. "Why are you here Cassian?"

"You're not okay," he said.

I crossed my arms. "Thanks for the reminder."

"You refused my help last night, but you can only push the inevitable so far."

I tilted my head. My eyebrows bunched in confusion. "And what am I inevitably avoiding?"

"Practicing. Training"

He said the words like they meant nothing at all. He said them as if I wanted whatever abilities I had just been cursed with. He said them like this whole situation was just another day to him, like it was all part of some plan.

I narrowed my eyes. "You want to *train* me."

He grinned. "Is that such a dirty word?" He dropped down onto the floor, patting the space across from him. "Come on," he said, voice lighter now. "I don't bite unless asked."

I didn't gratify him with a response. I walked over to my armoire, grabbing a shawl and wrapping it around myself. "Are you suddenly a master of mysterious magic?"

I turned, pulling the shawl tighter around me as my arms wrapped over my stomach.

He only shrugged. "Royal tutors leave no stone unturned." He sat with his legs crossed and his hands resting on his knees, palms up.

"How do I know you won't put some hex or curse on me?" I sauntered over, my steps slow. "Knowledge is power, and you seem to have the upper hand."

"No, Lyra. Power is power. And, remind me, who is the one with literal power at their fingertips in this very moment?" His eyes ran down my body, smirking at the shawl around my shoulders. They landed back on my own, the gold of his swirling in the light. "If you honestly believe knowledge is power, then come. Steal mine. I'll give it willingly if you ask politely. Though manners were never your strength."

I rolled my eyes so far back I swore they would get stuck in the back of my head, but I walked over and sat on the ground across from him.

Cassian's hands were still out and waiting, his palms up like an offering. He flicked his eyes from my gloves to his hands in a gesture for me to take them. I began to reach out, but he pulled back, just slightly.

He shook his head. "No gloves, Lyra. No barriers."

I hesitated.

I grabbed the fingers of one hand, sliding the glove from my skin. I set it down beside me, smoothing the silk before repeating the motion with the other glove.

The bareness made me feel vulnerable in a way I don't think I could ever explain.

Cassian didn't push. His teasing nature had subsided, giving way to someone patient. He didn't move or speak, just waited.

I reached out once more, slowly. I laid my hands in his, my palm against his own.

Everything crashed into me like a rogue wave.

Thoughts. Emotions. Images.

It all flashed from memory to memory quicker than I could comprehend. It was all too much.

I tore my hand away with a gasp.

He jerked his hands back too, his own chest rising and falling a bit too fast.

His mind was still swirling around my own, even without the touch. It was as if his memories and mine had become one, intertwining and mingling in my head.

I closed my eyes, squeezing them shut so forcefully it hurt.

"Again."

Something brushed and rested in my lap. I opened my eyes to see hands, Cassian's hands, open and waiting. I drug my gaze up to meet his. My mouth opened to object, but he spoke before I got the chance.

"Go again, Lyra."

I took a deep breath, filling my lungs with all of the oxygen I could muster. "What do you mean *again?*"

"Pick one, and step into it."

"What?"

"Anchor yourself. Don't let it drown you, just sink with it."

I stared at him in complete incredulity. I opened my mouth to quip back at him, but when my eyes found his, I only saw what can be described as hope. He was hopeful. He believed in whatever I was.

I nodded once as I took his hands. I let the flood surround me.

My name ran through his mind again, and again, and again. I saw the way he fought to keep his own hands steady in this very moment. The way he had waited outside my door, debating on knocking for over an hour. The way he had watched for me at breakfast before even that.

His mind ran over my own, each wave sending me deeper and deeper. In a way, it was beautiful. In a way, I wanted to keep sinking.

I released his hands for the second time.

Cassian's body sagged, his head falling forward before lolling back. His chin was up to the ceiling, his breathing audible. "Well, you certainly have that strategy down."

Panic raced through my veins, my blood drumming in my ears. "Did I hurt you?"

He exhaled with a laugh, his eyes meeting mine. Fire burned in his gaze. "No. No, not exactly."

His heart was racing.

I looked down at my hands. I stared at the smooth pale skin, the lines in my palms, the dirt under my fingernails.

"Look at me."

At the command, I did. My eyes moved to connect with the honey amber of Cassian's, and he stared back in complete awe. He stared as if I was now the inevitable.

"Try now."

"Try what?"

He leaned forward, his face a foot from my own. "Try to go in my mind now."

I began to stretch a hand out, but he backed away, shaking his head. "Just look. Don't touch for this one." He smirked. "Not that I don't want those pretty hands all over me."

I scoffed, waving my arms in disgust. He only chuckled, low and rumbling.

I sat my hands back in my lap and then looked at him. "I don't know *how*."

He only shrugged. "They say the eyes are the window to the soul. Use them."

I hesitated, then met his gaze. I pushed forward, imagining my power extending beyond my hands. It began to flow from my fingertips, the air becoming iridescent. I gasped as it slithered outward, a shimmering shining tendril of pure energy. It snaked across the ground, fighting against the path I forced it on. I stretched my power about halfway toward Cassian before it snapped back, the force of it throwing me back to my elbows on the floor.

I grimaced as I sat back up, rubbing at the bruise on my arm that was undoubtedly forming.

"Again."

My eyes flew up. "I just got mind-flung into the floor, and you want to try that again?"

"I do." Suddenly, no emotions ran over his face. Nothing broke through the mask of calm Cassian had schooled his features into. Nothing broke it, but I could.

I leaned forward, pressing my hands into the cool floor. I stared into his eyes, the golden brown of them seeming to become molten. I pressed my power outward again, allowing it to glide to him. I let it wander, let it flow. The silvery smoke-like strands floated up his body, curling around his head like a halo made of mist. It stayed there, rising and falling on his brow. His emotions flowed back along the same strand, softly and gently. He was amused, captivated even, but also...

"You're nervous."

Cassian gave a soft chuckle. "I'm usually better at hiding that."

I laughed, but barely. I let my power snake back, slowly. It flowed at its own pace, which was quite leisurely, at least for now. Once the air returned back to only sunlight and dust, I let myself breathe.

The breath came out as a shudder. "I did it."

Cassian smiled back, gently, and not teasing. "You did."

"But I—I felt things that weren't mine to feel. Those thoughts..."

Cassian only leaned forward, grabbing the gloves from beside me and holding the silk in his hands. "Anything can be yours. If you're brave enough to take it."

I didn't know if I wanted to take any more. I didn't know if I wanted anything else to be mine.

"I can never stop taking. I can't ever turn it off."

Cassian cocked his head, pursing his lips as if this was a question he hadn't anticipated. He exhaled and leaned back, his palms pressing to the floor behind him. "Would you like to turn it off?"

I thought of all of the whispers and thoughts that perilously ravaged my mind. Of the voices that shoved their way through my own and wove memories through my brain.

"I need it to stop. I need it to be quiet. Even if it's only for a second, I need the choice."

He sat up, folding his hands into his lap. "Okay then." He clicked his tongue, looking around the room. His eyes landed on the empty jars lining the copper bathtub.

"Those jars, on the tub there. When the lid is on, did the herbs spill from the glass?"

I laughed incredulously, leaning forward at him. "Was that a serious question?"

"Absolutely."

"No, Cassian. When the lid is on a jar, the contents of said jar do not spill." Sarcasm coated every word like grit.

"Then put your *contents* in your own jar."

I pinched my eyebrows together. "I don't understand."

Cassian brought his hands together to create a circle, his pointer fingers and thumbs connecting with those on the opposite hand.

"Close your eyes."

I let my eyes flutter to a close without hesitation.

"Picture a jar. Or anything really. Make it strong, sturdy."

I pictured a thick glass jar, like the ones form home. Hand-blown glass that had a slight yellow tint to it. Thicker at the base than along the sides. When I was done, I nodded.

"Make a lid. It impenetrable. It's perfect."

I imagined a solid silver lid. It was nothing I had seen before, but somewhere, somehow, I knew how it would look if it were a reality. Solid silver metal that screwed on top. My initials, L. S. were engraved at the top. It was mine, and mine alone. Again, I nodded.

"This is where your power lives. Where it sleeps and breathes and thrives. Where it's contained. It wants to go there. Coax it home."

I paused for a second. My power flooded every part of me. My skin, my blood, my breath. I wasn't sure where to begin, and Cassian knew it too.

"This power is yours, Lyra. It will listen."

I took a breath, allowing my lungs to fill with oxygen and my mind to slow. I slowly and carefully plucked my power from my body, pulling it from my skin and fishing it from my blood. Bit by bit it flowed into the jar I had imagined. Filling its space but never overflowing. I laughed softly when the last of it wound its way inside.

I could practically feel Cassian's grin.

"Now, put on the lid."

I screwed the lid onto the jar, and with each turn, the voices in my head quieted. Their volume lowered and lowered until eventually, silence.

I open my eyes with a gasp, looking up to Cassian immediately. Sure enough, a smirk was plastered to his lips.

I stared at him, and yet, I didn't hear a thing. I didn't even hear his own thoughts. That trickle that never quite stopped had ceased.

But even though his thoughts stopped, that golden thread was very much alive and well. It ran down my back from my shoulders to the base of my spine, warmth, and something close to pride shimmering with its touch.

Cassian stood, my new gloves still held in his hand. He held them out to me as I rose from the ground. I reached out to take them from his hand, the fabric cool in my grasp, but he didn't let go. He froze there, for just a second, but I noticed. He noticed too.

He cleared his throat, his hand dropped to hang at his side.

"Keep practicing, just be wary. People hide sharp things in the darkest corners of their minds. Don't sink too far."

I nodded sharply in agreement. "Thank you, really."

"Of course." His voice dropped, playful once more. "If you ever need a target…"

I raised a brow.

"I'd be more than happy to volunteer my thoughts." His eyes flicked to my lips and back. "For educational purposes," he added innocently with a wink.

I snorted. "Good to know, princeling."

He walked to the door as I made my way to the armoire, opening the doors and pulling out a cream cotton dress.

Cassian spun at the door, hand on the handle. "Want me to stay? Just to supervise of course."

My hands went to my hips, something his eyes immediately followed.

They hovered there even as he spoke. "Another time, then."

He swung the door open behind him, backing out of the door before pivoting and letting the wood hit its frame and close on its own.

Pompous Prince.

I changed quickly, sliding my nightgown off and the day dress on. I sat on my bed, legs folded under me, and closed my eyes.

The Prince told me to keep practicing, even if he didn't specify how. I let my power unfurl, filling my room as it flooded the space. I didn't force its path, I had at least learned that during our "training." I simply let it explore. It spilled through the door frame, the open windows. Through the cracks in the mortar and brick. It went where it chose, like a living breathing thing that was caged inside of me.

I heard the thoughts of everyone that passed by my door. I heard the thoughts of the servants that scurried through the halls. I felt the nervousness from handmaidens preparing nobles, and others in the halls. I felt Kaden's anxiety and fear as he stood outside my door but also felt his curiosity.

And if I was being honest with myself, I was curious too.

I stood and crossed the space, allowing my power to continue its exploration. I tugged the door open as Kaden turned to knock, his hand rising to strike the wood. I tried to smile at him, but he didn't believe any part of it.

I felt that, too.

"Seravell, this is uh— " He gestured at the singular handmaiden that stood behind him. "This is Eldra."

I waved. "Hello, Eldra. It's nice to meet you." My power shimmered in the air, leaking from my room into the hall. It didn't touch either of them directly, but their thoughts seemed to find their way into my mind, nonetheless.

Eldra stepped out from her hiding place and gave me a small wave in return, but she didn't look up from her feet. She was around fourteen years old, and her fear rolled off of her in waves. I fought to keep my face blank, even as terror flooded my head. This wasn't normal fear. This was blood-chilling.

I looked down at her hands. One held a basket containing a red dress, while the other held a small kit likely of hair styling tools. She noticed my stare, and her gaze shifted slightly up. Her eyes stayed down, but her face was just visible. I recognized her. She was one of the handmaidens from the first trial.

My eyes flicked up to Kaden's. His head was cloudy, as if his thoughts were running circles around even his own mind. I cocked my head slightly as my lips pressed into a thin line, sending a wordless message.

Why is she here?

He seemed to understand my question, clearing his throat as he placed a gentle hand on Eldra's back.

"Eldra is here to prepare you for a royal feast tonight." His eyes turned cold, hard. He knew more than he was letting on. He didn't speak the words, but he didn't need to. They flowed into my mind almost lazily, like a river stream.

The King had so graciously planned a feast for the remaining five candidates who had made it to the third trial. The trial which was to take place in two days time.

Both of those thoughts were news to me, and I couldn't help but wonder if Kaden was ever going to tell me either of them. I couldn't help but wonder what other secrets Kaden was keeping from me.

Irritation of my own burned. I crossed my arms, defiance oozing.

"I wasn't aware of any feast." I said coolly.

Kaden's jaw clenched, and he ran his tongue on his bottom teeth. "Good thing you were just informed then, hm?" He raised his eyebrows at me.

I huffed a laugh, but it wasn't from humor. I rolled my head around my shoulders as Eldra shifted her weight. It was clear she was wildly uncomfortable.

I looked back at Kaden, and his eyebrows had landed back where they belonged. Good. Forehead wrinkles would not be a good look for him.

I turned back to Eldra, and guilt began to eat at me. It wasn't her fault. She was told to come here. She was just following orders. It wasn't fair to take my annoyance out on her, so I fixed my face and threw a smile on my lips.

I clasped my hands in mock enthusiasm. "Well, good thing you are here then, Eldra." I stepped aside for her enter the room. She hesitated but did so slowly. Her eyes stayed glued to her shuffling feet. "I can hardly contain my excitement."

Kaden let out a sigh as he let his head fall to his back. He was just as agitated as I was, meaning I had accomplished my goal. I went to slam the door closed, but a hand stopped it on its hinges.

He leaned in, making sure whatever he was about to say didn't make it to Eldra's ears

"Listen Seravell. I know you don't want to be here. That is loud and clear, okay?"

I swallowed, hard.

"I didn't know about this feast until this morning. The King does what the King wants, and today, he decided he wants a feast." Kaden's eyes weren't harsh. They weren't cold or demanding, just truthful. And I felt that truth in every word.

"I am not your enemy."

I stared at him as he searched my eyes for any form of response, but I didn't have one. I felt now like nothing more than a spoiled royal brat. Maybe Cassian had rubbed off on me.

Kaden let out a huff of breath and glanced to Eldra in my room before he pivoted and walked down the hall. I closed the door slowly and turned to her. She stood in the center of the room, still clutching all of her supplies in her hands. Her eyes had yet to raise to meet my own, and I realized she didn't look at me when she was here for the first trial either. I moved towards her slowly, as if she were a wild animal that would dart at any second.

"Thank you for coming Eldra, really." I now stood a step away from her, and she shook like a leaf in a storm. I could practically smell the fear that rattled her nerves but could not for the life of me understand why she was so afraid.

"You can set your things down, if you like."

She slowly bent her knees until the baskets hit the floor, rising just as carefully. She folded her hands in front of her as she stood.

"Did they say you're not allowed to look at us?" I tried to tilt my head down to find her eyes, but she tucked her chin tighter. "Because if so, that's a silly rule that you do not have to follow with me at all."

I stood fully, giving up on trying to make her look at me and simply went to help her unpack her supplies. As I reached for the baskets that sat near her legs, I let my power slowly reach out. The shimmering tendril was barely visible, like heat waves on stone. When it brushed against her ankle wrapping and holding there, she gasped. She jerked her foot away, startled and afraid.

I stumbled back, my own heart now pounding. Cassian hadn't even flinched. I wasn't sure he had even noticed.

But Eldra had.

Her head snapped up, and in that moment, I saw eyes that I never thought I would see outside of a mirror.

Her eyes shone a beautiful silvery blue, but as quickly as her head snapped up, it fell back down. This time, it wasn't fear.

It was pure dread that filled the space.

I backed away, instantly. She trembled as if it took all of her effort to stay standing.

"Um—" I wasn't sure what to do. "You know, you must be busy today with the other girls. I could get ready myself if you would like to—"

I didn't even finish my sentences before Eldra walked out the door.

I never saw her again.

CHAPTER TWENTY

I STOOD BEFORE THE MIRROR in my chamber, the deep red gown cascading around me like liquid rubies.

The fabric clung to my frame, smooth and heavy, shimmering where the light caught the folds. The topmost buttons stayed undone as my arms were not long nor flexible enough to reach them. A new pair of gloves had been folded into the gown. The fabric was a light and airy mesh, but the color was the deepest black I had ever seen. My fingertips looked as if they were frost bitten, the black fabric darkest at my hands before gradually fading to crimson. Scarlet gemstones dotted along the length of them, clustering at the top near my elbows. It looked as if I had dipped my arms in blood. I could only do a handful of hairstyles on myself, so it laid in gentle waves down my shoulders, nearly hitting my waist. I had threaded a pin topped with rubies into each side near my temples.

Against my pale skin and white hair, I looked like some twisted fairy tale. Something beautiful, but wrong.

Kaden entered without warning, dressed in a tailored coat that showed all sharp lines and clean strength. The fabric was the color of storm clouds, and his face reflected the same turmoil. He wore gloves made of cold black leather. Looking at him now, he looked every bit the knight he was raised to be. After all, everyone is simply a product of their environment.

His gaze swept over me, and for a moment, something softened in his expression. His anger and frustration from our bickering earlier today had faded or at least dampened.

"You look lovely," he said, his smile faint.

"Thank you," I murmured. Embarrassment flooded my cheeks. "Could you...help me?" I spun around, pulling my hair to the side to show him the unbuttoned dress. I heard him inhale sharply. Footsteps sounded, bringing him closer.

His gloves left chills where they brushed skin. He buttoned the remaining few, his hands leaving when he was finished. They moved to sweep my hair back, the touch sending shivers running down my spine. He let his hand hesitate, his fingers running slowly through the white strands before he cleared his throat. He backed away as I spun around. I'm sure my face was as red as my gown, but at least so was his.

"Ready for this feast?"

"More like ready to survive it," I grumbled as I slipped my arm into his. Even if his warmth was fueled by fluster, or even residual anger, it grounded me as we stepped into the hall. The flicker of hanging lanterns lit our way. They burst to life in sequence as we passed, casting a golden glow against the ancient stone.

The mess hall had been transformed. Candlelight glimmered on polished wood. Flowers and vines trailed from the rafters like something out of a dream, or a trap. No windows lined the walls. There was only endless brick and flickering light. It was beautiful, but it felt like a cage dressed in silks.

I spotted Elena and Clara near the far side and made my way toward them. Elena offered a smile, sliding over to make room. I sat beside her, across from Clara, who looked pale and withdrawn. Like her mind had gone somewhere she couldn't quite return from.

My own head was no better. I could feel the pulse of thoughts, a constant churning tide of voices that didn't belong to me. The longer I sat among them, the worse it got. I tried to remember the training with Cassian. I tried to shut the door, tried not to drown, but every brush of someone's arm, every bit of eye contact or sideways glance bled into my skull like ink into water. My hands gripped the edge of the table until I was sure my knuckles were white under my gloves. I compressed all of my power into the silver and glass jar I envisioned in my mind. It lapped at the edge, fighting as I screwed the lid closed.

Some foolish part of me had assumed if gloves were on my hands, wrapping them protection, or a prison, then this curse would fade. It would quiet without me forcing it away. I peered down at my hands, looking at the mesh that coated them. Small holes fought through the thin fabric, open to the air, and to the people.

It wasn't gloves that didn't work, it was *these* gloves.

The wine shimmered in my cup, dark and red like the gown I wore. I took a small sip, hoping it might slow the storm, but nothing dulled the noise inside me.

"Are you alright?" Elena asked softly, eyeing the death grip I had on the table.

I released it, forced a breath, and smoothed my gown as if it mattered. "I'm fine."

I wasn't. Servant's brought plates out to each table. I cut the food, brought my fork to my mouth, chewed, swallowed. Again. The rhythm helped. A mantra of motion. My power was sealed, but Elena's thoughts were too loud. So were the rest. Everyone's mind seemed to press into my own as if I was a thousand feet under water. When it had just been Cassian, this had been easy. I had contained it. I had shut *him* out, but I couldn't shut *them* out.

Sorrow, envy, anger, disappointment, every emotion crashed and blended until I didn't know which ones were mine anymore. I had to release it. I had to let my power go.

So, I did.

The jar came undone. And it didn't just open.

It shattered.

The air hummed and vibrated with the abundance of energy. Power laced through the air, flowed under the table. It curled over people's feet, sending thoughts back with each and every touch. It slithered at its own will, ending and curving where it desired. I heard thoughts, felt emotions. None of which were mine.

This time, I was sure. Because they were about me.

That witch from the north needs to go home.

She's horrendous to even look at.

The Virellian nightmare is going to scare the children.

I'm disappointed that our Prince would even entertain that girl.

My power continued its venture, flowing forward until it hit the royal table. At the front of the mess hall was a raised stage. The King sat in the center, with Cassian to his right. On the other side sat a heavy-set man who was no doubt the King's seneschal. He had an empty goblet of wine, and a servant holding a bottle right behind him. He was whispering in the King's ear when the tendril of power raced under the table, hitting him. He hissed into the King's ear, his face red with anger while King Malik's was void of any emotion whatsoever.

The man leaned back and stopped speaking, but his thoughts only quickened. I couldn't make out what he had said, but his mind spoke more volumes than his words ever could.

She struts like a queen, snarls like a rebel, and dresses like a little girl who stole her mother's jewels. Did she claw her way up, or was she dragged like a stray dog?

My flinch was involuntary. I yanked back, and in doing so, pulled at the seneschal's mind. His head snapped up from his plate. His eyes met mine before I could look away.

Kaden, seated two down from the man, jolted as the seneschal stood with such force that his chair screeched back against the stone floor, toppling with a crash. Goblets rattled. Conversations fell into a hush. But the King paid no mind to him at all. In fact, his gaze wasn't on the scene unfolding beside him.

They were on me.

The man was red-faced. His cheeks flushed with wine and anger. His eyes, glassy and hazed, locked onto me with something feral in them. Spit gathered at the corner of his sneering mouth.

"Mind-thieving brat! I'll gut you like the snow-born filth you are!"

To everyone else in the room, the outburst seemed deranged. An unhinged member of the court who had too much to drink.

To me, it was a glowing target on my back.

At that, Kaden stood. His hand was already on the hilt of his sword, the blade withdrawn to show a few gleaming inches of unyielding steel.

The seneschal's head turned at the sound. "You." The man's voice cut through the hall like a cracked blade. "You're the one guarding that white-haired witch."

Murmurs rippled outward like a dropped stone into still water. I reached for my wine. I needed to break free from this nauseating reality. My name wasn't spoken, but it didn't need to be. All eyes flicked toward me. I froze, the goblet halfway to my lips.

"You're practically committing treason," the noble slurred, jabbing a finger in Kaden's face. "You think we haven't noticed you watching her like a dog with a bone? You think we're all blind?"

Kaden didn't move. Not yet. He stood there, coiled and still as a loaded trap. His gaze flicked to me once, barely a breath's worth of contact, and then returned to the man.

"Sit down, Edros," he said, quiet and even. Dangerous.

But the seneschal—Edros—was far from finished. He snarled and reached out, knocking over a silver platter of roasted duck in his clumsy lunge. Grease splattered across the table. He snatched a dinner knife from beside his plate and turned, not toward Kaden, but toward me.

My breath caught as the point leveled at my chest.

A collective gasp sucked the air from the room. The music stopped.

I didn't move. Couldn't. My skin burned cold as the blade gleamed under the chandelier light. My mind screamed to react, but my body locked tight with a fear so sudden and sharp it left me hollow.

Why were Aureans *so obsessed* with knives?

Then, motion. Kaden moved like a whip cracking through the air. One heartbeat I was frozen. The next, the knife was clattering across the floor, spinning out of reach in a flash of silver. Kaden had Edros pinned against the table in a blink. One forearm braced across the man's collarbone, the other gripping his wrist so tightly I heard bones grind. The seneschal gasped, eyes bulging in shock and pain.

The hall erupted.

Chairs scraped back. Shouts rang out.

But Kaden didn't so much as blink. He loomed over the man like a retribution carved in flesh, voice like iron dragged over stone.

"Threaten her again, and I will break your hand in six places. Try to speak her name again, and I'll cut out your tongue and feed it to the hounds."

The seneschal whimpered. He actually whimpered.

"Enough," came another voice, an officer. Guards were pushing through the throng now, steel flashing at their sides.

Kaden let go before they reached him. He backed away slowly, like a wolf deciding the prey wasn't worth the blood. Edros sagged into the table, wheezing and clutching his wrist.

The guards were shouting commands, but Kaden stood still as stone as they reached him.

My mouth opened to speak, to say something, anything, but Kaden didn't look at me. Not once.

The guards seized his arms and yanked him back. He didn't resist. Not a flicker of regret crossed his face, but his eyes were locked on Edros, cold and seething with a fury that burned like frost. The kind of look that promised this wasn't over.

They dragged him away, shoving bodies aside, but even then, Kaden never dropped his gaze from the man who'd dared point a knife at me.

And just before the doors slammed behind them, he turned his head.

He looked at me, and in that single, fierce glance, I saw everything he didn't say.

Loyalty.

Regret.

And pride, blazing like fire.

Then he was gone.

I couldn't breathe. Couldn't move. Couldn't stop the anger boiling in my veins.

Cassian sat at the head of the hall, watching. Calm. Cold. As though none of it mattered.

He didn't move.

He didn't speak.

He just watched.

My head spun, and the emotions of the room battered me like waves in a storm.

Excitement.

Pity.

Some were disappointed the knife hadn't flown true.

I felt that. I *knew* that.

And still, nothing from Cassian. His mask was as cold as ever.

Then he met my gaze. Tilted his head. Like he was curious.

"Miss Seravell," he said, voice smooth and low. "Are you alright?"

Of course I'm not alright.

I shoved my chair back so hard it screeched. I brought my goblet still full of wine back to my lips, effectively finishing the drink in two large swallows. "I'll take my leave."

I didn't wait for permission. I let the goblet fall from my hand as I stormed out, heels echoing on the stone as I ran down the corridor. My heart thundered, my hands trembling. I felt someone's gaze chase me, felt their presence shadow my thoughts, but I refused to turn around.

Kaden was gone. Dragged away like a criminal for simply guarding me. All the while Cassian had only sat there, unmoved.

And the thoughts—stars, the thoughts—they were still inside me. Not mine. Not fully. A blur of strangers' voices, emotions, hunger, judgment, desire. They clung to me like spiderwebs I couldn't tear away. I wanted to scrape them off my skin.

I tried to envision the same jar. I tried to shove and stuff my power into the glass, but it twisted free each and every time.

I threw my bedroom door closed behind me with all the force in my body. The sound cracked through the air like a whip, echoing off the stone walls of my chamber. My breath came in shallow, ragged pulls, and I pressed both palms to the door, as if I could somehow hold the world out. Hold everything out.

The room spun around me. My heart was a war drum, pounding so hard it shook my ribs.

I stumbled away, hands tangling in my hair as I let out a choked, ugly sound. A sob, a scream. I didn't even know what it was.

Then the wood shifted.

A hand emerged between the door and its frame. Cassian pushed the door open and mockingly shook his head, clicking his tongue as if to scold me.

He stepped in, slow and controlled. His long coat still perfectly arranged, his golden eyes unreadable in the low light. He closed the door with an audible click and leaned his weight against it.

"You weren't excused, Lyra," he said, voice low, soft. Dangerous. "You know better than to try and run from me."

I backed away a step.

He watched me like one might watch a storm cresting just beyond a cliff. Fascinated. Reckless. "Are you hurt?"

I laughed. Bitter and trembling. "You're asking *now*?"

He said nothing. Just studied me.

"You just sat there," I whispered, taking another step back. "You didn't even move when a man pointed a *knife* at me."

"He would have never reached you."

"That's not the point!" I shouted.

My voice cracked. I wrapped my arms around myself as if that would keep me from breaking open entirely. "I'm losing control, Cassian. Of something I don't even understand."

He took a step toward me. "Just remember what we talked about this morning. Remember how you controlled it then."

I shook my head hard. "No, don't. I didn't know then, and I surely don't know now. Just—don't come near me."

But he didn't stop. He kept walking. "Lyra—"

I snapped.

"You could have intervened. You could have, and you chose not to." My hand shook as I pointed at him. "You think I care about your perfect prince act? You don't feel it. You have no idea what it's like to hear everything, feel everything. Like it's being driven into you." My fingers crackled with energy. I pulled the gloves from my hands, throwing them to the floor. "People wanted me dead tonight. They were disappointed that knife didn't hit its mark. I felt it. And I don't even know if one of those voices were mine!"

Power curled from my fingers, thin snakes slithering across the ground like living beings. Tendrils snapped like lightening, whipping out towards Cassian's feet. One lashed at his ankle, wrapping around and winding up his leg.

The Prince froze.

"I didn't do that on purpose," I said quietly. My voice trembled like my limbs. "I told you. I can't control it." I brought my hand down, and the power snaking around his body receded.

Glass rattled in its panes. The air grew warm, the temperature climbing with the pitch of my heart. My stomach wound itself into knots. I sucked in air, my lungs heaving, but it did nothing. My chest was too tight. It *hurt*. Air wasn't registering.

"I can't breathe," I whispered, tears springing to my eyes. "I can't —I can't—" I pressed my hands to the sides of my head, squeezing my eyes shut.

I could hear as shimmering energy spun around the room. My power whipped around like a cyclone, knocking a vase from the mantle to the floor. I heard as the porcelain shattered, the shrapnel and water rushing across the wood. My blood rushing in my veins burned.

Cassian's footsteps came fast, but he didn't touch me. Not yet.

"You're unraveling," he said gently. "And it's remarkable."

"Stop." I opened my eyes as I turned away, letting clenched fists fall to my side. "Stop pretending this is something beautiful. I feel like I'm drowning."

He didn't respond right away. Then, softly, "Then let me help you breathe."

I couldn't take it.

I wanted to scream. Not with sound but with everything. Whatever power I had contained threatened to lash outward. Light spilled from my chest, my hands, my spine. It filled the room with silver heat, blinding, searing, shimmering. The window had burst open, the curtains flaring like wings. The wood panels in the floor shook. Books flew from the shelves, swirling in the whirlwind of color and magic.

Cassian stood in the eye of the storm, hair tousled by wind, coat billowing, and still, he didn't look afraid.

He looked awestruck. He stepped forward, silent.

"Magnificent," he whispered. "Stars, you're breathtaking."

A sound at the door.

Then, Kaden.

He stumbled into the chaos, blood trailing from a fresh gash along his cheekbone. His shirt was torn at the collar. One hand was braced against the doorframe as if it took everything in him just to stand. His eyes found mine, and he froze. He saw the tornado of shimmering silver power, of books and paper and wreckage.

He saw the magic. He saw me.

Silver light poured off my skin like mist, like flame, like something not meant for this world.

I began to stumble towards him, power sizzling down my arms, my fingers, sparking off my fingertips. But with each movement I made towards him, he flinched away. His hand slipped from the frame, the deadweight of his body pulling him down.

Kaden's knees buckled, and he dropped to the floor, gasping. "Stars," he whispered. His eyes moved back up, but he didn't look at me. "What... are you?"

His words were not meant to be cruel. They held reverence. He was terrified.

Kaden looked past the storm of power, to Cassian, who stood tall in the glow, and I saw something crack in his expression.

Rage. Pain. Grief.

Utter and complete disbelief.

He staggered up again and fled without another word.

"*Kaden!*" I cried, reaching out instinctively, but the door slammed shut behind him.

And I broke.

My knees buckled, magic still leaking from my fingertips like starlight, like blood. I was shaking so hard I thought my bones might come apart.

Cassian's hands caught my shoulders, sinking to the floor with me. He pulled me into his arms, holding me like something precious.

"Kaden. Kaden. Kaden..." His name tumbled out of my mouth again and again.

Cassian held me tighter, tucking me under his chin. The second his skin touched mine energy seemed to shove its way through. It rushed to the surface of my skin just as fast as it invaded him. Cassian clenched his jaw and ground his teeth as my power ran savagely between us. Each wave that came over me washed into him. His knuckles turned white as he grasped the fabric of my gown. His eyes squeezed closed, and his mouth shifted from barred teeth to pressed in a thin line.

He was taking everything, all the pain, all the suffering, all of the hurt. My body heaved with sobs, each one dragging a hoarse breath with it. My lungs gradually filled with more and more air as the storm inside me calmed. Cassian's fists unclenched, and the tension in his jaw dissolved. His head hung back, the column of this throat stretching, his Adam's apple bobbing. The debris swirling around us fell to the floor as the magic-laced air began to still.

I sat there for a while, breathing. Cassian's chest rose and fell in time with my own, and a piece of me wished this moment, right here, was where my story had ended. A piece of me wished he hadn't saved me.

"I didn't ask for this," I whispered. "I didn't ask to be this."

He pressed his cheek to the top of my head. "You didn't have to."

I turned my face up to him, angry hot tears rolling down my cheeks. "I don't even know what this is."

He pulled back, his eyes meeting mine. Slowly, gently, he leaned forward. His lips pressed against my cheek, kissing away each tear that ran down my face. Each featherlight kiss seemed to burn, as if the power beneath my skin had nothing left but fiery ashes.

"You're only beginning to understand what you are."

I flinched at the words. "A monster." I tried to pull away, but his arms locked around me.

"No, Lyra. You are not a monster. You are not broken. You are powerful, and raw, and untamed, and that terrifies them."

I couldn't breathe. I stilled, my body still wrapped in his arms.

He touched my jaw, soft as silk. The power in me stirred but burnt out as fast as it came.

"But it doesn't terrify me."

"Why?" I rasped.

His voice turned to steel.

He swallowed hard before saying, "Because you are a weapon. And you are my weapon."

My breath hitched.

"And you'll stay that way," he said, pressing his forehead to mine. "Even if it kills me."

For a long, broken moment, neither of us moved. I wanted so badly to hate him. I wanted to hate everything about this place, and I did. I hated everything.

Everything but Cassian Vaelros.

And for that, I hated myself.

CHAPTER TWENTY-ONE

Cassian didn't leave.

I woke with my head rested against his shoulder, and one of his arms was still wrapped loosely around me, as if even in sleep, some part of him refused to let me ever fall again. His breathing was steady, slow. I tilted my head slightly, just enough to see him.

Golden skin kissed by morning light. Freckles dusted across the bridge of his nose like stars in a night sky. His mouth was slightly parted, hair a curled mess, but still, somehow, he was as regal as ever. Peaceful in a way he never let himself be while awake.

I let myself study him for a moment longer. Just a moment.

Then, carefully, I slipped out of his arms.

Every joint ached, my skin still tingled with leftover energy, and deep in my chest, my heart thudded with a sick mix of shame and confusion. I pushed myself upright, weaving on unsteady feet as I made my way to the mirror and winced.

Stars.

My silver hair was tangled and wild, falling in uneven waves around my shoulders. My pins had fallen down, now hanging wrapping in white strands. My skin looked too pale, my cheeks sunken, but my eyes, that was what made my breath hitch. Dull silver now. Like moonlight through fog. Haunted and hollow.

I didn't look like myself anymore.

I pulled the pins from my hair, hissing as they yanked against my scalp. Still in the deep red gown from last night, I reached behind me for the buttons, fingers fumbling. I twisted awkwardly, muttering a curse under my breath.

"You always this dramatic in the mornings?"

Cassian's voice, low and thick with sleep, cut through the silence.

I froze.

He was still on the floor, propped up on one elbow now, smirking lazily at me like he hadn't just spent the night crumpled on my bedroom floor like a guard dog.

"I—" I started, then sighed, shoulders slumping. "I can't get this vile dress off."

He laughed. Actually laughed. "You know," he said, stretching like a cat as he stood, "if you wanted me to take your clothes off, you could've just asked."

Heat surged into my cheeks.

"Cassian," I scolded.

"Alright, alright," he said, still grinning as he stepped toward me. "Let me help."

His fingers found the buttons at my back with surprising gentleness. His knuckles grazed my spine, sending shocks trailing down with every touch. Each brush brought with it a whisper. A piece of a thought.

He had imagined doing this before, and not just once. He had wanted to do this.

I stood still, pulse thudding beneath my skin. One by one, the buttons came undone, loosening the fabric around me until I could finally breathe again.

"Kaden is terrified of me," I muttered. The sentence hung in the air like a ghost.

"Kaden is terrified of what he cannot control." Cassian's words were clipped and sharp. "He was raised to be a knight. A soldier. Discipline is everything to him."

I turned, even though a few buttons remained.

"You seem unlike your usual haughty self."

He smirked, but it was nothing like the mischievous ones from before.

"I guess we've both changed, haven't we?" He grabbed my waist and turned me back around, hands running up my sides to return to the buttons.

When he reached the last one, he turned away like a gentleman, but part of me wished he hadn't.

I changed into soft, cream day dress—simple, modest, and nothing like the blood-red drama of the night before. I brushed out my hair, taming the wildness into something resembling order. I didn't look regal or terrifying or powerful.

I just looked tired.

I could still feel his gaze on my back.

The silence stretched between us, charged and heavy with everything we didn't say. I couldn't bring myself to turn around. He didn't move, didn't speak, as if neither of us wanted to be the first to shatter it.

So, we both opened our mouths at once.

"I should show you something."

"Please don't tell anyone what happened."

We froze.

Cassian stepped closer. "Lyra," he said softly. "I'd never speak a word of it."

I turned to face him, studying him carefully. "You swear?"

"I swear," he said again, firmer this time.

I wanted to believe him.

But still, the doubt twisted inside me. What if the King found out? What if Cassian decided I was too dangerous to keep around?

"You're worried about the trials," he said, reading me too easily. "You think I'll send you away."

I didn't answer. I didn't need to.

He stepped in close, so close I could feel the heat of him, and cupped my face with both hands. I waited for the flood. I braced for his thoughts to pour in, to show me his words were truthful, but none came.

His voice dropped to something quiet, something steady.

"I'm not sending you anywhere. I've seen people lose their minds for less." His eyes flicked down to my lips. "Except, normally I'm the cause."

A smile crept up my lips. His curled just the same.

My eyes burned. Not from fear. From the way he looked at me like I was someone worth fighting for.

I simply nodded once.

For a heartbeat, we didn't move. His hands still cradled my face. His breath tangled with mine. I felt my own catch, fluttering inside me like something fragile and winged.

Is he going to—?

Cassian smiled then. Soft. Real.

He stepped back, and the moment shattered.

My cheeks flushed crimson. I stared down at the floor, butterflies crashing against my ribs like they were caged. I could still feel the warmth of his body so close to mine. The press of his presence.

Then his hands landed on either side of me, bracing against the desk behind me. Not trapping. Just... there. Close.

I cleared my throat. "You said you had something to show me?"

Cassian grinned, wide and easy. "Right. That."

He stepped back, offering his hand, but then he paused, frowning. I followed his eyes to the mess of a room around us. Books laid strewn across the floor, pages torn and parchment scattered. The vase from the mantle had been reduced down to glittering porcelain shards and a faint ring of dried water. The sheets and blankets so carefully arranged on the bed were haphazardly thrown about, debris speckling the once elegant fabrics.

I knelt down to the floor, beginning to use my hands to try and sweep the wreckage from the floor. Cassian bent over at the waist, finding my eyes.

"And what exactly are you doing?

I glanced down at the shattered pottery and torn paper in my hands.

"Cleaning. Something you could help with."

He huffed a laugh, standing back to his full height. "The palace has servants for a reason."

I dropped the mess in my hands but stayed kneeling. "You're going to call someone in here, have them clean a mess we cannot explain, all while they assume we made it together?"

Cassian blanched, just slightly.

I began to move the wreckage into a pile once more. "I thought as much."

He sighed, but by the grace of the stars, he bent down and began to pick up the ruined books. I found a dark gray tunic and used it as a rag to sweep the debris. Cassian stacked the books back on their respective shelves and moved to sweep up the shattered vase with the side of his golden shoe. We moved in silence, in tandem. The destruction slowly disappeared. The wreckage gradually cleared.

I gathered the silken sheets from my bed along with the thicker duvet. I shook the fabrics out, dust and debris falling to the ground before I folded them into a pile. I was not about to explain why the entirety of my room was a disaster to a servant, but having some laundry done didn't seem like the worst idea.

We finished up, and while the room wasn't in pristine condition, it was enough for me to finally collapse in my desk chair, my arms flung over the sides. I let my eyes fall closed, exhaling deeply. I could have stayed that way. Slumped in a chair, ignoring the mess of a world that surrounded me. I could have if it wasn't for that honey warm string that wound through my bones.

My eyes opened to see Cassian staring down, his gaze strangely soft. If I didn't know better, I would have called his eyes kind.

"Follow me." He offered his hand to help me from the chair. Before I could take it, he lifted a brow and gestured to the dress. "You'll want to change," he said, eyes sparkling. "Into something you don't mind getting wet."

I arched a brow at him, suspicious. But I obeyed. I stood, and this time, I went behind the folding screen to change.

When I returned in a gray blue tunic and navy pants, his smile deepened into something downright wicked.

"There she is," he said, already heading for the door. "Let's go."

"Where, exactly?" I asked. I grabbed my silk gloves as I followed.

Cassian just looked over his shoulder, reaching and snagging the gloves from my hands. He threw them on the desk, and all I could do was let out a breathy laugh.

"You'll see."

We snuck through the palace like we were children again, darting behind guards and skipping between patrol routes. I giggled, more than once, when Cassian dragged me behind hedges or motioned me into shadows with a flair of over-the-top stealth that made me snort.

We slipped past the last garden wall and into the hills beyond the palace, where the wind picked up, cool and salty. I closed my eyes as we walked, letting the breeze whip my hair behind me. It seemed to lift the weight that had settled on my shoulders since the day I arrived.

Cassian watched me. I could feel it.

We continued up the final hill, and when the view beyond grew above the flowing grass, the air seemed to leave my lungs entirely.

Before me stretched a lagoon, carved between jagged cliffs and framed in black rock. The ocean sparkled in impossible shades of white and blue, wild and bright, the waves crashing and hissing against the shore. Mist kissed my cheeks, and the scent of salt filled my head. The view stretched endlessly. Untamed, vast, beautiful.

I couldn't speak. Could barely breathe.

Cassian only grinned, like he'd known exactly what this scene would do to me.

He grabbed my hand and tugged me toward the edge of the water. My power sizzled, burning beneath my skin but never surfacing.

I hesitated. "I can't swim."

He blinked. "You can't?"

"The North is ice," I said. "If you're swimming…" I only shook my head.

His expression softened. He didn't laugh. Didn't tease. "Stay close," he said, voice low and steady. "I won't let anything happen to you."

So, I did just that.

Cassian threw his suit jacket and shoes on the rocks of the beach, my flats joining them.

We didn't go deep, just up to our waists, but the current was stronger than I expected. Cassian stayed near, always one step ahead, his hand grazing mine when I needed it, when the pull of the sea threw me off balance.

Then a wave surged harder than the rest.

The water slammed against my legs, and my feet slipped on the slick rocks beneath. I gasped and reached for the first thing I could grab.

My arms wrapped around Cassian's neck, and his hands caught my waist without hesitation. I clung to him, my face nearly pressed to his chest, his skin sun-warm against my cheek. His skin hummed against mine, his warmth seeping into me. Silver tendrils slowly found the connection, flowing between us like smoke. I wasn't sure if my power was exhausted from its explosion the night previous, or if it was simply dormant, but it seemed to brush against his mind as if walls surrounded the edges. No whispers attacked. No voices flooded in.

I didn't let go of him. Not even when the current eased away.

His chest rose and fell beneath my palms. His curls were damp. His lips parted like he'd been about to say something or perhaps laugh. I found his gaze, and he was already watching me.

His eyes flicked from my mouth to my eyes and back again.

The space between us burned. One breath. Then two.

The sea forgot how to roar.

Cassian leaned in the barest inch, and my stars, I did too, but then he blinked, and the hint of a smile disappeared. The moment snapped taut between us, a bowstring pulled too tight. He didn't back away, but he didn't move closer either.

"Do you want this?" he asked quietly, his voice rough and careful.

I swallowed. "Yes." My eyes flicked down to his lips.

"Are you sure? You looked ready to drown just now."

Oh, right. Swimming.

Embarrassment pooled in my stomach. "I'm fine," I said, but still, I didn't let go.

His fingers tightened at my waist before he finally gave me a slow, dazzling smile. "Still not letting anything happen to you," he murmured.

I snorted, the tightness in my chest too much to hold still. "Good luck with that during the trials." I retorted, chuckling, trying to ease the weight of the moment, but Cassian didn't laugh.

He didn't flinch. His gaze stayed locked on mine, golden, molten, unwavering.

"Especially during the trials."

I blinked, my smile faltering.

Then he said, softer now, "You think I'd put you through all of this if I didn't believe in what you are? In who you could be?" He looked to the horizon then, the sky painted in oranges and pinks, but his voice stayed steady. "This whole thing. The trials, the selection, the way it's structured… it was all my idea."

My heart thudded in my chest.

He turned back to me. "I'm doing what I want with it. And I'll do what I want with you."

No arrogance. No pride. Just truth. A quiet confession. Like he was giving me a piece of something no one else had.

I didn't want to process any of it. I didn't want to think about what he meant, what he was saying, so I flicked a handful of water at his chest. It smacked him square in the middle, soaking his shirt. He blinked, and the corner of his mouth twitched.

"Oh, so that's how we're doing this?"

I didn't get a second to brace before he splashed me back, hard. Cold sea hit my face like a wave, and I sputtered, soaked.

"You're dead," I laughed, launching a fresh attack.

Laughter echoed between us, mixing with the crashing waves as we chased each other through the shallows. Salt clung to my skin. The sun warmed my back. I ignored the words Cassian had admitted. I pushed the idea that somehow, somewhere in time, I could be something more.

Because as long as I did, the world didn't feel so heavy.

He taught me how to float, how to move with the water instead of against it. I learned quickly, bolstered by his praise and his constant presence, never far from reach.

By the time the sun slipped lower in the sky, a chill clung to the breeze.

We climbed the black rocks lining the shore, clothes clinging to our skin, feet raw and sandy. My cheeks stung from the sun. My hair was tangled with sea spray and wind.

Cassian laid back on the warm stone, arms behind his head, his curls damp and wild. The golden in his skin glowed. His head turned to me, the rocks below him knocking together.

"Better than your room?" he asked, eyes bright.

"Much," I said with a soft smile. "I think I've fallen in love with this lagoon."

His head swiveled back, his eyes fluttering closed. "Careful Lyra. Love can feel eerily similar to fear."

"I would never allow anything I feared to turn into love."

A deep chuckle sounded from his chest. "Weren't you terrified of being in this water only hours ago?"

I could only pause as a response because he was right. I was.

His eyes opened, the last of the sunset reflecting in the honey gold swirling there. "There was a time I used to believe the same as you. Now we both know we were wrong."

I let us fall into silence, listening as the waves crashed and rippled up the shore. We breathed in the peace. Soaked in the calm. I leaned back, sinking into the moment.

A horn. Deep. Sharp. Loud enough to shake the stone beneath us and echo through my bones like a warning from the world itself.

Cassian was on his feet instantly, grabbing my hand and yanking me up. The second his skin touched mine, terror surged through me like lightning, electric and overwhelming.

Not mine, but his.

"What is it?" I asked, my voice too thin, too high. My heart slammed against my ribs like it was trying to break free. I asked the question, but I already knew. Every instinct screamed it.

All I felt was fear.

He didn't answer. Didn't even look at me. He shrugged his jacket onto his shoulders as he shoved his feet into his shoes. I followed suit.

"We need to go," he said, and ran.

We sprinted through the hills, feet pounding over wet grass and slick rock. The air had shifted, heavier somehow. The garden came into view, and the scent hit me first. What had smelled lush and sweet now reeked of overripe decay, of something turned wrong. My stomach churned.

Something had happened.

Something terrible.

I could feel it, just beyond the horizon of my thoughts. Anger. Betrayal. A curl of sickening satisfaction. And fear, not mine, not Cassian's. Someone else's. A web of emotions bleeding through the world like spilled ink.

Cassian didn't slow. His grip on my hand was iron.

We rounded the final corner, the palace looming ahead.

He saw them before I did.

He stopped.

And when I looked up, my breath caught.

The entire Royal Guard stood at the gates, lined in precise formation, blue and gold armor gleaming. Waiting.

My blood turned to ice. The cold sank into my chest, thick and deep and absolute.

Cassian's expression went blank, cold and unreadable, but his emotions surged from him in waves, pressing into me like a sent message. Fear. Rage held on a razor's edge. Not for himself.

For me.

He dropped my hand and stepped forward, placing himself between me and the guard like a shield.

"Miss Seravell," one of them said, voice flat and formal. "The King requests your presence."

Cassian moved again, half a step forward already shaking his head.

But the guard raised a hand. "Alone."

The word landed like a blow.

Cassian froze, his jaw clenched so tight I thought he might shatter like glass. Droplets still fell from his hair, curling against his temple. He turned to me slowly.

He didn't speak. He didn't need to.

His eyes locked with mine, and what I saw in them made my stomach drop.

Whatever the King wanted, it would be unimaginable.

I would not walk out of that throne room unchanged.

I inhaled. My lungs felt too tight, like they might collapse. But I forced the breath in. Closed my eyes. Steeled the panic inside me.

Then I opened them. Lifted my chin. And said, steady and sharp, "Then let's not keep His Majesty waiting."

CHAPTER TWENTY-TWO

THE DOORS GROANED OPEN before me.

The same towering doors that had opened when I first arrived in Aurea. The same ones Cassian had led me through the night I had bled on the King's throne.

I stepped inside, and I froze.

The tapestry had changed.

I knew it the moment my eyes landed on it. The tapestry I first saw in the grand halls leading to the throne room had moved inside. The sweeping scene stretched across the left wall of the gleaming marble room. The fabric and string painted a picture of a phoenix ascending in triumph, its vast wings unfurling above a battlefield of golden thread. But the shimmer of silver that once flickered beneath the embroidery, the silver I had noticed when I first arrived, was gone.

Erased.

There was only gold now. Pure, blinding, unquestioned gold.

My pulse kicked hard against my ribs.

The throne room should have been magnificent. It was magnificent. Vaulted ceilings glinted flaked gold leaf and inlaid pearls. Marble pillars were curved into delicate arches, every polished surface reflecting fractured light. Thick silks draped and swayed on an invisible breeze. Sunlight filtered through the stained-glass windows high above, scattering rainbow shards across the floor like broken promises. The eyes imbedded in those windows looked down too, covering each surface with their gaze. The throne itself was a towering creation of golden spires and crimson velvet, crowned with banners bearing the imperial crest.

It should have taken my breath away.

Instead, it felt like walking into a tomb.

There were no guards. No advisors. No movement. Just the King.

The throne room had only ever been this empty when Cassian had brought me here.

King Vaelros stood before the altered tapestry, his hands clasped loosely behind his back. Not seated on his throne. Not looming.

Simply waiting, yet somehow, that was worse.

My skin prickled. There was always someone in the throne room. Always a murmur, a whisper, a shuffle of feet. Even in the quiet hours there was something, but now, nothing. The quiet was more unsettling than the noise.

I let go of whatever power sang in my veins, careful and slow, like dipping a hand into still water. I let it flow, just as I had learned with Cassian on a morning that felt like ages ago. It snaked through the space, wandering. Just a tendril of thought, barely a whisper.

But all I felt was slick ice. A frozen wall. Blank. Unyielding. Panic rose in my throat. A thin sheen of sweat bloomed across the back of my neck.

Then, something brushed against my mind. So faint it could have been a trick of thought. A phantom itch under my skin, but it was real. I tilted my head, unease crawling up my spine before I could stop myself.

The King turned slowly. His eyes were already on me.

"You noticed," he said softly, gesturing toward the tapestry. "It's new. I thought the design needed… correction."

I said nothing.

"A change I thought appropriate," he continued, his voice mild. "Don't you agree this variation is better suited for the room?"

I forced my expression to stay still. "Yes, Your Majesty."

"Do you like it?" he asked.

"It's… striking," I said.

He smiled like someone who didn't care what I thought. "Let's not make it a pattern to lie, Miss Seravell." His words cut like daggers, even as his face was carved from smooth stone. "Symbols must reflect reality. That phoenix is the kingdom. Absolute. Eternal. Untarnished. We do not fly on borrowed feathers. Only gold."

Still, I said nothing.

The King stalked down the grand stair, unhurried. His footsteps echoed too loudly across the marble floor.

"You've done well in the trials," he said, each word laid like a snare. "Made a name for yourself. Stood out."

It sounded more like a crime than a compliment.

"I've only tried to survive," I said, my voice stiff.

He hummed, almost amused. "Yes. That's what people like you always say."

My jaw tightened.

He stopped just a few feet away. His gaze slid over me like I was an unwelcome entry in a ledger. "You've spent time with my son."

The muscles in my throat twitched. "He's the Prince."

"He's naïve," the King said flatly. "Too used to thinking the game is his to play."

Then, with a voice like rope pulled too tight—

"He told you nothing would happen to you. Didn't he?"

I flinched.

The breath left my chest like a fist had landed beneath my ribs.

He knew.

Cassian's voice, quiet but sure.

I won't let anything happen to you.

It had been private. Sacred.

He shouldn't have known, and yet he did.

Now it was tainted. Dragged into the King's mouth like it meant nothing at all.

"*'I won't let anything happen to you,'*" the King repeated, his voice a mockery. Almost wistful. "Cassian means well," he said, watching me closely. "But he forgets the pieces on the board are not always his to move. He forgets how many eyes are watching. How many others are playing the exact same game."

My hands curled into fists at my sides.

"He's not the one in control," the King added, stepping even closer. "And neither are you."

I swallowed hard.

He studied me for a long, cold moment. "Aurea is a place of order, of legacy. Not of strays. You do not belong here, and the longer you remain, the more you endanger the balance we keep." His eyes burned into my skin like heat. Or like ice. "If you are wise, Miss Seravell, you will slip quietly back into the snow and shadows from which you came.

"The crown has little patience for outliers, and even less mercy for those who overstep. Best not to test how far the favor of Aurea stretches before it snaps."

I paused, feeling the weight of his words settle around me like ash after a fire. "You're asking me to leave?" I asked, my voice low. The King only stared back, extending the silence as long as it would go. "And if I don't?"

He smiled, a wicked, grotesque thing. "Then the board will rearrange itself. And you will find yourself on the wrong side of it."

He snapped his fingers, and a side door squeaked open. A royal guard walked out, his entire body gleaming with golden armor. A helmet rested over his face, covering whoever was underneath. They walked stiffly, as if the armor was robotic. The guard's heavy footsteps fell in rhythm and stopped a pace behind the King. His hand reached up to rest on the hilt of his sword, the blade rising a few inches to show uncompromising steel.

He was going to kill me. The King was going to kill me.

"But where are my manners?" The King gave me a sick grin and walked toward the guard, standing at his side.

"How could I ever send you away without a parting gift?"

He looked at the guard, and the other gold-covered hand slowly rose to grip the back of the helmet. The world seemed to slow down to this singular moment.

One second.

Two.

Three.

The guard pulled the golden cage off of his head, and nausea rolled in my stomach.

Before me was something worse than death.

Green eyes.

Green eyes stared back. Green the color of swirling vines. Green the color of the gardens and grasses. Green the color of safety, or of a time of safety. Green, that was now no longer a color I could call mine.

Kaden.

The man before me was Kaden.

He stood there, soaked in royal gold. His face deathly hollow as he looked to me as if I was air. There was no kindness. There was nothing.

A trembling hand rose to cover my mouth as a sob broke free. My lungs refused oxygen. I tried to move towards him, but my feet felt like concrete. My breathing was erratic, my mouth opening and closing noiselessly. I shuffled enough to be side by side with the King.

"Kaden…" I whispered, the name breaking in my throat like a plea already denied. I took another heavy step forward—

A shriek of steel split the air.

Kaden's blade was already unsheathed before I could blink. The silver edge flashed, arcing upward in a motion too smooth, too fast. I staggered back, but not in time.

Pain bloomed across my face.

The sword had grazed me. Starting at the curve of my cheek, just below my right eye, then cutting upward through the soft skin of my brow. I gasped, hand flying to my face. Warmth met me instantly. Thick, hot blood ran through my fingers, quick as spilled wine. The cut was shallow, but blood never cared for pity. It poured anyway.

And Kaden. He hadn't even blinked.

"Do you know how to kill a forest, Miss Seravell?"

My gaze snapped to the King, eyes glaring out from between the gaps of my fingers. I didn't dare try a response. My jaw quivered. My vision blurred. But I refused to entertain the King with my tears.

The King's voice was quiet, but it carried like thunder in a storm. "You don't strike the wood. You poison the water."

I couldn't keep the fury from my face. Couldn't keep the heat from searing in my veins. The tears from stinging my eyes.

"You're a complication," he said softly. "You've become loud. Difficult to ignore." Then, with the gentleness of a dagger sliding between ribs. "You are not meant to rise."

He turned his back to me then, as if I were nothing. As if I were no more important than the silver thread that had been stripped from the tapestry.

"I expect you will do what is right," he said.

I sank to my knees, the cold biting through my still damp clothes. I barely felt it. I stared at the marble floor as tears dripped down. And all I saw in that cold stone reflection was a girl who had knelt at the feet of the King and wept. Who had let the crown grind her into the marble and had conceded.

The King's footsteps echoed across the marble floor. Trailing behind were Kaden's, the metal armored boots clanking loudly against the stone. He stopped when he reached my side, but the King continued on.

I could smell the King as he passed me. Bitter cologne carried in his wake.

Kaden's scent used to be of leather and smoke. Of forests and fire. Of carriage rides and tavern ale. Of library books and starlight.

Not even that remained.

The King looked down at me with something worse than disdain, his face a warped image in the marble floor.

He smiled.

And then I felt it.

A thread of emotion. Deliberate. Directed. A single note he allowed me to feel.

Satisfaction.

Not hidden. Not masked. Given.

Another gift meant to shatter.

Tears slipped down my cheeks, but I didn't make a sound. Didn't sob. Didn't scream.

My heart pounded hard enough to break ribs. I lifted my eyes to the golden throne.

A hum, faint but certain, like an old song half-remembered. It rippled beneath my skin, threaded through my blood, humming in the bones of the room.

A pull.

A promise.

A vow.

I wasn't done here.

Not yet.

Not until the crown the King so desperately clung to turned silver instead of gold.

CHAPTER TWENTY-THREE

I DIDN'T SLEEP.

Not after the throne room. Not after the King's satisfaction sliced through me like a blade pressed against skin. Not after Kaden, or what the King had left of him, escorted me back to my room.

Sleep would've meant surrender, and I wasn't ready to fall apart, not completely. Not yet. So instead, I waited. I filled the copper washbasin with warm water and washed the dried blood from my face and hands. I cleaned the glancing slash and rummaged through the small cabinet near the bath until I found a minty ointment. I hissed as I spread it over the wound, but in an instant, the heat and pain dissolved. I sat at the edge of my bed, face smeared with cool balm and fingers twiddling, until I heard the metal of Kaden's boots scrap stone. I walked silently to the door, cautiously opening it and slipped out, moving like a shadow through the stagnant halls of the palace. The cold floor bit against my bare feet as I slipped into the library, unseen.

The scent of parchment and dust met me like an old, indifferent friend. Shelves loomed around me in the darkness, spines gleaming faintly under the moonlight filtering through the arched windows. I prowled between them, dragging my fingers across leather bindings and cracked titles, searching. Desperately.

Silver hair. Mind-bending. Magic. Anything that could tell me what I was. What Cassian saw in me. What the King feared.

After what felt like hours, I returned to my room with only a small stack of books. It was pathetically slim, as if the truth could be reduced to fairy tales and faded warnings. I shut the door behind me with a quiet click and curled up beneath the spill of moonlight on my bed. And I read. And read.

And read.

Tales of mirror-eyed witches and girls kissed, or cursed, by stars. Children who heard thoughts, who saw too much, who grew into heroes only to vanish beneath the weight of what they had become. Myths and rhymes and lullabies, cloaking fear with whimsy, but none of them were real. None of them were me.

Frustration clawed its way into my lungs. I shoved one of the books off the bed with a flick of my wrist, watching it tumble and thud against the floor. My eyes burned, the words on the last page blurring and pointless. I wanted to scream. I wanted to rip the truth out of the walls of this place with my bare hands.

Dawn crept in quietly, pale light seeping through the sheer curtains like a warning. The final book in my lap was more of the same. I read of a woman who seduced the King to give her offspring his power, only for her to rebel against him. It was entirely fantastical.

I wasn't even halfway through when the knock came.

It rattled the door like a threat.

My head snapped up, instincts bristling. I inhaled sharply and carefully let my power slither out, stretching across the floor, curling beneath the doorframe. I pulled at the silver tendrils, reigning them into control. I imagined that jar, that safety, and only took the amount necessary.

I brushed a mind that should have been familiar but was a void of complete nothingness.

I swept the books into the folds of my bedcovers and hid them beneath the quilt. I crossed the room and opened the door, slowly.

Kaden was dressed in deep navy leathers marked with gold. His hand was already resting on the hilt of his sword, like I was some threat to be managed before either of us had even spoken a word. His eyes flicked around my room before landing on the book I had thrown to the floor.

"You are to be escorted to the third trial in ten minutes' time," he said.

The third trial. Battle strategy.

I had completely forgotten.

Forgotten the stories we used to whisper by firelight in the library. Forgotten how we'd sit side by side on the edge of sleep and speak of wars and legends like they were fairy tales. Forgotten the diagrams he used to draw in messy ink on thick parchment, tracing lines of defense and siege. Forgotten all of it.

And maybe… maybe part of me had wanted to forget.

Forgetting was easier than remembering what he used to be.

Who he used to be to me.

Kaden's gaze returned to me. "I suggest her ladyship, Miss Seravell," he said, his eyes dragging down, scraping across my skin like grit, "change her attire."

His tone dripped with judgement. I felt it, tasted it, like spoiled milk. My heart shattered in my chest. Whoever this was, whatever had happened, this wasn't Kaden. Not anymore.

I simply nodded and shut the door.

I yanked the nearest dress from the back of the chair—a simple white thing, the only one not wrinkled from days of disuse. It slipped over my head with ease, whispering against my sliced face, but I didn't have the luxury of caring. I pulled the pair of white silk gloves on, not even pausing to smooth them up the entire length of my arm.

I didn't bother with anything else. My hair was still tangled from my sleepless night, my eyes shadowed and sharp. I didn't want to soften the way I looked. Let them see the girl who the King wanted sent away. Let them ask why. Let them wonder.

By the time I stepped back into the hallway, Kaden was waiting. He didn't offer me his arm. Just turned and began walking, expecting me to follow like a well-trained hound.

We walked across what seemed to be the entirety of the palace before climbing a staircase that seemed unending. My thoughts crashed like rogue ocean waves in my mind, rising only to fall and push the others further down. When we arrived at a narrow stone hallway, Kaden simply turned and began his way back without a word.

Five wooden chairs sat in a row before me, each cushioned with a different color and each precisely placed a few steps apart. The first two of the chairs were empty, their plush fabrics shining blue and gold. The next two were filled with the remaining representatives. I could only assume the empty chairs were meant for Clara and Rhea who had come and gone before I had even arrived.

The crown always arranged us in the same order, always the same silent hierarchy. And me, from the most northern region, always last. I moved and sat in the last chair, white silk wrinkling under my weight and melting into the folds of my dress.

The other girls were clothed in a way that could only be described as intimidating. Authoritative.

Naelle stood as her name was called, and sauntered over, the sleek black leather of her jacket and pants shining. Her shoulders seemed armored, her back paneled with a dull almost stone-like material. Even Elena, who sat in the chair closest to me was dressed in a way that made her seem militant. Her eyes were closed, lips pursed together in a thin line, but the brown supple suede of her vest made her look thoughtful, not nervous. Underneath, black velvet lined her arms and torso as golden buttons clasped the vest in place. Matching pants lined her legs from her waist.

I tugged at the skirt of my white dress as the door opened, and Naelle left. Elena's eyes snapped open at the sound, and she glanced at me with wide eyes before a man escorted her inside. I watched as the door swung closed behind her, whether to keep her in or me out I wasn't sure.

I waited alone outside the chamber, irritation prickling at my fingertips. Why a gown? Why hadn't I taken ten more seconds to dig for something practical? Something sharp and dark and commanding. Instead, the fabric floated like mist around my legs, too soft, too pale. I looked like a ghost walking to her own execution.

I leaned back, resting my head against the wall behind me and letting my own eyes drift closed. I tried to conjure up any memory from my studies with Kaden, but I could only see him in that throne room. Him soaked in gold. His sword against my cheek. I ripped my eyes open, sitting up and leaning against elbows propped on my knees.

"Miss Seravell."

The voice was gravel dragged across stone.

I lifted my chin to meet the speaker as Elena scurried away, her guard blocking her as she tried to peer over his shoulder. Her head dipped and swayed as she fought to catch my eye, but it was no use.

I stood and faced the man who addressed me. He was plump and sun-reddened with thinning gray hair sweeping across his scalp in stubborn denial. He looked at me like I was a smear on his schedule, his gaze pausing at the gash on my cheek and brow. Our eyes connected, and my power flared, as if the gloves on my hands were not thick enough to keep the energy at bay.

175

The silk was thin, airy. Light in a way that made you forget there was even fabric on your skin.

I wondered if my power could flow through these as it had once before with another pair. As it had at the feast.

I focused my power down to my hands, pushing it into my fingertips until it threatened to explode. And then I let it.

My power spilled form my hands and through the thin silk of my gloves, escaping as if there had been nothing there at all. I let the shimmering air worm its way to the man's feet.

And immediately, I regretted it.

Fraud.

Useless little parasite.

Just another pampered doll playing at power.

I said nothing. Just brushed imaginary dust from the sleeves of my dress, lifted my chin higher, and followed him through the carved archway.

The war room.

If the palace had a heart, this was it. Not a beating one. It didn't thrum with blood or heat, but with stone and strategy and centuries of conquest.

Light poured through towering windows that climbed like cathedral spires, casting long gold shadows across a floor of black-and-white stone. And beyond them, the kingdom unfolded. Rolling hills, rivers like threads of glass, cities in the far distance catching the sun. The edge of the world was visible here, but it was the table that caught my breath.

Not a table. A map.

The map.

Carved from smooth dark stone, it spanned nearly the entire room, a perfect rendering of the kingdom. Every mountain, every river, every forest was chiseled with breathtaking precision. The oceans were inlaid with obsidian glass, the capital's spires picked out in shimmering veins of gold. A golden plate was mounted to its edge.

Valerieth

My fingers found the carved edge of a mountain ridge before I even realized I'd moved. I jerked my hand back.

I looked up.

Seven generals.

Three lieutenants apiece.

All watching.

The general's uniforms were painted in their territories' colors: the deep oceanic blue of Seren, the burning oranges of Calem's plains, the emerald green of Hestel's wild forests, the rich plum of Delva's isles, the navy of northern Mirun, and the pristine white of Virellia.

My power still flowed from me, a cup perceptually overflowing. The shimmering tendrils looked like nothing more than heat from stone. They latched onto each general, winding and snaking up their bodies. Their metallic armor seemed to glow. I ran my eyes over each one, watching as that shimmering air enveloped them.

My gaze stopped on the Virellian general.

He didn't smile, but his thoughts offered something close to recognition. Begrudging, but not hostile. A faint tether of support and loyalty to the region, if not to me.

It was more than I'd gotten from most.

Their expressions were unreadable, polished to nobility's perfection, but their thoughts brushed against me like static.

Curiosity. Skepticism. Thinly veiled boredom.

Some wondered about the cut spanning my face, others simply enjoyed its existence.

It was all mundane if I was honest.

Mundane until I saw him, the Aurean general.

He was *drowning* in gold. A golden cloak, golden armor, golden crest shining against his broad chest. Even his ears were adorned with golden hoops and charms, a shining bar running across the top curve. He stood taller than the others by a full head, his skin bronzed and gleaming like a warrior sculpted from the sun itself. His lieutenants flanked him, silent and steady, but his mind was louder than any voice in the room.

His thoughts struck like a lash.

A flaw in the weave. A threat to the crown.

No control. No discipline. No place among us.

She should have been silenced in the cradle.

Her kind is everything we swore to destroy.

And I will not hesitate.

But beneath all of it, beneath the judgment and calculation and cold logic, was fear.

He was afraid of me.

The silence grew sharp around the edges, and I forced my eyes back to the table just as the gray-haired man began to speak in a bored, perfunctory tone.

"In the third year of the Fifth Reign," he droned, "the armies of Seren and Hestel attempted to flank Calem through the valley of Erist, while the river Vedan flooded the central fields. Describe how you would maneuver a battalion through that terrain without losing the high ground."

I blinked.

Nothing.

Erist? Vedan? High ground?

My stomach turned to ice.

I couldn't remember a thing. The names blurred together, the map blurred too, and I realized I was staring without seeing. A long, dreadful pause followed.

Then a sharp, irritated sigh cut through the air like a knife. I turned to its source, heart thudding in my throat. The general in blue. Seren.

His eyes, a cool pale cobalt, met mine across the map, and just for a moment, they dulled. Shifted... gray. Just slightly.

The thought came gently, deliberately.

Use the river for deception. Feign a retreat downstream, draw them in. Cross at the Caedes under moonlight.

The words echoed in my skull. Clear. Precise. Offered to me like a secret passed beneath the table.

I opened my mouth and repeated them.

Word for word. Steady and controlled. As if I'd known the answer all along.

The Seren general didn't flinch, but a pulse of thought flickered toward me. He was surprised.

The second scenario followed. This time, my eyes found orange for Calem.

The general there was older, with lines carved deep into his sun-browned face. He seemed careful, maybe even wary, but when our eyes met, his thoughts reached out.

Another answer. Another borrowed brilliance.

By the third question, I knew what I had to do.

The same monotone voice read out the last piece if his script.

"Your scouts report that an enemy force three times your number is advancing Aurea. You have two days to prepare, limited resources, and a population that refuses to flee. Do you fortify the city and risk a siege, retreat and regroup, or lure the enemy into a trap that could sacrifice a neighboring village? Explain your decision."

I turned to gold.

The Aurean general's eyes burned. And when our gazes locked, the strategy slammed into me like fire igniting dry grass. It struck hard, sharp, as if it had already been written in my blood.

Fortifying the city guarantees a siege, and retreating ensures they gain ground. We draw them into the village. Make it seem we're scattered and weak. Let them take the bait. Then we burn it with them inside.

His answer was vile. My lip twitched, the words like glue. I repeated the response aloud. I forced voice to be steady. It didn't shake.

The man by the door, the one who'd called me in, was quiet for a long time. His mouth was a thin, unimpressed line, but there was something unreadable in his silence now.

I looked at him properly for the first time. He wasn't a general. Not even a soldier. Just a piece of the palace's machinery sent to move me from one place to another. A facilitator.

He offered his arm.

I hesitated, then slipped my hand into the crook of his elbow. When our eyes met, his thoughts slammed into me like a crack of thunder.

How did she do that?

Pride rose through me like wildfire, sharp and hot. I didn't smile. Not yet. Not until the doors closed behind me.

A grin crept up my face slow and sure, uncontainable.

My steps were light as I walked the stone corridors, my reflection flickering in windowpanes and polished metal. Rain pattered down against the glass and wet the open corridors, the droplets falling in heavy veils. The dress still swirled around me like smoke, but it no longer felt like a shroud.

The facilitator said nothing as he led me back. We strode through the winding halls of the palace, and neither of us bothered trying to speak. I floated beside him, my mind still ringing from the trial, my body tense from holding myself together.

I stepped around the corner to my room, and Kaden was standing tall and still at his post. It was the exact place he always used to stand, but now, it felt more like a leash than a post.

I hadn't let myself look at him. I hadn't let myself see what the King had done, but with him here in front of me, I didn't have much choice.

His dark hair still curled slightly at the ends, a little longer than before. His hands still rested one on his side the other on his sword. Even his boots were still perfectly polished, but his eyes were unmistakably different.

The green was still there, but faded, dulled. A void stretched out where Kaden used to be, and it pulled at me like quicksand.

179

The boy who offered me his arm, his food, his protection wasn't there. Not anymore.

I didn't realize I was shaking until I felt the pressure of someone watching me. My head turned sharply and landed on the round man standing just behind me, arms crossed, and already smiling.

"I bid you good day, Miss Seravell," the man said, his voice slick and sharp, like he savored the taste of each syllable. I stared him down as he walked away, each step echoing with mockery. I didn't look away until he disappeared around the corner.

I turned to the door to my room, and for the first time, it didn't feel like a shelter. It felt like a cage. A box. A tomb.

I couldn't do it.

I couldn't stay there.

Not with Kaden outside. Not like this.

Rage boiled beneath my skin, tightening every muscle in my body until it hurt. My fists clenched at my sides. I bit the inside of my cheek until I tasted blood. Dread rushed through my body. I couldn't spend another second in this stars-forsaken palace. I couldn't stay in these suffocating hallways. My heart pounded out of my chest and my lungs refused to accept the air I heaved. I had to get out. Now.

My hands began to shake and sweat beaded on my temples. Why was it so hot in this palace? My chest rose and fell rapidly, sucking in breath after breath that seemed to do absolutely nothing. I couldn't stay here. I had to get out.

So, I ran.

CHAPTER TWENTY-FOUR

THUNDER CRACKED THROUGH THE sky like a warning shot, but I didn't care.

Lightning lit up the stained-glass in jagged flashes, painting the hallway in brief, violent hues. I barely registered the storm until I heard the second roll of thunder echo across the palace walls like a war drum.

I didn't think. I just moved.

The polished floor rushed beneath my feet, the hem of my white dress tangling around my legs as I threw myself through the nearest door and into the open back gardens. Rain lashed against my skin like punishment, cold and relentless, but I welcomed it. I wanted it. Needed it to wash away the anger and sadness curled so tightly inside me I thought I might rupture.

I ran past the willow tree Elena and I had once sat beneath. I sprinted past the stone bench by the pond where we had fed the fish, laughing as if our lives were ours to live. I didn't stop until I reached the greenhouse. I didn't stop until the door handle snapped open beneath my hand, and I stumbled inside, slamming the glass pane shut behind me like I could shut everything else out with it.

Water dripped from my hair, soaking through every inch of fabric and clinging to my skin. I paced the path between the overgrown plants and dying vines like a caged animal, my breath fogging the glass and sticking in my throat.

Then the door creaked.

I turned sharply, but it was him.

Cassian was soaked through, his golden curls plastered to his face, his cloak clinging to broad shoulders. Rain trailed down his cheeks like tears he'd never cry. He stepped inside the greenhouse, and the whole room changed.

Emotion flooded the room like incense. The room turned thick, heady, and impossible to ignore. Anger at the red line on my face. Longing to touch me. Desperation to dry the water from my skin and hold me until I was warm again.

No power of mine coaxed his thoughts out. It was all him. And I broke.

The tears came without permission, hot and furious, spilling down my face and mixing with the rain. I made no sound, just stood there, trembling, as my chest rose and fell with breaths that hurt more than any wound ever could. The storm beyond the glass roared, echoing the war inside me.

Cassian crossed the space between us in seconds. No hesitation. No question. Like he'd been waiting years, maybe even lifetimes, for me to finally welcome his touch. To want it. To need it.

His arms were a wall and a home all at once as they wrapped around me. One hand gripped my waist like he was afraid I'd vanish if he let go. The other slid up my jaw, brushing a soft finger over the gash that had begun to scab over. Pain laced through me, but it wasn't my own. It was his.

"A sword. This was from a guard—this was—" His hand moved into my soaked hair, fingers threading through the tangled strands with a gentleness that undid me. "Who did this?"

I could only shake my head. The name on my tongue sounded wrong to even think, nevertheless say.

I collapsed against him without grace, fists curled into the fabric of his drenched shirt, forehead resting against his chest.

He didn't speak. He didn't ask. He simply held me tighter.

His scent, rain and smoke and cedar, wrapped around me. It was intoxicating even through the storm. I could feel every inch of him, solid and real against my soaked skin. My tears drenched his collar, mixing with the rain, and he didn't flinch. He only pressed a kiss to the top of my hair.

I sobbed harder.

My body shook with the force of it, my face buried in the crook of his neck. The warmth of him seeped into my bones, thawing something that had been frozen for far too long. I didn't know how long we stood like that, only that time didn't matter. Only that when the storm inside me began to quiet, his hand moved from my hair to my cheek, tilting my face up just enough for our eyes to meet. His gaze flickered up to the rough scab on my cheek and brow. The touch left its own lightening in its path. His mind came with it, but it was gentle and soft. It was kind. It didn't push and prod but swirled inside me like a river meeting an ocean. But even while his mind was gentle, his thoughts were something else entirely.

His brows drew together. His jaw was tight. The muscles in his throat worked like he was holding something back.

It wasn't just concern etched into every sharp angle of his face. It was fury. Fury so controlled it felt like a bow drawn with an arrow, waiting for the order. But his voice, when it came, was quieter than a whisper, and yet somehow, stronger than the storm outside.

"What did he do to you?"

The air between us went taut.

I didn't answer right away. I couldn't. The words caught in my throat like shards of glass. I just shook my head as I stared at him, into those molten eyes that looked at me like I was both his salvation and his undoing. Into the eyes flecked with gold to remind me who he was. Who he is.

The truth slipped from me like a wound splitting open.

"Not to me. To Kaden."

Cassian's expression fractured.

His hands froze. His chest stopped moving for a breath, maybe two. The warmth between us flickered, and something shut down inside him. A gate slamming closed. A door locking.

I felt it as though it were my own. His mind sucked back into some hidden chamber, and with it, his emotions. I tried to follow it, tried to reach out with a tendril of power, but I slammed into something dense and jagged. A wall of stone. Layered and rough like a fortress hastily built.

I could tear it down. Stone by stone, I could unravel him, but I didn't want to. Not if he didn't want to let me see.

I let him go. I backed out of his mind.

And I met his eyes again. "The King told me to leave."

Cassian let go of me then, like my words physically broke whatever thread had been keeping him tethered.

He ran a hand through his soaked curls, turning away, the tension rolling off him like a second storm. Then, without warning, he grabbed a nearby pot and hurled it at the floor. It shattered with a piercing crack. Shards skittered across the tile.

I jumped, heart slamming against my ribs, stumbling back until I hit the edge of a table. It screeched beneath my palms, and the sound cut through the haze like a blade.

Cassian turned, eyes wild, and the fury drained from his face instantly. "I'm so sorry. Lyra—I'm not angry with you, I swear."

He moved toward me, but I backed further away. My breath hitched.

I had never seen him like that. My body was braced for impact. I didn't understand until I realized.

I was afraid.

For a moment all I could see in his face was his father.

Cassian froze. He saw the way I flinched. His hands dropped to his sides, and guilt poured off him like steam. I felt the crack in that stone wall. Felt it leak.

"I didn't mean to scare you," he whispered. "Stars, Lyra—I would never—"

"Don't," I said, voice brittle.

He swallowed hard.

"You can't leave," he said quietly. "We need you. I need you."

My gaze dropped to the floor. My eyes ran along the grout between the stones to steady myself.

"We'll fix Kaden," he said, voice thick with conviction. "I swear to you, we will. It's all going to be okay. You're meant to be here. You're exactly who you're meant to—"

"And what if I don't want to be?" I snapped, my head jerking up.

Cassian blinked. He didn't move.

"What if I don't want to be who you say I'm meant to be? What if I don't want to play your games and become your perfect little queen?" I moved toward him, every step defiant. The air crackled with energy.

Cassian held his ground. His breath came fast, erratic, but he wasn't afraid. He was fascinated.

I stopped inches from him.

"I'm done pretending. I'm done acting like any of this feels right. I'm done smiling like I want to be here when I never asked to be."

I was close enough to feel his breath against my face despite the cold soaking both of us to the bone. My rage trembled under my skin, power lashing against its cage.

Cassian didn't flinch.

His voice was quiet, but certain. "You're perfect." He reached out, his fingers brushing the wet hair from my face.

And it gutted me. Because he meant it.

"I don't care if you tear this place to the ground," he breathed. "Be whoever you want. Be cruel. Be a tyrant if that's what it takes to survive. Be a queen like my father is a king. But you and I both know you won't. If you loved this world how it is, you wouldn't be trying so hard not to drown in it."

He moved even closer. Our chests touched. His voice was a whisper, but it rolled through me like thunder.

"You're not here to rule this kingdom, Lyra. You're here to destroy it. To rebuild something better. And not by my way. Not by my father's way."

He leaned in, his lips brushing the shell of my ear.

"Your way."

A shiver ran down my spine, and I didn't know if it was the rain or the way his words lit something inside me that had been buried long ago.

He pulled back slowly. From somewhere inside his coat, he tugged a smaller jacket, folded tightly. He draped it around my shoulders, and tugged the fabric towards him, dragging me with it.

Then he whispered, soft and solemn, "Ask me to burn the world down. Ask me Lyra, and I'd do it with a smile"

And with that, he walked away. He stepped back into the storm, like the thunder and lightning were nothing more than background noise.

I stayed where I was.

Slowly, I backed into the table I had hit before and lifted myself up to sit on its edge. I pulled my feet up, knees tight to my chest, and let the coat wrap around me like a second skin. Rain still dripped from my hair. The cold still seeped into my bones.

But I didn't move.

I just sat and listened to the rhythm of the storm on the glass above.

CHAPTER TWENTY-FIVE

"LYRA?"

Elena's voice cut through the haze of sleep. The rain outside had dulled to a soft drizzle. The kind that whispered rather than roared. Water tapped against the glass panes above me in a rhythmic hush, and every so often, the wind sighed through the cracks, like the greenhouse itself was breathing in grief.

I groaned as I sat up, my neck and back aching from the wooden table I chose to be my bed for the night.

Elena stood in the arched doorway. The hem of her gown was soaked with mud. Her eyes swept over me. "Oh stars," she whispered, walking hurriedly closer. He hands moved up to hover over my cut cheek. "You're soaked. When you weren't at breakfast I panicked. I— I didn't know—"

"I'm fine," I rasped.

I wasn't. We both knew it.

I sat slumped on the table, my back against a trellis of ivy and dying jasmine, its petals heavy and browning from the cold. My hair clung to my face in wet tangles, rivulets dripping down my neck, seeping into the collar of my ruined dress. My face had scabbed over, but the cut was beginning to flake and itch. I felt wrung out. Hollow. Still trembling, like my body hadn't realized the storm had passed.

Her brows knit with worry as she crossed the moss-covered flagstones and pushed herself up to sit with me on the table.

"Come on," she said, gentle but firm, reaching out her hand. "Let's get you warm."

I stared at her fingers for a long moment. She wore gloves to combat the brisk morning. I glanced at my own hands, the white silk of my own translucent and sopping wet.

Maybe I was too tired to argue, or maybe I just didn't want to be alone anymore, but slowly, I slid my hand into hers.

We moved through the corridors of the palace. The rain outside blurred the stained-glass windows into shadowy mosaics of jewel-toned light. Elena said nothing. She didn't ask where I'd been or what had happened. She didn't press. She simply looped her arm through mine and walked in silence, her presence steady beside me. A lantern in the dark.

Her room smelled like lavender and honey when she opened the door. The fire was low, embers crackling softly in the hearth. A pair of thick wool socks had been discarded near the chaise. One of her hairbrushes lay beside a stack of books on the floor. She guided me to the center of the room and peeled the damp coat Cassian have given me from my shoulders, not even flinching at the cold. Then she moved to the small bathing chamber tucked behind a silk-draped archway and began filling the copper tub, her sleeves rolled to her elbows, her hair slipping further from its attempted braid.

"You're going to catch something, Lyra," she said quietly, almost chiding. "You're freezing."

"I know."

She returned a moment later with one of her own gowns, light blue and stitched with silver thread along the cuffs, and laid it carefully on the edge of the basin. I stood there dripping like a forgotten statue, unable to move.

Elena returned to my side and touched my shoulder. "Do you want help?"

I nodded before I could talk myself out of it.

Still wearing her gloves, she undid the fastenings at the back of my ruined dress with nimble fingers, peeling the damp fabric away from my skin. She worked gently, like I might break. Maybe she wasn't wrong. I stepped out of the last layers and eased into the tub, the hot water biting before it soothed, steam rising in curling wisps around me.

Elena busied herself with lighting candles and warming towels for after the frost melted from my bones. She even brought me a soft cloth and a bar of rose-scented soap but didn't linger. She gave me space, slipping back into the main room while I sank deeper into the bath.

I let my head fall back against the rim and closed my eyes.

Eventually, I found my way out of the water, my skin flushed and wrinkled, the sharp edge of exhaustion pulling at every limb. Elena returned with a towel, wrapped me in it, then handed me the gown. I dressed slowly, every movement dragging.

Once I was done, she reappeared holding a small tin of ointment that smelled of lavender. She gave me an apologetic smile, one full of pity that made my heart squeeze. She smeared the balm over my cheek and brow, the itch and burn of the scab fading with each brush of her fingers.

By the time I sat on the chaise, she was brushing my hair. Each stroke slow and deliberate. She hummed under her breath, some tune from Mirun, perhaps.

"Sorry," she said after a while when the bristles snagged on a particularly bad knot.

"It's fine," I murmured. "I've had worse."

She tried to braid it. Her fingers were awkward and too gentle, and the plait fell apart halfway through. She laughed under her breath, sheepish. Suddenly her own braided hair made sense.

"I'm better at battle strategy than hair," she joked, pulling the strands behind my ear.

I smiled, or tried to.

"I heard Clara was sent home," Elena said a moment later, more serious now. "After the trial."

My breath caught. "What?"

"She's gone. The servants told me. By royal order."

Clara. Quiet, steady Clara. I remembered her nodding to me in the corridor that morning, a quick, uncertain smile that never quite reached her eyes. The way she'd always stood to the side, watching, calculating.

"She had experience," Elena continued, running the brush through my hair absentmindedly. "Grew up near the trading ports in Seren. She once told me she used to help with the harbor patrols. Her father was an admiral. I thought she'd make it to the end, honestly. She knew more than most."

I swallowed hard.

I couldn't help but remember the moment in the hallway with Clara. Her eyes going silver and confused. How she was never quite the same after. It made me think of Selene, and what had happened back in Virellia. She had touched me for all but one second and had forgotten the entirety of the morning. I had held Clara much longer.

"She'll be alright," Elena said gently. "Maybe it's not a bad thing to leave. To go home."

Maybe. Or maybe the palace was chewing us up, one by one.

We sat like that for a while. She talked softly about the dresses her tailors were finishing, about the guard who winked at her in the courtyard, about the idiotic things Rhea said at dinner when she thought no one could hear. I nodded along only half-listening and simply letting her voice fill the space.

My eyes kept drifting to the window. The sky stretched deep and endless over the palace grounds. Swirls of clouds coated the horizon in grays, but a few spots let the sunlight shine through. Strands of sun poured down leaving honey gold spots on the ground.

I remembered standing on the balcony with Kaden. Remembered the way his arm had brushed mine. The way he'd looked at me like I was something he couldn't have. Now, when I saw him, there was nothing behind his eyes. Just darkness and silence.

Elena continued her rambling as my mind drifted. I wanted to be a good friend. I want to listen and talk with her, but I truly could not gather the strength.

"Thank you," I said quietly as I stood.

Elena paused her tangent and looked over. "For what?"

"For... this." I waved my arms down myself, gesturing to the hair and ointment and gown.

She smiled. "Don't mention it."

I wandered around the chair of her vanity and began to gather my old wet clothes into a pile.

"Would you like to stay?"

My eyes found Elena's, and they pleaded for me to say yes, but I shook my head. I needed my own space. My own silence.

I stepped back into the hall, the cool air prickling against my damp hair. The palace was quiet again. The rain finally stopped.

I turned the corner toward my room to see Kaden standing outside my door, guarding his post like a chained animal. The moment he saw me, his head turned slightly, but he didn't speak. His eyes weren't his own, not anymore.

I swallowed the lump in my throat and brushed past him. My hand closed around my door handle. I stepped inside and shut it gently behind me. A second passed. Then—

Click.

I froze. Turned. Gripped the handle. I shook it up and down, the door creaking under the rash movement. It didn't budge.

Locked. From the outside.

I pressed my forehead to the door and sighed. I was too tired to scream. Too drained to fight.

Instead, I turned.

There, on the center of my desk, lay a sheet of pristine white parchment.

Its edges were perfectly aligned. At the top was a thick gold wax seal that glinted in the low light. The royal crest stamped into it.

I walked over slowly, every step dragging.

I broke the seal with trembling fingers. Inside, in elegant, sweeping script, the words read:

Fourth Trial: Hand-to-hand Combat.

Training with Lieutenant Corvallis will begin tomorrow.

Of course it does.

I let the paper fall to the desk, sat down beside it, and stared at the locked door.

The King just made his opening move in our little game of chess.

CHAPTER TWENTY-SIX

I TRIED TO REST, but my thoughts twisted like thorns, sharp and inescapable. They curled around every corner of my mind, blooming with the memory of Cassian's shattered control, of Kaden's vacant eyes, of the way the King was always one step ahead.

I had barely slept in the greenhouse, and even while I was far more comfortable in my bed, I'd slept no more than a few additional hours. Maybe less. But I rose anyway.

I dressed in white—clean, precise. A tunic tucked into fitted pants, the same color as my hair. I opted for my silk gloves, tucking the long lengths of the fabric under my tunic to ensure no skin was vulnerable to the air. My pants ran long, the hem going over the tops of my boots.

I braided my hair tight, beginning at the crown of my head and working it down to my waist. A silver whip that glinted with every motion. I ran my fingers along the scab running from my cheek to my brow. The edges had dried out, flaking to reveal a thin white scar beneath. I quickly put on whatever mint slave I had found earlier before folding Elena's gifted gown carefully, laying it on my bed as a promise to return it.

I turned, my face appearing in my vanity mirror. I studied my reflection. Not for vanity. Not even for reassurance. Just to really look.

My eyes gleamed back at me, no longer dull, no longer desperate or pleading. They shimmered with something older than my grief and sharper than any rage.

A knock rattled. I didn't hesitate. I pulled the handle to find it unlocked and opened the door immediately to find Kaden standing there. Empty-eyed. Hollow. A ghost carved into flesh. He said nothing. Offered no arm. Just turned silently and began to walk.

I followed just behind, like a phantom waiting for a command. We passed Naelle and her quiet guard in the corridor. Kaden fell into step behind them without a word, and I the same, letting their path take me where it would. The route wound past marble columns and fogged windows until we reached the same training pavilion from the maze trial. The morning air was crisp, the humidity falling with the previous rain. The pavilion was no longer bare beneath, but covered in faded red mats, sun-bleached from their years of use. My boots echoed on the hard concrete before we reached the padded sparring area. The others were already there.

Rhea stretched like a cat preparing to strike. Elena adjusted her simple day dress. Her cheeks were pink. Whether from the brisk air or nerves I wasn't sure. Naelle stood silent, as if she was trying to go unnoticed. I felt it. All of it. And I could feel Thane's attention on us too.

He stood like a statue carved from stone. Dressed in black, arms crossed over his chest, his shirt cut to reveal every muscle honed for war. His gaze swept over us like we were prey. He didn't smile until we stood in front of him, and even then, it was a cruel, twisted thing.

"Welcome," he said, his voice like a blade drawn in silence. "Today, we prepare for the fourth trial. Hand-to-hand combat. Unlike the others," he continued, pacing slowly, "this isn't about your titles, your lineage, or your dresses." His gaze landed on Elena and her dress. Her blush deepened. She smoothed the fabric with trembling hands.

"It's about whether you can survive the moment someone wants you dead."

The silence that followed stretched long enough to make even Rhea shift.

"You'll be paired at random," Thane went on. "You'll know your opponent the time of the trial. You have five days. Consider this day one. Use them wisely, because if you lose…"

He stopped near Naelle. His gaze flicked from her to me.

"You'll be eliminated. Not just from the trials. From the palace."

A beat.

"Immediately."

I didn't flinch. Neither did Naelle.

"No tricks. Just fists. Just instinct. And sometimes..." His eyes landed on me again, sharp as a scalpel. "Sometimes instinct is the only thing standing between a crown... and a grave. Sometimes," he added, louder now, "running isn't enough."

The smirk he gave me was cold. How Cassian could call this man a friend was something I don't think I would ever understand.

"Pair up," Thane ordered. "Let's see what you've got."

I moved toward Elena without a word. We met each other's gaze and nodded. A silent pact. We wouldn't break any bones today.

When Thane signaled, I cracked open the lid on my power just enough.

The threads slipped through the seams of my being, silver and slithering like mist. They curled outward, invisible to the eye but searching, hungry. Snaking from her ankle up to her head, they found Elena's mind quickly and her thoughts mingled with mine like smoke.

I could feel the beat of her pulse, the split-second flicker of decision before her arm moved. My body reacted before my mind could catch up.

She stepped in with her left foot, shoulder dipping low. I lifted my arm and blocked it clean, twisting her wrist with enough force to throw her off balance.

Defense was easy. Almost too easy. It was like dancing with music only I could hear. But offense? That was different. The moment I stepped out of her head and tried to lead the fight, everything vanished. Even in her dress, she still held the advantage. Her mind became static, her intentions a haze. I couldn't see how she would react to my strikes. Couldn't predict the counterweight of her body. Couldn't cheat.

And every time, every single time, I missed.

Again. And again. And again.

Elena ducked beneath my elbow, spun, and jabbed her fist into my ribs. Not hard enough to bruise, but enough to sting.

"Focus," she muttered, not unkindly. "You're quick. You're strong. But you're hesitating."

I shook my head, jaw tight. Embarrassment pooled in my chest, hot and sharp, rising like bile. I ground my teeth and stepped back into my makeshift stance.

We circled. Her stance low and loose. Mine tense and tight.

Then she charged. Fast, faster than I expected. She aimed for my left side, but her shoulder feinted at the last second. I followed the feint, dropped my guard, and she slipped behind me.

A solid foot to the back of my knee sent me stumbling forward. I caught myself. Barely. My hands scraped against the mat as I twisted, spun, and lunged forward with a swing. She dodged. Of course she did.

I snarled under my breath and threw a second punch. Too wide. She ducked. Came up from beneath me, elbowing me in the stomach. I staggered back, air wheezing from my lungs.

"You're fighting like someone who doesn't want to hurt me," Elena said, panting. "Don't protect me. Try to beat me. Control yourself and try to win."

I straightened, wiped the sweat from my brow with the back of my hand. "I *am* trying to win."

"No, you're not," she said, steady now. "You're holding back."

She was right, and that made me want to scream.

I clenched my fists and charged again.

This time I threw all of it into the swing, my frustration, my fury, my shame.

She blocked it with both arms and under a pink swish of her gown, swept my legs out from under me.

I hit the mat hard.

The breath left my chest in one sharp gust. I stared at the ceiling, my braid fanned out like a silver rope beneath my head. My lungs burned. My ribs ached.

Elena offered me her hand. I ignored it and rolled to my feet.

"This trial's not going to care how kind you are," she said, eyes flinty.

"I'm not kind," I snapped.

"Okay, then you're afraid."

The words struck harder than her fists.

I said nothing. Just lifted my hands again.

She nodded once. "Prove me wrong."

We sparred again, harder this time. She was all fast footwork and sharp hits. And me, I was anger and instinct and the thrum of power just beneath my skin, aching to be unleashed. But still, I struggled.

Then, I felt it.

Warmth. Golden and thick like honey. A thought, not mine, slid through the connection I hadn't asked for.

A vision of me, soaked through in my white dress. Rain clinging to my skin. My eyes narrowed in defiance. My mouth parted in breathless fury. Pure adoration for every bit of that memory.

I didn't need to turn to know Cassian was watching. His gaze burned into me like sunlight through glass, unrelenting and magnifying, but I didn't stop. This wasn't about him. Not anymore. Not about stolen glances or shared thoughts. Not about the memory of his hand in mine or the weight of his voice whispering my name. This was survival.

And part of me couldn't shake the memory of the pot he had shattered. I still felt the fury in his gaze, even if it was aimed at the heart of someone far from mine. Still felt the tremor of his voice when he snapped. Still heard the echo of his blood. He was the King's son, and that was starting to become ever so clear.

Eventually, Thane barked for a break. I stalked off the mat and began walking towards a filled basin to grab some water. I hoped the cold could do something to numb the fire roaring under my skin.

Cassian was already there, that slow, ruinous smile curling his lips.

"Let me help you," he said softly.

"No." I grabbed a glass and the dipped it into the water. "Elena and I can handle it."

His brow pinched. He shifted, dragging a hand down his jaw like the motion might steady him. "You're not seeing—"

"I said no." It came out harder than I meant. Sharper. But I didn't take it back. "You made me a promise," I added, quieter this time as I faced him. "My way."

The flicker of emotion ran through me. Not anger, not hurt, but rejection. He nodded once and stepped back. He didn't argue, but his thoughts didn't leave.

Even as I turned my back to him. Even as I tried to focus on Elena's next move, the next strike, the next breath.

He was thinking about the way I looked at him. Like he was worth saving. I saw the way he looked at me. Like maybe I was worth loving.

And he hated himself for it.

Elena was waiting on the mat when I returned. We went again, and this time she didn't hold back. Her strikes were sharper, her footwork faster. She called out tips as we moved—low, quick instructions between every breath and hit.

"Don't turn your hips like that. You're giving away your next move."

"Lead with your left shoulder. No, tighter. Good."

"Eyes up, Lyra. Look at me, not the floor."

I listened, I adjusted, and slowly, very slowly, I got better. But the progress I made was nothing compared to the refined instincts of the other girls.

My power had no doubt given me a competitive edge that I had abused, but this? This was raw and brutal and required a kind of effort that felt unnatural. A kind of effort that felt barbaric.

By the time Thane called for us to stop, my body was slick with sweat, and my arms shook from holding form too long. My braid stuck to the back of my neck. My chest heaved with every breath.

I didn't look at Cassian. I knew he'd been watching. I could feel his stare like heat trickling up my spine. Could feel the tangle of his thoughts chasing mine even as I turned away. They ran rampant in my mind—longing, hungry, bitter. They pressed against me like a tide, trying to pull me back.

I wanted to let it take me. To wrap me in that golden warmth and drag me towards him. I wanted to, but a part of me couldn't face him. A part of me didn't want to even think about the confusing mess of emotions that surrounded Cassian Vaelros. And if I allowed myself to stay, to go to him, I wasn't sure I would leave.

So, I didn't stop. I didn't glance back.

I walked past him without a word.

CHAPTER TWENTY-SEVEN

I FELT RESTED.

I wouldn't say I felt joyful, but for the first time in what felt like forever, the bruised shadows beneath my eyes had faded. My limbs, though sore from Thane's training regimen and Elena's brutal sparring, felt lighter.

Like they belonged to me again.

I sat at my vanity and ran a brush through my hair. I split the strands to begin my braid, but I stopped. I ran my fingers down the length and let the white waves fall where they pleased. The scab on my face had all but vanished, leaving a pale scar in its wake. A bit of my eyebrow has disappeared with it, leaving a thin line in the hair.

I slipped into a cream day dress, the fabric a bit thicker as autumn began its arrival. I slipped my silk gloves over my hands as a finishing touch.

When I reached the door, I paused. My hand rose not to the handle, but to the wall beside it. I pressed my palm flat against the stone, closed my eyes, and let my breath slow.

I reached with a thread of the power that lived beneath my skin, beneath my bones. I let it drift outward, like a ripple over still water, brushing the air beyond the door. My power, this energy, whatever it was, had become a piece of me. A continuously intertwining part of my life. It flowed through the silk of my gloves, just as it had before.

The pulse of magic slipped through the corridor like smoke, curling in invisible spirals, brushing against cold stone.

Kaden wasn't there.

He was always gone now. Always just out of reach in the emotional aspect but was beginning to make physical disappearance his forte as well. Here one second, then gone the next. He was present only as a whisper of footsteps. The glint of a blade in the distance. I tried to convince myself that's why he had begun to lock my door at times. He was protecting me. He was still my guard.

Even if the King had stationed a ghost at my door.

I stepped out, closing the door softly behind me, my heart pounding a rhythm that didn't quite match my steps. In the mess hall, I swiped a still-warm muffin without slowing, then made my way through the silent corridors to the library. The palace hadn't stirred yet. Perfect.

I needed the quiet. I needed answers.

The books I'd read before hadn't been enough. They were wrong somehow. Too polished and curated. Stories dressed up in poetry. What I needed wasn't legend, it was something truer. I just didn't know where to look.

I started with myths again, just in case I missed something. Heroes and monsters. Bedtime tales from kingdoms that didn't exist anymore. They offered nothing but riddles in fancy ink. Metaphors that were strung together like lullabies and tied neatly with pretty lies shaped like a ribbon bow.

So, I moved on.

Lineages. Histories. Architectural texts. Anything that might hold a clue to the bones of this palace. I looked for anything that might tell me what the King had done to Kaden, but every trail ended the same way. Silence.

It was like the world had been erased before the Vaelros name took root. Every book had been rewritten by the same unseen hand, scouring away anything that didn't serve them. Even the volumes I had poured over days ago had vanished from the shelves, leaving only dust behind. It was like they had never existed at all.

Frustration flared in me like a spark, but I clamped down on it. In the space it left behind, warmth bloomed. Honey sweet and golden.

It began low on my spine, curling upward like a slow-blooming flame. A familiar presence. Like sunlight had spilled across my back and decided to stay. It traced the line of my neck, soft and steady, and when it brushed my jaw, I knew.

Cassian's gaze burned like always. I didn't turn. I didn't need to.

A small smile tugged at the corners of my lips before I could stop myself.

I moved swiftly, tugging a thick architectural tome from the shelf and slipping behind a marble pillar before he could speak. My heart pounded in my chest, the book tight against it. I let my head rest back against the stone and exhaled.

I felt him follow. The tether between us grew taut. He stopped just around the pillar.

"Lyra," he said softly. "I've missed you, little flame." His voice, low and golden, nearly unraveled me. I stepped around the pillar, spine straightening, face schooled into calm.

"Prince Vaelros," I said coolly.

Cassian blinked. "Formal today, are we?" He smiled, but it was off. Edged with something sharp and sad. He stepped forward, close enough that I could feel the heat of him but not close enough to touch. He always did that. Danced at the edge of distance.

The sunlight filtering through the stained-glass painted his skin in shifting blues and violets. He looked like something from a dream.

"I've been looking for you," he said. "You haven't exactly made it easy."

I didn't answer.

"Are you alright?"

"I'm fine."

"That's not what I asked."

The book in my arms trembled. I tightened my grip, hoping he didn't notice.

"I'm still here," he said, voice gentler. "Whatever happens, I'm right here."

It hurt. The way he said it. The way he meant it. My chest twisted and something in me screamed to reach out, to trust him, but I stayed still. I had to.

"I'm sorry," he added after a beat. "About the greenhouse. About the pot." He reached for my hand slowly, like asking permission without words. "I never meant to—"

I flinched before I could stop it. Just a twitch, but he saw it. He let his hand fall. The hurt that flashed across his face was quick but unmistakable.

"I know you're avoiding me," he said. "I just want to understand why."

"I'm not," I replied, voice sharper than I intended.

He gave a hollow laugh. "You were never a good liar, especially not to me."

The bond shimmered between us, invisible but undeniable. I could feel his thoughts brushing against mine. He was holding back, but just barely. It would've been so easy to close the space. To listen. To fall. To drown in him.

But I couldn't. I wouldn't allow myself to.

"I have work to do," I said, trying to keep my voice steady.

He glanced at the book. "Work pertaining the blueprints of the palace?"

I hesitated. "I'm curious. About what's changed over the years."

He arched a brow, the ghost of a smirk playing at his lips. "Of course." He stepped back. "I'll leave you to it, Lyra."

It was just my name, but he said it like it was something sacred.

As he turned, something shifted in the air. Not sound. Not thought. Just feeling. A gentle warmth brushing against the edge of my mind like a silken hand.

I didn't mean to reach, but I did.

Not with power, not with magic. Just with the part of me that still felt something for him. Felt anything for him.

I reached with the bond that hummed between us.

Cassian paused. He didn't turn, but I saw the way his shoulders stiffened, like he'd felt it, too. Like he was fighting the urge to come back to me, but then he walked away.

The space he left behind felt cold in his absence.

I turned back to the shelves, forcing myself to breathe. My eyes drifted toward the return rack, and there he was. Cassian's fingers trailed along the spines of the very books I'd been reading. Every myth, every failure. He was following my trail in his own quiet way, and then it happened.

My world shifted.

It wasn't a vision. It was sharper than that. Clearer. Like my own memories had been replaced by someone else's.

His.

Cassian's mind, his memories, surged into me.

They pressed into me like a second heartbeat, deep and unrelenting.

He was thinking of the lagoon. Of the way the wind tangled my hair the night we stood on the beach. My laughter torn away by the waves. My eyes full of stars and lashes full of salt. He remembered the way I'd looked at him then. Completely unguarded. Like he could reach into my chest and steal whatever he wanted of my heart, and I might've let him.

He was thinking of the ballroom. Of the moment I stepped through those gold-veined doors in that shimmering backless dress, all fire and silver defiance. His thoughts dripped with hunger as he remembered the feel of my waist beneath his fingers, the scent of me. Moonlight and something wild. He hadn't stopped thinking about it since.

And the greenhouse. His mind reeled with it, got drunk on it. He thought of my soaked white dress clinging to me, of the way the rain had plastered my hair to my skin. He had wanted to press me against the glass walls, to kiss the storm right off my mouth. He wanted to drown in me, again and again.

Then the throne room. The way his heart stopped when I entered alone. The helpless fury at his father. The pain. The bruises he covered with long sleeves. The care he had to give to himself because no one else would.

And then, the ache. The waiting. The want.

Me.

It was gone as fast as it came.

I gasped, stumbling back, one hand catching on the shelves as the other clutched the tome.

Cassian didn't move, but when I looked up, he was already watching me. His eyes were soft, sad, shining.

I blinked. Once. Twice. Then I turned and walked away. Back to my room. No guard stood at the post.

Relief hit me like a wave. I collapsed onto the bed, arms flung wide, and finally let myself breathe.

The sun was glaring into my window, still hanging in the sky high enough to say it wasn't time for bed, but a nap would suffice.

Sleep took me slowly, like the pull of the tide, and in that darkened space where thoughts blurred and softened, I saw Cassian once more.

Not as I knew him now, but as a child.

His curls were wild and untamed, a natural crown of bronze gold that glinted in the sun. Freckles spilled across the bridge of his nose, and his eyes, those golden eyes, held a kind of wonder I hadn't seen before. He couldn't have been older than five or six, his limbs still coltish and thin. He knelt in a field of pale blue flowers, whispering to something, or someone, hidden in the tall grass.

I stepped closer, though I wasn't sure if I was myself in this dream, or something else entirely. Still, I followed his gaze and there she was.

A girl.

Tiny. Barely more than a toddler. Her hair was a silvery white, bright and soft as moonlight. She sat in the grass, legs tucked beneath her, fingers curled around a cluster of wildflowers. Cassian reached out a hand toward her, cautious but kind, and she didn't flinch. She smiled.

But before his fingers could brush hers, the dream shifted.

The warmth bled away, replaced by shadows and firelight. Stone. The throne room.

I was inside his memory now. I could feel it in the weight pressing against my chest, the ache behind my ribs.

Cassian stood in the corner, half-hidden by a curtain of shadow, smaller and younger than he was now, but older than in the field. Maybe fifteen. Maybe sixteen. His face was pale with fear, his fists clenched at his sides. I could feel the tension vibrating from him, his panic like a drumbeat beneath my skin.

In the center of the floor stood a boy. A boy no older than ten.

His head was bowed, white hair hanging like a curtain to shield his face. Ropes bound his hands behind his back and lashed his ankles together. His knees trembled. His shoulders shook with quiet, shuddering sobs that echoed across the marble.

I wanted to move toward him, to lift his face and look into his eyes, but I couldn't. I could only watch.

And there, kneeling in front of the King, was the Queen.

Cassian's mother.

She was pleading. I couldn't hear the words, but I saw them in the way her hands shook, in the tear-streaked desperation on her face. She shielded the boy with her body, arms outstretched, a human barrier between him and the King.

He stood at the top of the dais, golden armor catching the firelight, casting harsh gleams across the cold stone. His face was contorted with rage, his mouth twisting as he bellowed at the Queen. He pointed at her, demanding. Threatening.

"Get away from him," Cassian whispered, echoing his father. While the words were angry, his voice held nothing but fear.

The King drew his sword with a slow, deliberate motion. It hissed from its scabbard like a live animal. The Queen's body shook, but she didn't move. She only knelt lower, curling her hands into fists and sobbing with the boy behind her as she bent over on the floor. I could have sworn I saw the boy reach out towards the Queen, perhaps in a final plea for mercy.

The King descended the rolling staircase.

"Stay down," he roared, and this time, I heard it, clear and violent and rattling through my bones.

Cassian didn't breathe.

Neither did I.

The sword lifted.

The white-haired boy froze in fear.

And then, just before the blade could fall, the Queen rose.

She surged upward with a cry, her hands flung upward begging for mercy, but it was too late. The King couldn't stop his sword.

The dream shattered.

I shot upright in bed with a strangled gasp, lungs burning as if I'd been underwater. My heart slammed against my ribs like a warning drum. It was dark now. My sheets tangled around me. Sweat clung to the back of my neck. I clutched my chest with both hands, trying to steady my breath, but my thoughts were a blur of white hair and Cassian. The Queen. His mother.

That boy.

CHAPTER TWENTY-EIGHT

THE SKY HAD DARKENED when I woke from my nap, but sleep was no longer an option. I tossed and turned beneath the covers, but every time I closed my eyes, all I could see was the Queen standing before that white-haired boy. And in the shadows, young Cassian, frozen in place, watching it all.

Eventually, I threw off the blankets and swung my legs over the edge of the bed. The floor was cold beneath my feet as I made my way to the balcony. Leaning against the railing, I turned my gaze to the left, toward the far edge of Aurea. Even cloaked in shadow, the city glittered. The music of the night drifted up, a soft, delicate symphony that reminded me of nothing and everything all at once.

I tilted my head back, searching for constellations. I used to do the same in Virellia, tracing the stars with my fingers as I whispered their names. I remembered how frustrated I'd been when I first arrived here, at the lack of stars above the palace. And how Kaden had told me, back then, of all the supposed opportunities I'd gained instead. The memory stung more than I expected. I dropped my gaze.

That's when I saw the movement in the gardens.

I had never seen someone wander out this late, not unless they had a reason. The figure swept through the garden like a breeze, graceful and slow, pausing at each flower bed to examine the blooms. I leaned forward, breath held. They moved with intention, each step purposeful.

The figure crouched and shifted through the roses, then stopped. There was one, nearly hidden beneath the others. Small. Pale. With a quick, practiced snip, the figure clipped it. A single rose. Then they turned and vanished back into the palace.

I didn't know why I felt so disappointed to see them go. I didn't even know who they were.

The floor bit at my feet again as I slipped back inside and crawled beneath the duvet. I tried to sleep, but I only drifted in and out of shallow dreams. By the time I gave in and opened my eyes for good, the sun was still low in the sky, casting soft gold through the curtains in fragile patterns.

I slipped from bed, every movement careful. I padded barefoot across the room to the door and let my fingertips skim the wood, reaching out with my power. Just a taste. Just enough to feel.

No trace of any guards. No flicker of thought or shadow of presence, but there was something else.

I flung open the door.

There, sitting at my feet, was a flower. A small yellow rose, bound in sparkling gold ribbon and still damp with dew. My breath caught. A flutter stirred in my chest, tight at first, then blooming wide.

I slipped back into my room and set the flower on the small drawer near my bed. I stared at it for a moment, heart aching and wishing to keep it alive forever.

A knock startled me.

Kaden's voice came through the door. The words were flat, and emotionless. "Breakfast is in the gardens."

I swallowed my frustration. "I'll get ready."

Turning to my wardrobe, I hesitated, then reached for a pale yellow dress—the color of the rose. It shimmered faintly in the light, its hem catching hues of gold. My gloves hit an inch below the short cap sleeves. I braided my hair tightly, remembering the strength I'd felt the last time I wore it like a crown.

When I stepped into the hall, I found myself hoping that it would be the real Kaden waiting. The one who used to walk beside me with lazy grins and too-loud whistles. The one who would likely joke and say, "*Trouble in yellow? That's dangerous*," with a teasing smirk and offer me his arm.

But it wasn't.

And stars, it still stung like the first time.

We meandered through the halls, Kaden marching in front like a perfectly broken solider. We exited the palace and reached the gardens. The path we followed led us by the greenhouse, and I watched as the glass caught each bit of the morning sun. I slowed, my heart catching. "I tripped over your shoes the first time we danced in there," I said, my voice light, almost wistful. "You told me I'd never survive a royal ball if I kept stepping on your toes. And then we made up our own dance." I grabbed the skirts of my dress, quickening my pace until I walked at Kaden's side. "You told me to name it, and I never came up with a good one. It was your favorite, or so you said."

I laughed softly, glancing up at him.

Kaden didn't smile. Didn't even blink.

By the time we reached the gardens everyone had already found their place. Servants bustled about carrying trays and dishes. Guards stood at attention surrounding the space, and nobles filtered in.

My chest was tight and aching, but it loosened slightly at the sight before me.

The breakfast table was mesmerizing. It was made entirely of glass. A gleaming pane that reflected the high-arched windows and the blush of morning spilling through them. The chairs were clear, delicate-looking things that somehow still managed to seem solid, and every plate, every cup, every fork was crystal. There was no metal, no wood. No harshness.

The only color came from the food, like someone had spilled a painter's palette across a still life.

Ripe fruits were heaped in blown-glass bowls. Slices of ruby watermelon, plump blueberries, glistening grapes, and wedges of honey-dripping pear. There were golden croissants and sugared rolls nestled beside warm cinnamon pastries and buttered toast still steaming. Carafes of thick, dark coffee sat beside pitchers of rose-colored juice and something that shimmered like lavender and starlight. There were cheeses dotted with herbs, trays of cured meats, and tiny dishes of honey, jam, and clotted cream.

Sunlight danced across it all, casting prisms of yellow and pink and orange into the air. A living watercolor. A dream.

And at the head of the table sat Cassian.

My heart stopped.

The King wasn't here—thank the stars—but Cassian was. Regal, poised, and devastating in the morning light. His button up was open at the throat. He had a casual elegance to the way he sat, even while his fingers were only wrapped loosely around a clear mug of coffee.

His golden eyes found mine again and again. I didn't reach for his thoughts. I didn't need to.

I could feel him.

Like a river meeting the sea. Like gravity deciding I belonged near him. He liked the dress. I could tell.

Perhaps a bit too much.

I broke the stare before I drowned in it and searched the table. My eyes landed on Elena, and the smile curling on my lips came easily.

I rushed over and claimed the seat beside her, grateful for something solid, for someone familiar.

"I need to learn how you braid your hair," she said immediately, noticing. "I saw it during sparring, too. I've been trying to teach myself, as you suffered through."

I laughed softly. "I could braid yours. For the fourth trial."

Her eyes lit up. "Would you? That would be... perfect." Her gaze darted to the now scar running along my cheek. "And by the way, you look good with a scar. Makes you look all intimidating." She threw her hands up in mock terror. I only laughed.

It felt easy, slipping into conversation with her. The tension of the morning melted as we giggled like ordinary girls.

We both reached for the fruit first. I bit into a piece of peach, sweet and so soft it melted on my tongue. Elena passed me a slice of watermelon next, grinning as juice dripped from her fingers. "They always serve too much of everything," she said, rolling her eyes affectionately. "And yet I eat like I haven't seen food in weeks."

"Same," I said around a mouthful of pear, then reached for a pastry that caught my eye.

It was small, coiled like a rose, the dough flaky and layered with a golden sheen. I broke off a piece and stopped, my jaw mid-chew.

It was filled with spiced apple and cream, a hint of citrus tucked in, like sunshine folded into silk. It wasn't just good. It was stunning.

I blinked, looking down at the rest of the pastry like it might vanish. "What *is* this?" I whispered.

Elena leaned over, grinning. "You found the sunrise pastries. I've been dreaming about those since the first trial."

I took another bite, slower this time, savoring the way it melted in my mouth. I'd never tasted anything like it. "I'd sell my soul for a basket of these," I murmured.

Elena laughed. "Careful. Someone here might take you up on that."

I looked down the table toward Cassian without meaning to, only to find his gaze already on me, unreadable.

I turned back quickly, cheeks warming.

I reached for a slice of toasted bread, spreading it with sweet plum jam and a dollop of cream, but that pastry stayed on my plate, slowly disappearing bite by bite as we talked and laughed. But beneath the light conversation, the jokes, the laughs, tension pulsed. The fourth trial loomed over everything.

Elena was first to say it aloud. "There's a chance we'll fight each other, isn't there?"

I nodded. "If it happens... we'll fight fair. I swear we will."

I wouldn't use my power on her. I promised myself that, too.

She tilted her head, meeting my gaze. "I won't let them make me hurt you."

She didn't have to say more.

I let my attention drift down the table and reached out with just a thread to Rhea. Her mind was filled with images of blood, bones, and violence. Her imagined visions of the day hit me all at once. She wanted to be paired with me. She wanted to carry out a plan she had longed for.

I pulled away, bile rising. I suddenly wished I hasn't eaten so much.

Then I reached again. Naelle this time.

She was quiet, still but sharp. Her thoughts moved like blades in the dark. She was confident, but no images or visions came with the emotion. She didn't have a plan, or at least not one that I could see. She seemed eerily calm, as if she was aware of the outcome long before it ever happened. A chill prickled down my spine.

I turned back to Elena, who had launched into a rant about Will again. How his forearms were *"sculpted by the stars"* and how his crooked smile made her drop dishes.

"If I'm rejected," she said with a wink, "but they let me stay, I'm marrying him. Or running away with him. Haven't decided yet."

I about spit out my drink with laughter. "Let me know how that works out for you."

After breakfast, the others filtered out slowly, their chatter fading into the background. I spotted Kaden at the far edge of the garden, nearly hidden beneath the shadow of a tall, skeletal tree. Something in me sparked—hope, maybe, or something close enough to hurt just the same.

I moved to him quickly, clinging to the last ember of possibility. But as I drew close, he turned without a word, staying two paces in front.

I sighed. "How was your morning?" I called forward, trying to stir something from him, anything.

He responded with silence.

Not even a flicker of reaction.

He just continued on, escorting me like I was nothing more than a responsibility.

When he returned me to my room, I waited. I stared at the door until the faint presence outside finally vanished.

I stripped off the yellow dress, a new favorite, and changed into a navy tunic and matching pants.

I let out a breath, pulled at the door handle, and felt it click softly. He only seemed to lock it at night, thankfully. I slipped into the hallway and shut it gently behind me.

The training yard was quiet. I had half expected Thane or one of the other girls to be there, but it was completely vacant. Just the echo of wind brushing over the stone and the dull thud of my boots against the floor.

I walked to the center mat, the same place where Elena and I had sparred. I tried to get into the stance she'd shown me, but it felt wrong. Forced. I threw a few fake punches into the empty air, imagining Rhea's sneer in front of me. I swept my leg under an invisible opponent, pretending she was the one crashing backwards to the ground. I ducked, dodged, turned, and twisted. It all felt stupid.

Frustration clawed at my throat, and I let my hands fall to my sides. I stood still for a moment, breathing hard, and let my head fall into my hands.

This was ridiculous.

"Maybe a little ridiculous."

I spun around at the sound of that golden voice, but I already knew who it was.

Cassian strolled in like he owned the place, which technically, he did. He wasn't in the elegant attire he wore at breakfast. Instead, he wore a soft cream shirt and deep brown pants. His sleeves were rolled up to his forearms and the buttons at the top were undone. Every movement pulled softly at the muscles beneath his skin. His hair was a little messy, like he hadn't meant to be seen but didn't mind the invasion of certain eyes. Dirt and sand clung to his bare feet, and I had no idea why that detail made my stomach twist.

I straightened. "I didn't ask for help."

"I know," he said, stopping just a few feet from the mat. His expression was unreadable. "But I watched you return to the palace after breakfast. And something told me you weren't going to sit in your room all day."

I crossed my arms. "Spying on me now?"

"No. Just noticing you. That's different." His brow arched, just slightly. His eyes ran down the white line on my cheek and brow. "You're lucky I'm into scars."

I turned away to hide my flush, trying to focus. "You can go. I can train alone."

"Clearly." He gestured lazily to the imaginary battle I'd been waging. "You just defeated four invisible enemies with stunning mediocrity."

I narrowed my eyes at him, my hands settling on my hips. "Was that supposed to be encouraging?"

He grinned. "If you want encouraging, I can lie. You hit like a court lady. A particularly angry one, but still." He wandered ever closer, the scent of cedar moving with the breeze. "But if you want to win, maybe try combat training when there's actually someone to combat."

A laugh escaped before I could stop it, sharp and reluctant. "Well, I'm sure you've seen it, but I don't think there's a person on this planet that I can *combat*."

Cassian's smirk lit his whole face, and stars help me, it lit something in me too. "Don't take it easy on me, Seravell."

He stepped into the circle of the mat with fluid ease, falling into a stance so natural it looked like breathing. His feet were staggered, his hands loose, ready. Even with his knees bent, he was still a full head taller than me, and I wasn't short. I hadn't worn any gloves. I hadn't expected anyone to join me. My hands were bare, but I wasn't the one vulnerable. Not anymore.

"Let's see what you've got."

I sighed, shaking out my arms. "Fine. But don't complain about the bruises tomorrow."

"Land one hit and I'll bruise wherever you ask me to."

He lunged forward playfully, and I immediately let my power sink into his mind, just enough to glimpse his next move. I spun away easily, like it was some choreographed dance.

He circled me slowly, appraising my stance. "Feet apart, wider. Bend your knees more. Now, again."

I struck out, and he blocked it with ease. My hand hit his forearm, the touch sending shocks running along my skin. I twisted, jabbed, missed. He pivoted around me like smoke.

"Use your hips more," he murmured. His hand pushed my left hip back to match my feet. The touch was nothing. Fabric separated us. He was just helping me train, but I couldn't help the butterflies that fluttered in my stomach.

I swallowed. I swung harder this time, and my fist grazed his side.

A mischievous grin curled on his lips. "Impressive. I almost felt that one." His smile broke, showing teeth. "Stop pulling your punches. I can take a hit."

I pulled my hip back like he had showed me and swept my foot low. He avoided it easily, but that was exactly what I wanted.

While his eyes were down, focused on my leg, my fist was colliding with his shoulder.

The hit was solid, hard, but still he barely even moved.

Cassian paused and glanced to where my fist had met its target. Then looked back up with a slow, proud smirk. "There she is."

My breath hitched. He was too close. Too steady. Too much.

I cleared my throat. "Again," I said, my voice lower now.

We fell into rhythm. Strike, block, twist, reset. The silence between us changed. It thickened. Shifted. Our hands brushed. His fingertips grazed my wrist, my shoulder, my back as he adjusted my form. Each touch sent his thoughts racing into my own. I hated the way I noticed it. Part of me loved it too.

Cassian tried a few more attacks after that, testing my reflexes. I evaded each one with ease, slipping into the rhythm like I'd been born for it. I saw every strike before it happened—a flicker of muscle, a shift of weight, a fleeting thought blooming in his mind just seconds before his body followed through. It felt almost unfair, how easily I could predict him when I reached into that golden mind of his.

But then, all at once, his thoughts vanished.

It was like someone had slammed a door shut in my head. That stone wall had reappeared in his mind, rough and enclosing. The rough stone had begun to smooth, and I couldn't gain traction, not fast enough.

I staggered for the barest second at the sudden silence in my mind, and in that heartbeat of hesitation, he lunged forward. It was a straightforward move, something I should have been able to dodge, but without the echo of intent to warn me, without his mind open to mine, he got through.

His hands closed around my upper arms, firm but not painful, and I gasped. Not from the grip, but from the look in his eyes. No thoughts ravaged my mind. Nothing slipped though the connection he had created.

There was nothing. Nothing but us.

Cassian stared down at me, golden eyes molten with some unreadable heat. The edges of his mouth curled into a slow, wicked smirk.

"Careful Lyra. I'm staring to think you want me to catch you," he said, voice low and pleased.

I could only stare up at him, breath frozen in my lungs. Stars, he was beautiful. Incredulously so. Beautiful in a way that was too much, too overwhelming. That messy hair. That sun-warmed skin. That mouth I shouldn't be staring at.

The lump in my throat grew. "Guess that means I need more practice then, huh."

His gaze dipped down to my lips, to the column of my throat, before lifting again to find mine. The weight of it sent a shiver straight through me. Heat bloomed at my core, molten and impossible to ignore. Cassian didn't look away. He held my stare like a vow, like a challenge. His grip tightened slightly, just enough to make my breath catch.

"I'll be sure to let Thane know his training needs work," he murmured, and there was a dangerous sort of amusement in his tone, one that told me he was very aware of what he was doing.

He lingered a moment longer, one heartbeat then two, before slowly releasing his hold on my arms. His fingers slid away like a snake, leaving fire in their wake. And still, his eyes didn't leave mine.

He stepped back, measured and slow, every movement controlled. He was always so composed, so sure of himself, and the worst part was that it wasn't arrogance. He had every right to act exactly how he did.

I let out a breath, my lungs grateful for the air, even as my chest still burned.I wasn't sure how much this tension could build before it snapped, but I had a feeling we were going to find out.

I shook my head, trying and failing to clear it. I couldn't afford this. Not now. I needed to push him out of my mind, but he was already there, taking up space I hadn't meant to give.

Gritting my teeth, I turned back to the center of the mat. I started again, punching at ghosts, ducking invisible strikes, practicing until the sting in my muscles matched the ache in my chest.

I fought until the evening chill settled into my bones and the sun dipped low enough to kiss the edge of the sea, painting the sky in fire and gold.

Only then did I stop.

Only then did I let myself breathe.

CHAPTER TWENTY-NINE

THE SUN HAD JUST begun to crest the horizon when I stepped into the training yard again. This time, it wasn't by choice. The fourth trial loomed, set for the day after tomorrow. And this, Thane's last brutal session, was mandatory for every contender.

Autumn had unfurled in Aurea. Dew clung to the grass like silver dust. A thin mist drifted low across the yard, curling around the stone pathways and dissolving in the chill air. The gray of the sky matched the gray of my clothes. The slate tunic and pants covered every inch of skin possible, my silk gloves finishing the rest.

My breath fogged in the early morning air. I scanned the edge of the sparring ring out of habit. Hoping and half-expecting to see him, to see Cassian. He sometimes lingered in the shadows when he thought no one noticed, arms crossed, golden eyes watching like a flame behind glass.

But today, nothing.

Kaden trailed in front of me, silent as ever. I felt him there, the dull weight of his presence, but when he glanced back, his gaze was distant. Unreachable. Like he was watching something far beyond this world.

My chest ached. Disappointment curled quiet and sharp beneath my ribs. It settled into my bones, leaving me slightly off-balance as I walked toward the gathered girls. Their voices quieted as I approached, and it wasn't until Thane's voice snapped through the air that I realized I was the last to arrive.

"Well, well. Look who decided to grace us with her presence." His voice was a blade, honed and mocking. "Late today, Seravell?"

"I—" I started, but he cut me off before the excuse could even form.

"No need," he said smoothly, already stepping into the ring. He rolled his shoulders, the slow stretch of muscle that spoke of blood to come. "Since you're clearly so confident you don't need the full training session, let's put your expertise to the test."

The girls shifted behind me. I hadn't even known I was late. I caught Naelle's smirk as Rhea nudged her with the point of her elbow. She whispered something behind her hand. Her lips curled in cruel amusement. Elena said nothing, but I saw the tight set of her jaw.

Thane gestured toward the ring, smiling like a man who thought he'd already won. "You and me. On the mat."

I stepped forward. My steps crunched on the gravel as I crossed into the ring, each movement slow, deliberate. The chill air bit into my skin, but I barely felt it. My pulse pounded loud in my ears. I cracked open the door to my power just enough to let it breathe. It slid through my limbs like breath, like smoke, like memory.

It flooded my gloves before spilling through the thin fabric, winding its way up Thane's body.

His movements hadn't begun, not truly, but I felt them coming. The subtle shift in his weight. The twitch of muscle before he struck. The thoughts burning behind his eyes like sparks pressed to my skin.

He swung.

I ducked beneath it before I even thought to move.

Another low strike, a feint. I pivoted, the world narrowing to the stretch of mats and the rhythm of his body. A block. A sidestep. A twist that let the strike pass clean over my shoulder.

I wasn't fighting. Not really. I was just defending. I flowed, moving the way rivers swirled around stone. There was no need for retaliation.

I read him like music, like a poem I already knew by heart. His emotions poured into me with every swing—frustration, disbelief, something darker curling underneath.

He gritted his teeth. "Stop playing with me," he hissed below his breath, venom filled each word.

He lunged again. I slid out of the way with a twist at my waist.

"I'm not," I replied into his ear as he staggered past.

But maybe I was. Just a little. Because I could feel it. I could feel his anger building sky high, cresting into something hot and volatile. His chest heaved under his frustrated breaths and his hands clenched in and out of fists. He came at me harder.

His foot swept low. I jumped. He twisted, elbow slashing toward my ribs. I leapt into the space beside him and let it pass. The air split from the force of it, but he never touched me. Each time I moved, his frustration cracked wider.

She's making me look like a fool.

This shouldn't be possible.

He was right.

Where.

Is.

Cassian.

I blocked the next blow with my forearm, but the force of it sent me staggering. I caught my balance, then set my feet the way Cassian had taught me. Wider. Ready. I caught Thane's next strike once again and let it roll off my frame like water. Another came, higher, closer. Close enough to shear strands free from my braid. Gasps rippled through the others.

He wasn't pulling punches anymore, and I wasn't sure I could keep him back.

Naelle's smugness wavered, Elena's eyes lit with pride so bright it pierced through the fog in my chest, but it was Rhea who burned. I could feel her fury from across the yard, bitter and dense like smoke choking the air.

Thane roared and struck again, this time with every ounce of his frustration.

He was faster now. His precision lost to his rage. Wild and sloppy, driven by the knowledge that this wasn't the overwhelming defeat he had imagined. He swept low again, angling toward my knees. I leapt back mid-air as he twisted to strike at my side.

I turned my body, narrowly avoiding the blow, and landed light on the balls of my feet.

My lungs burned, but I knew his did too.

"*Enough!*" Thane barked, voice rough with exhaustion and humiliation. His chest rose and fell in sharp bursts, sweat darkening the collar of his shirt. He lifted his hands to the air in surrender, though the word never crossed his lips.

He didn't look at me as he turned and stormed away, disappearing into the still morning fog.

I stood there for a moment, heart hammering against my ribs. I'd danced on the edge of a knife. I bowed my head slightly and stepped back toward the others.

Their stares followed me. Naelle wouldn't meet my eyes. Elena grinned openly now, pride warming her face. Even Rhea's scowl had twisted into something more uncertain.

They each drifted away, moving toward the water basins or collapsing onto the stones to stretch aching limbs. My body ached too, but not from the fight. I didn't hurt the way Thane had hoped I would.

I found myself turning, my gaze slipping back toward the palace without meaning to.

Cassian stood in the corridor just beyond the stone archway, flanked by guards, scribes, and a pair of advisors. His head was bowed in conversation, one hand lifted in that elegant, fluid way of his as he gestured. Regal. Composed. Distant.

Until his eyes met mine.

The world dropped out beneath me. Whatever connection we had, whatever bounded us together, surged to life like a storm. No warning. No mercy. He crashed into me like a wave that had been building in silence, waiting for the moment it could break.

His voice wasn't spoken, but I felt it everywhere.

The rose was from me.

It echoed through my blood, my bones, the deepest part of myself that wasn't entirely my own anymore. The petals of that memory unfolded in my mind.

I haven't stopped thinking about you.

The longing that followed was unbearable. Not mine, *his*. Thick and golden, honey-warm and aching. His emotions slid through me like silk, winding around my ribs, curling behind my lungs, pulling so tight I could hardly breathe.

His want was raw and terrible and beautiful. It wasn't clean or controlled. It burned.

The force of it shook me. Shook the air in my lungs and the walls I'd tried so hard to keep up. I dropped my gaze, blinking fast as if I could erase him, but nothing could keep him out.

Cassian's presence clung to me like fire, like breath in winter, invisible at times but deathly obvious at others. Every inch of my skin felt too hot. Every beat of my heart thundered in my ears, in time with his.

I looked around as the training yard dissolved into motion again. Thane had long vanished under the far arch leading back to the palace. The girls stood in loose clusters, not yet dismissed, lingering out of habit.

I couldn't stay. Not with Cassian stuck in my head.

I walked across the yard, past the arch, past Kaden who didn't so much as blink, and past Cassian. I didn't look at him. I couldn't. Not without falling all the way in.

The hallways blurred as my walk turned into a jog, my flats hammering the stone. The air felt thinner the higher I climbed, and yet it still wasn't enough. I needed distance. I needed air that didn't taste like him.

When I reached my room, I was in a full-out sprint. I slammed the door behind me and pressed both palms flat to the wood. My breath came fast and uneven, my heart still galloping, but the sensation of him hadn't faded.

If anything, it had followed me. Burned hotter.

I stumbled to the basin in the corner of my room and wrenched open the spigot. Cold water filled into the copper tub, and I splashed my face again and again. My skin went numb. My fingertips turned blue, but it didn't help. The fire inside me hadn't dimmed. It licked at my spine, my throat, curled beneath my ribs like smoke.

I gripped the sides of the basin, arms trembling, chest rising and falling in sharp, shallow bursts.

What was happening to me?

To *us*?

The bond was no longer just a thread of thoughts. It was a force, living and pulsing and tethered to my every breath. I could feel him even now. No power, no touch, not even *seeing* him. I could feel Cassian's frustration at being surrounded by people, his need to break free of their voices, his silent, unbearable want for me to have stayed just a little while longer.

I pressed the heel of my palm to my chest, as if that could shove him out. As if I could silence whatever had taken root between us.

But there was no escape from it. No shutting him out anymore. The bond had deepened, become something more than emotion, more than thought.

It was instinct.

It was real.

I tried to reread the books I had borrowed from the library. Tried to shift through the thousands of words that stared back at me. I tried to sit on the couch before the windows. I tried to allow the sun to melt away the feeling of him. I closed my eyes, pressing my hands into the plush fabric.

I cleaned my room.

I took a bath. Then another.

I washed, brushed, and again braided my hair.

I organized my armoire yet again, pushing more dresses I would never wear behind spills of colored fabric.

I watched as the sun crested, then began its descent.

I tried to lie down, but my limbs wouldn't still. My body felt like a battle I'd lost without even realizing I'd gone to war. I stood again, pacing the length of my room in tight, agitated circles. My skin continued to buzz, like the sizzle of lightning.

Eventually, I opened the window and stepped out onto the balcony, desperate for air. For anything that didn't reek of cedar and cologne and soft promises I couldn't afford to believe.

The sky had shifted while I'd been spiraling. The day had deepened into evening, and the clouds were tinged with silver. The breeze tugged gently at my braid as I sat on the cold stone floor outside my room, knees drawn to my chest, arms wrapped tight around them. The air swept over my bare feet, but I barely felt it. Below, the palace still pulsed with life—soft footsteps, hushed laughter, distant voices drifting like ghosts through open windows.

I rested my cheek against my bent knees and closed my eyes just before a knock, soft and tentative, sounded at my door.

I went still. My power stirred in me, instinctual now. I reached out with just a thread, a whisper of silver through the air.

Elena.

I exhaled, tension loosening. My heart lifted, unspooling some of the tightness in my chest. I stood and padded across the room, already knowing before I cracked open the door.

There she was.

Elena stood barefoot in the corridor, wrapped in a flowing white sleep dress, her long black hair unbound and curling softly around her shoulders. She looked so unlike the sharp-tongued girl I'd sparred with. She looked young and fragile and insanely scared.

"I couldn't stand being alone anymore," she whispered.

I didn't hesitate. I stepped aside and let her in.

She slipped inside without another word, hands knotting in front of her. The candlelight painted warm gold across her features, casting long shadows that made her eyes seem darker, deeper.

"I thought I'd be fine, honestly," she began, her gaze fixed on the rug. "In the garden earlier, for training, I even convinced myself I was. But now—now all I can think about is the trial. What if I lose? What if I go back to my region with nothing?"

Her voice cracked. She blinked quickly, her fingers twisting in the sleeve of her gown.

"They'll all expect something of me," she said. "Something great. Something perfect. And if I fail…"

She trailed off, the words unfinished. Her eyes went glassy with unshed tears. I didn't need to hear the rest to understand.

Before I could think, I crossed the room and wrapped my arms around her.

Fabric stayed between us, but I held on tightly. No rehearsed politeness. No calculated comfort. Just the simple act of holding someone because they needed it.

It felt strange, but real and right. It was the first genuine hug I could remember giving.

"They'll be proud of you no matter what," I murmured against her hair. "I know I would be."

She blinked up at me, her lashes clumped from spilled tears. She just gave a small nod, just once.

Trying to lift the mood, I stepped back and managed a faint smile. I grabbed the dress she had let me wear when she had comforted me, and I returned it like an offering. "Want me to braid your hair? Like I said earlier?"

Elena's face lit up like the moonlight from the night sky outside had reached her. She took the dress and her shoulders relaxed, the tightness in her posture softening.

"Yes. Yes, please."

We sat on the edge of my bed, close enough that our knees brushed. I gently gathered her thick black hair into my hands, fingers parting it with a slow rhythm. I was careful of every touch, keeping space between my fingertips and her scalp. Her hair was soft, heavier than I'd expected, and shimmered like liquid ink in the firelight.

My hands moved on instinct—twisting, weaving, looping. She closed her eyes as I worked. Her breathing slowed. I coiled the braids up at the crown of her head, pinning them delicately into place. She looked like a painting, strong and luminous and untouchable.

When I finished, she turned her head side to side, squealing softly. "It's perfect. I love it. Thank you—*thank you!*"

Her joy was infectious. I laughed, and it was real. It was the kind of laugh that cracked something open inside me, and for a little while, we were just girls.

We sat on the balcony's edge, chins up towards the sky watching as the sunset gave away to the star-dotted night sky. We whispered about the trial, half-joking and half-dreading what we'd wear—if anything could help us survive with our dignity intact. When the wind bit and whipped at our hair, we moved inside. I closed the glass windows as she crawled into my bed.

She yawned as I joined her, her body slowly curling into the lush pillows and blankets.

"Will finally admitted he liked me," she murmured. "He asked me to stay here, with him. He said he'd marry me."

I nudged her gently with a pillow. "He'd be a fool not to."

She smiled sleepily, eyes fluttering half-closed.

Then, so soft I barely heard her, she asked, "What about the Prince?"

My fingers stilled.

Elena blinked up at me, drowsy but steady. "I've seen the way you look at him. And how he looks at you."

I swallowed, suddenly aware of every breath I was taking.

"You don't have to say anything," she added quickly. "I just wanted you to know…I would never take that from you."

I opened my mouth to respond, but no words came.

She smiled faintly. "You deserve to be happy too," she murmured, and closed her eyes.

The silence that followed wasn't heavy. It wasn't strained. It was warm, like an embrace left behind. I laid, watching her curl up in the silk like something soft and wild that had wandered into my life without permission.

You deserve to be happy too.

The words sank into me, deeper than I expected. Like seed into soil. I didn't know if they would bloom, but I let them settle there, untouched.

The moonlight spilled across the floor, painting silver lines over the blankets. The balcony door was still open, and the breeze whispered gently through the room. And it didn't feel like a cage tonight.

It felt like mine.

CHAPTER THIRTY

THE MORNING PASSED IN a blur of dreamy grogginess and nervous laughter.

Pale light streamed through the glass doors, coating everything in soft hues. It felt strange, waking with someone else nearby. Familiar, in a way I hadn't felt since being with Selene. Elena moved with quiet ease, already looking in the mirror at her braided crown before my feet had even hit the ground. She twirled her sleep dress around her as if the woven hairs on her head were solid gold.

I had only just pulled open the armoire when Elena let out a delighted sound behind me. She reached toward the very back of the wardrobe and tugged something free.

"Can I...?" she asked, holding up the pink ruffled dress.

I stared at it. All rose and blush layers, cascading satin ribbons. It looked like spun sugar—overly sweet, overly delicate. I'd shoved it back there for a reason.

"You actually want to wear that?"

Elena laughed, but there was a dreamy softness to her expression. "It's the most romantic thing I've ever seen."

I snorted, but I couldn't help smiling. "You can just take it. It'll get more use from you than it ever will from me."

Her eyes widened. "I could not possibly take this. I—I couldn't."

I leaned toward her, resting a hand gently on her shoulder. Her skin was warm beneath my palm, even through her nightgown. "Elena, you can have a dress I never planned to wear. Especially with all you've done for me."

For a heartbeat, I thought she might cry again, but her lips just spread into a glowing smile, radiant and soft, like she was holding something too fragile to speak aloud. Then she turned to the bed, grabbed the gown she'd given me and held it up with both hands.

"Then I guess this must be yours."

I rolled my eyes but grinned anyway, taking the gown with a huff of mock-exasperation. "Fine. You win."

I hung it up neatly and reached instead for the bottom drawer of my armoire. I pulled out the dress that had been saved for me. The one I had worn when chosen for this madness. The one I had purchased with Selene.

We dressed in comfortable silence, helping tie each other's laces and smooth out wrinkles. It felt easy, natural. The pale blue fabric was thick on my body. The layers were more than I had grown accustomed to here in the Aurea heat, but that was no deterrent. I slipped on my silk gloves, welcoming the cool fabric against my skin.

When I finally opened the wooden door, I was already bracing myself. The lock clicked open, unlocked and waiting.

And there he was. Back from whatever depths he was hiding in. Or hiding from.

Kaden stood in the hallway, already waiting. His posture was rigid, hands clasped behind his back, face carved from stone. That same unsettling stillness clung to him, the hollowness I'd come to dread. Beside him stood a guard I could only assume to be Elena's.

She leaned in close, her voice barely a whisper. "He's different lately, isn't he?" Elena tilted her head towards Kaden.

The question pulled something tight in my chest.

I gave a small shrug, pretending not to feel the chill crawl down my spine. "He was promoted. I think he's just... taking it seriously."

Breakfast in the mess hall was chaos.

Nobles and servants swarmed the long tables, filling the space with chatter and nervous energy. Rhea and Naelle lingered near the walls like vultures, watching, calculating. I kept my head down as I grabbed a plate—fresh fruit, a lemon pastry, a steaming cup of tea. My stomach fluttered too much to eat most of it, but the tea helped soothe the edge of dread rising in my throat.

Across from me, Elena barely managed a bite before a familiar figure approached.

Will wore the same crisp servant uniform, but he looked less formal somehow, like he couldn't quite contain the smile tugging at his mouth. His bow was awkward, endearing, and Elena lit up like a lantern.

I grinned at her and waved them off. "Go. He's been waiting for you."

She didn't argue. Just blushed furiously and slipped away, laughing behind her hand.

That left me alone.

Which, truthfully, was fine. I needed focus. Centering. Something to make me feel like I had any form of control over what came next.

I grabbed my plate and made my way to the library once more.

The room was quieter than usual, almost eerie. Sunlight filtered through the tall arched windows, painting the marble floor in gold and shadow. I combed the shelves for anything useful. After far too long, I finally found a heavy, dusty tome tucked in a corner.

Aurean Martial Lineage: Discipline Through Design.

The title alone made me want to fall asleep, but I dragged it to a table near the window and cracked it open.

Dense didn't even begin to cover it. The pages were lined with diagrams, archaic terminology, and rigid stances that seemed better suited for statues than humans, but Rhea was Aurean. If there was even one move in here that could help me avoid getting my ribs crushed tomorrow, it would be worth it.

I pressed a hand to the edge of the open page, trying to focus, but my mind kept drifting. I was halfway through skimming a chapter on reverse blade sweeps when I felt it.

A pull.

Subtle at first, like the whisper of a breeze against the back of my neck. Then firmer. Warmer. A golden thread, invisible and pulsing, curled around my ribs and gave the gentlest tug forward. It wasn't physical, not exactly, but I felt it as surely as if someone had placed a hand to the small of my back.

It felt like him.

That same maddening softness and steel. Gentle and kind, yet unyielding. Passionate. Determined. Fire clothed in silk.

I closed the book without thinking, not even marking the page, and left it on the desk. My feet were already moving.

Down one corridor, up a wide marble staircase. Around a bend I didn't recognize. The palace shifted around me like a dream, familiar yet not. Like a place I had walked through in memory rather than waking life. I didn't question it. I just followed, letting that golden thread wind through me, guide me.

The thread brought me to a room I'd never seen before, and the second I stepped across the threshold, it stole the breath from my lungs.

Paintings covered every inch of the room. Not just the walls, but the ceilings and floor too. Art bled across every surface, saturating the space with color and memory. Soldiers in battle. Coronations. Sunlit fields thick with poppies. Storm-dark oceans. A child running through a meadow of stars. Every canvas glowed with life, the light catching on metallic frames and rich oils until it felt like the whole room shimmered. Even the windows were covered in paintings on thick canvas, turning the sunlight into stained-glass—gold and crimson and sapphire bleeding into each other.

The marble floor beneath me reflected it all, illuminating painted shapes with a dreamlike glow.

I drifted through it like a ghost, trying to soak in every brushstroke, every hue. There was a reverence in the air, like a chapel made of memory.

At the far end of the gallery, something small caught my eye. Tucked into a corner, nearly forgotten.

A tiny frame, no more than a foot across, nestled low along the base of the wall. I knelt in front of it slowly, knees touching the cold marble. It was empty. The decorated frame glistened silver, but no painting filled the space inside.

I reached to brush my fingers along the empty frame's edge when the thread stirred and pulled me yet again.

It coiled up my spine, soft and burning, and filled me with warmth. I stood, breath shallow, and turned toward the end of the gallery.

An archway waited there, and beyond it, an armory.

This wasn't a training space or a weapons cache. This was a gallery of relics. Of kings and soldiers. Golden suits of armor stood in perfect formation, lined up like sentinels. Each one shimmered with embedded gems—sapphires and rubies and emeralds, armor that looked more like treasure than something meant for battle.

They glistened in the sunlight like fragments of the sun itself.

I let out a soft snort. "Like anyone could actually fight in that." I said, just to myself.

Still, I wandered through them, drawn forward. I dragged my fingertips along the cold metal as I passed. Each suit was more ridiculous than the last. Rubies in the shape of roses. Shoulders shaped like lion heads. Capes threaded with golden beading.

But one caught my eye.

A set of charcoal armor covered in deep blue sapphires, dark and cool and gleaming like the sky after a storm. The exact color of the skies over Virellia after a storm. Calm and rain-washed. It was smaller, dainty in a way that shouldn't be possibly when speaking about armor. It tugged at something inside me, something nostalgic, but the thread didn't want me there.

It pulled my eyes farther. Not my body, just my gaze, and I saw it.

Tucked away at the very front, almost hidden behind a pillar. A suit unlike the others.

Black obsidian.

No gold. No jewels. No ridiculous flourishes. Just black shards in the shape of knives that gleamed despite their deep black, absorbing light and shadow both. It looked ancient. Older than anything else in the room.

I approached slowly, like I was walking toward a beast that might stir at any second.

The armor wasn't beautiful. Not in the way the others were. But it was staggering. Powerful. It radiated something else. Something heavy. Like it had seen things. Endured things. Carried the weight of a hundred battles.

I raised my hand, fingertips just shy of the metal, though I wasn't even sure if it was metal. It vibrated faintly. Buzzed with a kind of energy I didn't have a name for. Magic, maybe. Or memory. The golden thread hummed louder in my chest, but I couldn't bring myself to touch it.

I lowered my hand. Let the thread lead me forward again.

Past the obsidian armor. Around the edge of the room. A small servant's door was tucked into the wall behind it, nearly hidden. I eased it open and found a narrow spiral staircase leading upward. Passages sprawled out, all leading here. To this one tower. I wonder where they began. I wonder who had traveled them.

Dust clung to the steps. The air thinned as I climbed, tasting like age and forgotten time.

At the top was a small arched door.

The wood was old, faded gray with age, a long crack running from base to center. A sliver of sunlight bled through it, spilling across the stone floor in a golden line.

I pushed it open.

The turret was small. Empty. A narrow space with a large square window cut into the far wall.

The world stretched out before me in soft, endless color. Rolling hills unfurled like a painting, each one kissed with light. The palace gardens spread below in waves of green and bloom. Just beyond them, the lagoon glittered in the morning sun. And farther still, like a mirage, the sea shimmered like poured glass, silver-blue and endless.

I stepped forward, hands pressing to the low stone sill. The wind kissed my cheeks. The silence was sacred. I didn't know what this moment was supposed to be, only that it felt like something.

Like the beginning of something new.

I felt that golden thread pull once more, but this time it wasn't toward a place. It was toward him. I turned.

Cassian stood in the doorway.

His crown sat slanted on his head. It caught the last thread of light, casting fractured gold down his cheekbones. That lavender coat he wore shifted gently with the breeze, catching the air like waving water. His curls were unruly and wind-swept, as if the world hadn't dared tame them. His eyes—stars, those eyes—honey-gold and burning, brighter than the horizon behind him. Like the sun had set just to rise inside him.

And in that very moment I knew that he had brought me here. I wasn't sure how, or why, but he had led me to this moment, to this place.

It had been him. It had always been him.

He didn't say anything. He just stepped forward, slowly, carefully, as though I might vanish if he moved too fast. I felt the restraint in him. I felt the way he wore his control like armor. Every movement precise and cautious. His logic wove through the air like chainmail, holding him back, so I broke first.

Not with words, but with truth.

I opened myself to him.

I unlatched the lid I kept locked tight and let my power unfurl. It spilled out like a ribbon through my gloves, threading through the space between us. I let it whisper. Let it ache. Let it want.

The wave of it circled him gently, like the tide curling around stone.

I saw the exact moment it found him. The slight hitch of his breath. The way his eyes flared. How they dropped, flicking down to my lips like a prayer he wasn't ready to speak.

Another step. Closer.

He was within reach now. If I moved, I could touch him, but I didn't. I stayed rooted where I was.

I let him come to me.

I let my power brush his skin, just a nudge, or maybe a plea.

Whatever it was, he understood.

Cassian surged forward, and then his mouth was on mine.

The kiss wasn't soft, not at first. It was fierce, like the sea crashing against shore. Like a wildfire that had waited too long to burn. His hands found my waist and pulled me in hard, until my chest pressed to his, my body caged against his heat and breath and fire.

He tasted like honey and sunlight. He was warm and sweet.

My hands rose along his arms, but he stopped me. Without breaking the kiss, he pulled my hands into his and slipped the gloves from my skin. The fabric whispered as it hit the floor.

"Wha—" I began to ask, but his hand only tangled with my hair, cutting off the words as he deepened the kiss.

His hand slid down to cradle the back of my neck, fingers still threaded through my hair, anchoring me like I might dissolve into the air if he didn't hold me tight enough. The other moved to hold firmly at my waist, grounding me. His fingers dug into my side, wanting me close. Wanting all of me.

My knees nearly gave out.

Our emotions tangled instantly—his, mine, both. I couldn't tell them apart. All I knew was that I was drowning in the flood of it. Need. Longing. Desperation. Devotion. It all surged between us like a second heartbeat.

And then—slower. Softer.

Like he couldn't bear to let go but remembered he had to breathe.

He drew back just enough to rest his forehead against mine. His breath was hot against my lips, unsteady breaths rasping. His voice was barely a whisper, hoarse and breaking.

"I know what my father did."

My stomach twisted. Cold slithered up my spine.

"I know what happened to Kaden," he whispered. "I'm so sorry, Lyra. I never meant—" His voice caught, cracked. He brushed his thumb down my scar. "I never meant for this to happen."

He kept apologizing. For everything.

The trials. Thane. His father. The greenhouse. Me.

It all spilled out of him like a wound he'd been holding too tightly shut.

But I didn't want the apologies. So, I kissed him again. Soft this time. Not to silence him, never to silence him, just to hold the moment still. His lips met mine again like he understood, and when I finally pulled back, eyes still closed, I let myself savor that last brush of his warmth.

When I opened them, he was already looking at me. His eyes traveled down my face, studying every feature as if he was committing it to memory.

Something had shifted in his gaze. Something deeper, something steadier. Passionate.

Understanding, maybe.

He didn't say another word.

Instead, he stepped past me and walked to the low windowsill. The cold stone barely seeming to register as he sat down. He held out his hand.

I didn't hesitate. I reached for him.

His fingers wrapped around mine, and he pulled me into him until I stood between his legs. His skin hummed beneath mine, electric and alive like the world had lit a fuse just beneath my bones.

He guided me up onto the ledge, and I let him. His arm curled around my waist, my head found his chest, and we sat there, tangled in each other. I imagined a painting of this moment. I pictured the window being the frame and the swirls of color that would create the flaming sunset and the scene before it. The sea shimmered below us like melted glass. The lagoon glittered. The garden sighed beneath us like it had waited its whole life for this stillness. And for a little while we just breathed.

Cassian was the one to break the silence. "I see you finally received my gift. Or finally decided to put it to use."

I rolled my head across to his shoulder, craning up to meet his eyes. "What gift?"

He chuckles, low and soft. "After you were so incredibly upset I burned your gloves, the least I could do was save your Drawing Day gown."

My heart seemed to stop beating. My lungs stopped breathing air.

"How—how did you know it was mine?"

"Virellian carriages are always white. And I assumed since you were the only lady traveling, the gown belonged to you."

The dress had been from him. All this time, it had always been him. My eyes suddenly went glassy, and the only response I could muster was a small smile.

As the sun dipped lower, the stone beneath us began to cool. The golden light that had turned the world soft and safe slipped behind the edge of the ocean. I didn't want to move, didn't want to break the

228

spell, but Cassian pressed a soft kiss to the top of my head before shifting underneath me.

He held my waist as I slid down from the ledge and then followed behind me. His fingers caught mine again, interlacing them like it was the most natural thing in the world. We paused at the window one last time, watching as the sky turned navy blue, as the hush of evening settled over the land.

We didn't speak as we descended the tower. Our steps were slow and quiet, but the silence wasn't empty.

When we reached the base, he turned to me. His gaze flicked in the direction of my room, an unspoken question in his eyes.

I gave the smallest shake of my head. No. Not yet. I didn't want to be alone. He didn't push. He just understood.

We slipped through the palace halls together and stepped out into the night of the gardens. Moonlight painted the marble paths silver. The roses were drenched in misty white. The breeze carried the scent of jasmine and sea salt, a reminder that somewhere out there, the ocean kept breathing.

Cassian was the first to speak. "You can pick who you fight," he said, his voice soft and careful, like one wrong word might shatter me. "Just say a name, and I'll see to it."

I paused. The King's voice coiled through my mind like smoke

"The pieces on the board are not always his to move."

I shifted to look at Cassian, letting my gaze settle on his face. His eyes were molten amber in the low light, threaded with worry and something heavier.

"I want it to be fair," I said quietly. "I only want to win if it's deserved."

His features tensed. Pain flickered there, sharp and raw. He turned toward me fully, his voice lowering. "Lyra, I don't know what constitutes losing."

Dread bloomed in my chest, but I didn't let it show. If my opponent sought to kill me, stars have mercy, I'd put up a fight.

"No," I said. Just that. Firm and steady. I couldn't afford to let fear decide for me.

He sighed and pulled the crown from his head to run a hand through his windswept curls. His fingers knotted in the strands before dropping to the back of his neck. He rubbed there absently, like he was trying to work out a tension that had lodged itself in his bones.

Then he turned and walked a few steps ahead, his shoulders slumped in a rare show of defeat. He sat down on a stone bench, the same one where Rhea had once tried to stab me. That moment felt like it belonged to another life. Another version of me.

Cassian sat in silence, then looked up. Something passed between us. Unspoken. Real.

I crossed the space slowly and sat beside him. Without really thinking, I slid down and laid my head in his lap. My braid had come undone. Loose strands of snow-white hair spilled over his legs like threads of moonlight, messy and wild.

He stroked the strands gently, careful with the tangles. His callused fingers caught now and then, rough against the silk of it, but there was something grounding in the imperfection of the touch. Something so delicately human.

"Would you like to hear a bedtime story?" he asked, teasing. A smile tugged at the corner of his mouth, soft and lopsided.

I snorted. "That's what you're going with? The night before the trial?"

He chuckled. The sound wrapped around me like warmth. "Don't judge it yet."

And so, beneath the hush of stars and the soft breath of roses blooming in the dark, Cassian told me a story.

"There were once two bloodlines," he began, his voice slow and rhythmic, like the beginning of a myth. "Both gifted by the stars. One could know their people. Feel them, read them, understand their thoughts and emotions better than even they could themselves. They were gold blooded, and their people were called Aurum."

His fingers kept stroking through my hair.

"But the other... the other was different. More powerful, some would say. They could control minds, emotions, even memories. They could create thoughts and dreams and fears with nothing more than their will. They had silver blood. Argentum."

My body went still. His hand didn't stop moving. If anything, it gentled.

"People feared them," he continued. "Called them witches. Monsters. Eventually, the Aurum rose to power. They used their gifts in quieter ways. Persuasion. Manipulation. They took the throne and the Argentums became scapegoats. Controlled weapons... until one of them wasn't.

"She was wild. Powerful. She led a rebellion—a coup. She had a daughter, white-haired and silver-skinned. But the rebellion failed. The mother was executed, and the daughter was stolen away, hidden far from the kingdom. Taken to a place where she would never discover who she was."

His hand slowed in my hair. I didn't dare move.

"The King ordered all Argentum killed. Some tried to flee, but day after day they died. One was a boy. A child. The Queen begged for his life. She wanted to raise him as their own, but the King refused. When he tried to kill the boy, the Queen threw herself in the way. She died protecting someone everyone else feared."

I couldn't breathe. I sat up slowly, and as I did Cassian's hand left my hair. He placed his crown atop my head. It settled crooked there, sitting there as if it had no where else to rest. He looked at me then, and as his eyes met mine, I saw it. The dream, it hadn't been just a nightmare. It had been real. His mother. His story. This wasn't some bedtime fable.

"They never found the girl," he said, voice barely above a whisper. "It's said she still lives. Somewhere in the kingdom. Waiting. Gathering strength. For the next rebellion."

My lungs burned. I hadn't realized I'd been holding my breath until my ribs started to ache.

That story was a story in name only. Every word had been laced with something far too fragile, far too haunted, to be fiction. It had been history. I sat up slowly, my body stiff and coiled tight. The night air felt thinner now, like it couldn't hold the weight between us.

Cassian met my gaze with quiet intensity, and I felt it. The truths we hadn't spoken. The pain we couldn't name.

"You should sleep," he said gently, brushing a loose strand of hair away from my face. His hand lingered. His eyes flicked to the crown on my brow. He cupped my jaw, and I leaned into the touch, just for a second. Just long enough to feel like something in this world might still be stable. Sparks sizzled there, but no thoughts came in their wake.

"You'll win tomorrow, Lyra," he said. "Because you have no other choice."

The garden suddenly felt too vast. The palace beyond it, too cold. I gave the faintest nod, then rose to my feet. I took the crown from my head and sat the metal ring on the bench. I turned and walked away, his words echoing behind me. The warmth of his hand still ghosted across my cheek like a promise. Or a farewell.

He didn't follow me, but I could feel his eyes on me the whole way back, watching until the palace swallowed me whole.

CHAPTER THIRTY-ONE

THE SKY OUTSIDE WAS barely awake, dusted with rose and ash. I sat with my back pressed to the cold stone of the balcony ledge, knees pulled to my chest, the air biting at my skin through the thin fabric of my nightdress. This ledge had become the only peaceful corner of my room. The rest of it was full of polished floors, elegant drapes, gold-framed mirrors. It all felt too beautiful and carefully arranged. A cage disguised in velvet clothing.

I turned my head back toward the desk. A leather uniform sat waiting, laid out in careful symmetry. Strips of brown, soft to the touch but built for war, not pageantry. Kaden must have delivered it while I was with Cassian in the gardens. The memory flickered through me. His voice, his story, the way his hand had moved through my hair like it belonged there. His crown on my head. I had returned to my room only to carefully pack away my dress once more and stretch the hours as long as they allowed.

But now, that world had ended.

I rose and padded barefoot across the chilled floor. The leather caught what little morning light seeped through the curtains, its buckles gleaming faintly. No frills. No silver threading or embroidered crests. Just clean, functional violence. The black nightdress slipped off me like a solid shadow, pooling at my feet. The leather hugged tighter than I expected, like it remembered me. The torso straps crossed over my ribs and shoulders like an armored corset. Each buckle looped into place with finality. My arms felt stronger. My breathing steadied. I tugged on my leather gloves and boots, fastening them tight.

I sat at my desk and tugged a brush through my hair. The strands were soft from Cassian's touch, tangled only at the ends. I braided it like I had Elena's, weaving each section tightly and pinning them around my head until it resembled a crown of snow. No loose strands. Nothing for someone to grab.

I opened my door before the knock could land.

Kaden stood there, arm raised mid-motion. His eyes widened slightly, surprised. He let his hand fall back to his side.

He looked… different this morning. Still distant and unnervingly still, but his gaze lingered longer than usual, drifting down my face, my shoulders, the uniform. He didn't speak. Just nodded once and turned to walk. I followed, falling into step beside him.

For once, he didn't trail in front like a shadow stuck to the wall.

We entered the mess hall together.

The shift in the air was immediate and thick with unease. The silence wasn't total, but it hovered above every whispered word and scraped fork. A room of predators pacing the edge of their cages, pretending to be calm.

The long tables were half-filled. Servants moved quietly along the edges, laying out food no one seemed interested in eating. Rhea and Naelle sat across from each other at the far end, their trays untouched save for clear glasses of water sweating against the wood. They both wore their own leathers, the thick material twisting over their own bodies as it did mine. They didn't speak. Just watched. Rhea's eyes flicked up at me once, then away. Naelle stared at her hands like they held a weapon no one else could see.

Elena wasn't there.

My chest tightened, but I forced myself to keep moving. I sat at the far corner of the table, Kaden silently dropping into the seat beside me. The plate before me was filled with things I normally loved. Slices of melon, sweet berries, soft rolls with golden crusts, and warm honeyed tea stared back at me, as if chosen by someone else.

My stomach curled in on itself. Everything smelled too strong, too sharp, too sweet. I picked up a piece of fruit and moved it to the side of the plate. Then another. My fork tapped gently against the porcelain, marking time I didn't want to measure.

I sipped my tea, but the taste was bitter today, like ash in my mouth. My nerves were a live wire beneath my skin. Every clatter of cutlery made me flinch. Every brush of fabric sounded like a blade being drawn.

No one said anything out loud, but we all felt the tension in the air.

A horn sounded, the noise soft and distant. Naelle and Rhea stood, and their guards immediately joined them at their sides.

I rose and left first. No words. No glances. Just motion. My body moved before my mind caught up. I didn't wait for Kaden. I didn't need to. I knew where to go.

The arena was already roaring.

Not the eerie silence from the maze trial. Not the collective hush of suspense. This was something else entirely. The noise poured down the palace halls like smoke through a keyhole. The sound was thick and choking, alive with fire. I didn't have to see it to know. The crowd had come for blood, and this time, they would get it.

The corridors under the arena ran like a rectangle, each tunnel extending down the sides. A guard stood at the intersection between two of these halls, jerking his head right to signal me along. I followed his directions, and eventually a narrow passageway broke off towards the deafening sound of people above. A small wooden sign was hung above the opening.

Miss Seravell

I entered the mouth of the passage and stopped. The cheers thundered above me, loud and violent, the crowd stomping and chanting, drumbeats slamming into my bones like fists. Dirt and small stones crumbled from the ceiling, hitting my shoulders as they fell. Every step above reverberated through the stone walls, a heartbeat not my own.

Metal scraped behind me, rough and screeching along the stone floor.

I spun around just in time to see a heavy steel door stop shut. A royal guard stood there, grinning faintly as he locked it. I hadn't even noticed him until it was too late.

"Locked in," I murmured, more to myself than him. "Perfect."

He didn't speak. Just turned and walked back into the shadows.

The bars shimmered in the torchlight. The metal was thick and roped. This was the kind of metal used in cells, not corridors, but perhaps that was the point. Perhaps this was a cell.

I stared at the door for a long beat, feeling the newfound instinct rise—to reach out, to brush against the edges of the guard's mind, to see what was lurking there—but I stopped myself. I didn't want to know what he thought of me. I didn't feel like gaining another enemy this morning.

Instead, I turned toward the light.

The tunnel stretched out before me, straight and narrow, the end glowing with harsh, blinding sunlight. I started walking, the sound of my boots echoing off stone. My breaths came slow but shallow. The leather of my uniform creaked softly as I moved. The sunlight hit my eyes like a blade. I lifted a hand to block it, squinting until my vision sharpened.

The thoughts. The emotions. The minds.

They pressed in from all sides. Thousands of voices, shouting and screaming, not with their mouths but with their souls. Every flicker of rage, thrill, bloodlust, and anticipation flooded toward me like a wave crashing against my skull.

It felt like my head had cracked open. Like someone had pried apart the edges of my mind and poured in the chaos of a city's worth of people. Too many thoughts. Too much noise. A thousand fragments stabbing in from every direction. I couldn't focus on a single one. I couldn't pluck one from the crowd, couldn't focus my power. They came by their own will.

I'd rather kneel to the King a thousand times than see her with a crown.

Virellian trash, parading through the palace like she belongs.

She should be shackled.

She's a ghost from a dying bloodline.

Just another northern brat.

Let her burn.

She's beautiful.

She's a monster.

Weak.

Fraud.

Silver.

My knees almost buckled.

I couldn't fight like this.

I clenched my jaw, forcing myself to breathe. In and out. In and out. The powers inside me, always lurking and waiting, tore at my skin. Hungry. Restless. Begging to be loosed. I shook my head. Not yet.

Not now.

I imagined the jar again. My mind wrapped tight around the lid, clamping it closed with iron will. I sealed it. Locked it. The thoughts dulled, fell away like distant thunder. My breath returned.

I could breathe again, just barely, until I looked up.

Now I knew who those thoughts had belonged to.

The stands stretched higher than I'd ever imagined, rising tier after tier into the sky. Thousands upon thousands of people filled them, all pressed shoulder to shoulder, standing, shouting, leaning over the rails like gods watching mortals wage war below. The energy in the air was tangible, buzzing like static beneath my skin. It wasn't just a crowd. It was a storm.

They were chanting. *Screaming names.*

I wondered briefly if mine was among them.

The arena floor beneath my boots was hard-packed sand, bordered by a low stone wall. Across from me, I could see three more tunnel openings—one on each side wall, and one to the left of where I stood.

Above it all, like the eye of the storm, sat the royal pavilion.

The gilded structure looked almost delicate from a distance, strung with trailing flowers in white and violet. But it wasn't delicate, it was deliberate. Every petal, every drape of silk had been placed to elevate the man seated at the center of it all.

The King.

He sat on his golden throne, unmovable, unshakable, and untouchable. His face seemed carved from the same marble as the palace and was utterly void of humanity. To his right, seated slightly below him, was Cassian. His chair was simpler. No jewels or grandeurs adorned him, but he didn't need any.

The sun hit him like it had chosen him, coating his honey blonde hair in molten light. His posture was relaxed, but his eyes were fixed on me. I felt it like heat against my skin. His gaze didn't waver, and there was something in the way he looked at me that made the roar of the crowd fade for a moment. Not gone, but just... distant.

I turned slowly, my hands curling into fists at my sides. My heart thundered in my chest, loud enough I was sure someone could hear it.

The others entered one by one, each from a different tunnel.

To the right, Rhea strode in first, her steps slow and confident, her head high like a champion before the battle had even begun. She didn't scan the crowd. She didn't need to. She knew they were watching her. Feeding off her fire. Her golden hair shimmered beneath the sunlight, and her smile was already the kind meant for a victor's circle.

To the left, Naelle emerged. Her usual smirk played across her lips, her eyes flicking toward the stands as if she were drinking in the adoration, but there was nothing behind her eyes. She was just a mirror reflecting what others wanted to see. I could sense it. Confidence that was empty and bright yet fragile.

The crowd erupted. Cheers and stomps, whistles and claps. Thunderous approval.

Not for me.

Never for me.

And then, Elena.

She stumbled from the tunnel to my left, her figure small and uncertain as she entered the sunlight. Her face looked paler than I'd ever thought possible, like the color had been drained from her skin. Her hair once braided into a crown hung haphazardly with rogue strands. Her arms curled slightly around her middle, as though she were already wounded.

"Elena?" I whispered.

She didn't look at me. She didn't look at anyone. Her gaze was fixed straight ahead, unfocused. Her steps were slow, like she might fall apart if she moved too fast.

Something was wrong.

I turned toward her fully, worry rising fast in my chest. I took one step forward—

Pain exploded through my side.

A sharp, burning burst just beneath my ribs. I gasped—an involuntary, broken sound—and staggered. My hand flew to my right side instinctively, and when I pulled it away, my palm was slick.

Blood.

I stared at it, blinking, as though my brain couldn't comprehend what I was seeing.

A firm hand pressed against my other side, shoving me into the blade, into the pain, into her.

"Don't fall," came a voice beside me. Soft. Sweet. Familiar.

Rhea.

I turned my head slowly, the edges of my vision going white with pain.

She stood beside me, her expression the picture of innocent curiosity. Smiling like an old friend might when checking in after a long absence. Only I could feel the heat of her breath at my ear. Her blade was no longer than two inches and slid out from the side of my uniform, disappearing just as quickly. The tip of it still glistened red.

No one had seen.

No one had even looked.

"Just a reminder," she whispered against my ear. "Consider this my warning. *Walk. Away.*"

I didn't answer. I couldn't. My teeth were locked against the scream trying to claw its way out. My knees buckled slightly, but I forced myself upright. I would not give her the satisfaction.

Instead, I took a shaky step back like nothing had happened. Like she hadn't just *stabbed* me.

The leather was soaked already, warm and wet, the blood blooming through the brown like a spreading flower. I pressed my hand to my side harder, trying to get the bleeding to at least slow down. The sight of so much blood was beginning to make my head spin. Or maybe it was the loss of it.

I couldn't breathe properly. Every inhale was fire. Anger flared, but it wasn't mine. It surged from somewhere else, a storm pressing against the edges of my mind, thick and hot and furious.

Cassian was sitting still, but his hand gripped the armrest of his chair so tightly I could see the whiteness in his knuckles from across the arena. I felt the flare of his fury brushing against my thoughts, his presence sliding into the corners of my mind like a familiar shadow.

He knew.

I slammed that jar of power shut. Sealed it. Barred it. I couldn't let him in. Not right now. Not when everything was unraveling.

I forced myself to stand straight and lift my chin. No one else had noticed, or maybe they had and simply didn't care.

The announcer stepped forward toward the great iron horn, the sunlight catching on the gold trim of his robe as he raised it to his lips. When he spoke, his voice thundered across the arena, thick and formal and final.

"The fourth trial. Two rounds. Miss Rhea Damaris versus Miss Elena Morwyn. Miss Lyra Seravell versus Miss Naelle Zarathos."

My name echoed in my ears, but it wasn't the sound of it that stunned me. It was the pairings.

To my left, I heard a horrible, wet retching noise, and when I turned, I saw Elena doubled over, her hands braced against her knees, vomiting onto the sand.

She looked ghostly pale, her skin almost translucent beneath the harsh sun, and now her lips had taken on a bluish tinge. She was shivering, barely able to stand.

The arena floor had been marked with two massive circles made of blue-colored sand. Each was wide enough for a full duel but close enough that every clash, every fall, every drop of blood would be seen by both the crowd and the combatants.

The matches would happen at once.

A guard gestured for us to move forward.

My legs obeyed, but every step toward the ring was agony. The gash in my side screamed with each movement, the torn leather of my uniform pressing hard into the wound. It felt like the edges of the cut were pulling wider with every breath I took.

Naelle had already reached the circle. Arms folded in front of her chest. One foot cocked casually to the side. She looked like she was waiting for someone to bring her a glass of wine, not like she was about to enter combat.

I stepped into the circle, my boots smearing the blue sand ring out of place. A gust of wind stirred dust into the air, and the sun beat down on us both. My legs trembled beneath me, not from fear, but from the sheer force of the pain. The horn sounded.

Naelle didn't charge. She began to circle, slow and deliberate, as though she had all the time in the world. Her gaze flicked down to my side once, then back to my face. She smiled.

A predator hunting wounded prey.

I knew I couldn't win like this, so I opened the jar.

Not all the way. Just enough. Enough to let my power slip free like a mist, unseen and quiet. I pushed it again the leather of my gloves, trying to force the shimmering silver through the thickness, but nothing came. It was trapped.

I ripped the wrist straps from my gloves, tearing the buttons off with the rough movement. I pulled the leather from my hands, throwing them down in the sand. My power rushed, free from the prison that now laid discarded below me. It coiled outward, invisible to the crowd, slithering across the sand and up Naelle's boots, winding around her thighs, her waist, her chest. Whispers from the crowd leaked in more frequently than ever, but my power knew its target, and I felt the instant it reached Naelle's mind.

Thoughts flowed like ripples in water, faint and fleeting, but they were enough.

Naelle lunged, her hand pulled back for a strike.

I stepped sideways and caught her wrist before it could land.

She twisted into a low kick.

I ducked, narrowly missing the sweep.

She grunted in frustration and moved faster, but her thoughts betrayed her before her body could.

Every movement sent pain tearing through my side. My limbs were heavy and sluggish, and my reactions started to slow. I could read her, but my body was a second too late in answering.

She clipped my jaw with her elbow. Her boot slammed into my thigh.

I hit her, once. A solid kick to the stomach. I felt the impact up my leg as she staggered backward a few paces, coughing. Her expression cracked just slightly, but I didn't get time to enjoy it.

A scream pierced the air. It was louder than the roar of the crowd, louder than the drums.

Elena.

I turned, eyes locking on the other ring.

Rhea was straddling her. Elena was on her back, pinned down in the sand. Her arms flailed weakly, unable to protect herself. Blood streaked her forehead, and one of her eyes was already swelling shut.

Rhea's fists came down in a blur. One after another. Like she'd lost herself to the violence, like she'd been consumed by it. Elena's fingers dug lines into Rhea's shoulders, but it did nothing to slow her spew of attacks through her leathers.

Her snarl echoed through the arena, animalistic and awful.

A single red line ran on her face from her temple to her chin, her own wound dripping freely, but it was nothing compared to what she was doing to Elena.

Elena was sobbing through bloodcurdling screams, trying to twist away.

"Stop! *Stop—!*" she cried, but her voice broke halfway through the word.

Rhea didn't stop. She didn't even hesitate.

Blood splattered across the floor, flecked onto her face, her fists, the sand. Elena's body gave one final twitch. Then nothing.

Her screams fell silent. The crowd didn't care. They howled louder, and something inside me snapped.

My body went still. My breath caught in my throat.

Heat bloomed beneath my skin, fast and rising.

My hands trembled, but not from pain. No, this was something else. My power pounded against the walls I had built inside myself, furious and desperate and wild. It seemed to hiss in my mind,

Let me out. Let me out. Let me out.

A second horn blew. The match beside us was over.

Rhea rose from the blood-soaked sand like some unholy goddess. Her chest was heaving, her knuckles dripping red. The triumph on her face was a mask of cruelty.

I stood there, burning, shaking, barely breathing.

Her fight had lasted less than two minutes.

Elena's body was dragged from the ring. At first, I thought it was one of the healers, but then I saw his face and everything inside me stilled.

Will.

His eyes were wild with terror, rimmed red, his arms tight around her limp frame. His mouth moved in frantic bursts against her temple. He whispered words meant to hold her here, to tether her to life. He was begging her to stay, and then Elena moved. The softest shift of her breath pulled her chest up, but it was enough. She was alive.

Relief slammed into me so hard it nearly knocked me off my feet. I took a breath, but even that was sharp and cold.

It could have just as easily been me, and Naelle hadn't forgotten that.

Her foot slammed into the back of my knee.

Pain fractured through my body as if I had been made of glass. I crumpled, my leg folding beneath me. My hand rushed to my side as the floor came rushing up. My ribs hit the ground hard, driving the air from my lungs, the gash in my side tearing wider. My scream caught behind my teeth. Sand rushed into my mouth. My vision went white at the edges. I pulled my upper body straight, my knees digging down into the sand as a fist, brutal and sharp, collided with my jaw.

My head snapped sideways. A sickening crack echoed in my skull. The taste of blood flooded my tongue, warm and thick and bitter. My ears rang with a high, keening sound, muffling everything else.

The sky spun. Blood dripped into my mouth, metallic and warm. Naelle's shadow loomed above me, pausing as if to savor her triumph. I could hear the crowd cheering, already writing the end of my story. I was down. Broken. Defeated.

But they didn't know me.

Not yet.

I plunged my hand into the sand, fingers trembling. My side screamed. My vision blurred.

No.

Not like this.

I was not born to kneel.

Let them drive me into the ground. Let them bruise me, cut me, bleed me dry. I would still rise, because I was never theirs to destroy.

I am not delicate. I am not soft. I am not the queen they hoped to mold, nor the martyr they wished to bury. I am not the heroine in this story, just as I am not the villain. I am not the light. I am not the dark.

I am kindling, and I am flame.

I am present, and I am future.

And stars help the ones who thought I'd stay down.

I ground my teeth and shoved myself upright. Every breath was a blade in my chest, but I rose, nonetheless.

My limbs felt slow, unsteady, but I stood.

And I shattered the jar.

A surge of power erupted from inside me, something pure and raw and furious. It tore through me like a river breaking a dam. I could feel it ripple through my blood, down my spine, into the marrow of my bones. The air seemed to shimmer in waves of cold silver, ebbing and flowing like liquid metal.

I seized the thread I had already anchored to Naelle. I drove my power through the thin tendril that had coiled around her like a halo.

This time, I wasn't kind. I wasn't merciful. I wasn't afraid. I was exactly what I needed to be.

Cruel.

My power split apart and rushed inward, prying her open like a locked door kicked from its hinges. I felt the resistance of her mind. I felt the walls built from pride and that relentless, unearned confidence, and I burned them down.

My power twisted and writhed. Once a whisper, now a spear. It tunneled past the shallow surface of thought, past the half-formed emotions and flickering instincts that usually swam in my awareness, but I didn't stop there. I went deeper. Deeper than instinct. Deeper than memory.

I pushed past all the layers that made Naelle who she was and reached something central, something raw. I didn't know what it was, but I knew I wasn't supposed to be here.

Her mind resisted at first, like flesh flinching from fire, but it didn't matter.

My power shattered her defenses like thin glass underfoot.

Naelle flinched. Something visibly involuntarily. Her shoulders twitched. A tremor ran down her arms. Her body shuddered like it had been struck by cold wind, though the air was heavy with heat.

Her eyes found mine. Deep brown, ringed with disbelief, and I saw it then.

The fracture.

It wasn't dramatic. Not at first. Just the smallest flicker, the beginning of a crack in stained-glass. Her lips parted. Her grin twitched once, like she was trying to hold onto it, like if she just kept smiling, she could stay in control, but the mask was slipping.

The corners of her mouth dropped. Her brow tightened in sudden confusion. Fear began to rise in her gaze, swelling like black ink in water.

She knew something had gone wrong.

Her limbs stopped resisting gravity. Her shoulders sagged, her hands fell limp at her sides, but she didn't fall. Some invisible string kept her upright, suspended in the air like a marionette whose puppeteer had gone silent. Her chest rose and fell, her heart still beat, but Naelle wasn't inside anymore.

Her mouth opened, slow and uncertain, as if she were about to speak or scream or beg but nothing came out. Her eyes locked on mine, wide and trembling, as if she were watching herself from inside a glass coffin. Terror bloomed there—pure, instinctive, animalistic terror.

And for one awful moment, I could feel it too. I felt her struggling, trying to claw her way back to herself, but she would never reach the surface.

The color in her eyes began to fade.

From rich brown to shining silver.

Gone.

She didn't collapse. She didn't cry. She just stood there, breathing. She was still standing in front of me, still solid and whole, but there was no one behind those eyes.

Naelle was no longer Naelle. She was mine now. The ego that had made her so smug, so mocking, so cruel, was nothing. My power had taken root in her mind, and it was now all she knew.

I wasn't simply in her mind. I *was* her mind.

I should have felt guilty. A sharp twist curled deep in my stomach, deep and dark, but it wasn't guilt, not quite. It was satisfaction.

It crept through my veins like warmth, like the first taste of something forbidden and sweet and utterly addictive. I had taken everything from her, and she hadn't even seen it coming. And stars help me, I didn't feel sorry.

I had won.

I looked at her again, at the slight sway of her body, the lifeless tilt of her head. She was a puppet waiting for orders. My orders. Watching the strings I held in my hands.

And I wanted her to feel the pull of each one.

My power curled tighter around her mind like smoke with no air left to breathe. Naelle's breath hitched. Her hands began to shake.

I stepped forward, slow and sure, until I was just beside her. Close enough to feel the tremble in her spine, to see the thin sheen of sweat beading along her temple.

I leaned in, my voice a hiss of wrath against her ear.

"*Yield.*"

For a breath, nothing happened, then she crumpled. Her knees struck the dirt with a hollow, graceless sound, and she let out a strangled, gasping sob. Her body bowed under the weight of my command.

"I yield," she choked, the words scraping out of her like something broken. "I yield. I yield. *I yield! I yield—*"

Her voice cracked and kept going, a litany of surrender tumbling from her mouth like she didn't know how to stop. She bent at the waist, arms shaking, fingers digging into the sand as if she could find something, anything, to anchor her.

But there was nothing.

I didn't pull away.

I let my power stay exactly where it was. It coiled tight around her, pressing down like a second skin she couldn't shed. I stood still, quiet, my heart pounding so loudly it felt like it echoed in the air around us.

The horn blew again. A single, sharp sound that sliced the air in two. The crowd didn't cheer. No one rose to their feet. There were no gasps, no clapping, no triumphant shouts.

I lifted my head and met his eyes. Cassian was still, surrounded by noblemen and guards, but his gaze locked on mine like a rope between us. And in that moment, all of it, the storm I'd summoned, the pain, the blood, it quieted.

Sunlight.

Honey.

Warmth.

The power that had been threatening to shred Naelle recoiled, slithering back into the place where I kept the jar in my mind. I felt it go, reluctant but obedient, curling into itself like smoke in a sealed bottle. Naelle dropped completely then, her body folding as I severed the strings.

I didn't smile. I didn't bask. I simply stood there, breathing hard, my face carved in ice.

The King was seated in his high throne, cloaked in crimson and gold with that sickening crown resting on his head. I expected outrage, anger, something, *anything*.

His jaw twitched. The flicker of emotion across his face, quickly masked behind regal boredom. He watched me like a man realizing the wolf at his feet had grown teeth long enough to bite.

Cassian didn't move, but I could feel our golden bond humming.

Pride, sharp and gleaming, pressed beneath a heavier tide of fear. Not fear of me, but fear for me. Fear of what I'd done.

He'd wanted to intervene. I felt it so clearly it nearly knocked the breath from my lungs. The desire to touch me, to wash the blood from my skin, to press his hands to the wound on my side and hold me like I wasn't something dangerous.

It pulsed from him like heat, like longing so intense it scorched.

Cassian had seen me, all of me.

Naelle still knelt in the dirt, gasping and breathing like a panicked child.

I turned to her one last time.

Her head snapped up as our eyes met and for a second, I saw it. The brown was back, but it wasn't the same earthy, coffee brown it had been before. It was dull now, like something had been drained from her, something vital.

She flinched. Her breath caught audibly, and then, like a spooked animal, she scrambled back. Hands clawing at the earth, legs slipping under her, she fled in a graceless scurry across the arena floor, as if just being near me burned.

She didn't look back, and I didn't wait.

I didn't wait for the King to label me as a champion. I didn't wait for the applause that would never come. I didn't wait for the guards to rush forward or for any kind of celebration. I didn't even glance at Rhea.

I turned toward the tunnel from which I'd entered and walked.

Every step sent a bolt of pain through my side. I could feel warm blood seeping beneath the waistband of my uniform, trickling in slow, sticky rivers down my hip. My head throbbed and my vision hazed. My jaw ached with every swallow, and my breathing became ragged gasps. My knees were raw, caked with sand and blood, but I did not limp. I would not limp.

The arena gate loomed ahead, iron bars crusted with rust and dust. As I approached, the guard stationed beside it jerked the lever almost too quickly. The gate creaked open with a groan, and I watched him from the corner of my eye. He had been the same one who'd smirked when I first arrived. Cocky and condescending. The kind of man who thought power belonged only to people like him.

Now, he couldn't meet my gaze. His eyes stayed glued to the ground. His face had gone pale, jaw tight with the effort of keeping still. The sharp tang of fear radiating off him like sweat.

Satisfaction curled low in my gut.

I passed through without a word.

The palace stretched before me, quiet and gleaming. I walked through them like a ghost made flesh. Blood stained my collar and splattered down the front of my uniform. A red river flowed in my wake, marking my warpath through the marble halls. My fists were still clenched at my sides, streaked with grime. No one dared speak to me.

Servants turned away. A nobleman flinched and pressed himself against the wall, as though I might touch him and turn him to ash. I kept my head high. My expression unreadable.

I didn't stop moving.

Not for the pounding in my head.

Not for the ache in my chest.

Not for the gash in my ribs.

I reached my room. The door swung shut behind me, hitting its frame like a clash of thunder. I didn't care if locked behind me, didn't even care if it closed. Only then did I let go. The mask slipped, cracked, and finally shattered.

My knees gave out, and I sank to the floor shaking. I pressed my hands to the wooden panels just to feel something solid. Something real.

I thought about the King, smug and unreadable, standing beside Kaden like an owner with their leashed dog. I thought about Elena's crumpled body and Rhea's cruel, triumphant grin. I thought about the lagoon, the secrets I still didn't understand, and Cassian. Cassian, the boy who made me feel like I was something more and something awful all at once.

Tears followed. Quiet at first, like a leak in something long held back, and then louder, messier. I laid down at the foot of my bed and curled into myself. I cried until my throat was raw. I cried for the girl who had first stepped into the palace. I cried for the girl who now knew she was a weapon and who wasn't sure if she could be anything else.

I cried because no one could see me here, because I was alone, and because, stars help me, some part of me had liked what I'd done.

And I didn't know what that meant.

CHAPTER THIRTY-TWO

My CHEEK WAS PRESSED to the wood, stiff with dried blood, sweat and dirt. I didn't remember falling asleep, but the ache in my every muscle and bone told me otherwise. For a moment, I just laid on the cold floor. I just breathed, sucking air through clenched teeth, trying to remember how I'd ended up here at all.

The palace was quiet, but it wasn't the soft, peaceful hush of afternoon. It was heavy and hollow. It coiled around me like invisible chains, pressing into my ribs, into my spine, into the gash that pulsed with heat beneath my clothes.

When I finally moved, I did it slowly, groaning as I rolled to my side and pushed myself up on trembling arms. My lip was swollen, or swelling. That I knew for sure. Pain lanced through my ribcage, sharp and hot, and I bit down on a whimper. My head spun, vision swaying as the walls seemed to stretch and tilt. I blinked hard even as my split cheekbone screamed, trying to anchor myself. A red ring had formed under me, drying into a deep brown in the hours I had drifted off.

My leathers clung to me, stiff and soaked with blood. I unbuckled the belts with shaking fingers and peeled the fabric away, hissing as it tugged at the crusted wound beneath. The moment the last strap fell, I saw it—a deep, angry wound stuck between my ribs and the curve of my hip. Just more than an inch wide, but about double that in depth. The blood had dried almost black, cracked and flaking, but still seeping at the edges. I had forgotten to clean it or just forgotten to care.

I pressed a palm against the floor, bracing myself as I stood. Stars sparked at the edges of my vision. Lightheadedness, no doubt from the blood loss, buzzed and filled my brain.

Staggering to the washbasin, I turned the brass knob. Warm water sputtered out and splashed against the basin's copper like a heartbeat. I eased down into a chair at its side and sat still as I let my stiff muscles readjust to the movement. I grabbed a cloth from the edge of the basin, soaked it, then pressed it to the wound.

The pain was instant and blinding. I sucked in a breath, but it came too fast, too sharp. My vision blurred and the edges went black. Bright white sparks shot up my side, winding around each rib, but I didn't stop.

I washed the blood away, slowly and carefully, biting down on every noise trying to escape my throat. I cleaned it until it no longer looked like part of me, until the rawness beneath looked vaguely human again. I grabbed at the minty ointment I had used on my cheek and hissed as the green salve blurred into brown with the blood. I ran the rag over my face and arms, streaking blood across my skin.

I dragged myself to the armoire and pulled out a white linen tunic, ripping the sleeve from the bodice. I threw the destroyed shirt to the ground, not bothering with the cloth carcass. I wrapped the strip of fabric around my waist and ribs in a makeshift bandage. It was loose, uneven, and wouldn't last, but it was better than bleeding out in this stars-forsaken palace.

I stripped off the rest of the leathers from my lower body, wincing with every bruise I uncovered. Blood speckled my legs and knees, but I was too tired to care. I didn't even bother trying with the rag. I found a soft cotton shirt and loose pants in the bottom drawer and slipped them on. They clung to my dirtied skin. My body felt foreign. Heavy.

I crossed to the door, fingers brushing the handle. I reached outward to search for Kaden, and I found him, but not just him.

My blood went cold.

There were others. Dozens.

A sea of minds just beyond my room, all muddled and tense, packed tightly together like a wall. I couldn't even count them.

My pulse stuttered, panic clenching my chest. My blood ran cold, and adrenaline coursed my veins, blinding me from the pain in my side.

I twisted the handle. It didn't move.

Cold crept down my spine.

I tried again, harder this time. Nothing.

I knelt, careful of my side, and plucked a pin from the vanity. I eased it into the keyhole, twisting and jiggling, but nothing. Not even a whisper of movement from the mechanism.

My stomach dropped.

"What in the stars..." I breathed, backing away.

The balcony.

I could use the balcony.

I crossed the room limping and flung open the glass doors. Wind rushed in instantly, sharp and wild, tearing through my hair. The braid I'd worn during the trial had all but collapsed from its crown. Loose strands snapped in the gusts like smoke.

I stepped into the open air and gripped the railing. The courtyard below was a dizzying drop. It was high, too high. Solid stone walls slid smoothly down with no vines, no trellises, no escape. Just the wind and the height and the cold.

I backed away, the air too thin and sharp in my lungs. They had trapped me. An animal in a cage.

My hands flew to my scalp and tore out the last of the braid, letting my hair fall wild around my shoulders. It whipped in the wind, but the release didn't help. The tightness in my chest didn't ease. I dropped to my knees. My chest rose and fell too fast for the oxygen I was dragging in to register. I stayed there on the floor, arms wrapped around my center as if I could physical hold myself together when a voice shattered the stillness.

Sharp. Raised. Furious.

I froze. Still kneeling, I crawled toward the door. I pressed my ear to the wood, heart thundering like it might drown the words out entirely.

"... command you to open it!" Cassian's voice. There was no mistaking it.

This wasn't the warm, smooth tone I'd become accustomed to. This voice was ragged and quickly unraveling. Laced with fury so sharp it almost cut through the door's lock itself.

A guard replied, low and hesitant. "We were told she was not to be disturbed, by order of the King—"

"*I am your Prince!*" Cassian roared. His voice hit the corridor like a blade scrapping across stone. "And I will be your king. If you do not open this door at my orders, I swear on every god you pray to, I will see your names wiped from history and your bloodline broken beneath mine."

A long, terrible silence followed.

I didn't breathe.

Boots shuffled. Armor scraped. Keys clattered to the floor, fumbled by shaking hands.

I stood, slowly, my feet shuffling backward to the center of the room before the lock even turned. I didn't know if I wanted him to see me like this, to see me broken, but I couldn't look away from the door handle that shifted with the key.

The lock clicked. The door groaned open.

Cassian stood in the center, the frame of the door making the scene look like a painting. He held a black cloak in the crook of his arm. He wasn't smiling. He wasn't soft or playful or golden. He was his father's son, and they felt it.

Kaden stood off to the side, still and unmoving with a face carved from stone. The other guards stood frozen, their gazes locked forward but not really seeing. Their faces were pale, their spines straight with terror. They withered beneath Cassian. One even bowed his head, whispering a prayer as if he thought Cassian might strike him down where he stood, but the Prince didn't look at them.

His gaze dropped to the blood staining my shirt, soaking slowly through the linen. His eyes lingered on my arms, bruised and scraped, then the split on my lip, the pallor in my face. My hair was loose and wild, tangled from wind and sleep and pain. My shoulders hunched like I might fall apart if I stood too long.

"All of you are relieved of your duty at this post. Leave. Now." The words were thrown over his shoulder as he snapped the door shut behind him. He crossed the room in two long strides.

"Stars, Lyra," he breathed, voice frayed at the edges. "Stars…"

His hands hovered near my arms, trembling slightly. He didn't touch me, not yet, but the heat of him was close enough that I could feel it brush my skin, warm and grounding. My legs wobbled beneath me. I wasn't sure if it was the pain or him.

"What did you do?" he asked, almost whispering. "Why didn't you call for me?" His eyes searched mine like they were looking for what was left of me. "You left, and I assumed you only wanted to be alone. I didn't—"

He shook his head.

I didn't know how to answer.

"I'm fine."

250

He knew immediately that was a lie. His brow furrowed while his hand ran slowly down his mouth and jaw before paused at his chin. Golden eyes connected with mine and that hand moved to brush a strand of hair away from my face, his fingers finding the white scar. His thumb ghosted the edge of the split on my lip. The touch was feather-light, but I felt it like lightning striking. His thoughts hovered over the edge of whatever wall he had built, but I didn't have the energy to reach out.

"I never should have let you walk away." His voice cracked.

His gaze burned into me. It ran along each bruise, each scrape, each tint of blood like he could erase everything that had happened.

The problem was, he couldn't.

"I can't do this anymore." The broken words fell from my lips, desperation clinging to every one.

Cassian cocked his head, the anger beginning to melt into something else. "Why do you say that?" he whispered.

"You told me I was here to rebuild something better, but that…" Tears spilled down my cheeks. "That didn't seem better."

Cassian paused, his hand stopping just under my ear. Something like surprise crossed his face.

"Lyra," he breathed, "Naelle would have *killed* you. You have to understand that." His last step stopped close enough for him to bring a gentle hand up, his bent forefinger resting under my chin.

He pulled my head up to meet his gaze. "You showed her mercy by giving her a fate far less than she deserved."

It hadn't felt like mercy. If anything, death would have been kinder than whatever had become of Naelle.

"Do you want to see why you're here?"

I pulled my head from his hand, confusion obvious on my face. "What do you mean?"

He glanced again at the blots of red that dotted me and my room. "You can't know who you're fighting for until you see who's already bleeding." His eyes hovered on my side. On the green ointment and red blood seeping through the tunic. He knelt before me, one hand moving to cup the back of my thigh.

Cassian's other hand ran along the bottom hem of my shirt, but he paused, glancing back up at me.

I raised my eyebrows at him, but he just sat there, waiting as if time obeyed his commands as well. I let out a sigh.

"You can pull my shirt up, Cassian."

A grin curled on his lips, charm and arrogance exuding from every pore. "I can," he agreed, his voice silky-smooth and maddeningly smug. His eyes returned to my own, the honey gold of his molten. "But where's the fun in that, when I can make you ask for it?"

I rolled my eyes, and he gently lifted the shirt. His face quickly changed from being anywhere near flirtatious. The ripped fabric had all but turned red, the center becoming almost black with the saturation. I took my shirt from Cassian's hand as he began to peel off the blood-soaked cloth. I gritted my teeth when it reached the final layer. The wound was swollen at the edges, a clear liquid oozing alongside the blood.

Infection. I knew it from helping my father. I needed a honey salve, maybe even something stronger. I opened my mouth, but Cassian cut me off before I could respond, his hand raising in the air to silence me.

"Yeah, infection. I know." His eyes snapped back up to mine. "I'm not a complete moron."

He grabbed the torn shirt from its place on the floor and torn off the other sleeve. He wrapped it around my waist and tied the cloth in a firm knot, my side protesting at every shuffle of the fabric against my skin.

He stood and held out his hand. I accepted, and he led to to my armoire as I held my stained shirt off my skin. He opened the drawers, digging until he pulled out a black tunic and matching pants. He laid the clothes over my free arm, and I slipped behind the folding screen to change. When I walked out, Cassian was already standing in the doorway, his cloak back in his arms and mine pulled from my armoire and folded at my desk. The guards that were there only minutes ago were nowhere to be seen, including Kaden.

"A friend of mine requires a brief visit." He threw his cloak over his shoulders, clasping the golden latch at his throat.

I didn't question it. I simply grabbed my own cloak and walked through the door, leaving my bloodstained room behind.

We walked through the palace as if the hallways answered our every beck and call. We wound down through the lower levels and reached a corridor that was coated in moss and vines. Old and hidden, but beautiful. The tunnel opened to a back garden, overgrown and wild and undoubtedly gorgeous. Maybe even more so than the palace gardens themselves. We continued down, walking around the outer walls of the palace onto a gravel and dirt path not made by anyone in particular, but years of use. A path made purely by the desire of others to escape into the city that opened below.

We reached a cobblestone street and entered a place that didn't possibly look real. Stars, it truly was unlike anything I had ever known.

The Aurean streets wound like vines through neighborhoods of colored tile and sculpted glass. Warm golden storefronts were tucked into corners like treasure chests. Buildings rose sky high, their towers made of air and stone and glass. They wound upward, the spiraling structures mesmerizing as they danced in the sun. Vendors were bustling with customers. Shops with open doors and carts lining the streets were filled with flatbreads drizzled with honey, painted pottery, embroidered fabric. Dried meat and salted vegetables filled the air with a scent that was downright mouth-watering. Fruits of all shapes and colors filled baskets tilted to show off their possessions to those walking the streets. Others sold silk ribbons in jars like candy, or vials of oils and spices arranged in rows that caught the light like tinted glass.

Women wore light silk dresses, all splashes of color and beautifully laid over their olive tan skin. Golden bangles and necklaces shone like poured sunlight on their arms and collarbones. Earrings drooped and dangled from piercings running the entire length of their ears.

Some men wore long golden chains, the metal dipping down to the center of their stomach where a token or totem fell. They tended to favor light billowing pants and often, no tunics at all. Not that I was complaining.

Children darted between alleyways, laughter ringing like chimes. Musicians played on the steps of old cathedrals, their melodies weaving through the air like smoke. Their instruments were light, airy, but the lyrics seemed darker. History concealed within song. Lanterns flickered in second-story windows. Somewhere nearby, people danced. The rhythmic falling of their feet echoed in the streets.

I turned in every direction, my eyes wide. I had lived within the palace for weeks. I had stayed between the stone walls, veiled by etiquette and silence, but this, this was life. This pulsed and breathed and laughed and wept. This moved.

Thane had called it a maze.

He hadn't been wrong.

From here, the kingdom flourished. It looked every bit like the places spoken about in fairy tales. The birds seemed to sing songs as the sun made the golden buildings shimmer like light itself.

My power unfurled, brushing over every passerby. Their thoughts slid into me like water through cracks in stone.

A first kiss. A final goodbye. A father's laughter. A mother's lullaby.

Their memories slipped into me, subtle and intimate, stitching themselves to the hollow places in my chest. Cassian walked at my side, silent. We didn't speak, but we didn't need to. The city whispered enough.

Cassian led us through the pulsing heart of Aurea.

He moved without hesitation, even as the streets narrowed and the cobbles turned to cracked stone. Even when the lights dimmed and the air grew quieter. Even when the musicians were too far to hear. We kept walking past the glow and glamour, into something quieter, something forgotten.

We crossed through a stacked stone wall, moss filling the gaps like mortar. It was only about as tall as Cassian, but crossing through the small opening was like stepping into another world.

All of the glamour, all of the splendor, it was gone. Music didn't reach this place. The road we walked upon was crooked and dim, flanked by shuttered shops and ivy-choked windows. Lanterns burned low in rusted iron sconces. No one passed us. No one watched. It felt like the edge of the world, like the place Aurea exhaled and turned away.

I placed a hand over my mouth.

A man was on his knees, begging a farmer pulling a cart for an ear of corn. A child, her face streaked black with soot, dragged a wagon of coal toward a sagging house. People crouched in doorways, holding out empty cups that jingled with a single coin. Dogs moved through the shadows with ribs pressing sharp beneath their skin. A baby wailed somewhere, unseen, and still more voices whispered in my head—ragged, raw, forgotten.

There were no colored fabrics or ribbons. No candies sold in painted jars or honey covered pastries. No voices ringing in song, or laughter filling the air.

This wasn't in the fairy tales.

I turned slowly, heart hollowing. For every story I had heard of Aurea's splendor, there had been this.

Cassian's hand pressed to the small of my back, gentle but grounding.

When I looked up at him, sorrow bloomed in his eyes. His stare was deep and wordless and old. He had known. He had always known.

This had been here all along. While I'd been scraping half-eaten meals into polished compost bins, they were starving. I pressed my hands to my ears, but the cries still pierced through. I didn't know if it was the noise that hurt more, or the knowing.

This wasn't just neglect. This was cruelty in slow motion. This was evil, disguised in silk and ceremony. This was what he wanted to show me.

He didn't say anything. He just reached up and brushed his thumb softly along my cheek, a silent promise. Then he turned, and I followed him down the crooked road, past the lanterns, and deeper into the shadows that Aurea didn't dare name.

Cassian stopped at a modest house pressed against the side of a darkened apothecary. The door was plain wood, chipped at the corners. There was a flower box below the window, empty save for dried stems. He walked up the steps to the front door. I followed and stood behind him on the narrow staircase.

He knocked three times. A heartbeat passed. Then another. It opened.

A woman stood framed in the doorway, backlit by candlelight and the faint scent of metallic copper. She exited the house and closed the door behind her. I couldn't see her well from behind Cassian, but she wasn't tall. Her frame was frail, and she seemed anything but intimidating, yet when she looked at Cassian, she narrowed her eyes like a blade being drawn.

"Cassian," she hissed, her voice sharp as cut glass. "Tell me you didn't let anyone see you sneaking off again. I swear by the stars—"

Then her gaze shifted.

To me. Her voice changed mid-sentence.

"Oh, Cass…" she said quietly. "You've brought company."

That nickname—Cass. No one had ever said it other than Thane, but even he didn't say it like that. Not with familiarity.

"Good to see you too, Moira."

Moira, as Cassian called her, opened the door and gestured for us to enter. I followed behind him, the scent of herbs hitting me the moment we crossed the threshold. There was something else mixed in the air though, something slightly foul and decaying…

I had to force the bile back down my throat as we walked inside. Cots lined the space with people dotting them, laying curled and unmoving. Ribs and bones wrapped in thin taut skin. I wasn't even sure if malnourished was the correct term anymore. They were rotting. The walls were lined with jars and vials. Bowls filled with sludges cluttered a small worktable.

She was a healer. Just like my father.

I felt that familiar glow in my chest. The bond, golden and taut, anchored me to Cassian. My attention moved back to him and Moira. They both watched me, Cassian's eyes matching the grief inside my own. He felt it, too. The outrage. The helplessness. The fury turned inward.

He gave the bond another gentle tug, and I walked over to stand by his side. He wrapped an arm around my waist and pulled me flush against him. He was careful of my wound, shifting me forward so my back rested against his chest.

"This is Lyra Seravell," he said, voice low, unreadable. "She's from Virellia."

Her eyes flicked up to meet Cassian's, and then, I saw it.

I had no idea how I hadn't noticed it right away. Maybe I'd been too consumed by the people, but now, standing face-to-face with this woman, I saw it clear as day.

Her eyes.

Stars, they were Kaden's eyes.

The same shade of vivid green. The same edge to them, the same weight that made you feel like you were being seen too deeply. It was like looking into a window from a different life—one that had been fractured, scattered, and partially lost.

She was Kaden's mother.

I knew it with a certainty that made my stomach twist. I inhaled sharply, trying not to stare. She didn't seem to notice, or maybe she did, and chose not to comment. She seemed too intrigued by Cassian's introductions.

Moira turned to look at me now, clasping her hands in front of her.

"Oh, well. How lovely to meet you."

I wasn't sure how she was having this conversation as if people were not dying in the same room. I went to turn around, but Cassian's hand moved to my hips, holding me firmly forward. He nudged me gently with the bond, pushing a thought through to my own mind.

It would be polite to respond, little flame.

I took a breath and brought my eyes up to meet Moira's. "Lovely to meet you as well."

I tried to break the awkwardness by offering her my hand to shake, but her eyes flicked from my bare hand back to her own, and I let mine fall before words needed to be said.

She tucked her hands into the pockets of the green apron she wore as she shifted her eyes back up to Cassian.

"Well, get on with it. You never stop by unless you need something so, best ask now."

"I'm only here for a visit." He gave me a small glance. "But Lyra here might need some stitches…"

Moira nodded once and immediately moved to a small dresser, pulling out jars of salves, rolls of gauze, and a small kit holding needles and thread.

"Kaden is usually my visitor." She tried to force yet another smile, but this one dropped almost instantaneously. She walked over to a circular table, pulling a chair out and gesturing for me to sit. "Have you seen him lately?"

There it was. The killing blow.

I moved to sit in the chair, but my steps dragged. I didn't know if the devastating sadness blooming heavy in my chest was mine or Cassian's, but it filled me all the same. I swallowed it down, tasting its weight in the back of my throat.

Cassian's eyes didn't leave Moira's as he spoke. "You know I'll always take care of Kaden."

Moira pressed her lips together. She gave the slightest of nods. She knelt at my injured side, pausing for the slightest of moments. "I'm just glad that…" She huffed a breath and brought her gaze back up. Her eyes met mine, and they turned glassy with emotion. "I'm glad you found what you were looking for." She waved her hand at my cloak and tunic, silently asking me to move them.

I peeled back the fabrics and hissed at the pain along my side. My shirt was soaked through along with the makeshift bandage, dark with dried blood. The wound beneath was torn and angry. The swelling brought with it a nauseating throb.

Cassian dropped to one knee before me. Not as a prince. Not even as a soldier. Just as a man.

He gathered my hands in his own, enveloping them in his grasp. Nothing poured through the raw connection. No thoughts, no emotions. Nothing.

Moira hovered her hands over the wound, eyes scanning it with focused intensity. Then, without a word, she slipped on a pair of green leather gloves and laid everything out with quiet precision.

Salves. Bandages. Scissors. Thread. A small flask of clear liquid that caught the candlelight like ice.

She opened salve jars that smelled of honey and lavender.

I froze.

My father. He'd used the same ones.

A memory surged—his hands, steady and sure, pressing balm into my scraped knees when I was a girl. His quiet humming. The warmth of his lap as I clutched his coat.

The memory was warm, and every piece of it made me long for home.

Moira filled the metal tin with warm water from a kettle. She dipped a cloth in and gently began to clean the wound. Her touch was deft but careful. Every movement was measured. Every pause was weighted. When I flinched, Cassian's grip on me tightened, his own jaw clenching.

The honey salve stung when it touched my skin, a sharp jolt of clarity, but nothing more than the pain of a paper cut. She worked it in with the lightest pressure, the scent soothing, familiar. Then she reached for the needle and thread—clear and fine as spider silk.

Moira didn't so much as hesitate, but Cassian stared into my eyes.

He hated this. He hated that what she was about to do would hurt like no other.

"I'm sorry," he murmured, his thumb rubbing idle circles on the back of my hand.

I didn't trust my voice. I just grabbed a rag from the desk and bit down on it, nodding once.

Moira stitched slowly, carefully.

The needle pierced skin, and a gasp escaped me before I could stop it. Tears blurred my vision. Cassian's jaw clenched with each wince I made. But even as each pass sent shivers through me, the pain began to dull, to fade, until none remained.

Cassian was as stiff as stone, frozen with his eyes down and closed. He didn't speak, didn't flinch, but I saw it in him. I saw the tension in the set of his shoulders, saw the tremble in his breath. As if he was the one getting stitched, and not me.

When Moira tied off the final stitch, Cassian leaned forward and pressed his forehead to my shoulder, letting out a breath. I felt the sweat that had beaded there, cold and clammy. I hadn't even realized she was done.

She smoothed a lavender scented balm through the stitches, the faint ache dissolving under the brush of her fingers. Gauze was pressed against the sticky ointment as a bandage was wrapped around my torso. Moira tied the ends together tightly, brushing her hands off when she finished.

Cassian's hands left mine, and I could have sworn the ache in my side increased in his absence, filling what space he left behind.

Moira stood, gathering and cleaning her supplies. Cassian followed suit, rising to his feet, but he only wrapped Moira in a gentle hug. His large frame engulfed her, and her hands grabbed at the fabric on his back before she pulled away, turning her back to us and grabbing a mortar and pestle. She began crushing whatever herb laid in the bowl as she spoke over her shoulder.

"You two should head back. They'll know you're missing soon, if they don't already. Keep that cut clean." Her eyes turned to Cassian. "Change that gauze when you get back and use this on her other wounds." She pressed a metal tin to his palm.

She glanced between us with a warm, weary smile. "Come back. Visit."

Cassian nodded to Moira and turned back to me. He grabbed my hand and gently guided me back towards the door. Rain had begun to fall in soft drops outside. He gently pulled the hood of my cloak over my head, running his thumb down my scarred cheek as his hand fell. He pressed a gentle kiss to my forehead, pausing there for just a breath. I sunk into that touch, waiting and wanting his mind to meld with mine. But it never did.

He pulled on his own hood, and we stepped out together.

CHAPTER THIRTY-THREE

WALKING BACK TO THE PALACE, I couldn't stop the whispers from slipping into my mind. They came fast and sharp—people's thoughts, fears, stray memories, broken dreams—and scraped against me like glass. I couldn't hold them back. Couldn't slow them down. They flooded in with every step I took, layering over one another until the noise was too loud to separate. I tried to pull my power back. Tried to imagine that jar that could contain it.

Cassian glanced at me, concern etched into his features. His brows pulled together, and he tilted his head toward me, silent but asking.

Are you all right?

I shook my head, dismissing him. I hadn't heard his thoughts, but I didn't need to. Not that I could. His mind seemed complete separate from mine, locked down and away into a sea I should surely drown in.

I gritted my teeth and shoved my fingers down into the pockets of my cloak. I shut the voices out as best I could. I forced my power to pull back and shoved the pain down into the pit of my stomach.

Cassian said nothing. He just watched me stare blankly at the ground as we continued on. The palace gates loomed ahead, tall and cold in the moonlight. Beyond them, life went on. Servants murmured and boots scuffed along stone. Kitchens housed shelves upon shelves of food, and waiting rooms were warmed by firelight. It was the world I was supposed to return to, and I hated it.

Light from the city reflected and burned, as if the city was on fire. Part of me wished it was. Laughter echoed from the inner city of Aurea, where no one even knew of the starvation and suffering happening less than a mile away. Or maybe they knew and chose not to care. I was done with all of the games this region, this city, this palace loved to play. I was done holding my tongue. I was done with it all.

"They're dying," I whispered. My voice trembled and I clenched my fist, digging my nails into my palm to anchor me.

"They're starving and dying and the palace—" I threw my hand up toward the glittering gold towers. "They have feasts with ridiculous amounts of food. They drink wine and get drunk. They party and turn their backs on children. On mothers starving." I stared at Cassian.

I wasn't really angry at him in particular, not really. But the fury was so overwhelming, I just wasn't sure what to do with it. It coursed through my veins like it had always belonged there, like my anger was kindling to the power burning under my skin. Deep, heavy breaths puffed from my lungs, mixing with the night air.

Cassian's expression stayed smooth as stone. "*You* also have feasts with ridiculous amounts of food. *You* drink wine and get drunk. *You* party."

Not a lick of emotion left him. My rage boiled hotter under my skin. "I apologize deeply for my horrid mistakes after I was swept away alone to a kingdom known for its cruelty. Forgive me, my dear, dear Prince."

Cassian didn't so much as flinch at my abundance of sarcasm. "I don't need your apology. They do."

I scoffed, hard. "Because I'm the reason they're starving? The crown let this happen. *You* let this happen." I hurled the insult like a knife, piercing and sharp. I didn't mean it, truly I didn't, but a part of me would always know I belonged with the less fortunate. Just as the other part would know Cassian belonged anywhere but. Tears began to roll down my cheeks, leaving small wet drops on the cloak bunched under my chin.

Cassian looked at me, emotionless. His hand rose to brush my jaw, but I moved away, taking a step back.

"How can you not care? How long have you known about this and done nothing?" My eyes were wide, chest rising and falling irregularly. Emotions seemed to burn into my skin from the inside out, peeling away layers of my control one shred at a time. I felt like I was going insane. Perhaps I was.

His eyes wandered around the city sprawling before us, landing anywhere but on my own. "I brought you here, didn't I? I very clearly care." His hand flexed in and out of a fist but still, his expression remained unchanged. "Politics are never that simple, Lyra." He looked like a carved statue.

I shook my head as I really looked at him. "People starving isn't politics. That's not nearly an excuse and you know it." I reached out with my power, letting the silvery tendrils crawl to him. They wound around his legs, up his body, to his head. They circled there, like vultures to death. His jaw ticked, clenching at its side. He felt the invasion, but I didn't care. I reached inside, hitting nothing but a smooth stone wall. Not a thought crossed his mind.

"You really have nothing else to say, Cassian?"Anger welled within me like a storm of fire. As much as I had wanted, yearned, begged, for him to be something I could want, he never would be. His heart would always beat with royal blood. He would always wear a golden crown. He would always be a Vaelros.

"You really are your father's son, aren't you Cassian."

I barely even finished the sentence before complete misery flooded every part of me. The palace gates blurred in the distance. The world pitched sideways. I doubled over, gasping. I clutched at my skull as if I could somehow hold my mind together—keep the pieces from shattering further. The wall I had felt second earlier in his mind had dissolved away, and nothing but agony met the strands of power still hovering there. Vomit rose again in my throat, and I couldn't hold it back. I lost food I didn't remember eating in the rocks under me.

"You think I don't blame myself for every single child that even thinks about hunger? You think my nightmares aren't filled with images of that house? Those people?"

I dragged my gaze back up to face Cassian. He looked down at me, his golden eyes molten and liquid. Whatever mask he had worn was shattered. My whole body shook, overwhelmed by the pure despair coursing through my veins. I crumbled, head falling into the rocks and hands clutching at anything that found purchase.

"Tell me, since you're so intelligent Lyra. Why did we have breakfast in the gardens?"

I opened my mouth to respond, but I couldn't. Grief and anguish were all I knew. I tried to raise my head to him but failed. He crouched down and picked my chin up with his hand, turning my face up to look at him.

"I did it so they could eat your *leftovers*." He swallowed, hard. "I am doing all of this for them." His own eyes went glassy, a lone tear escaping. "I am *nothing* like my father."

I choked down a sob, my hand trembling terribly as I raised it to wipe the shining streak that ran down his face. "I'm sorry." The sound was wet, broken. "I'm so sorry."

His expression didn't soften, but the flood of emotion lessened. My chest lightened just enough for me to suck in a real breath. I forced my body to sit up, kneeling in the gravel. Cassian stood above me, towering with his chin in the air. His arms were slack at his sides, his fingers flexing repeatedly.

I didn't dare move, but it wasn't out of fear. I wasn't afraid. I wasn't afraid of what he had made me feel or what he had said. I wasn't afraid because it had all been the truth. He felt every bit of their pain. All he had done was break down the wall that kept it hidden. Guilt ate me away inside, making my stomach flip and my heart race. He was nothing like his father. I, of all people, knew that.

"Cassian—"

"Don't ever compare me to the King."

His chin stayed skyward even as he said it. I crawled forward, reaching a hand out in the gravel to touch his boot.

"I was wrong. I *am* wrong, and I am so sorry."

He brought his gaze from the stars down to me. He paused there for a while, just looking. He crouched down and took my hand slowly into his.

"Show me."

Confusion bunched my brow and my mouth hung soundlessly. "Show you what?"

"Show me how sorry you are."

I exhaled sharply. I tried to pull my hand from his grasp, but he held fast. "And how would you like me to do that? I'm not some plaything you can just—"

"Stay with me tonight." He fully knelt before me, his knees hitting the gravel that shifted beneath his weight. "Nothing more, I swear it. Just don't leave me for your room. Don't leave me to be alone." My breath hitched, or maybe I just stopped breathing at all. "Stay. Stay and show me I'm not the monster you believe me to be."

I couldn't form a proper response, so I just nodded. He closed his eyes as he let out a sigh of utter relief. He rose to his feet and helped me with the hand he had yet to let go of. My fingers curled into his, and he gave them a gentle squeeze. Once, twice, three times.

I didn't argue. I didn't ask where we were going. I simply let him guide me. We didn't go through the main gate. He knew better. Knew exactly where to slip through the cracks in the palace's golden perfection. We darted past the walls, cutting through a narrow garden passage I'd never noticed before, half-hidden behind an overgrown hedge of white roses. We entered the side of the palace where the marble lost its shine, and the torches burned dimmer.

Servants' passages, I realized. He moved like he'd done this a hundred times—ducking through low archways and slipping between quiet shadows, always watching ahead for guards or listening ears. I followed close, barely thinking, just matching his steps. We climbed a narrow staircase, the walls close and warmed with our breath. The silence between us was thick but not heavy. When we reached the landing, Cassian paused. No guards lurked in the corners. No swords were drawn in protection. The only barrier to his quarters were two tall wooden doors. Not grand like the royal chambers. Sturdy, plain, but polished, the handle gleaming faintly in the low light. He glanced back at me once, eyes searching mine. I nodded.

Cassian pushed the door open, and it moved without a sound, silent as breath on well-oiled hinges. I froze in the doorway, but the power inside me didn't. So, this was the Prince's room. My power reached outward, unruly and raw, curling from my fingertips, slipping from my hands like mist. Silvery-blue tendrils brushed the air, delicate and searching, tracing faint patterns along the walls like smoke stirred by a storm wind. They clung to the stone like they recognized it, like they had found something to anchor to. I hesitated, and then I felt that golden thread that always tugged faintly between us. It hummed like a low note beneath my ribs. It pulsed once, gentle and warm, and I felt his hand on the other end.

He gave it the slightest tug. Not a pull. Not a command. Just a feeling. And that was enough. I stepped inside. The air changed immediately. It stilled, going quiet and warm even in the night. His room was nothing like I expected. I had pictured something cold and pristine. White marble, a perfectly made bed, and a neatly organized desk. But this, this felt lived in. This was real. The scent hit me first— cedar and woodsmoke, and beneath it all, him.

To the right sat a desk cluttered with books and parchment, most of it half-unfurled. A leather journal rested in the center. Small pots and quills scattered the surface, leaving splotches of dark black ink. I caught sight of a paper filled with scrawled handwriting. I took a step closer, and my hand flew to my face. I took the note carefully, holding the edges gingerly. The script was scratchy, as if written in haste.

Kaden Thorne

Stolen by whom?

Throne room and my ~~father?~~

Silver or gold? Voided.

Books missing from library?

Touch the flame.

My head snapped towards Cassian.

"Is this about Kaden? Did you find—"

His shaking head dried up the words on my tongue.

My eyes returned to the words scattered about the page. I read them over and over, trying to see them through glazed eyes. I had to physically tear my hand from the paper. It fluttered back down to the desk, drifting down and landing without a sound, as if it never existed.

I continued to sweep my gaze over the room. To my left was a large tapestry. Embroidered thread showed a knight on a horse, rearing into battle. Behind him stood a crowd of people, their arms raised in a cry. They were storming forward. Forward to a palace. The palace shone a dull yellow, as if the iridescent gold had lost its shine with the moving time.

The doors to the balcony were wide open, silk curtains rippling gently in the breeze. Moonlight spilled in, casting silver across the polished stone floor. Beyond the archway, the city shimmered in the distance, glowing like a glass sea reflecting the star-lit sky.

His bed stood against the far wall, large and carved from dark wood, the posts reaching upward like spires. Rich purple velvet draped from the canopy, embroidered with gold thread that caught the light with every shift of the breeze. The duvet was thick and luxurious, folded with an easy kind of care, and pillows, so many pillows, were stacked with near-military precision.

There was a decanter on a small side table near the fireplace, half-full of something amber and aged. Two tumblers sat beside it. One perfectly clean while one was still smudged with fingerprints and dried liquid. On the same table, a wild yellow flower sat wilting, as if he had forgotten, or simply not wanted, to throw it out.

Everywhere I looked, I saw signs of Cassian. Not signs of a prince or an heir, but just him.

He simply watched me with that quiet stillness he wore like armor. I let out a shaky breath, turning back to him. When Cassian's eyes met mine, he moved. Slow. Intentional.

His hands found my waist first. Broad, warm palms anchored me like he'd done it a hundred times before. He eased me in, pulling me against him until there was nothing between us but breath and heat and the ragged edges of everything I couldn't say.

I leaned into him. My forehead met his collarbone and stayed there, tucked beneath his chin like I'd always fit in that space, like we'd been carved to stand here, just like this.

"I should have never said that." I breathed out the words into his shirt. His chest rose and fell against mine, steady and grounding, the rhythm of it syncing with my own.

"I didn't mean it. I swear I didn't mean it."

Cassian exhaled shakily, and I felt it ghost along my scalp. His fingers moved to my hair, slow and lazy.

"I know you didn't."

I let out the smallest sigh of relief and curled into him tighter. The longer I stayed tucked into his chest, breathing in that scent of woodsmoke and rain and something wholly him, the more I felt the exhaustion take root. The storm inside me had gone still, but the wreckage remained. I felt it in my limbs, in the hollow ache behind my ribs.

Cassian pulled back slowly. Not far. Just enough to see my face.

His knuckles brushed the side of my cheek, then he tucked a piece of hair behind my ear with aching tenderness. He ran a finger down the scar cutting my brow and cheek. The look in his eyes was unreadable but heavy.

"Let me see it," he said, voice low and rough around the edges.

I blinked, confused for a beat.

Then I remembered.

I pulled back my cloak and lifted the hem of my shirt just enough for the white gauze to peek out.

Cassian knelt down as he reached around me. He began to untie the thick bandage knotted on my opposite side, unwrapping the cloth and peeling the bloodied gauze from my skin. The stitches had pulled the gash into a thin line, but the sight still made my knees weak. Cassian reached into his cloak pocket and opened the metal tin of balm. He opened it, placing the lid on the ground before an arm raised at my back to steady me. Lavender filled the air, and he gently smoothed the salve across the stitched line. The relief came fast—cool and numbing and sweet. I let out a shuddering breath and sagged deeper into his touch. He pressed clean white gauze over the stitches, careful to touch only the edges as he wrapped the bandage around my middle once more. He tied the knot at the side of my waist.

Cassian's hands paused there for the briefest second, but he didn't stop.

He moved on to coat the bruises and the scrapes with the ointment. His fingers skimmed over the split in my lip, the tender cut along my jaw, the soreness blooming across my collarbone and shoulders like violet shadows under skin. His touch was never harsh. Just quiet. Present. Like each movement carried unspoken vows.

He stood, grabbing my hand with his free one and led me to his chair. His was much larger than mine, the cushions deeper and the velvet lusher. I sat down without complaint, sinking into the seat as if it would heal every ache.

Cassian reached for my hair.

Gently, he began brushing out the tangles, careful not to pull too hard, working through the snarls with patience. His knuckles grazed my cheek more than once, and every time they did, I closed my eyes.

When he was done, he crossed the room and came back holding a white tunic. It was simple, soft, and unmistakably his. It smelled faintly of him too.

I took it in trembling hands. He turned away without being asked, giving me space. No teasing. No lingering gaze. Just a quiet respect that only made my throat tighten further.

I changed quickly, wincing as the fabric brushed over the healing wound at my side. The tunic fell past the middle of my thighs, the sleeves hanging loose around my elbows. When I finished, I eased back into the soft chair, the cushions sighing under me. The sound must have told him I was done, because Cassian glanced over his shoulder and wandered back.

His eyes swept over me once, from bare feet to mussed hair. He walked to stand in front of me again, resting one hand lightly on the armrest beside mine, the other brushing a final touch down my cheek.

"You should lie down," he said, voice low.

"I'm fine," I murmured, though my limbs were growing heavier by the second.

My eyelids fluttered. My head dipped slightly, lolling to the side. The soft cotton of his tunic wrapped around me like a cocoon, and for the first time in what felt like hours, the pain had ebbed enough for the warmth to seep in.

And then, without warning, Cassian swept me up into his arms.

A startled yelp punched from my throat. "Cassian—!"

But his only response was a low chuckle, warm and rumbling from deep in his chest. It vibrated against my cheek, where my head now rested just above his heart.

"Don't fight this," he said. "Don't fight me."

So, I didn't. I melted into him instead. My skin brushed his and sparks seemed to strike like lightening. My arms curled around his neck as he carried me with unshakeable calm. Like it was nothing. Like I weighed less than air. Like I wasn't a weapon born for war.

He crossed the room in a few smooth strides and gently laid me down on the bed. The mattress dipped beneath me, soft and thick, like clouds had been sewn into its seams. I sank into it instinctively, every muscle in my body loosening, surrendering.

Cassian pulled the covers up to my chin with a care that made my chest ache. I watched him as he leaned over me, his shadow cast long across the canopy overhead. He brushed his lips across my forehead. A kiss so soft I barely felt it, but it landed. My heart squeezed.

"Goodnight, Lyra," he whispered. He hovered there, as if he wanted to say more. Then he turned and walked back toward his desk.

"You're not sleeping in the bed?"

He let out an airy chuckle, a corner of his mouth rising. "I'll join you soon."

The scattered work and parchment waited for him, but I could tell his mind wasn't on it. Not really.

I gave him a small smile back before burying my head back into the pillows. I didn't fight the exhaustion.

I let it take me.

CHAPTER THIRTY-FOUR

I WAS DREAMING.

I knew it even as it continued to unfold around me. The edges were too soft, the air too golden. Everything moved with a hush, like the world itself was holding its breath. A gentle hum threaded through the haze, vibrating low in my chest. I felt weightless, but not free.

The fog peeled, revealing a familiar space. I stood in the ballroom.

Empty now. No music. No laughter. Just candlelight dancing in quiet flickers across the marble floor and faceted crystal. It was beautiful in a haunted sort of way. It was grand and hollow, but the stillness wasn't cold.

I was back in the first trial.

In the mirrors lining the walls, I saw the way my dress had draped over my skin like moonlight, spun from shadow and metallic silver. I smelled the bitter wine I hadn't been used to. I heard the laughter that had slipped too loudly from my lips. I watched the way I'd twirled and smiled and tried so hard to seem unbothered.

A sound stirred behind me just loud enough to break the stillness. I turned.

Cassian stood near the far pillar, cloaked in shadow while the candlelight cast gold across his shoulders and jaw. He didn't move.

His arms were crossed, and though his body was controlled, his gaze was already on me.

No, not me.

Her.

The version of me from that night. Twirling and laughing. Faking ease with every breath. The memory version of me bumped into someone, apologizing with a grin that never reached her eyes.

At first, his expression was cold. Analytical. Like he was watching a puzzle unfold with no exact promise of a solution. He wore the face of a strategist. A prince.

But then, it shifted. The sharpness in his eyes melted, just barely.

Judgement became curiosity. Curiosity softened into awe. Awe melted to form admiration.

He didn't smile. Didn't move.

Just watched.

I turned, unable to look at him any longer, my heart aching from the weight of a memory I hadn't realized I'd kept.

As I walked forward, the ballroom dissolved behind me. I passed through an archway and into the throne room. It was empty. No courtiers or guards occupied the space, but only the golden seat atop the dais and two figures at its base.

Me, again.

Standing before the throne, my hand smeared with blood that dripped on the carved gold. The glowing words alive and dancing on my back. My chest rose and fell too fast. I remembered that moment too vividly. The surge of magic. The whispers. The way the world had seemed to split open around me. Cassian stood nearby, jaw clenched, fists balled at his sides. But his face.

His face was unguarded. Open. Fractured wide with something too raw to name. I watched him stare at me again, only this time, it wasn't awe, or admiration.

It was devotion. Terrifying. Reverent. Absolute.

"She doesn't even know what she is," his voice whispered from the air around me, bodiless, like smoke curling through shadow. *"And yet she belongs here more than any of them."*

I turned again. The memory crumbling behind me like ash.

I sat on the floor of my room, gloves beside me. Cassian sat across, his hands out and open as mine slowly slid into his. I watched as he trained me. I watched as he let my power snake into his mind. I watched as he controlled each flinch, each shiver, each moment of doubt.

His eyes stared into mine. His words echoed in my skull.

Eyes are the window to the soul.

I turned to my vanity, looking into my own eyes, but the scene behind me had changed once again.

With a splash of sound, I was suddenly beside the lagoon.

The sun hung low, stretching light across the water like spilled paint. It shimmered with every ripple. Golden. Soft.

Two figures moved in the shallows.

I saw myself soaked and breathless with laughter. My hair slicked back from my face, lashes clumped with sea water. And Cassian, waist-deep beside me, arms out to steady me as I floated. His gaze flicked to my face again and again, like he couldn't help himself. Like he had to keep checking that I was real.

I looked down at the surface of the water.

Our reflections swayed with the ripples. I watched his fingers trail down my back. I'd never seen his face that soft. No tension. No calculation.

The image bled away with my next breath.

I stood now in his chambers.

The same ones drenched in gold and velvet, but they looked different in this light. They were disheveled. Messy. Human. Real.

He sat at a desk, hunched over parchment. The candle had burned low, wax spilling in lazy drips. Paper was crumpled and cast aside in piles. Only one sheet remained unwrinkled.

And at the top was a name. My name.

Lyra

He stared at it, unmoving. His quill hovered above the page, stilled. His other hand tapped against the desk like he was trying to think without feeling.

Then, softly, and barely audible, he spoke.

"She's not mine to have."

He didn't shred the paper. He didn't curse.

He folded it. Carefully. Tenderly. Like it was something precious.

And he slid within the pages of a leather-bound journal.

Then, he stood.

And I followed him.

Through winding halls I didn't recognize. Down a corridor I had never seen in waking life. Until we stepped into a garden half-overgrown, bathed in moonlight.

Cassian knelt in the middle of it, among wild yellow blooms. He picked one buried beneath the taller flowers small, bright, ordinary.

He walked barefoot back through the palace. Silent. Straight to my door. He knelt again. Laid the flower down.

But then, he picked it back up. He brought the wild unnamed bloom to his own room and snipped a golden rose from the gardens. He placed that one outside of my door.

Golden and royal for me, and wildness for him. He melted into shadow, just around the corner, and he waited for me to find it.

Another doorway pulled at me, and I stepped through it, going up the winding stairs to the tower. I stepped into the cool night, the sharp air brushing against my skin. Inside, the space hummed with memory. My other self sat at the window, knees drawn to her chest, the view stretching out below her—the gardens, the forest, and the silver-black shimmer of the lagoon.

Cassian sat behind her. He didn't speak when her hair blew into his face. He looked at her like he understood. The ache. The exhaustion. The terrible weight of being both too seen and never seen at all. I watched, standing in the doorway, heart thudding in my chest.

Cassian turned then.

He looked straight at me.

Not the version of me in the scene.

Me.

My breath caught. I whipped around, and I fell into one final place.

A courtyard bathed in silver moonlight. The stars above shimmered like something divine. Something endless and bright. The grass was soft beneath my feet. The flowers glowed faintly, like constellations blooming from the earth.

Cassian stood in the center. He looked like he'd been sculpted from gold. He shined sharp against the starlit dark, and he saw me.

And this time, he smiled.

Not with flirtation.

Not with the practiced edge I'd grown used to.

He stepped forward and reached out, brushing his knuckles across my cheek like he had so many times before.

Tears welled in my eyes before I could stop them.

And then, he whispered, *"Did you see?"*

I gasped as my eyes flew open.

CHAPTER THIRTY-FIVE

HIS VOICE CLUNG to my skin, warmer than the fire, sharper than any blade. I didn't know how long I stayed like that—curled beneath the sheets, unmoving, haunted by shadows that didn't belong to the night.

Eventually, the morning light grew too bold to ignore. It spilled through the windows, bright and molten, gilding the stone floor in morning sunlight. I blinked against it, dragging myself upright with slow, heavy limbs. The sheets tangled around my waist, soft and wrinkled, and the air in the room held a faint chill that kissed my bare arms.

Cassian didn't wake.

He was still asleep, his head buried in the pillows and lips slightly parted. There was no tension in his face, no weight bunched in his brow. He looked peaceful. And stars, he was breathtaking like that.

I rose carefully, easing my legs over the edge of the bed, not wanting to wake him. The tunic he'd given me still clung to my frame. It was warm from sleep and still carried the faintest trace of his scent. My hair lifted in the morning breeze as I stepped barefoot onto the balcony.

The view struck me like a held breath.

His balcony sat higher than mine, angled toward the rising sun. The light spilled across everything—the city, the distant hills, the sliver of water far beyond the trees—turning the world into something golden and otherworldly. I leaned against the railing, hands resting on cool stone, and I stared.

This was his city.

The place he would one day rule.

I tried to picture the woman who would stand beside him. A queen worthy of his crown. I tried to imagine her face, her bearing, the perfect composure she'd wear, but every time I tried, I saw myself. I saw the way his hands had rested on my waist in the tower. The way he'd knelt among the roses just to lay one gently outside my door. The way he'd looked at me in the dream, like he was already undone by me and didn't care to put himself back together.

And stars help me. I wanted it. Not just the crown. Not just the power. I wanted him, but I wasn't supposed to be here. I wasn't supposed to be anything. The King's voice echoed through me, jagged and cruel.

You are not meant to rise.

I gripped the railing tighter, my knuckles going white.

Cassian was the Prince. He belonged to a future written in gold and history. The King would never let me stand beside his heir.

So, no. I couldn't afford to dream of him. I couldn't afford to feel this way, to want this life, this softness, this warmth, this impossible hope. Not when the cost of it could be everything. Not when the fire in me might be the very thing that consumes him, too.

The wind shifted. The scent of sun-warmed stone and faraway jasmine drifted around me. I closed my eyes. A soft sound stirred the air behind me.

I turned. Cassian was waking. The sunlight had crept its way up his body, turning the hard lines of his arms and shoulders into something warm and gentle. He shifted in the bed, arms lifting in a lazy stretch, a yawn slipping past his lips, barely muffled. His eyes opened slowly, hazy with sleep. And then they found me like he'd known I'd be standing there.

His smile was soft and unguarded, still tame with sleep. He stood, bare feet brushing the floor, the hem of his creased shirt clinging to him. He didn't speak. The morning didn't need words. There was only the breeze met with the golden hush of early light and the quiet rhythm of his steps as he padded toward me. I turned back around as he reached me, staring again towards the city that would one day bow to him. To their King.

His chest brushed against my back, warm and solid like the sun itself had come to press against my spine. I closed my eyes as he leaned in, his lips brushing my temple in the gentlest of kisses, light as breath. Then his arms came up slowly, resting on either side of me along the railing. Not to trap. Not to cage. Just to be there.

Yet, I froze.

Not outwardly. Not enough for anyone to notice, but inside, I tensed like something was about to break. I wanted to lean into him. My body ached for the familiar weight, the safety of his warmth, the way the world always seemed to quiet when he was this close. But I couldn't.

I shouldn't.

I pulled back. Cassian felt it. I knew he did. He didn't move at first, but I felt it in the shift of his chest, the slight furrow of his brows, the way his mouth parted as if to ask—

"Is something—?"

"No," I said, too fast. Too quiet.

Because what was I supposed to tell him?

I saw every thought, every feeling, every ache you've ever had, and it undid me. I think I love you for it, Cassian, and now I can't bear to look at you.

Not an option. So, I forced a smile, small and practiced, but it didn't reach my eyes. He saw that too.

His face faltered, the edges of it dimming, softening into something more resigned. Wordlessly, he stepped back, withdrawing his arms. But as he did, his hands ran up my arms, just barely.

And the golden thread between us lit up like a struck match.

I inhaled sharply.

In that instant, I felt it all. The sting in his chest when I pulled away. His joy. The quiet, stunned kind just from seeing me in his shirt, like it was the most beautiful thing in the world. The subtle, careful way he'd looked me over when I wasn't watching, checking for bruises or any signs of pain. His worry about my stitches, my bruises, my scar. The constant thought of who could have given it to me. The ache. The hope. The quiet, trembling wish that this moment could happen again.

Me in his room. Me in his clothes. Morning after morning.

Always.

He didn't touch me again. He just stepped back inside, leaving the balcony door half-open behind him. It swayed gently in the breeze, the fabric of the curtain brushing the floor like a whispered farewell.

I turned back to the view and gripped the railing until my hands threatened to cramp.

A sharp knock at the chamber door shattered the quiet.

I flinched, heart leaping, and instinctively ducked out of view. I slipped around the curve of the balcony into its farthest corner, the stone cool against my back. Cassian moved across the room, calm and unhurried, and I watched him through the thin veil fluttering in front of the windowpanes.

He opened the door. A guard stood in the hallway, his golden armor gleaming with reflected sunlight. "As you requested, Your Highness," the guard said, voice clipped and formal. He handed something I couldn't see to Cassian. "Lady Morwyn is in the infirmary. The healers say she should recover."

Any breath I held left my lungs.

Cassian nodded once. "Thank you."

The door clicked shut again, quiet and final. For a moment, I couldn't move. Elena was alive. She would recover. That truth flooded through me like a tide I hadn't realized I'd been holding back.

I stepped out of hiding slowly, the relief still humming in my bones. Cassian turned to look at me, his gaze steady.

Just *'I knew you'd want to know'* written in the soft set of his lips.

Then his eyes flicked down to a small pile of neatly folded clothes in his hands. Clothes meant for me with a pair of gloves resting on top.

He'd thought of that too.

We dressed without speaking, moving through the room like twin flames, the hush between us somehow soothing instead of strained. I stopped to check my split lip and cheekbone in the mirror, surprised to see both already scabbed and healing.

Cassian turned to the door and unlatched it. I followed, hesitating only a heartbeat. We slipped out into the corridor, footsteps silent on the palace floor. We wound our way down through the lower levels of the palace, the corridors narrowing with each turn. The air grew colder the deeper we went. It melted from a coolness to a sterile chill, sharp and stripped of comfort. Our footsteps echoed too loudly against the smooth stone floors, and every sound seemed to vanish too quickly, swallowed whole by the quiet.

This place didn't feel like the rest of the palace. No gilded mirrors. No carved moldings. No silks or gold-threaded tapestries. Just stone and silence. As if forgotten by the rest of the palace.

The infirmary was buried in the east wing, out of sight and tucked away like a secret. The moment we crossed its threshold, everything shifted. The walls were blocks of pale quartz, smooth and too clean, like polished bone. The light filtering through the square windows was thin and colorless. Bright but without warmth, like it had been wrung of everything good before being allowed in.

There was no perfume here. No rich parchment or ink. No incense. Just the sharp bite of isopropanol, the bitter tang of ointment, and a tinge of blood beneath it all.

Everything was white.

The tiles. The curtains. The uniforms of the healers. The beds with their narrow metal frames. Even the air felt bleached. Curtains hung like ghostly veils between the rows of cots, most of them empty. The hush in the room wasn't peaceful, it was clinical. Cold. Like the quiet here didn't come from rest, but from suffering being muffled behind linen drapes.

Then I saw it. The far cot had its curtains drawn tight. Closed all the way to the floor. Too deliberate. Too careful.

Elena.

I didn't wait. My legs moved before I even knew what I was doing. I darted forward, footsteps loud in the hush, and yanked the curtain open with a screech of metal rings against the rail.

Will startled in the wooden chair beside her. He'd been half-asleep, arms folded across his chest, eyes heavy with worry. He jolted upright at the sound, but I barely noticed him.

Elena was lying in that bed.

My chest constricted so fast I could barely breathe. She looked better than I'd feared, but stars. It was still bad.

Her right eye was swollen shut, the skin around it a sickening blend of purple and green, like the bruises were still blooming. A bandage curved over her brow, the edge tinged with pink where the wound beneath hadn't stopped bleeding entirely. Her lip was split wide, raw and jagged, the stitches puckering her skin unevenly. Her ribs were bound in tight linen, but even the wrappings couldn't hide the bruises that spilled across her torso. There was dried blood along the shell of her ear and at the top where it had torn. The dark crescent made my stomach twist.

Then, I saw her hair.

It had once been so sleek. Glossy. Always pinned back or done in some makeshift braid, something Elena had put so much effort into, but now.

Now it was matted. Her braid crown was tangled beyond recognition. Crusted with dried blood in black-red clumps, stiff and wild against the pillow. Some of it had stuck to her skin, some to the cot beneath her. The mess of it, the sheer neglect of it, made my throat burn.

They hadn't washed her hair.

They'd stitched her up. Wrapped her ribs. Applied the salves and checked her breathing. But they hadn't spared even a moment, not a second, to clean the blood from her scalp.

No warm cloth. No gentle comb. No kindness.

Just cold hands and bandages.

To them, Elena wasn't a person. She wasn't a girl who had laughed with me on my bed or rolled her eyes at Thane's smugness or smiled with such mischief while stealing loaves of hangover bread. She was just another broken body. Another patient on a cot, lined up with the rest of the wreckage this palace liked to call marriage trials.

My hands curled into fists at my sides.

Elena would've hated this. She would've loathed the idea of anyone seeing her like this. She would've wanted her hair smooth. Her spine straight. Her chin lifted like she was still a threat. Still in control.

She would've wanted to look like herself, and they hadn't even given her that.

Will cleared his throat, the sound thin and uncertain. My eyes snapped to him, and he froze like a cornered animal. He looked at me as if I might strike him, wide-eyed and stiff in that rickety wooden chair, but then Cassian stepped forward, just a simple shift in his tall frame.

"P-Prince Vaelros," he stammered, leaping to his feet and bowing so deeply I swear I heard his spine crack. When he rose, his fingers fidgeted over one another, nervously tangling and untangling.

"Thank you for watching and protecting Miss Morwyn," Cassian said gently, his voice a break against the sterile air.

He meant it. Every word.

I felt it ripple off him. The sincerity, the gratitude. It tightened something in my chest. An ache that was sharp and sudden.

Will's shoulders eased. He gave a small, curt nod, eyes darting between us. I turned back to Elena, unable to bear the tension in my limbs anymore.

I opened the narrow drawer beside her cot and found a shallow metal tin inside, its edges dented from years of use. Beside it, a clean cloth. Across the room, a small brass spout jutted from the wall above a deep stone sink. I filled the tin with warm water as steam ghosted off the surface, then carried it carefully back to her bedside. The heat warmed my palms, steadied my hands.

I knelt behind the cot, setting the tin just beneath the edge of her pillow, and gently slid one arm beneath her neck, cradling her with care as I tilted her head back into the water.

Her hair dipped in like strands of spilled oil, the braid black and tangled and soaked in dried blood. The moment it touched the surface, the water bloomed pink, curling with crimson threads that unfurled like smoke. I sucked in a breath, blinking against the sudden burn in my eyes.

I reached for her hair with both hands and began to work through the worst of it. The mats were stubborn, tangled tight by blood and time. I used my fingers gently, slowly, never pulling, never rushing. I threaded my forefinger through the woven strands, loosening and undoing the braid as the water burned scarlet red. Bits of blood loosened and swirled in the basin. Some hair came with it too. I swallowed hard and kept going.

I found a bar of soap in the cart nearby. It was simple and scentless, but it felt like luxury. I lathered it in my hands until suds foamed at my fingers, then ran it through her hair again and again. The water turned murky, then pink, then clear again as I worked, over and over.

When her hair was clean, I rinsed it one last time, watching the final cloud of grime drift away. I lifted her head gently from the basin and wrapped it in the soft cloth from the cart, drying it with care. I combed it out with my fingers, smoothing each section until it fell in dark, silky strands.

Then I braided it again into a single, thick plait, tight and neat. I imagine she would have liked this style for training. For when she felt most like a warrior. I laid it gently over her shoulder.

Only then did I glance up.

Cassian stood across from me, silent. Will looked guilty now. His lips pressed together in a thin line, his fingers clenched tight in his lap. As if it had only now occurred to him that he could have done this. Should have done this.

I caught his gaze and offered him a small smile. Not one of pity. One of understanding. I wasn't angry with him. I was angry with the world that had made this feel normal.

I rounded the cot, coming to stand at Elena's side. I brushed a piece of hair from her forehead, smoothing it with gentle, careful fingers.

Cassian's voice came softly behind me, his tone low. "They said she'll make a full recovery. She's strong."

I nodded, though my throat tightened at the words.

She would survive. But survival felt hollow.

I sat in silence and felt fury curl inside me. Not loud or wild, but slow and heavy. Like embers burning beneath ash. I didn't want her to simply wake up. I didn't want her to carry this agony in silence, wear her scars like trophies.

I wanted justice. Not the kind handed down from gilded crowns, crimson oaths, or hollow thrones. Not the kind given by blood-stained hands and numb hearts.

Justice is what fate gives to those who mistake mercy for weakness.

And I no longer dealt in forgiveness. Not anymore.

Cassian and Will stood watching, and without looking away from Elena I whispered, "I need some time."

Will moved forward in protest, but Cassian laid a firm hand on his shoulder. It wasn't a threat, but Will didn't argue further. They turned and left without another word.

CHAPTER THIRTY-SIX

A DINNER TRAY SAT untouched beside me, the steam long since vanished. Only the faint aroma of rosemary and lemon and something spiced I couldn't name lingered in the air. I didn't have the appetite for any of it.

I sat in a wooden chair on the wall opposite Elena as I watched a healer scurry around her cot. I hadn't left yet, and for a heartbeat I thought the healer might lift her gaze and ask why I'd stayed. Her backwards glances told me she was curious, but she barely paused in her work, and for that mercy, I was grateful.

The air inside was cool, scented with dried herbs and the faint tang of something medicinal. Lavender. Willow bark. Linens freshly laundered and still holding the scent of soap.

Elena lay half-draped in the evening shadow. Pale. Still. Her chest rose and fell in slow, even rhythm, each breath a quiet victory.

I heard the infirmary door creak open, and in the hall, stood Will. He looked at me, desperation in his eyes. I let my power crawl, the shimmering silver air crashing against his feet.

His thoughts drifted to me like leaves in an autumn breeze. His mind was gentle, but his emotions were anything but. It was killing him to be away. Enough that he had disobeyed Cassian, and part of me respected him for that fact alone.

I crossed the room on quiet feet, each step careful. When I reached the side of Elena's bed, the healer backed away, leaving whatever balm she was using on the end of the bed. I brushed a gloved hand down her cheek, tracing the edge of an angry purple bruise under her eye.

I looked at her. At the dark lashes resting against her cheeks. At the swollen red split in her eyebrow. I gently tucked a stray hair behind her ear as I pressed a gentle kiss to her forehead.

"I'll see you again," I whispered. My voice was barely a breath, almost swallowed by the quiet. "I promise."

I turned and walked away.

I passed Will and gave him a small nod as I walked back into the marble halls. His gratitude pulsed in waves, and he practically sprinted back to her side, only slowing when he worried his steps might disturb her. He gently picked up her hand and held it near his lips. He whispered soft things against her skin that I couldn't hear. The moment wasn't mine to listen to anyway.

My footsteps echoed softly as I moved through the palace like a ghost. Unseen and untouched. I didn't have a destination. I let my feet carry me. The open air passages let in a slight breeze. The wind outside was thick with warmth, but not the kind that clung like sweat. It wrapped around me gently, like a whisper brushing across skin. It smelled of florals and salt, of sun-baked soil and something else. Something sweet I couldn't name.

The leaves had changed. Flashes of red and amber whispered through the treetops like the sparks of an inevitable fire. It was the kind of day that hummed with transition. The kind that told you something was ending, even if you didn't know what exactly it was just yet.

Somewhere nearby, a fountain trickled. Water against stone. Birds chirped lazily in the hedges, and a bee buzzed past my ear with no real urgency. The gravel paths beneath my feet crunched faintly with each step.

Everywhere I went, I found pieces of memory.

Elena's scream still rang in my ears sometimes. Sharp and raw. I could see her falling, over and over again. The way her body crumpled, and how her eyes had gone deathly void.

Then there were Cassian's hands—steady one moment, trembling the next. The way he had looked at me in the greenhouse, like I was both his ruin and salvation. Like he knew something I didn't. Maybe something I didn't want to know. Maybe something I couldn't.

Kaden's eyes, empty but now flickering. Changing. Haunted.

And then, without even realizing how I'd gotten there, I found myself in the southern tower.

The place where Cassian had kissed me.

The stairs wound tightly, a narrow spiral of stone that stretched high. Few guards came this way. Most didn't know the stairwell led anywhere at all, but I did.

I placed one hand on the moss-covered banister and climbed. Each step pulled gently at my legs, reminding me of my bandaged side, of my body that was still tired, still healing. I climbed with a strange calmness, like I was moving toward something inevitable.

At the top, the wooden door creaked open. The terrace welcomed me like an old friend. The view stretched endlessly. Palace gardens rolled out below like a painting, all color and curve and motion. Beyond them, hills drowsed in the sun's warmth, golden and green. And further still, the lagoon shimmered like glass, the water catching the sunlight and scattering it like spilled diamonds. A willow tree leaned heavy near the edge of the gardens, its silver-green arms trailing toward the pond below, swaying gently in the breeze like it was reaching for something just out of memory.

And beneath it, still, solitary, and unmistakable stood a figure.

Cassian.

Even from that distance, I knew it was him.

The tilt of his head. The way he moved.

He didn't wear his princely mask or the heavy cloak of duty. He wasn't the charming heir or the watchful commander. He was just Cassian.

He looked like he was made of sunlight, like the last kiss of day had chosen him alone. Gold streaked his hair, brushed his cheekbones, lit the edge of his shoulders until he almost seemed unreal.

Something twisted inside me. A sharp, aching pull beneath my ribs. I turned from the terrace. Down the narrow stairs. One after another, my hand trailing the cold stone as the walls closed in and then opened again as I reached the corridors below.

The palace watched me as I passed. Servants halted mid-step, startled eyes flicking toward me before quickly dropping. A few pressed themselves against the walls to let me by, their shoulders taut with unease. Guards straightened and looked away. Fear clung to them like a scent. I didn't know what had changed, only that something had. I didn't blame them.

I crossed the lawns with my flats brushing through the grass, dew still clinging in the shadows. The gardens were quiet now. Empty. Even the birds had gone still. The willow tree loomed ahead, its branches low and swaying gently with the breeze. And there, slouched against its trunk like it might be the only thing holding him upright, was Cassian.

There were two wine bottles beside him. I recognized the label even from a few paces away, the memory of that ballroom wine churning in my stomach. One bottle was already empty, lying sideways in the grass like it had given up. The other still dangled from his fingers, swinging gently as his thumb traced idle circles over the glass. Only half full now.

Cassian Vaelros, Prince of the realm, the King's golden heir, was drunk.

And stars. He looked remarkably human.

His collar was unbuttoned. His sleeves were rolled up, forearms resting on his knees. His legs stretched out in front of him like he'd simply collapsed there and decided not to get up again. The breeze moved through his hair, softening the sharp lines of his face. His eyes were closed.

For a moment, I just stood there and watched

He didn't notice me, not at first. He looked far away. Like whatever world he was in was far from this one. Like the bottle in his hand was the only object anchoring him to anything at all.

I took a step forward, and then another.

His head tilted lazily in my direction, his eyes slow to open. They were glassy, dark, a little unfocused, but when they landed on me, something behind them sparked. Recognition. Surprise. Maybe even something like relief.

"You," he said, his voice a strange mix of too loud for the quiet garden and too soft for everything he seemed to be holding back.

I arched a brow. "Me."

A crooked grin curved across his lips, slow and lopsided. "Come to save me, little flame?"

He lifted the bottle and took a long pull. A single drop of deep red wine caught on the corner of his mouth. I watched it slide down, trailing the sharp edge of his jaw. Stars, it should've made me laugh, but it didn't.

I remembered how he'd carried me once, when I was completely and helplessly drunk, and now here he was. Sitting beneath a willow, lost in a bottle, wearing sorrow like a crown.

"Why are you drinking Cassian?"

He looked at me like it was the most ridiculous question in the world. "I am the Prince. I can do whatever I please, and today," he lifted the bottle in a solitary toast, "I choose drinking." He slugged another portion of the wine.

I stepped forward and sat down in front of him, my knees brushing his own. "We both know that's not the reason."

His head fell, his chin meeting his chest. I bent my own down, shifting so I still met his gaze. His eyes found my own and utter anguish filled me. He was in pain, but not from anything physical.

I held out my hand, resting it on his leg. "Come on," I said softly, my fingers moved to brush against the inside of his upper arm. "Let's go, my Prince."

Cassian blinked at me, as if trying to make sense of the words. Then he let out a sound, half laugh half sigh, and leaned into my touch, my hand moving to press against his chest.

"I am forever yours," he murmured, his hand rising to grab a piece of hair that flowed in the breeze. He stared at the strand as if he was hypnotized.

"But never call me Prince. If anything," His eyes lazily dragged back to my own. "I should call you Queen."

His voice was rough velvet. That particular kind of raw that only came after truth or ruin.

I cleared my throat as I jumped to my feet. "Good to know that you lie when you're drunk," I said, trying to keep my tone level, unaffected.

He clawed at the tree, forcing himself to his feet. "I'm a lot of things, but a liar isn't one of them," he shot back, and then, without asking, slung an arm around my shoulders.

I steadied him as best I could. His weight dragged me down, but I didn't pull away. He stopped walking and dropped the bottle in his hand to the ground. The red wine spilled like bloodshed. The arm Cassian had wrapped around me jerked back, spinning me into him.

"I just... I don't know what you want from me."

I looked up, startled, but he wasn't done.

"Should I stop, or should I continue?" His brow furrowed, and his breath hiccuped on the exhale. It smelled sweet. "Is it effort you want? Or proof? Please, Lyra. I'll give you whatever it is you want." His head tilted toward me, curls falling across his eyes. "If I haven't earned you yet, tell me how. Tell me and I swear I'll do it."

My mouth opened. A protest. A plea, maybe. I didn't know, but he just kept talking.

"I feel it too, Lyra," he said, and stars, the way he said my name. Like it tasted better than the wine. "The pull. That little silver string that is absolutely relentless."

His hand found my waist for a moment, his fingers running down from my ribs to my hip, landing on the curve and curling inward to stay here. He pulled me closer.

"It's become more than want. I can't stop thinking about you. Can't stop *needing* you. I'm not like this." His voice cracked slightly. "Not with anyone. But you…"

His eyes met mine, and I swore I could feel it. The heat of his desire. The admiration. The ache. And not a lick of it was my power. It was just him and this unbearable, golden thing between us that refused to burn out.

I tried to back away, to give myself room to breathe, but I tripped slightly on a root in the grass, my breath catching. "Cass—"

He grabbed at me slowly, the wine tearing at his movements. Too slowly to catch me, though I hadn't really fallen.

A boyish smile spread on his lips. "You called me Cass," he said, his face lighting with something drunken and wild. It was as if his entire speech was nothing but a memory. "A nickname and a declaration all in one night?" His grin curled, wicked and slow. "Tell me, Lyra, how do you feel about the last name Vaelros?"

The name rolled off his tongue like a purr—soft, teasing, dangerous.

I rolled my eyes so hard it almost hurt. "Stop talking," I muttered, grabbing his wrist and tugging him forward again. "You're insufferable."

But my voice wasn't steady. My pulse thundered against my ribs, echoing in my ears like war drums. Part of me wanted to laugh, part of me wanted to slap him, and a shamefully large part of me wanted to lean in and kiss the wine right off his mouth.

He said it himself. Cassian was many things. Beautiful, dangerous, infuriating, far too clever for his own good, elegant. Even now, even like this, he carried the ghost of grace in the way he spoke, but my stars, was he a noisy drunk.

He stumbled from one side of the corridor to the other like the palace walls were conspiring against him, hands slapping against marble to catch himself before his face met the same fate. I kept a tight grip on his wrist, half dragging, half guiding him forward as we made our way toward my room.

We passed a tall window along the corridor. Moonlight had begun to pour in like water as it painted silver across the floor.

Cassian yanked me gently back with the hand I still had wrapped around his wrist, his fingers rising to curl around my forearm. I turned, confused, but before I could ask what he was doing, he pulled me flush against him.

My chest met his, the warmth of his body soaking through both our clothes. One arm wrapped firmly around my back. Not rough, not desperate, just there.

His eyes were glazed, yes, unfocused around the edges, but they never left my face. Not once.

"Tell me this doesn't feel like we were created for each other," he whispered.

And then he kissed me. Not on the lips. Not yet.

His mouth brushed the sharp line of my jaw, slow and devout. I felt my breath catch. Felt something else, too. A ripple, subtle and instinctive, of silver power surged between us like it had a mind of its own. My power slipped, tangled with the bond, wove through him, and wrapped around us both.

Warm breath ghosted against my skin as he pressed another kiss, just below my ear this time. A softer place. A weaker place.

"Tell me," he murmured, "and I'll stop."

The words wrapped around me like silk and steel. He meant them. He meant each one, but he didn't want to stop.

What if I don't want you to stop either?

The thought surged up before I could swallow it back, full of heat and hunger and longing that scared me more than any blade.

I forced it away.

Cleared my throat. Pulled gently from his grip, just enough to place space between us and the truth trembling in my bones. I stepped out of the moonlight. Out of the cocoon we'd created.

"You've had too much wine," I said curtly. The words scratched my throat on the way out.

Cassian gave a small shrug, half amusement, half defeat. "I have," he admitted, his voice low, almost rasped. "But you know I'm not a liar."

His gaze dropped then, moving from my eyes to my lips, to the curve of my waist, lingering like a hand I could almost feel.

"I can't get enough of that," he said, tapping his temple with one finger. "When you do that *thing*. It's *maddening*. You feel like the water in the lagoon. Suddenly I'm drowning." He took a step forward. "And I don't care."

I didn't move. I should've, but I didn't.

We were inches apart. I could see the flecks of gold in his eyes, the way the shadows framed his face like he was something carved from light and trouble. He leaned into and brushed his lips against the shell of my ear. His breath tickled my cheek, wine-sweet and burning.

"Go in my mind again," he whispered, voice husky. "Let me feel more of you."

He tilted his head, just slightly, just enough to turn temptation into something living, something electric. I didn't have to use my power to feel the tension. It was a storm inside me. A pull I couldn't name. A fire I wasn't ready to feel.

I could barely breathe.

"I will," I said, brushing a hand through his curls, pushing them from his eyes. It landed at the back of his neck. "When you're sober. Maybe then you'll remember it."

He threw his head back with a groan of pure, dramatic exasperation, his whole body radiating frustration and something perilously close to affection.

I let my fingers linger a second too long before I pulled away for good because if I didn't, I wasn't sure I'd walk away at all.

We made it to my room by some miracle. By an even greater one, Kaden was still nowhere in sight. I didn't question it. I didn't want to break whatever fragile thread of fate had decided to give us this one quiet moment, unobserved.

I reached for the handle and shook it gently, testing the lock for resistance.

"Unfamiliar with opening your own door, little flame?" His voice was slurring, and yet he still had quite the tongue.

"My apologies, Prince. My door hasn't always been unlocked recently. Fun little game me and the palace like to play."

He huffed a laugh, as if my prison-of-a-room was comical. "I handled that the day I found you bleeding out on your floor." He leaned against the doorframe, his head canted sideways. His curls fell into his eyes.

I slipped us inside and shut the door quickly behind us, leaning against it for half a second to exhale. Cassian stumbled as he looked around like he'd never been here before, which was ridiculous. He had briefly, once. But tonight, everything seemed new to him.

And if I was honest, the room looked new to me too. No blood stained the wooden panels. No dirtied rags hung on the copper tub. No torn tunics or makeshift bandages littered the floor. I whipped around, unspoken questions filling my head, but they were all answered with a singular sentence from wisdom only granted by wine.

"The palace has servants for a reason."

Something close to gratitude squeezed at my heart.

Then, without warning or ceremony, Cassian sat down. On the floor. With all the elegance of a sack of flour hitting the ground. He flopped back onto his elbows, gazing up at me with that same crooked grin he wore far too often for his own good.

"This is nice," he said breezily, his voice thick with wine and mischief. "You should have visitors more often."

"You are not a visitor," I chuckled, crouching near his feet. "You're a hazard."

His nose scrunched up, watching with mild curiosity as I reached for his boots.

"What are you doing?" he asked, head tilting lazily.

"Returning the favor," I said, tugging at the laces.

He blinked slowly, as if trying to work through what I meant, and then simply let me. One boot came off, then the other, clunking down by the door. He relaxed further into the floor as I stood back up, walking over to the sit at my vanity.

"You're sweet when you're bossy," he murmured, eyelids drooping.

"You're loud when you're drunk."

His smile deepened. He looked at me in the mirror. Something quiet passed between us. Then, with a huff, he sat up and gave the fireplace a truly venomous glare.

Even though autumn carried summer heat, the nights had begun to dip coolly. The flames crackled softly, casting a golden glow across the stone. He muttered something I didn't catch, then fumbled with the buttons of his shirt, scoffing under his breath.

"It's too *hot* in here," he complained, slurring only slightly. "This shirt's always been itchy. Stupid royal fabric."

I arched a brow but said nothing. I watched in the mirror as his fingers worked clumsily, undoing the last few buttons until the shirt fell open entirely.

The cloth still clung to his shoulders, but bronze skin, sun-kissed and golden, stretched over his abdomen. And the stretching bands of muscle were anything but decorative. Every line of him had been carved by battle, by repetition, by grit. He wasn't delicate or polished like I had imagined a prince to be. Cassian was raw strength wrapped in lazy charm. There were scars, too. Faint, but real. Evidence of the life he lived under all the silk and ceremony.

I didn't mean to stare, but I did.

He yawned, stretching like a satisfied cat, and his body shifted beneath the light. Muscle rippled, defined and unrepentant.

I looked away too late.

He caught me, and the grin that followed was nothing short of scandalous.

Cassian stood, swaying like the wind had suddenly changed direction. He sauntered over and placed both hands on the back of the chair I sat in, shirt hanging open, curls mussed from my hands and the wine. And when he reached for me, it wasn't to tease. His finger brushed beneath my chin, tilting it up until I had no choice but to meet his reflected gaze in the mirror.

"Yours," he whispered, voice low and slurred, but strangely certain. "Little silver flame."

I didn't know what to say to that.

Luckily, I didn't even have time to breathe it in before he turned from me, stumbled two steps toward the sofa by the window, and collapsed into it like it had always been his final destination.

And then he passed out. Just like that.

I sat there, caught somewhere between a laugh and a sigh, staring at the ridiculousness of a man unconscious on my settee.

Stars help me, I thought, dragging a hand down my face.

I stood frozen, my pulse still humming from the chaos he left in his wake. His words echoed in my head like a song I couldn't shake.

"If I haven't earned you yet, tell me how."

"Yours, little silver flame."

I swallowed hard, chest tight. The room had gone quiet except for the soft crackle of firewood and the faint sound of his breathing. I slipped my shoes from my own feet, setting them gently beside my vanity. I moved slowly, as if any sudden movement might shatter the fragile stillness hanging between us.

My armoire was closed, and when I opened the doors, each dress seemed to be washed and pressed to perfection. I grabbed a flowing silver nightdress, the fabric opaque and iridescent in the moonlight. I slipped the clothes Cassian had gifted me from my body, pulling the dress overhead and letting the shimmering silk fall where it may. Crossing the room, I climbed into bed without a word. The sheets were cool, untouched, and I curled into them, drawing the blankets to my chin.

I looked at Cassian one last time. I looked at him slumped in my chair like a drunken fool, his boots off and shirt gaping. Bronze skin caught the firelight, casting shadows across the lines of his chest, the curve of his throat. His lips were parted slightly, like even in sleep, he had more to say.

I watched him, silently. Half of me wanted to wake him. Shake him. Ask him if he meant it. If I was really his.

But the other half...

The other half wished he had finished that second bottle. That he'd let the wine dull the line between restraint and desire. That he'd been just drunk enough to forget his decency and crawl into my bed without hesitation. Wrap himself around me like I was something warm and safe and his. Like in another life he could be mine, too.

But he hadn't.

So, the chair would have to do.

CHAPTER THIRTY-SEVEN

SLEEP FELT LIKE A DRUG as it pulled me further and further down. Reality lingered under the veil of exhaustion that seemed to make the entire world look off-kilter. The colors bled at the edges, too bright, too soft. Sound came like it was filtered through water or cotton stuffed in my ears. My thoughts moved slowly and syrup-thick, each one trailing behind the next.

Then—

CRASH!

The sound shattered the fog like glass.

Steel on stone.

A curse, sharp and breathless.

My eyelids were heavy as I fought to pry them open just in time to see movement—fast, dark, violent.

Cassian was already up. He was a blur of motion between me and the door. I blinked hard, struggling to shake off sleep as my mind scrambled to catch up. There was another figure, sizable yet fast, and then a flash of moonlight on steel.

Four royal guards had swarmed the room.

Cassian lunged. One guard didn't even have time to raise his blade. I heard the grunt as Cassian collided with him, then a sickening crack. Bone on stone or skull against wall, I did not know. The sword slipped from the attacker's grip, and Cassian caught it like it belonged to him. In one fluid, brutal motion, he drove the blade up beneath the man's ribs.

Blood sprayed. A wet, horrifying sound. The attacker gasped once, blood gurgling and bubbling from his mouth, then slumped to the floor in a heap of armor and limbs, the clang echoing off my stone walls like a bell tolling too late.

Cassian turned to me, the sword dripping, but his eyes weren't on me. They found something beside me to focus on.

"*Lyra—!*" he barked.

I tried to move, but I was tangled—wrapped in the blankets of my bed like a trap. My legs were caught, arms pinned beneath the weight of fabric I'd once curled into for comfort. Now it felt like a noose.

I thrashed, kicked, cursed.

A second shadow moved. I saw another man. Another guard turned assassin. His fist twisted in my hair, yanking me back with enough force to wrench a cry from my throat. The air left my lungs in a choke as my head snapped sideways, the ceiling spinning above me. The guard pressed a cloth to my mouth and nose that smelled sickly sweet and slightly metallic, the scent coating my lungs and throat.

He didn't strike, not yet. He was waiting, gloating. I saw the glint of something raised, steel again, and I knew.

Cassian's roar split the air behind us. "*Don't you dare!*"

Then chaos.

I was yanked from the bed like a rag doll, limbs limp and useless, my voice still caught in my throat. The attacker stood behind me. They held me above the ground, my toes brushing the floor as I struggled. Whoever held my hair began to lower me, but then they kicked the back of my knees, pulling my head down to the floor from behind me.

The back of my skull slammed into the cold wooden floor, and for a moment, I couldn't even breathe. White-hot pain exploded behind my eyes. My vision blacked out as my ears rang. My entire body seized, curled inward from the shock of it. I tried to move, tried to scream, but my muscles refused. Everything was wrong. The room flipped and spun and everything was too loud, and yet somehow so far away.

Steel screamed against steel.

I blinked, forcing my vision to focus. Cassian was a whirlwind of gold and shadow, holding back two guards at once. One staggered back, blood pouring from a gash at his shoulder, while the other advanced, fast and ruthless. Cassian met him head-on with a clash that sent sparks into the dark.

I tried to call out. Tried to warn him that there were more but I was already being claimed in a fight of my own.

I willed forward any power I had, but the pain was too overwhelming. I couldn't reach anything. The jar in my mind was empty, void of anything at all. My head swam, from the sweet cloth scent still echoing in my mouth or from the collision I wasn't sure.

A thick, calloused hand snatched me from the floor. One arm wrapped around my waist like a vice, while the other twisted in my hair and slammed me hard into the wall.

Stone. Cold. Unforgiving.

I cried out, but it was barely a sound. More breath than voice.

The shock paralyzed me. I was pinned like an insect under glass. My limbs trembled as I struggled, but the man was stronger, heavier, pressing his body into mine to hold me still. He smelled like rot and old wine, and his breath was a rancid fog as he leered down at me, dagger in hand, its blade cold against the base of my throat.

"Look at you," he murmured, almost lovingly. His voice made my stomach churn. "Pretty little prize. Bet you're soft all over."

His hand moved, slowly, deliberately.

Over my waist then up my ribs. To the neckline of my dress and down my chest, his fingers claiming and cruel. My skin crawled beneath his touch. I gasped, choking on a sob, on fear and disgust and helplessness. My body squirmed, instinctively trying to retreat, to escape, but there was nowhere to go.

His hand gripped my hip, bunching the fabric there, pulling until the seams threatened to rip.

Cassian saw.

His scream shattered whatever silence was left in the room.

"No—don't you lay a hand on her!" he bellowed, voice breaking like a dam. "Don't you *dare* touch her!"

He surged forward, but a guard crashed into him, forcing him back into the fight. Cassian's face was pure fury and unfiltered terror. He tried to claw his way toward me, and still, they didn't recognize him. Not in the dark, not like this. Not when he bled like any man.

The assassin chuckled, low and amused. "That your lover, little girl?" he sneered against my skin. "Pity. He can't save you. Might as well enjoy what's left of you while I can." His blade scraped along my cheek, a faint line of fire kissing my skin, but it was his hand, his bare hand, that moved after it.

Skin to skin.

And that was his mistake.

In that moment, I broke. Not with panic, or fear, but rage. I didn't need to reach for my power this time. No, it flooded through the brush of his fingers as if it had awoken from a slumber of its own. No caution. No restraint. A violent surge, raw and unfiltered, poured from my skin to his.

His eyes flared sterling silver.

The knife clattered to the stone floor with a sharp clang, but I barely registered it. He broke the touch and expected relief. He staggered back, gasping with wide eyes, but I already had him. I had him, and there was no escaping me.

He screamed, but I didn't stop.

His knees hit the ground with a dull thud, his body tense and convulsing as if struck by lightning. His hands clawed at his own face, fingernails raking deep gouges through his skin like he was trying to rip something out.

Blood filled in the paths his hands left, leaving perfectly circular drops of red on the floor. There was a grim beauty in their pattern. I shoved deeper. I wasn't gentle. I didn't creep. I slashed through his thoughts like a knife through flesh, tearing them apart as if they were pages in a book I never wanted to read again. Memories splintered under my grasp. Flashes of women crying, of pain dealt without remorse, of dark corridors, of screams that went unanswered.

The scent of blood filled the room, a sharp and metallic thing. Sweat clung to his skin and mine, the air thick with the stench of it.

He arched backward violently, the veins in his neck bulging as another scream ripped from his throat. His voice was no longer human. It was primal, broken, and still, I didn't stop.

I turned the current inward, twisting it like a blade. I forced him to feel the fear he caused, the anguish, the helplessness. Every cry he'd drawn from another soul, I threw back into his own. Every hand he'd laid, every vile word whispered was forced back down his own throat.

I let him feel it. I let him suffer.

Cassian's voice reached me again, but it was distant, my name murky.

I didn't hear him, not truly. He was a whisper against the hurricane roaring through me. I had claimed this man's mind as my own. I had claimed the rotted, snarling husk of a soul who didn't deserve another breath. I gripped pieces of him, shredded what I found. I twisted his memories, squeezed the worst of them until they cracked and bled fear.

Blood began to seep from his ears and his eyes, each struggling blink pulling the red up into a thin sheen over his nearly white irises.

I should have stopped. I meant to stop, yet something inside me kept going. A deeper, colder current pulled me further in. I reached for the very center of him, the core of his mind. The final piece. The part that made him *him,* and I crushed it with a single, brutal twist. His mouth opened for one last scream, but it was silent this time.

He toppled like a man emptied of soul and sinew. Slack. Twisted. Wrong. He slumped sideways on the wooden floor, eyes wide, staring up at nothing. The whites of them gleamed like frost, his irises one in the same. There was no breath. No flicker of thought behind them. No mind left to speak of.

I stood over him, gasping. My whole body was shaking. My lungs burned like they didn't know how to breathe anymore. My skin was slick with sweat, my dress clinging to my back.

My hands trembled, silver threads of power still weaving through my fingers, refusing to settle.

I looked down at the thing I'd created. Not a corpse. An absence. He wasn't just dead. He was gone. Erased like nothing more than a simple error.

I felt my knees buckle. The only thing that kept me upright was the fury that still pulsed like a second heart in my chest, but it was fading now in a slow, painful ache. This silence was worse than the screaming.

Cassian's voice cut through the haze like lightning in fog. "Lyra!"

I turned as he gave his final lunge. His sword plunged clean through the last guard's chest, sliding into the narrow gap between the man's chest plate and belt. His mouth opened in a gasp, a wet, choking sound spilling out as blood poured down his front. He grasped uselessly at the armor, then crumpled to the floor.

Cassian stood above the body, panting, the blade still in his hands.

His chest heaved with each breath. Blood streaked his forearms, smeared across his jaw and cheekbone. His hair was a wild tangle, damp with sweat and carnage where it clung to his skin. Red flecked his face in sharp, angry splatters.

That blood wasn't his own.

His eyes locked on me, then they shifted downward to the white-eyed corpse at my feet. I saw the moment his breath caught. Not with fear, but with fury.

It mirrored the heat inside me, tight and coiled and consuming. His rage was not separate from mine. Our fire blended, becoming one. As if we were always meant to exist in the same space. We burned the same now. We understood each other in a way that had no name. I didn't look away. I didn't flinch. I felt it too.

Silently, I stepped over the body.

The air was metallic and reeked of copper. The floor beneath my bare feet was warm and sticky. I didn't want to know why. I didn't want to breathe. I didn't want to look down. I tried not to slip as I knelt beside one of the fallen guards, my fingers numb as they curled around the hilt of his sword. Still warm blood coated the leather grip. I fought the vomit and nausea that rose in my throat.

I pulled it free, rising to my feet as the blood dripped from the tip of the blade. The sword was heavier than I expected. I stood straight, my spine taut with purpose, and walked across the blood-slick floor to Cassian.

His eyes never left me.

When I reached him, I didn't speak. I couldn't. Words didn't exist for this moment or for the storm in my chest. Our eyes met, and I saw his. Red-rimmed and wide with adrenaline and something unspoken. I felt it in myself, too. The tremble of what had just happened, what we'd just survived. The fire of what we'd become. What we were.

His fingers reached for mine. Rough, blood-warm, steady. He didn't say anything, and he didn't need to. I already knew. I laced my fingers through his, sword gripped tight in my other hand. My heartbeat was loud in my ears, echoing against stone and silence and the wreckage we'd left behind, and together, without a word, we walked into whatever waited next.

We stalked through the palace like shadows, like ghosts, like soldiers on the edge of war. Each step echoed with purpose. With fury. Blood marked our path, and while his was from the slaughter he'd left behind, mine was from the sword that proved the wreckage true. The corridors blurred around us, tapestries and golden trim bleeding together as we climbed spiraling staircases that reached higher, higher, higher. My heart beat not with fear, but with fire and vengeance and the steady thrum of power still alive beneath my skin.

The halls were lined with guards, each one adorned with the same golden armor. Their heads wore helmets. Their hands held a sword pulled free from its sheath. None of them dared stop our path. The only movements were quiet flinches as we continued on.

We reached the doors. Two enormous slabs of mahogany that stretched to the ceiling and were tall enough to welcome mammoths through. They were carved with a thousand twisting symbols, each one more arrogant than the last. Gold leaf shimmered in the torchlight as rubies winked in dragon's mouths. Sapphires glittered in the eye sockets of crowned figures locked in eternal poses of glory. The crown's vanity was on full display, and that alone made me snarl.

Cassian stood to my right, sword tight in hand, face hard and unreadable. He didn't need to speak. We were aligned now. A perfect, deadly silence stood between us as a single guard stood between the doors. He stiffened at the sight of us, all blood-slick, weaponed, and wild-eyed, but his hands trembled where they rested on the hilt of his sword. The blade was unsheathed and pointed down, the tip of the blade quivering.

I stepped forward. One step. Another. Measured. Controlled. I let him feel it. I let him feel how close I stood to the edge of unleashing something far worse than steel. I smiled. Slow. Sharp. Something cruel curled at the edges of my mouth, and I let it linger.

"Hello there," I said, my voice a velvet purr laced with venom. "Would you open the door?" I reached out, but not with my hands, with my mind.

I let my power slip from me, like smoke winding from a fire, under his armor, curling up his legs, into his spine, to the fragile shell of his thoughts. No subtlety. No care. I wanted him to feel that I was already taking root in him. That I had him before he could even finish drawing breath to speak.

He stuttered, blinking. "By order of the King, I cannot permi—"

I shoved, hard. His mind cracked like dry bark beneath my boot. I didn't have to scream. I didn't have to strike. I just leaned in a little more and watched him break.

His eyes glazed silver.

"I said—" I whispered, stepping close enough for him to taste my rage, "open the door. Before I have to say *please*."

His fingers fumbled for the keys on his belt, hands shaking so violently he nearly dropped the metal ring numerous times. I let the pressure build just a little more, just enough for him to understand what waited if he failed.

He opened the doors.

A groan of hinges. The shimmer of gold light spilling from within. The stench of expensive incense and rot.

I released him as he staggered back. The moment my power left him, his entire body slumped with relief.

Then, he ran. Smart man. A coward by definition, but at least a wise one.

I stepped forward, Cassian at my side. We crossed the threshold together, bloodied and burning, into the lion's den.

The King's chambers glowed with the soft flicker of firelight, golden and warm, but it all felt like a lie. The hearth crackled, casting long shadows against the high walls and gilded trim, catching the crystal decanters and silks in a comforting glow that no longer held any comfort at all.

And there he was, the King. Seated in a high-backed chair of carved obsidian and velvet, legs crossed, wine glass delicately balanced in one hand. He didn't even look up as we entered. He just sipped like nothing had happened at all. He acted like he hadn't just sent a man to kill me, and like I hadn't killed him in return. He acted like Cassian hadn't carved his way through each of his guards. Like his chamber doors hadn't just been flung open by a blood-soaked girl and the son who had caused the massacre.

Cassian moved first. He stalked into the room cloaked with wrath, his fury radiating off him in waves. His breaths came hard, his steps louder than they should've been on the carpeted floor, like thunder rolling in from some far-off war.

I followed, slower, quieter, but no less dangerous. I could feel the power simmering beneath my skin, coiling like smoke in my veins. I must have looked like a ghost with my silver tattered dress, stained in blood and ash. My skin streaked with blood and sweat, and my hair loose around my shoulders. Cassian, who was still bare-chested, looked equally as barbaric, face grim and furious and smeared with blood.

The King finally raised his gaze. His eyes swept over us as if we were no more than an inconvenience to his night. He quirked a single brow. "Is this scene supposed to intimidate me?" he said, voice smooth, unconcerned. He wagged a finger between us, and a smirk grew on the corner of his mouth.

Cassian's answer was silence. He stepped forward and slammed his sword down, point-first into the floor between the King's feet. The steel punched through the thick carpet and lodged in the wood beneath with a heavy, satisfying thud.

"You sent men to *murder* her," Cassian growled.

Still, the King did not flinch. He just swirled the wine in his glass, watching it slosh lazily against the crystal. "I sent men," he said mildly, "to correct a mistake."

Cassian bristled. "You tried to gut her in her sleep."

The King met his gaze. "A mercy, really. Quick. Clean."

Cassian's teeth were bared, his body a coiled weapon ready to strike. Anger rippled off him in violent waves, something I felt before he even thought of moving, but I was faster. I stepped in his path, catching his arm with the lightest brush of my fingers. It was enough. He stopped.

His chest heaved, eyes wild and bright with fury. Rage twisted off of him like fire, and his thoughts seemed to scream through the touch that provided a direct connection.

I'll kill him. I'll kill him right now. He'll never touch you again.

My heart pounded, but I wouldn't let him do this for me, not when I could do it myself, so I walked forward. The King didn't so much as blink when I approached. His expression was mild, almost bored. He took another sip of his wine, as if I were merely a child come to tattle.

I reached for him, my power burrowing to depths I wasn't aware possible. I leapt inside, enveloping myself within the King's own mind.

I expected resistance. I expected to tear through layers of flesh and sinew. I expected rot. Expected the foul stench of cruelty, of decay and blood and darkness, like the assassin in my room. I braced myself for it, but what I found instead was ice. A vast, frozen sea stretched beneath a sky as pale and endless as bone. Wind swept across it in soundless currents, dry and cold enough to steal breath from lungs. The silence was absolute, pristine, and beautiful, in a way that made my skin crawl, and at the center of it all, he stood waiting.

The King.

His hands were clasped behind his back, his posture relaxed. He looked like he might have been standing there for centuries. As if this place, this impossible landscape of cold and silence, was not just inside him. It was him.

He smiled. A small, patient thing. Almost kind. That made it worse.

"You don't belong here," he said. His voice was quiet, but it echoed across the ice.

I ignored the chill crawling up my spine. I struck. I reached for him the way I had with the man growing cold on my floor. I coiled my power and drove it inward, shoving it into the shape of a blade, aiming for the cracks in his armor, but there were none.

My power hit something slick and sheer and impenetrable. Polished smooth and cold as death. I had no traction, nothing to grab, nothing to pull. My blade of thought slipped and splintered. It shattered. I reeled back and tried again, sharper this time, faster, more violent. I threw everything I had at him.

The ice didn't even crack. He was stronger, older, and he knew. He knew exactly what I was trying to do, exactly how to counter it, and exactly how to win.

"You think you're powerful?" His voice was soft, the faintest amusement curling at the edge. "You are nothing compared to what I've seen. What I've done. You are a child playing with matches at the center of a forest. You have set a fire *you will never escape*."

I reached again, desperate now, and clawed toward him, rage burning like fire through my veins.

He moved one step, and he was there. He grabbed me, not my body but my mind, with hands made of iron and frost, and he shoved. The world lurched. I felt myself hurled backward, out and away, as though yanked through a void at the speed of a scream.

My consciousness slammed into my own skull as the real world rushed back into focus in a sickening wave of nausea and fire. My legs gave out, and I hit the floor, gasping. My skin felt too tight. My mind was ringing with the echo of his voice.

You will never escape.

I collapsed. The carpet-covered floor hit me like a wave. It should have felt soft, warm even, but all I felt was merciless cold. My sword tumbled from my grasp, the blade glinting. My body folded, breath gone, my skull pounding with a pain so deep it felt like it was splitting me open from the inside. My lungs fought for air. Blood dripped from my nose, warm and metallic on my lips. I tasted copper and rage and defeat. The King only grabbed the bottle, pouring more sour red wine into his glass.

Cassian caught me before I hit the ground completely. He held me. One hand cradling the back of my head, the other pressed against my ribs, and kept me from crumpling entirely. He forced me back to my feet, holding up the weight I couldn't.

He turned, slow and precise, to the King. His sword was still planted in the floor where he'd slammed it down, but now his entire body became a weapon. Shoulders squared. Jaw tight. Eyes blazing like a dying star.

"If you ever come near her again," Cassian said, his voice shaking with fury barely held in check, "I swear to whatever stars are listening, I will cut you down myself. Father or not." He ripped the sword from the floor.

The King stood. He didn't flinch. Didn't blink. His movements were smooth as oil, quiet as falling snow. The fire behind him crackled softly, casting golden light against his dark silhouette. His eyes found mine as he spoke, but there was no soul behind them. Just depthless cold.

"Royals do not kill their own bloodline," he said, each word calm and perfectly measured.

Cassian's snarl cut through the room. "As if you haven't."

The King's expression didn't change. But something darker slipped into the air around him, like a shadow made of intent.

Cassian turned from him, and his eyes found mine once more. I tried to stand on my own, but my knees buckled. The moment I faltered, he slid his arm behind my back and held me firmly, silently, one hand steady under my arm.

Still, he didn't carry me. He made sure I stood.

He made sure I faced the King on my own two feet. Strong and very much alive.

We said nothing more. We turned, and together, we walked from the room. Just as we crossed the threshold, Cassian paused. His voice was low, venom-laced, and aimed like a blade.

"You started this war," he said. "Don't be surprised when it ends with your crown at her feet."

CHAPTER THIRTY-EIGHT

WE DIDN'T SPEAK AS we left the King's chambers.

Silence hung between us like a veil of fog, something dense and heavy. Like the smoke from a fire that hadn't burned out quite yet. Our bare feet echoed over the marble, every step trailing the blood of the fallen guards growing cold on my bedroom floor. It smeared the once-pristine floors with crimson streaks. Proof of the violence we'd carved through the palace like a fault-line splitting the earth.

Cassian didn't lead me back to my room. He took me to his.

We walked up flight after flight of stone steps, side by side, scorched by the fury still burning in our bones. His chambers were dim. Quiet. He shut the door behind me silently, the gentleness of the action a sharp contrast to his blood-soaked body. The fire in the hearth burned low. Soft light casted faint golden streaks against dark wood and stone. I'd only been here once before. Now, it felt different. It was too large, too private. As if I was a trespasser in the aftermath of a war, a ghost pacing through the ruins.

Cassian crossed the room without a word. He stopped at the washbasin, poured warm water from a kettle into the bowl. His arms were covered in scattered slashes, red speckles and streaks scattered down his body. The waistband of his pants was darkened with blood, some of it his, but most of it not. His jaw was clenched, his mouth a hard line, his eyes unreadable and distant. He dipped a rag into the water and scrubbed at his arms. The motion was rough and mechanical, as if it caused him no pain at all.

For some reason, it seemed to hurt me more than it hurt him.

I stood in the center of the room, staring. I crossed the space without thinking. My fingers brushed his, and I took the cloth from his hand.

He looked at me, and for a heartbeat, neither of us moved. He didn't stop me. He didn't pull away. Cassian simply let his arms fall to his sides and exhaled like he'd been holding that breath since the moment I opened the doors to the King.

I slowly reached for the sides of the once white button up he wore. The fabric was shredded, slashes raking across the sleeves. I eased the sleeves from his shoulders, letting the tunic fall behind him. He shrugged it off, but laid the cloth over his shoulder, saving the floor from the blood.

I dipped the rag into the warm water, wrung it out, and reached for him. The first pass of the cloth across his arm was slow. His skin shone with a sheen of scarlet and sweat. His eyes never left mine.

"I didn't know he'd do that to you," he said quietly, voice raw.

"We're both alive," I said. "That's all that matters."

He didn't answer. His jaw twitched.

I moved the cloth to his other arm. Closer now. His breath stirred a piece of my hair that had fallen free. I could feel the heat radiating off him, the strain in his muscles as he stood there. I pressed the cloth to his temple, where blood had dried at the edge of his hairline. His eyes drifted shut.

"I would've killed him," he murmured.

"I know."

I lowered the cloth, and he opened his eyes again. I saw unintelligible whispers there. Whispers of everything he hadn't said. Everything he couldn't.

The next swipe dragged a smear of blood from the inside of his forearm. The one after traced over his shoulder, red streaks disappearing beneath the damp fabric. My touch was light, careful, but every inch of him told the story of what he'd done to those guards. Slashes curved over muscle, grazes slicing through skin. Shallow, mostly. Glancing blows. But still, my chest pulled tighter with every mark I uncovered.

I worked in silence, rinsing and wiping, the motions slow, steady, deliberate. There was something almost reverent in it, as if this was an offering, or something sacred that belonged to me alone.

Every time my fingers brushed his skin, that golden thread between us lit up. It coiled around my ribs and tugged, gentle but unrelenting, like it knew something I hadn't yet admitted, even to myself. It slid down my spine with a sensation like warmth and thunder. An ache that wasn't pain. A spark that wasn't fire.

Cassian watched my hands. I felt his eyes burn into my skin. A physical heat. His jaw tightened, and though he didn't speak, I could see the restraint in him. The effort it took not to lean into my every touch.

When the worst of the blood was gone, I set the cloth aside and crossed the room to his desk. I began to reach for the drawer when his voice rang out from behind me.

"Second drawer down. Satchel that's in the back."

I tugged on the handle, revealing miscellaneous papers and quills. Pots of dried ink and discarded parchment. Behind it all though, laid a brown leather satchel. I freed it from the drawer, walking back over to Cassian.

I unbuckled the worn straps and let the cover flop open. Inside were jars of salves and balms, each sealed with wax and labeled with careful script. The scent of juniper and mint rose the instant I cracked the first one open. It hit something in me, something familiar and unexpected.

A memory of my father's steady voice guiding my hands, the first time he taught me how to mix healing creams from dried herbs and pressed oils. I had never used them, not on any real patient at least. My fingers dipped into the cool paste.

"Hold still," I said, my voice hoarse as each scream seemed to cling to my throat like ash.

Cassian didn't move. Didn't flinch. Didn't speak. I stepped back to him and smoothed the balm over a gash on his upper arm. He hissed through his teeth, low and sharp.

I pressed the salve gently into each wound. My fingers moved in slow circles, rubbing the minty cream into his skin, grounding us both with the simple motion.

And as I touched him, I memorized him.

The shape of his arms, the way his chest rose and fell, the exact spot just above his ribs where a bruise was beginning to bloom. The snaking muscle that ran along his upper arms, the hard planes of his stomach, his cheekbones and jaw. He stood still under my hands, as if I was the only thing tethering him to the ground.

When I reached his wrist, I paused.

His hand turned in silent offering, palm up and open.

I stared down at it. At the lines of his palm, the dark smear of dried blood near his thumb. My own hand trembled as I reached for him, and I didn't know if it was from exhaustion or something else, something that had been building between us long before tonight.

I brushed my thumb over the inside of his forearm, just above where his pulse beat steady and strong.

He didn't speak, and I didn't ask him to.

What could be said after a night like this?

I quickly wrapped layers of gauze and bandages around the worst of the gashes on his arms and sat back in his chair, letting my head fall and eyes close with a sigh.

The sun had just begun to rise, pale gold light filtered through the curtains, brushing over the stone and silk like a well constructed lie. It painted the room in soft hues that didn't belong here. The morning was gentle and warm against the lingering scent of copper and iron that still cloaked us like a second skin.

Cassian stood in front of me silently. He grabbed the same damp cloth and knelt before me. His hand wrapped around my ankle, sliding up to my calf. He wiped at the blood drying on the bottoms of my feet. He cleaned the speckles dotting my legs and arms.

His hand moved to slide behind my neck, angling my face down for him to look over the red lines flowing from a place on my head. His fingers dipped into the warm water and ran over each one. He ran his fingers through my hair, cleaning the scarlet streaks as I had once done for Elena.

He ran the cloth through to the end, the white of my hair once turned pink returning to its pale hue. He stood, setting the cloth in the water once more, before continuing towards his armoire. He pulled out a dark gray tunic and slipped the clean fabric over his head, the cotton catching briefly on the fresh bandages that still lined his arms. He pulled out a pair of pants in a similar color, and I turned away as he slipped off the ones stained with the proof of his massacre. At the sound of the armoire doors clicking shut my head swiveled back towards him. He walked over and reached for the small table beside the bed, where a white shirt sat folded. It was the same one I'd borrowed before.

He didn't say anything. Just placed the tunic in my lap with the cloth and basin nearby and turned away, facing the wall.

I took the tunic with quiet fingers and turned my back to him. My dress peeled off in slow, sticky movements. Tacky blood had dried in the fabric, attaching it to my skin. It hit the floor in a muted thump. I quickly ran the cloth over my worst of it before slipped the shirt over my head. The linen was cold against my chest. The white fabric too clean for the night we'd just endured.

When I turned around, Cassian hadn't moved.

I cleared my throat. He turned immediately at the sound, and his eyes swept over me. Then, wordless, he reached for my hand. His fingers laced with mine, and without hesitation, he led me to the bed. In his other hand, though, he still carried the sword. The same one he'd driven through blood and bone less than an hour before. Its edge was still coated in a thin layer of pinkish red. He set it against the wall, close enough to reach.

I climbed beneath the sheets. The silk was cool against my skin, and the mattress dipped slightly beneath me. I turned my head back to him, and he followed. Cassian didn't just lie beside me. He wrapped himself around me like a shield, like armor. One arm slipped into the crook of my neck, the other curled firm and certain around my waist. His chest pressed to my back, steady and solid. His chin came to rest on the top of my head, and for a moment, for the first time in what felt like days, I let my eyes truly fall shut. And I breathed.

The silence stretched, heavy and golden, and then I whispered it. Not to him. Not to myself. Just to the air, or to the shadows still curled in the corners of the room.

"I killed him."

The words didn't sound like mine. They came out flat and hollow, like a confession offered to the dark.

Cassian didn't flinch. Didn't pull back. Didn't quicken his breaths.

"You did," he said. He was calm, certain. It wasn't a question, just a statement. His hand found my forearm, fingers gliding gently over my skin, drawing soft circles as if he could coax me back from wherever I was unraveling. "If you hadn't..." His voice was low, rough, rasping with something sharp and aching. "You might've been in his place."

I knew that. I knew that even in the moment, felt it in the scream still echoing inside my head. The terror in the guard's mind. The way he'd tried to escape, to lie, to survive, and still, I hadn't stopped.

That was what haunted me. Not that I'd killed him, but that I hadn't stopped. I could have. I could have pulled back. I could've severed my power, cut off the screaming, walked away, but I didn't. And worse, some part of me, buried deep and dangerous, had liked it.

I had liked the way his mind had crumbled. Like the way I could bring a man to his knees without ever lifting a hand.

It had answered something in me I didn't know I'd been asking.

Cassian's breath ghosted across the crown of my head. His arms never loosened. If anything, they pulled tighter around me, like he could hold me together with sheer force. Like he believed if he stayed close enough, he could keep the memory at bay, but I already knew the truth.

This wasn't something that could be shielded.

This was something I carried now, and there was no going back.

CHAPTER THIRTY-NINE

I DIDN'T WAKE UNTIL the light outside the window had turned a hazy, dusty blue.

The sun had climbed too high in the sky to be ignored, its filtered glow spilling across the stone floor and warming the silk sheets tangled around me. I blinked slowly, my lashes sticking together from sleep, my body reluctant to move. For the first time in what felt like a lifetime, I hadn't woken with my fists clenched or my heart pounding like war drums in my chest.

Cassian's arms were still wrapped around me.

His breathing was steady and slow, each rise and fall of his chest brushing gently against my back. One arm was draped across my waist, anchoring me to the bed, while the other lay tucked beneath his pillow, his fingers curled softly in the fabric of the cover as if he was standing guard.

I could have stayed like that forever.

Warm. Safe. Held.

But then the knocking started.

Firm. Fast. Urgent.

Cassian stirred behind me instantly, the stillness in him snapping into tension. His breath hitched, his arm tightening slightly before he exhaled and pressed a kiss to my temple.

Light. Silent. Fleeting.

Then he was gone.

He slid from the bed and crossed the room barefoot, tugging at the collar of his loose shirt as he approached the door. His body moved with quiet purpose, but something about the way he froze just as the door swung open made my skin prickle.

Then I heard his voice.

"If Miss Seravell is here, I need to speak to her."

Kaden.

His voice was rough. Sharp at the edges. Hoarse like smoke and sleepless nights. I sat up on instinct, heart kicking hard against my ribs.

Cassian didn't turn, didn't open the door right away. His shoulders went rigid. His fingers flexed against the handle. Then he cracked the door open, just enough for Cassian to see him fully.

"Stay in bed, Lyra," he muttered over his shoulder, voice low, taut.

The door swung wider, and Kaden stepped inside.

He stopped dead.

His eyes found mine, and the world seemed to tilt.

His gaze dragged over me, and I felt every inch of it. My white hair spilled around me like snow. The blanket had dipped dangerously low, and Cassian's shirt, far too large for my frame, had dipped with it. I scrambled upright, heat rushing to my cheeks as I pulled the shirt tighter around myself and flung the blankets off with a breathless gasp.

"Kaden—" I tried. My voice cracked, too soft, too full of something I didn't know how to hide. "Wait—"

He didn't move. He didn't blink. He just stared like something in him had been carved wide open.

He looked at me like I was a wound he couldn't stitch shut. Like I'd taken a blade to something sacred.

And in his hand, trembling, was a folded letter.

Kaden walked over, the buckles of his boots clinking softly with each step. He reached me and held out the parchment without a word.

His face was unreadable, frozen into something cold and distant, but his eyes—

His eyes burned.

Not with anger.

Not with hate.

But something raw. Something bleeding and betrayed. Something I didn't have the right to name.

I couldn't breathe.

He didn't say a word as I took the letter from his outstretched hand.

The parchment was still warm from his grip.

I unfolded it slowly, almost afraid of what I'd find inside.

Only one word stared back at me, penned in bold, exact strokes like a sentence carved into stone.

$$\textit{Veritus}$$

"Veritus?" I read aloud, my voice catching.

I didn't understand, but Cassian did.

His spine snapped straight, shoulders going taut with a force that vibrated through the space between us. A sharp breath cut the silence, and then the temperature seemed to drop and rise all at once. That same fury from the night before began to stir in him again.

My gaze darted between them.

Cassian, standing like a storm barely leashed, and Kaden who was already retreating, that careful mask of his cracking in a way I hadn't seen since the day we met.

Then he turned and walked out.

Just like that.

"Kaden—no!" I called after him, clutching the edge of a blanket tightly as I threw it around Cassian's shirt and stumbled toward the door. I held the paper tight in my fist, crumbling and wrinkling the parchment. "Please—wait!"

I only made it two steps before a hand closed on my waist.

"Lyra," Cassian said, and my name on his tongue stopped me more than his grip did.

His voice wasn't sharp. It wasn't commanding. It was desperate.

"Don't." His fingers tightened just slightly. "Just stay. Please."

I turned back to him slowly. His eyes searched mine like he was looking for something already lost.

There was no force in his hold. Just ache.

"Don't run from me again," he said, his voice breaking. "Not after everything. Not after last night."

My throat bobbed. I felt the words before I said them.

"I have to."

"You don't," he said, as if willing it to be true.

"I do," I whispered. "You know I do." And it was my hand that pulled away.

He flinched like I'd struck him.

Like something inside him had shattered right there in the doorway.

His hand dropped to his side, and I left.

I didn't stop to think, didn't look back. The blanket fluttered behind me like wings made of silk and shame as I darted into the hall and sprinted after Kaden. I found him just before he reached the corridor that led to my room.

His pace was fast, too fast for someone with nowhere to go. He wasn't heading toward anything. He was trying to escape.

"Kaden—" I called out again, breathless now. "Please." He didn't stop. Didn't turn. "Kaden!" I gasped.

He paused now, but still, he didn't face me.

"What."

His voice came out sharp and empty.

I caught up to him, the pace more run than walk, my bare feet stinging against the cold floor, the blanket still clutched around me with one hand. "What's wrong?"

He let out a breath, but it was all edge. "I don't know."

"Then think," I pleaded. I hadn't heard a word from him besides orders regurgitated from the King. Hadn't even seen a glimpse of the man I used to know. I reached for him again, my hand brushing over the sleeve of his shirt. He flinched away, pulling his shoulder away from my fingertips as he stalked a few steps further down the corridor. His chest rose and fell erratically, his breathing audible and echoing in the hall.

"Kaden, please. I just want to help—"

Finally, he turned, whipping towards me so fast his sword swung in its sheath. And stars, his face carved open something in me that had been buried as soon as he took off that helmet in the throne room.

"I'm angry," he hissed. He rushed forward, his strides long and quick, and suddenly, he stood only inches from me. He grabbed my shoulders, his fingers digging through the fabric to bite skin. My eyes widened, flickering down to the hold that would leave thumbprints. "I'm angry, and I don't know why. I saw you with him and—" His voice cut off. He looked down at his hands and released me, his hands hovering in the air. One moved back to run through his hair, but it didn't make it halfway up before they both fell back to his side.

My throat tightened. I forced my breathing to slow, to calm. I blinked away the fear in my eyes. "You know me, Kaden. Somewhere in there you know me."

He shook his head slightly, like he was trying to dislodge the ache lodged behind his eyes. His hands raised to press into his temples. "I don't know *anything*," he whispered. "I don't know how I got here. I don't know this post." He threw his hand down towards the stone, finger pointing to the exact place he so carefully guarded. He pointed between his eyes. "I'm only supposed to know what he tells me I know. And yet—" He threw his hands up at me, but they were anything but accusatory. "And yet, I know you."

Tears began to glass over in his eyes.

Stars. Kaden was still in there.

Somewhere behind all that careful obedience carved into him, behind the silence, the precision, the numbness, he was still there.

"Kaden," I said quietly.

He paused and glanced at me.

"Have you been to the greenhouse lately?"

His entire body froze. He brought his head back up, blinking away his glassy eyes. He looked at me like I'd spoken a word he hadn't thought of in years.

He straightened, his expression shuttered once more. "No Miss Seravell. I have not."

"Would you like to?"

He hesitated. Just for a second. He glanced down the hall like he was expecting someone to call him back, to remind him who he was supposed to be. Then he looked at me again, really looked, and whatever crack had let my voice in widened.

He stepped back and extended his arm down the hall, silently accepting.

My heart lifted the moment he stepped into stride behind me. I led us through the corridors in silence, my bare feet echoing softly on the stone. I was still wearing a blanket as a gown, but I didn't care. Every step toward the greenhouse felt like breathing again, like waking from something too still, too long. The light shifted as we passed beneath the arched windows, golden and dappled, falling in long slashes across the floor. The closer we came to the greenhouse, the more I felt the weight of the palace ease off my shoulders.

The gardens welcomed us like an old friend. The air smelled of cool autumn, of flowers just past their peak and fruit ripe on the branch. The trees had fully given away to blush with reds and golds.

Vines crawled up the walls like living lace, and roses still bloomed in bursts of velvet, defiant and untamed.

I slowed, smiling at the ponds as we passed. Sunlight scattered across the surface like glitter, and below the shimmer, fish darted between the shadows of lily pads. Dragonflies skimmed the water, wings catching the light. It was beautiful.

I didn't say a word. I just kept walking.

The greenhouse waited at the far end of the garden with its panes fogged slightly from the warmth inside. I reached for the handle and pushed the door open. Humid air rushed out to greet us, warm and damp, thick with the scent of soil and sun. It wrapped around me like a memory.

Kaden hesitated at the threshold, then stepped inside. I watched him as the light touched his face. His eyes wandered slowly, unhurried and curious in a way that made my breath catch. He took in the moss-covered stones, the orchids suspended in midair like stars, the vines that tangled through the rafters and spilled over railings. Silver-veined leaves glistened in the glow of the glass ceiling above. He didn't speak, but he looked. As if something here tugged at a piece of him he hadn't touched in years.

I held still. Didn't move. Didn't breathe too loudly. Hope stirred inside me. Such a fragile, fluttering thing. Maybe this place could reach him. Maybe it already had.

Then, I saw it. The way his shoulders tensed, the way his jaw locked tight. That flicker of clarity dulled again, shuttered like a door closing against the light.

It wasn't all gone. Not like before. But it was enough to make my chest ache. I wanted to scream.

Not at him, never at him, but at the one who had done this. At the King who had broken him down until even sunlight felt like a threat. At the silence that replaced his laughter. At the lies and poison and all the time we'd lost.

Still, I would not give up.

We walked deeper into the greenhouse, past rows of ferns and curling ivy. The air shimmered faintly with heat, and my skin dampened with it. I let my fingers trail along the edge of a broad leaf, traced the pattern of veins like I could read the language of the earth itself. My hand moved across a blooming heliotrope, its purple petals lifting toward the glass above, chasing the light. I understood the feeling.

Reaching for something you aren't sure will ever be yours.

I wondered what Kaden knew of this place, if anything. I wondered what had survived inside him. I didn't need him to speak. I didn't need some grand sign or apology or revelation. I just needed this. Him here. Breathing. Feeling. Even just for a short while.

And I would stay in this quiet as long as it took. I would walk this path again and again, until the hollow inside him cracked wide enough for light to flood in.

Because I had known him, once. And I believed, no matter what the King had done, that I could know him again.

By the time we returned to the palace, the sun had risen to its peak. The sky was clouded, but a singular patch of clear blue shone directly above us. It was kind of blue that used to remind me of Virellia. Now it brought memories of salt on my lips and wind in my hair, of sunlight dancing across the sea's surface like spilled gold. That color lived in my bones. The color of before and after.

We stopped at my door. Kaden didn't say a word, but I turned to glance at him anyway. He didn't meet my eyes.

The last memory I had in this room was less than fond, and I wasn't sure if I could face the scene behind that door alone. Memories of the previous night came crashing back. The blood coating the floor. The coppery tang in the air. The guards Cassian had cut down. The corpse I had created. I closed my eyes as Kaden's hand gripped the handle. I listened as the door swung on its hinges, near silently but squeaking just enough to hear if you were truly listening. I filled my lungs with air and exhaled as I opened my eyes to whatever carnage lay before me.

I expected gore. Bloodshed. I had braced myself for red speckled golden armor. For scarlet-stained wooden floors. I had pictured every possibility for how my room may look in the daylight but this.

It was pristine.

I leaned into the doorframe, unease spilling into my veins. I think I would have preferred some sort of sign that something had happened. My room looked as clean as the day it was assigned to me. My bed was made with fresh sheets, the smell of laundry soap heavy in the air. The floors shined with polish and the windows glass was so clean I couldn't tell if the panes were open or closed. For some reason, it felt more tainted now than ever. I stepped inside, and then I paused, standing just behind the threshold. I waited for the illusion to break. For the veil hiding reality to drop, revealing some twisted nightmare. I stood still for several heartbeats. I held my breath.

Behind me the door softly clicked closed. I waited for the lock to slide into place. I waited, but no sound came. Then slowly, I turned to grab a hold of the handle. I pushed down, and it moved. Kaden didn't lock it. For the first time in days, maybe longer, I wasn't trapped in my own space. I wandered to the center of my room and stopped, staring at the unsullied walls, the bed with its speckless linens, the empty scrubbed hearth.

My eyes flicked down the crumpled paper in my hand. Just one word, etched into my bones like a brand.

Cassian had known what it meant. I'd seen it in his eyes the moment I said the word aloud. That silence, heavier than any words he could've spoken, had wrapped around him like armor.

I folded the letter carefully, even though my hands were shaking. I set the parchment on my desk as I trudged over to my armoire. A deep navy tunic and pants greeted me as I pulled open the drawer. I shed Cassian's shirt and pulled the navy fabric on, tucking the white tunic into my drawer before pushing it closed. As I walked toward the door, I slipped the parchment message into my pocket, pressing it flat against my thigh, like the paper might steady the thunder in my heart.

Then I grabbed my cloak, slipped my boots and gloves on once again, and left.

Because I was going to the only person who wouldn't hide me from the truth.

CHAPTER FORTY

THE STREETS OF AUREA felt different in the light of day.

Or maybe maybe it was just this particular day.

The sky hung low overhead, a dull slab of gray that seemed to press down over the rooftops. Clouds clustered like they were waiting for something, heavy and unmoving. The spots of blue had all but disappeared, buried under the high fog. A strange light spilled over the city in muted, pale washes. It was as if the sun itself had dimmed. The air held a weight I couldn't name. Mist curled through the alleyways like smoke without fire, a ghost of something burned long ago. The whole city seemed to hold its breath.

I wrapped my cloak tighter around me, my fingers gripping the edges as my eyes swept across every face I passed. People moved quickly, heads ducked, voices low. Their conversations were sharp, clipped, spoken in fragments meant only for those close enough to already understand.

A group of soldiers marched past, boots striking in perfect rhythm. I kept my head down, letting my hair fall forward, heart thudding until the clatter of metal faded behind me.

This wasn't the city we had fled through days ago.

Back then, the streets had pulsed with sound and color. Music, shouting vendors, spices curling through the air. Now, it was like someone had wrung all the life from it, leaving only gray bones and polished steel.

The guards were everywhere. Their armor gleamed too brightly, swords practically begging to be seen. Their hands hovered near hilts like they wanted a reason to draw.

I didn't give them one.

I turned down a narrow lane flanked by ivy-covered walls, my boots echoing between the crooked homes and slanted windows. Wrought-iron balconies sagged under the weight of forgotten flowerpots, and rust dripped down stone like old blood.

At the end of the lane sat the house I remembered. The stone crunched under my feet, the sound slicing through the air like a warning. My fingers were shaking as I lifted my hand and knocked thrice on the weather-worn door. It opened only a moment later.

Moira stood there. Her green eyes were sharp, almost too sharp, and her silver-brown hair was tied back in a braid that had started to come loose. For a heartbeat, her eyes lit up with something like hope. She smiled, but then she saw me. And the light vanished.

Her expression faltered, the corners of her mouth dipping not quite into a frown, but something sadder. "Oh," she breathed. Her voice was soft. Disappointed. "I thought…"

She didn't need to finish.

"I'm sorry," I said quietly, and I meant it.

Her gaze dropped to the floor for a moment. She gave the smallest shake of her head and stepped aside. "Don't apologize, I just wasn't expecting you is all. Come in."

I slipped inside, letting the door close behind me, and immediately the scent of firewood and herbs wrapped around me like a memory.

"Did you break a stitch? Probably time for them to go anyway."

I shook my head. "I came to ask you a question."

She cocked her head at me, confused.

"I didn't know who else to go to."

She paused before nodding once. "Well, ask while I take that thread out from you then, hm?"

She led me through the house and away from the makeshift hospital, my boots scoffing softly on the worn wooden floors. I passed a narrow kitchen with hanging herbs and cluttered shelves, a bedroom filled with cracked portraits and dusty books. Time lingered in the corners of the house, settling in places untouched by the world outside.

We entered a small sitting room. There stood a round table with four chairs, each one splintering and cracked. She sat in the far chair, and I drug the one closest to be directly beside her. I pulled my cloak off my shoulders and around the chair. I folded the tunic I wore up and away from the bandages. Moira gently unwrapped the fabric. Underneath, the gauze only had the thinnest line of pink. She peeled away the gauze to reveal a perfectly straight, inch wide line. The stitches puckered the skin where they pierced the sides. Moira reached into her pockets and pulled out a small pair of steel scissors. She lit a candle and ran the blade through the flame, sterilizing the metal. She slowly snipped each stitch, pulling them out as I hissed breaths through my teeth. She set each one on the table, the string knotted and stained a deep red.

I winced as she pulled the last one out.

"Perhaps it's good you came alone." Moira whispered, her brow knit with concentration. I peered down, bracing my stomach for the sight of my side, but the line stayed closed, healed in a way that seemed impossible. Once the last stitch fell to the table, she walked quickly into the hospital, grabbing a cloth that smelled of mint. When she pressed it to my side, the pain melted instantly.

I sat there in the stillness for a few seconds, letting myself breathe, before I reached into my pocket and pulled out the crumpled slip of parchment. I smoothed it flat between us and slid it toward her. Her eyes dropped to it, even as she continues to press the cloth into my side.

"I got the final trial," I said, watching her face like it might hold the answer. "That's all it says."

Moira's reaction was instant. She froze—her entire body going rigid, breath catching hard in her throat. Color drained from her face like someone had pulled the plug. "No," she whispered. It wasn't a protest. It was a plea. "No. He can't—Does Cassian know about this?"

I blinked. "What?"

Moira dropped the cloth on the floor. She ran a shaking hand across the parchment repeatedly, as if she could erase the word.

"I mean, yes. He does, but why is that important?"

She looked at me then, truly looked at me, and the fear pouring from her was stark, unflinching. "You don't understand what this is."

"That's why I came to you," I said. My voice wavered, but the words were solid.

"You don't know what this word means," she said through gritted teeth.

"Then tell me." I grabbed the cloth from the floor, holding it against my healing wound. I leaned forward, the tremor in my chest impossible to hide. "Tell me what it means. What are you so afraid of?"

For a moment, she didn't answer. Her eyes fluttered shut, jaw tight, shoulders curled like she was bracing for impact. "It's not a trial of skill," she finally said. "Or strength. It's not even of magic." Moira shook her head slowly. Almost in disbelief. "It's truth."

The word hit harder than I expected. My breath caught in my throat. "What kind of truth?" I asked. The air felt thinner suddenly, like the room itself was shrinking.

"All of it," she said hoarsely. "Veritus is an ancient rite. Older than the palace. Older than the court. It's something I only ever read about, and even then, only in the restricted archives before I was...." She shook her head, breaking off the sentence. She looked up at me again, and this time, I saw something different behind her fear.

Dread.

"It's forbidden for a reason, Miss Seravell," she said. "It's invasive. It's horrifying. You don't fight. You don't cast spells or wield weapons." She pressed both hands to the sides of her temples. "You are seen. Completely. Your thoughts. Your memories. Your truths. Past, present... even the ones you've never said aloud."

My pulse thudded like thunder in my ears.

"You cannot control what they see," she said. "Everyone will know."

She didn't have to explain what she meant.

A chill rolled over my skin. I tried to swallow but my throat was too dry. "Is there anything I can do?" I whispered.

Her gaze locked with mine. I saw defeat before the trial had even begun.

"Please. Tell me there's something."

"Not unless you are..." She hesitated. "Not unless you can protect your own mind."

I sat back slightly, the weight of it all settling in my chest like a stone. The letter on the table felt heavier now, as though it knew the outcome before I did. A long silence stretched between us. I shook my head. "I refuse to give the King what he wants," I said quietly. "Not after what he's done."

Her eyes went sharp, like a freshly cleaned blade. "You don't understand what you're just throwing away," she snapped. "You know *nothing*." Moira hissed the last word, and it felt like a slap.

I stared at her, stunned. Before I could even respond, she surged to her feet. In the next heartbeat, she was beside me, twisting the cloth of my sleeve in a hold that was firmer than I'd expect from a woman her size. Not cruel, not violent, but desperate.

"I won't let you kill yourself trying to prove a point," she said, dragging me out the back of her house.

I dug my heels into the floor, trying to twist out of her grasp, but she kept pulling, the urgency in her body like a fire, racing toward the edge of reason.

"You're leaving," she said. "Now. I'll get you out of the city. Away from the palace. Away from him."

I yanked harder against her, breaking free from her vice-like grip. "*Stop!*"

Moira's hands rushed to try and find purchase on my arm once more. "Please," she breathed, and now I heard it—panic, threading through every syllable. "You're the only chance we have. You don't know what it's like to starve. You don't understand suffering. You'll never—"

"Aurea isn't the only region who starves." The words exploded out of me before I knew I'd said them. "Virellia has people killed for their hunger." A pulse surged from my chest, a raw wave of power rolling off me in all directions. Not violent. Not meant to harm. But it swallowed the air in the room. The candlelight flickered out. The silence that followed was absolute, like the world itself had paused to listen.

"I won't be some pawn in a game. I won't be controlled my anyone but myself. Not you. Not the King. Not Cassian."

Moira stumbled back a step, eyes wide. I could see it on her face as the ripple passed through. Her breathing slowed, her shoulders dropped, and for a heartbeat she looked at me as if seeing something divine.

Awe. Astonishment. Reverence.

"Argentum," she whispered.

The word curled like smoke between us, but I didn't let it settle. My voice cracked like thunder.

"My name is *Lyra Seravell*."

She stared at me like a woman standing before a storm she hadn't seen coming. Moira's voice, when it came again, was quieter. Not a plea. Not a command. Just a truth too heavy to hold in silence. "Miss Seravell," she said, "you need to understand. It's not just your mind they'll see. Not just your…abilities. Or your pain." Her eyes searched mine like she was hoping to find some piece of me still innocent enough to be spared. "Veritus reveals everything. Your every truth. The people you love. The woman you are. The woman you'll become. Every hope. Every fear. Every dark corner you thought you'd buried." She shook her head, grief heavy in her throat. "They will see everything."

I didn't answer.

Not at first.

The silence settled thick around us. I snatched the paper from the table and walked to the back door. Moira didn't try to stop me. She knew she couldn't. My back was to her, but I felt her gaze like heat against my spine.

I turned my head just enough to look at her.

My chin lifted, and my voice was cold and sharp and unyielding, forged from everything I had survived to become what stood before her.

"Good." I said. "Then they'll see the crown they'll place on my head."

I didn't wait for her answer.

I walked through the door and made sure it closed behind me.

CHAPTER FORTY-ONE

I RETURNED FROM THE CITY with Moira's warning thundering through my skull.

Not unless you can protect your own mind.

The words chased me with every step, echoing like thunderclaps against the cobblestone beneath my feet. I couldn't stop hearing them. Couldn't stop feeling them. They slammed again and again, each syllable sharpening the edge of my fear.

My mind was swirling with solutions to the cautionary riddle Moira had given me. I had always just assumed my mind *was* protected. Naelle had known when I had entered her mind. Just as Cassian had. And the guard.

But I had wanted them to know. I had emphasized my invasion as a point of its own.

What of those who may never know? Like Thane. Or Elena. Or Will. Or Clara.

What if someone had already been in my head? Prying and raiding. How had the King known of Cassian's words from the lagoon? Had guards overheard and fed him the message? Or had the King twisted his way into my mind and tainted the promise himself?

I needed answers.

And there was only one person in this cursed palace who might have them.

Cassian knew. He had to. The way his expression shifted at the mention of *Veritus*—sharp, unguarded—wasn't meaningless. He knew what the word meant in its entirety. He would know what Moira's forewarning meant. And whatever it was, I needed to know too.

I *needed* him. I needed *him*.

Maybe I shouldn't have ran this morning. Maybe the moment I climbed out of his bed to chase someone else, I had silently cemented any assumptions he had of his meaning to me.

A means to an end.

It was wholly untrue.

There was something between us. Something intangible, something impossible. Something I felt pressing beneath my skin, impossible to ignore yet too fragile to speak aloud. It wasn't a word I could say, not yet. It was a quiet ache, a weight resting deep in my chest that both comforted and terrified me. I wanted to push it away, to tell myself it was nothing more than gratitude or fear. But his own words rang in my head.

Love can feel eerily close to fear.

I was afraid. And every time I thought I had it buried, it stirred— subtle and relentless—like a whispered promise I wasn't ready to claim.

I didn't entertain the thought of my fear becoming anything else.

I went to Cassian's rooms first. I knocked, softly at first, then a little harder when no one answered. I cracked the door open and peeked inside.

Empty.

I tried the gardens next, winding through tall hedges and blooming roses, past the silent fountains where light once danced on water like glass. No sign of him. I moved faster.

Our tower was next. I climbed the steps two at a time.

Nothing.

I tore through the mess hall, ignoring the stares from the other contenders, ignoring the hush that followed me. I didn't care. The library came after. Then the gallery.

Gone. Always gone.

By the time I reached the throne room, I had all but given up.

I stood just outside the open doors, heart pounding, breath caught somewhere between hope and foolishness. This was the last place he'd could possibly be.

Something tugged at my spine. A pull. A whisper without sound. It curled, icy and cold, around my ribs and clenched at my heart.

Look inside, it seemed to whisper.

So, I did.

I stepped through the doors.

The throne room buzzed with the usual, hollow grandeur. Soft chatter from silk-draped nobles bubbled as advisors gathered like circling hawks near the steps. Servants moved with purpose, each shuffling from place to place as they were told.

They retrieved scrolls, wine, platters of food.

Sycophants. All of them. Cloaked in gold and glass and the illusion of grace.

But I didn't see them.

I couldn't see them.

Because there, just to the right of the King's monstrous throne, stood someone I could not bear to see.

Kaden in golden armor.

My heart stopped. It didn't falter. It stopped.

He was rigid in posture, spine arrow-straight, head held high like a knight from the stories we used to laugh at. His armor gleamed beneath the latticed sunlight. Not steel. Not shadow-forged iron, not the rough, worn metal I'd seen on him a hundred times before. Gold. Studded with blood-bright rubies and glinting sapphires, gemstones so absurd and opulent they looked fake.

My stomach twisted, flipping once, twice, rising so fast into my throat that I nearly gagged on the food I'd forced down at some point. I reached for the wall beside me, fingers shaking, pulse wild.

I couldn't breathe.

He stood in the place of the guard I had killed.

I killed him. I killed him, and now Kaden was the one who had to suffer.

They didn't see me, the courtiers. I was just a shadow in the doorway, a girl in plain clothes tucked into the corner of a painting.

But the King did.

He looked at me the way a wolf watches a rabbit realize too late that it stepped into a snare. That crown on his brow glinted like the blade of a guillotine, catching the filtered sunlight and casting soft golden halos over his hair. Halos that did not belong.

His lips curled into a slow, cruel smile like he'd been waiting for this exact moment. That terrible, oily slither crossed my mind, but this time, I didn't retreat.

This time, I let my power rise.

Quietly. Carefully. I shaped it into a single thread, then sent it slithering across the stone floor—fast, silent, unseen. It crept over his polished boots, up his legs, coiled like a serpent along his spine. I drove it through his skull like an arrow loosed from a bow, except, he didn't flinch.

He only smiled wider.

Teeth gleaming like pearls in blood.

I felt bile rise in my throat. My breath quickened, shallow and sharp.

This wasn't real. It couldn't be real.

My vision blurred. My legs moved before I made the choice.

I turned, and I ran. I ran like the palace was on fire.

My boots slammed against the stone floors, the sharp rhythm echoing off the columns and ceiling like a war drum. My cloak snapped behind me, catching on corners, fluttering like a wounded wing. People turned as I passed, but I didn't see their faces. Didn't hear their words. My vision tunneled until all I could see was the hallway ahead. Until all I could feel was a fire burning in my lungs.

I rounded the final corner, and my breakfast caught in my throat.

There was a royal guard standing at my door.

His back was to me.

For a moment, everything stilled. Even my footsteps, even my heart.

The man turned. And my world collapsed.

Older—forty, maybe more—with graying stubble and hard, sun-damaged skin. His armor was pristine, polished, dull with disuse. His gaze met mine. Emotionless. Indifferent. Cold.

My heart cracked open in my chest. Not in silence, but with a deafening, internal rupture that left my ribs shaking. I forced a nod, stiff and mechanical, and stepped past him.

He opened the door without a word.

I didn't look back.

The door closed behind me with a heavy thunk.

Click

The latch. Locking. From the outside.

Just like before.

I just stood there, staring at the wood.

Cassian was nowhere, Kaden wore golden armor, and soon I would be forced to stand before the court and bare my soul to a trial I still didn't understand.

I was completely, utterly alone.

I stumbled toward the mirror like something half-dead. My knees buckled once, but I caught myself on the edge of the vanity, fingers curling into the carved wood.

I looked up, and what I saw broke the last piece of me still clinging to denial.

The girl staring back at me was a stranger.

Her silver hair was wild. Knots and mats snarled in her hair from wind and sleepiness nights. Her cheeks and collarbone were smudged with grime, faint streaks of dirt I hadn't even noticed. Her skin had lost its warmth, its color. It was pale now. Sickly. Hollow. Shallow cuts now scabbing and flaking streaked along her cheekbone, with a split running though the corner of her lip.

And her eyes—stars, her eyes.

They were rimmed in shadows, sunken and bloodshot, shining with something too close to desperation.

No wonder Moira looked at me like that. No wonder she tried to drag me away.

I didn't look like a queen.

I didn't even look like Lyra.

The mirror warped as tears filled my eyes, but I didn't let them fall.

I couldn't fix Kaden.

I couldn't fix Veritus.

But I could fix this.

My hands trembled as I turned the tap, watching the copper basin begin to fill with steam and silence. The pipes groaned in the walls like a warning, but I ignored it. I poured the lavender oil into the stream and watched it ripple, watched the perfume cloud the surface in soft spirals of violet.

I stripped, layer by layer, until the girl in the mirror was bare and cold. I peeled each cloth off of my body, the gash at my side now a pink line. Whatever minty solution Moira had used worked.

I climbed into the bath, and the heat hit me like a rushing tide.

It stole my breath for a moment, making my limbs ache as if they were waking from a long, cruel sleep. I sank deeper, until the water kissed my shoulders, until the lavender wrapped around me like arms that didn't judge me for falling apart.

I scrubbed until my skin flushed red.

I scraped the dirt from beneath my nails, scrubbed my scalp until it tingled, until my fingers shook from effort. As if I could scrape the failure off of me. As if I could undo the things I'd seen. The way

Kaden had stood beside the King. The sound of that latch clicking behind me.

I stayed until the water turned murky, until it began to cool.

When I finally stood, my skin was pink and raw, but I felt lighter. Not healed. Not fixed. But cleansed. As if I'd clawed my way back from some edge, even if the world around me still burned.

A sound startled me.

A soft rustle.

I froze.

Then a small rectangle of parchment slid under the door, catching on the edge of the wood.

I wrapped a towel tight around myself and crossed the room with wet feet and a pounding heart. I knelt, scooping the letter up with damp fingers. It was small. Light. Only a few words.

She's awake

Elena.

I didn't think. I didn't pause. I moved.

I threw open the armoire and tore out the first dress my hand touched. The fabric clung to my still-damp skin as I pulled it over my head. I shoved my hands into my gloves and my feet into my shoes, not caring they were mismatched. My hair hung wet and tangled down my back.

I grabbed the door handle, yanked.

Locked.

"Open it," I snapped.

The guard on the other side didn't answer. I pounded once. Twice. "*Open the door!*" I hissed. My power pooled at the floor, the shimmering air rippling and waiting for the order to strike.

I pushed a thin tendril under the door just as I heard a metallic *click.*

I didn't wait for permission. I recoiled my power and shoved it open, bolting past the guard without looking back.

The halls blurred around me. The infirmary wasn't far, but it might as well have been on the other side of the world. My lungs ached, my throat burned, but I kept running.

When I threw open the infirmary doors, I half expected to find her still unconscious. I braced myself to see her pale and unmoving, surrounded by silence and grief, but instead, she was laughing.

Elena sat upright in bed, a wool blanket draped around her shoulders. Her cheeks were flushed. Her eyes sparkled with mischief.

And across from her, in that same old chair, was Will. His shirt was wrinkled. His eyes rimmed with exhaustion, but he was smiling at her like she was the sun after a hundred-year storm.

My heart lurched. Relief slammed into me so hard I had to grip the doorframe to stay upright.

"Elena," I whispered.

She turned.

And when her eyes met mine, full of warmth and light and life—

I broke.

And this time, it wasn't from despair.

The braid I had woven into Elena's hair was still there.

It was messy, barely holding together, frayed and twisted by sleep and pain, but it was there.

Without thinking, I crossed the space in a sprint and threw my arms around her, clinging tight. Her skin was warm even though her clothes. Her pulse still beat beneath it. Real. Alive.

"Oh stars," I whispered, my voice breaking apart, "I'm so glad you're awake. I'm so glad you're alive."

Elena gave a soft laugh, tired but real. She weakly wrapped her arms around me. "I'm glad *you're* alive," she murmured into my shoulder. Her fingers trembled where they curled against my back.

But when I pulled away, when our eyes met again, the smile faded from her lips. The light dimmed.

Her gaze sobered. "When they dragged me off..." Her voice was quiet now, careful. "I really thought they were going to kill me."

My heart twisted. I sat down on the bed beside her, setting a hand on the blanket draped over her legs.

"But then," she continued, her brows drawing together, "everyone froze. Like something had snapped. They looked scared. They were staring at you. Or Naelle. Or both—I don't really know. I wasn't sure if you were alive. What... what happened?"

I opened my mouth.

And nothing came out.

The truth tangled in my throat, sharp and heavy. How could I explain it? That it wasn't a match. That was retribution.

So, I said only two words.

"I won."

Elena's frown deepened. "That's not what I asked."

I dropped my gaze to her hands curled in her lap. Her fingers were thinner than before, paler, but still moving. Still real.

I couldn't look her in the eyes. I couldn't confess what I'd done.

Silence stretched between us, thick as tar. I wanted to speak. I wanted to be brave enough to tell her, but the words wouldn't cooperate. I couldn't ask her to carry that weight after what she'd been through.

I shook my head, softly, slowly.

She didn't press. Elena only gave my leg a gentle pat and let it go.

After that, we talked of smaller things. Safer things. She asked about the gardens, and I told her the leaves had turned to burning red and oranges. We laughed about the time we'd stolen bread from the kitchens and were convinced we were master thieves. She thanked me again for the braid, but the guilt didn't leave.

It clung to me like a second skin. Heavy. It scratched at the back of my throat, throbbed behind my eyes. I smiled, I nodded, I played the part but inside, something coiled and unspoken stayed tight and sharp.

When Elena's eyelids began to droop again, her laughter fading into hums, I reached for the blanket and pulled it up to her chin. My fingers lingered there, just for a moment. It reminded me of the night Cassian had done the same for me, when I'd been too broken to sleep, too scared to breathe.

Funny, how we all took turns being shattered.

I stood slowly, giving Will a plastered smile.

I lingered in the doorway, watching Elena's chest rise and fall in the soft rhythm of sleep before I left.

CHAPTER FORTY-TWO

WHEN I TURNED THE CORNER to my room, Cassian stood in the hall facing my door. No guard was in sight.

A stack of books rested in his arms, the covers bound in black leather, their spines stitched with silver thread that shimmered faintly beneath the flickering lantern light. I didn't recall seeing anything like it on the shelves of the library. His head was bowed slightly, as if he'd been waiting there for a long time. Tension radiated from every inch of him—tight shoulders, clenched jaw, his grip on the books too rigid, too still. The muscles in his jaw flexed and released, again and again, like he was trying to hold something back.

The golden thread between us, dimmed and frayed from their past day, suddenly pulled taut. As if time folded in on itself and erased the space between us.

His head lifted slowly.

A searing heat surged down my spine, curling low in my belly. I swayed, caught in it. His longing slammed into me like a storm tide, pouring into me in golden waves. I felt him in every inch of my body.

It was like sunlight breaking through storm clouds.

Like warmth returning to frozen skin.

His lips didn't move, but the words still came. Silken and intimate, whispered directly into my mind,

I missed you, little silver flame.

My knees nearly buckled. The bond between us pulsed like a heartbeat, alive and aware and pulling me closer. My steps slowed, tentative. I took one stride forward and the thread between us throbbed again.

Cassian's eyes softened, dark lashes lowering slightly. His grip tightened on the stack of books, like it was the only thing keeping him tethered to the ground.

Everything inside him came rushing into me. Wanting. Yearning. The sharp, breathless burn of desire that made my own heart twist in answer. But it wasn't just want. It wasn't hunger alone.

He ached for me.

The way I looked at him without seeing a crown. The way I challenged him, without fear or pretense. The way my power curled around him like wildfire and moonlight. He missed my voice, the sound of my laugh. He missed the feel of me, even in silence, the weight of my presence filling whatever void he tried to hide behind all that restraint.

His feelings for me weren't soft. They were fierce, wild things. Full of claws and teeth. They held no apology. And when I felt the full weight of them, it didn't just break something in me. It unmade me, gently and completely, like I'd been waiting my whole life to fall apart in his hands.

He hadn't come here just to give me books.

He had come because he couldn't stay away.

The emotions he sent me sharpened. They morphed from hunger and longing to memories.

The lagoon.

The laughter I hadn't realized he'd memorized.

The sound of my breath catching when his thumb had ghosted down my cheek. The way I'd looked up at him, his body against mine, and yet he hadn't kissed me. Had only looked at me like he was drowning in the want and the war of it.

His throat bobbed.

I felt the effort it took him to stay still. To keep his hands to himself. He was holding himself back with everything he had. Slowly, I reached out, arms trembling. My fingers brushed the topmost book, just barely, and his fingers grazed mine.

The world ignited.

Flames roared through that golden tether. It screamed between us, incandescent, like a live wire had snapped and buried itself in my spine.

My breath left me in a gasp. Cassian sucked in air through his nose, sharp and harsh, like I'd burned him.

He whipped his head away.

Stared down at the marble floor like it held the only escape from whatever had just broken loose inside him, but the bond didn't stop. It surged, tearing into me like a storm tide crashing over a broken dam, and suddenly, it wasn't just his need I felt.

It was his fear.

I don't know if I can watch them tear you apart.

I don't know if I can stay away.

I will kill them all. I will burn this palace to the ground.

The words were not spoken. They didn't need to be. They flooded through the bond in raw, unfiltered emotion. No guards. No walls.

My breath shuddered out. "Cassian…"

His name broke on my lips, and my stars. It wrecked him.

He didn't flinch, but I saw it—the slight twitch in his jaw, the flicker of pain in his eyes. His composure cracked, just enough to let me see how close he was to snapping. A hand dropped to his side. His fingers flexed, aching to reach out, but still, he didn't.

When his voice came, it was low, rough, ragged with restraint. "I thought you'd want these."

He placed his hand back on top of the books, lifting the stack an inch higher, but he wouldn't look at me. His eyes stayed fixed downward, fixed on the silver-threaded spines.

I furrowed my brow. "What do they say?"

His gaze rose slowly.

"Read them," he said softly. "Before tomorrow."

Another wave rolled down the tether between us. Not desire this time. Not fury or pain.

Hope.

A lump rose in my throat. My voice barely made it past my lips. "I don't know if I want to survive it." His breath hitched. I pressed on, afraid to stop. "I don't know what you'll see."

Cassian's jaw clenched so tightly I thought it might snap, and then, finally, he moved.

He stepped forward slowly, like he was testing the weight of each footfall, like he was giving me the chance to run again. Like I had only this morning.

I didn't move.

He stopped a breath away. Leaned in, slow and reverent, until his forehead hovered just above mine. Close enough that I could feel his heat, feel the air between us humming. His eyes fluttered shut, and he held his breath like this moment was a thread he could stretch forever, if only he didn't breathe.

His voice broke through the stillness, soft and rough and mine.

"I'll see *you*, Lyra," he whispered. "Because I already do. I see all of you. And I will not let them take a single piece."

His breath brushed against my lips.

Warm. Steady. Dangerous.

My heart stuttered in my chest. My lungs barely remembered how to function. The space between us was a breath, a heartbeat, a choice, but he didn't close it. Neither did I.

Instead, he placed the books into my arms, one by one. Like offerings at an altar. As if I were something sacred. His fingers lingered on the last one, just for a moment longer than they should have.

I couldn't breathe. Couldn't speak. I only clutched the books to my chest, as if they could keep me upright, as if they could keep me whole. The golden thread between us was alive, buzzing, thrumming, aching with everything unspoken.

Cassian took a step back, and the space he left behind felt like a wound. He started to walk away.

"Stay." The word tore out of me before I could stop it. My voice cracked open, raw and aching. "Stay with me, Cass. Please."

He stopped. Turned slowly. His face was cast in torch light and shadow, but his smile—stars, his smile—was soft. Gentle. Breaking.

"I wish I could."

I stared at him, confusion thick in my chest, pressing against my ribs. I didn't understand. Why couldn't he? Why was he continually *almost* mine?

If I spoke, if I asked, my voice would shatter.

He exhaled. The sound of it was full of restraint—like he was holding something back. Like he'd been holding it back for ages.

"I've already caused enough trouble today," he said. His eyes dropped to the floor. And when they rose again, they weren't soft anymore. They were cold. Composed. Hardened like steel. "Best he takes his anger out on the right person."

And just like that he turned again, and he left.

CHAPTER FORTY-THREE

I NEARLY THREW THE DOOR off its hinges.

The lock was open and welcome, and the moment it clicked shut behind me, I was already moving across the room in long, frantic strides. I flung the books in my arms across the desk like they were too heavy to carry for another heartbeat. They landed with soft thuds, silver-threaded spines catching the last glow of candlelight like dying stars.

But one caught my eye immediately.

It didn't belong with the rest. It didn't shimmer silver like the others. It gleamed gold and black.

My eyes snapped to an open silver book, the thickest in the stack, and saw the inside was completely carved away. Just wide enough for the gold book to slip inside. Cassian had hidden it well.

My breath stilled as I reached for it, fingertips grazing the cover like it might dissolve under my touch. My hands trembled, a rush of heat and something close to fear rising in my chest. I opened it carefully.

It wasn't printed. It was written. His handwriting. It was his voice, tucked into every loop and curve of ink.

Forgive my distance.

I couldn't give him any more weaponry against you.

Use the power you've been given.

Veritas is an Argentum ritual. It's built for you to

control.

My eyes stung. My hands clenched around the edges of the page.

I've read all the others. Don't waste your time.

It's all here. Please read it.

For you, little silver flame.

Tears blurred the letters. I pulled the chair out roughly, sat down, and flipped the page of the journal. And I read.

Cassian's notes were sharp, layered with ancient texts and interpretations, handwritten annotations tucked between lines. They spoke of the old powers—of the great divide between Aurums and Argentums. Of how Aurums required years of discipline, how they wove mental shields brick by brick, thought by thought. Iron dedication, forced boundaries. But Argentums, Argentums were different.

Your mind is not a void, Lyra.

It is a sea. Control the tide.

I stared at those words for a long time.
A sea.
Not a fortress. Not a locked room.
A tide.
I closed my eyes. Breathed deep. And then I began.
I dove into my memories, forcing myself to relive them. I sat there, jaw clenched, muscles tight, and cracked myself open like a sealed vault. Each image, each vision, each relived nightmare came in a wave. They drowned me, only to give me a gasp of air before the next came crashing.

The golden throne beneath my skin. The pain of the pin-prick edge and the bright flare of blood down my finger. I watched it fall, drop by drop.

The guard's body. The moment he obeyed me.

I forced myself to feel it. Not just remember, but feel.

Naelle's sobs. Rhea's fury. Elena bleeding on that arena floor. Kaden's eyes. Empty, absent, and yet still watching.

And Cassian's voice in the dark, whispering my name like it was the only thing in this world.

And then I reached inward.

There, coiled like a snake of fire and light, that power waited. It pulsed silver-bright behind my ribs. I cracked the jar of it open and let it swirl through me like mist, like smoke, like flame.

Control the tide.

I imagined vaults. Doors. Domes of silver light. I pictured each memory, each pain, and locked them away one by one. Carefully. Tenderly. Not to forget, but to wield.

The throne.

The girls.

Kaden.

Cassian.

I filed them away. I coated them in silver, sealed each vault with flame.

And I did it again.

And again.

Faster. Sharper. Until my hands stopped shaking. Until my tears dried on my cheeks and all that remained was a calm so precise it felt like the eye of a storm.

Grief. Fury. Love. Fear. I forged every sharp edge inside me into armor.

The knock at the door was a thunderclap.

Not gentle. Not soft.

It was brutal, like a threat slamming through wood and air and bone.

"Yes?" I called, my voice catching.

No answer came.

Only the sharp, deliberate click of the lock sliding open from the outside.

I froze.

The door burst inward.

Two guards stormed into the room like a gust of metal and silence, their armor gleaming dully in the candlelight. I slammed the book shut. My body moved on instinct—grabbing a dress from the floor and flinging it across the desk.

Their eyes were covered in golden helmets. Their hands were cold as they grabbed my arms. Chainmail gloves kept their skin separate from my own.

They didn't look down.

They didn't speak.

They seized me by the elbows and dragged me into the hall. Something about their silence told me this wasn't about punishment.

It was about control.

I walked where they forced me to walk, the cold of the corridor crawling into my skin. Every turn tightened a noose around my neck, and when we reached the end of the hall, I knew where they were taking me.

The throne room.

One guard opened the gold-veined doors.

The other shoved me through them.

They slammed shut behind me with a thunderous finality. The echo of it rolled across the marble floor, louder than my own breath.

Moonlight spilled through the high windows, pale and sharp. It washed everything silver. The throne room looked different like this. The golden walls didn't shimmer. They sagged. And the throne itself, that gleaming monstrosity, looked brittle. Fragile.

Yet, there he sat.

The King.

Draped in velvet and cruelty. A serpent clothed in jewels.

"Miss Seravell," he said, rising to his feet with a smile like a slit throat. "What a lovely night for a reckoning."

His voice slithered through the air.

Power coiled in my chest, rushing to cloak my thoughts, locking down everything behind those walls I'd spent the whole night building. I felt him. I felt his probing touch brushing against my shields.

I snapped my eyes to his.

He felt the resistance.

"Practicing, I see?" he said lightly, as if amused. His eyes ran down me like acid rain. "Care to tell me who whispered that in your ear?" He stepped down from the throne like a man strolling through a garden. Leisurely. "No?"

I felt the pressure of his magic with every movement. Testing me. Stretching. Pressing. He clicked his tongue, cocking his head to the side, as if I was nothing more than a disobedient child. "Pity."

My shields strained, but they held.

He circled me slowly.

"I wonder," he mused aloud, "when they watch your memories tomorrow, will they be more shocked by the one you killed—" he paused, his eyes glittering with delight, "—or the ones you love?"

My heart stuttered. A bolt of cold fear struck down my spine.

"What?" I breathed.

He turned his head. "Bring them in."

The words cracked like lightning.

Kaden entered, but it wasn't him. Not truly.

He didn't even look at me.

That wasn't my Kaden.

That wasn't the boy who trained beside me, who bled for me.

That was someone truly numb.

He dragged a girl behind him. She was thrashing, fighting like a storm.

"Elena," I gasped. Her name tore from my throat.

Behind them came another guard dragging a lifeless figure. Blood smeared in his wake.

Will.

The boy who was here only for love.

I wonder when that love turned to fear.

"What is this?" I demanded, my voice shaking.

The King's grin widened. It wasn't a smile. It was a mask of dominance sharpened to a blade.

"Insurance," he said simply. "I needed a reminder. For you."

Elena bawled through her cloth gag, straining toward me, her entire body shaking.

But the boy, he didn't scream.

He just looked at me through bruised and swelling eyes.

And he looked horrified.

Throughly and utterly horrified.

I didn't even know his last name. I didn't know the name Elena had hoped to receive.

I had never asked.

The King lifted a hand. No flourish. No speech. Just—

Snap.

A sound, clean and cruel.

Will crumpled.

He just... fell.

Elena's scream was bloodcurdling and raw, breaking with each sob that thrashed free from her throat. The gag in her mouth did little to dampen the sound that seemed to reverberate through my bones.

His blood spread beneath him, blooming like ink across the marble from his nose and eyes and mouth.

"No," I whispered. My voice cracked. *"No—!"*

My scream split the air, and so did my power.

It erupted out of me like a dying star. Silver flames surged in every direction. The torches shuddered. The windows quaked. The very floor cracked beneath my feet.

It was all there, bursting through me.

Elena scrambled away, as if I was a wild burning fire. Her eyes were wide, the glassy tears reflecting the shining silver air coiling through the throne room. I felt her terror as soon as her eyes hit mine.

I felt everyone's terror, yet I couldn't stop it.

The King only smiled.

"Ah," he said softly, with something like delight. "There she is."

I lunged. Silver power lashed from my fingertips. My heart screamed louder than my voice.

But then, something smothered my head.

A bag.

A bag that smelled sickly sweet.

"Let go of me!" I thrashed wildly, every limb burning with magic and grief. I struck something, maybe someone. A scream tore through the dark.

I didn't care.

I couldn't see.

Couldn't breathe.

I saw nothing.

Only darkness.

And it swallowed me whole.

CHAPTER FORTY-FOUR

THERE WAS NOTHING. Not pain. Not sound. Just dark.

It wasn't cold, exactly. Or warm. It simply was. A black so deep it felt soft, like velvet turned inside out.

I didn't know if I was standing, or floating, or dissolving. Somewhere, in some distant version of myself, I knew I should be fighting.

But I wasn't, and I could've stayed. That was the terrible part of it.

How easy it would've been. To let go. To let it all fall away. The blood, the fire, the screaming. The boy with no last name. The boy with no more soul. The boy with eyes like honey. The crown.

It would be so easy to float here forever. I didn't have to hurt anymore. Didn't have to win or lose or fight or survive. All I had to do was drift. But then there was a thread.

Thin. Silver. Burning.

A voice, maybe. Or a memory. Or just the truth I'd buried deep some long time ago.

You are not born to kneel.

I didn't want to go back.

I wanted to rest.

I opened my eyes anyway.

CHAPTER FORTY-FIVE

I WOKE WITH A GASP—violent, ragged—as if the world had yanked the air from my lungs before I remembered how to breathe.

Cold struck me first.

It wasn't gentle. It sank through my skin, into my ribs, into the marrow of my bones. I didn't open my eyes right away. I didn't want to. I already knew something was different. Something was amiss.

The stone beneath me pulsed. Not warm, but alive. I felt it, humming just beneath the surface, ancient and aware, like the heartbeat of something that had been sleeping too long and had finally opened its eyes.

When I forced mine open, I found myself lying on a massive obsidian platform, polished black and veined with silver. The veins glowed faintly, pulsing like a living breath. The platform was circular, elevated, suspended above a vast abyss of shadow.

I pushed myself up, staggering as pain flared through every limb. My knees trembled. My head throbbed. The ache wasn't clean. It was residual, like whatever they'd drugged me with still lingered in my veins.

My clothes hung in tatters. Dirt clung to the torn hem of my tunic. Blood dried at the seams. My hair felt like a snarl of brambles and ash, half-matted from the sack they'd shoved over my head. My throat was raw. My skin ached. I looked like I'd been dragged through a war.

Maybe I had.

I was an animal on a pedestal. A sacrifice on display.

When I lifted my head, I saw her standing directly to the side of me, on her own obsidian pillar.

Rhea Damaris.

She looked untouchable. Dressed in a gown of amethyst that caught the chamber's cruel light, her golden hair coiled up like a crown ringing around her head. Her spine was straight. Her chin high. She looked perfect, but her hands betrayed her. Clenched into fists in the side fabric of her dress, white-knuckled and trembling.

She was just as terrified as I was.

I turned, slowly, taking in the chamber around us.

It was vast and cavernous. The walls, floor, and ceiling were carved entirely from jagged obsidian. The stone caught and fractured phantom light like broken glass, reflecting it back in slivers and shards. The air felt heavy, metallic, humming with the weight of what was about to unfold.

And the room was full. People were everywhere.

The full court was in attendance. Both walls to my left and right glimmered with people half-seen. Nobles sat draped in silks and jewels. Court members wore gleaming, gold-threaded robes that flowed like honey, their faces masks of frozen indifference. Palace guards lined the walls, their armor black and glinting with flaxen sashes, hands resting on hilts, eyes fixed forward.

Above them all, on a raised black dais directly ahead, sat the King.

A grand stair ran from wall to wall, its steps pitted and crumbling in places. His throne was hammered gold—ridged and jagged, like it had been pulled from the wreckage of a sun. He didn't slouch. He didn't blink. He just watched, draped in deep crimson and layered velvet, the weight of his gaze like a brand pressed into my skin.

And beside him sat Cassian.

My breath caught in my throat.

He was seated stiffly, shoulders too straight. His honey curls were combed back, his face clean-shaven, every detail pristine except for the hollow in his eyes. There was no fire. No smile. No rebellion curled at the edge of his lips.

A high-collared shirt was buttoned to his throat, sleeves to his wrists. But I saw them, peeking out just beneath the fabric, where the cuff had ridden up slightly.

Bruises.

Ugly and blooming.

His gaze flicked to me, just once, but in that one look, I knew.

He had paid for the books.

I curled my fingers into the stone beneath me, teeth clenching so hard my jaw ached.

Whatever trial this was, whatever horror they meant to play before the court, it wasn't just a performance.

It was a punishment, and I was the main event.

A silence stretched so taut I thought the stone beneath me might snap with the weight of it.

Then, a horn sounded.

Low. Ancient. Violent.

The sound invaded the chamber like a storm that had been bottled and released. It boomed from nowhere and everywhere at once, vibrating in my chest, splitting the air like a scream too old to belong to the living.

My knees buckled slightly as I watched the mist pour into the room.

A surge of cold poured from the far corners of the room. Liquid silver mist spilled from seams in the obsidian walls, flooding the sunken space between the pillars like a rising tide.

It wasn't natural. It didn't feel natural.

The mist moved with intention, coiling around the base of my pillar, brushing against my ankles like it had fingers, like it was tasting my skin. I staggered back a step on the slick obsidian, every hair on my body standing on end. The cold seeped in beneath my skin, wrapping around my ribs and tugging.

It wanted something.

Flickers of light danced in the fog. I squinted my eyes, leaning forward to peer off the edge of the obsidian platform. I saw pictures flash as quickly as they came. I saw swirls of laughter and heartache. Of fear and love. Images I didn't understand shimmered just beyond reach. A glint of morning dew in the gardens. A mother brushing a young girl's hair. The halls of the palace at night, lit only by the moon. A bottle of half-drank red wine.

Realization hit me like a lightning strike.

Memories.

They were memories.

Memories made physical.

All there and gone in an instant, like reflections in water broken by a stone.

Rhea flinched across from me. Her eyes darted to the mist, then to the King. Her hands trembled.

I knew what this was.

My mouth went dry. My knees locked.

This was Veritus.

Panic clawed its way into my throat.

The horn died away, leaving only the soft sound of the mist curling along the stone. The chamber held its breath. So did I.

I braced myself, fists clenched at my sides, heart hammering.

I couldn't run. I couldn't fight.

This time, the battlefield wasn't made of blood or blades.

It was made of memory and minds.

It was made of truth.

And it was already clawing its way out.

The King's voice rang out, sharp and merciless, carving through the thick silence like a blade.

"Miss Damaris. Who are you?"

She barely had time to register the question before the mist struck her.

Rhea didn't speak. She didn't even try to answer.

Her head snapped back with a sickening jolt, her spine arching like an overdrawn bow. A cry tore from her throat—half gasp, half scream—and then the silver mist surged into her, plunging into her chest like smoke funneled into unwilling lungs.

I stepped back instinctively, my heart hammering.

The mist above her shifted, swirled, and then ignited.

Images bled from the haze, unfolding in perfect, brutal clarity.

Rhea as a child in the palace gardens, blonde curls and velvet ribbons. I almost let out a breath until I saw her hands. Small. Precise. Tearing the wings from a butterfly, her face calm as the creature twitched in her grasp.

Someone in the audience let out a soft gasp.

The scene changed.

Rhea again, now here in the palace, standing in front of a table in the library. Before her sat Elena, who poured over the same fighting technique books I had attempted, and failed, to read. Her fingers slipped something from her sleeve as she rambled on—a fine pinch of powder. She flicked it into the steaming mug of tea sat before the very distracted Elena, the white dust dissolving into the depths of the liquid. Rhea turned away before Elena could lift it, but the outcome was clear.

Anger bloomed harshly in my chest, spreading over rib after rib until the entirety of my body burned.

I would kill her for what she did. If this trial doesn't handle that for me.

Then darker even still.

Rhea, looming over a kneeling servant. Blood already pooled from the girl's nose. Rhea didn't blink. She didn't flinch. Her voice was a dagger.

"Make it look like an accident."

My stomach turned.

Then it all vanished. The mist retreated. The light receded.

Rhea crumpled to her knees like her strings had been cut, gasping for breath as if she'd drowned and only just been pulled from the water. Her hands trembled in her lap. The amethyst gown shimmered like the beginning of the night sky.

The room filled with gasps, whispers, a shuffling of silks and polished boots. A woman in emerald beside the dais turned her head sharply away. One of the advisors leaned toward the King, his brow furrowed with unease. The air was turning. The court was watching.

I swallowed hard and reached for my power.

Not to attack, not this time, but to shield.

I had no idea what the mist would attack. I had no idea what it would drag out. My memories had teeth.

I shaped my magic like a veil, thin but iron-strong, wrapping it tight around my mind, my thoughts. I pushed it outward like a second skull, built of silver wind and sheer desperation.

Pain lanced behind my eyes as the strain set in, but I held.

The King's gaze moved to me, slow as a guillotine.

"Lyra Seravell," he said, voice steeped in amusement. "Who are you?"

And then it hit me.

Not a physical blow, but stars, it felt like one.

The mist slammed into my skull like ice cracking down the middle. I felt it sliding in, probing, peeling, ripping. My jaw clenched. My arms trembled at my sides as I forced my body to remain standing.

Images pushed against the edge of my mind. Familiar. Precious. Dangerous.

I could feel it trying to pull them free—Kaden, Cassian, Elena. The child I'd been. The girl I had become. The things I had done to survive.

"I—" My voice cracked. I forced the words out. "I am Lyra Seravell. Daughter of Dalen Seravell. Of Virellia."

The mist paused. And then, nothing.

No images. No projections.

Just silence.

It stretched out around me like the eye of a storm. For a single breath, no one moved. Then the murmurs began.

Low. Staggered. Shocked.

I heard it ripple through the crowd, a wave of disbelief. A man in silver silk leaned forward, blinking like he'd just seen a ghost. A few guards exchanged uncertain glances, their stances flickering with something that looked dangerously like fear.

And the King, the King was watching me like I had just confirmed something he had long suspected. His jaw twitched slightly, but enough to betray the crack beneath his polished facade. Then he turned from me, sharply, his eyes back on Rhea. The mist followed, leaving my body shaking and shuttering, but my mind untouched.

"What is your greatest ambition?" he asked, his voice as flat and cold as steel left in snow.

Rhea swallowed. This time, she answered. "To—rule. To serve this court."

I saw the flicker in her eyes, the slight delay in her voice, and so did the mist. It surged upward again, quick and vengeful.

The haze above her burst into light, forming another projection. Rhea, older now, standing in a candlelit corridor beside her mother. Her posture was arrogant, her tone dripping with disdain.

"I'll make the throne mine," she said with a sneer. *"Prince or not."*

The image flashed and died. Rhea let out a raw, visceral scream and collapsed forward, her hands catching the polished obsidian as she hit the ground. She coughed once. Then again. Her trembling fingers smudged the reflection beneath her.

For the first time since I'd known her, Rhea Damaris looked afraid.

Not just of the King. Or the court. Or even me.

But of being seen.

Of being known.

Of the armor being stripped away and realizing she had nothing left underneath.

"Get up," the King ordered with a hiss.

His voice cracked across the chamber like a whip.

Rhea obeyed, barely. Her limbs were shaking as she dragged herself to her feet, jaw clenched so tightly I thought she might chip a tooth.

His gaze slid back to me.

"Lyra Seravell," he said, voice quieter now, more pointed. "Do you, too, wish to take the crown for your own gain?"

The mist lunged for me.

I didn't even have time to brace before it slammed into my mind again, harder this time, like it had learned where the cracks were. I felt it clawing, snarling, digging. My legs locked. My back arched painfully.

My power surged in response, the shield I'd formed earlier fighting to hold.

I forced my jaw open. "No," I rasped. "I want to protect the people your rule has broken."

The words rang true in me, sharp and bright like a silver bell. I meant them. Every syllable. And yet the mist didn't relent. It twisted around the truth like it didn't trust it. Like it wanted to corrupt it.

I felt it pressing at the edges of my memories, testing my certainty, but I held. I held until the mist yet again fell away, crashing down into the ocean of fog below.

The court began to shift uneasily. Their reactions were more subdued this time, like they didn't quite know what to make of me.

I risked a glance at Cassian. His knuckles were white where they gripped the armrest of his chair. His jaw was clenched so hard a vein stood out along his throat, but he didn't look at me.

The King leaned forward slightly on his throne, his velvet robes spilling down like the folds of a curtain closing around a hanging noose.

Then, with venomous precision, he asked, "As Queen of Aurea, will you love this city and its people as your own?"

I flinched. That question was piercing. The mist struck with force, slamming into me so hard I staggered. My knees buckled slightly, but I didn't fall.

I despised this city. The cruelty. The masks. The glimmering lies draped in gold and velvet. I hated how it took and took and smiled while everyone else burned.

But that was my purpose. My reason.

Something needed to change.

"Y-yes," I choked out, my voice cracking under the weight of it. "Because I will make it my own."

The mist didn't like that answer. It tore at my shield again, searching for deceit, but there was none. Just truth.

My legs gave out. My muscles strained and my head split. I hit the obsidian hard, the jolt rattling through my bones, my teeth clacking together. I didn't collapse fully, but my hands slammed down to brace me. My head bowed, white strands of hair falling across my face, sweat clinging to my temples.

And the mist withdrew. Dissolving once more, it fell to the stone and dissipating as fast as it came.

I forced my head up, feeling warmth trail from my ears. I didn't look, or touch, but I saw as Cassian's face flushed with anger. He stood. I felt the sudden rush of heat in the room, his fury igniting like dry tinder, but it lasted only a heartbeat. The King slammed his fist down on the armrest of his throne with a crack that echoed through the obsidian chamber. "Sit. Down."

The words reverberated like a command carved into stone. Cassian obeyed, but slowly.

The room blurred, my vision swimming from the mist still clinging to me like frostbite. Each breath I took felt like I was inhaling snow. It burned. It numbed. It weighed.

Rhea was still beside me, hunched and broken, her silhouette trembling. One of her arms wrapped around her head, her hair bunched in her grasp. She didn't speak. Didn't move.

The King stood. He moved with deliberate weight, his golden robes trailing behind him as he stepped toward the edge of the dais. His voice rang out, smooth and sharp. "Miss Seravell. How would you achieve this feat? What power do you have?"

He knew what he was doing. He wasn't asking a question. He was drawing a blade. The moment the words left his mouth, the mist thickened again. It surged into my throat, up my nose. I gagged on it. It was like drowning in the silence.

My lungs seized. The pressure closed around my ribs like a vice. My voice, what little I had left, caught and died at the back of my tongue.

I forced the words out, one shuddering breath at a time, scraping them from the fire in my bones. "I… have… *justice*."

The King's face went red. Not just anger, but rage. Pure, choking rage. His eyes sparked as he stepped down from the platform, one heavy footfall at a time. He moved like a god descending from a throne to smite whoever dared oppose him.

And then, he struck.

Not with his hands, but with his mind.

I didn't scream aloud. I screamed inside.

I felt him, cold and ancient and cruel. His presence crashed through the mist like a predator into snow. His power was practiced, honed, like a scalpel slicing through layers of flesh. He tore.

I felt the edges of my mind peel back. My thoughts were splintering under his intrusion. He moved with the confidence of someone who had done this too many times before. He knew where to look, what to sever, how to break.

I convulsed. My body arched against the obsidian floor, my teeth gritting so hard I thought they'd shatter. Sweat beaded and poured down my neck and spine.

He kept going. He kept pressing and tearing, until—

I felt it.

His mind was pressing so wildly into mine that he forgot something.

Himself.

He was forcing his power elsewhere, meaning the space left behind was mine for the taking.

After all, anything can be yours. If you're brave enough to take it.

I reached out. Just a flicker at first. Just the barest thread of thought. Like casting a line into deep, black water, and there it was.

Ice.

His mind was a fortress of it. Slick walls and no purchase, but I was wind and current and memory. I flowed. I slipped across the frozen stone, searching for a weakness, for a crack. And I found one.

Hairline thin. Barely visible, but real.

I dug into it. Slithered through it like smoke. I let my power fill every corner of his mind that he'd left unguarded. And then, I struck.

I slammed my power into that fracture. Into the thinnest places, where the weight of all his power had thinned the ice.

I didn't wait.

I drove into him.

A mental snap cracked through the air. Not sound, not quite, but I felt it in my bones.

The King reeled.

He ripped away from me, but it was too late.

I'd seen it. I'd seen what he'd buried so deeply.

He wasn't afraid of the regions.

He wasn't afraid of failure.

He wasn't afraid of death.

He was afraid of me.

He was afraid of Lyra Seravell.

The King stumbled back as if I'd physically struck him. His face was pale now, his chest heaving. His crown glinted like a knife's edge under the torchlight. His eyes were wide.

He knew.

And I knew too.

I pushed myself up from the floor, trembling but unbroken.

I didn't need to say a word.

The truth had already been found.

It had nearly destroyed him, and I simply smiled.

It was slight. Just a curve of my lips through the haze and the sweat and the agony, but it was there. It was real. I smiled as I felt his power retreating and recoiling like a wounded beast.

The ice in his mind began sealing itself again, the cracks filling, the fortress reassembling. He was scrambling, trying to pull himself back together.

It didn't matter.

I was already inside.

All he was doing was sealing me in.

My knees screamed in protest. My limbs shook so badly I thought they might fail, but I made them obey. I rose, spine straight, chin high, shoulders back.

I let my power stretch, slow and deliberate, slithering through the spaces in his mind like smoke curling beneath a locked door. I forced him to feel me. Let him know I was there. That he could hide behind his walls all he wanted, but they would never keep me out.

I pressed one word into the dark cold of his thoughts. One truth, wrapped in steel and silver and flame.

Kneel.

It wasn't a suggestion.

It was a command.

He collapsed.

The sound of his knees slamming into the obsidian rang like a bell tolling the end of an era. Harsh and final.

The silence that followed was deafening.

The crown slid from his head. It hit the black stone and rolled, the gold gilding scuffing away as it spun, faster and faster, until it reached the base of the pillar beneath me.

It vanished into the mist.

No one moved.

Not the guards frozen at attention. Not the nobles with hands over their mouths or fists clenched at their sides. Not the courtiers who had once whispered my name like a curse.

They stared at me like they were witnessing a myth come to life. Perhaps they were.

I barely noticed them. My heart thundered so violently in my chest I couldn't hear anything else. My vision flickered. My body was breaking, crumbling beneath the weight of what I had just done.

And still, I stood.

A figure cut through the stunned crowd.

Cassian.

He ran. Across the black stone, past the still-kneeling King. The mist drew back like it knew him. Like it feared him. It parted for him in ribbons, retreating into the walls with a sound like a thousand sighs.

He reached me just as my legs finally gave out.

The world tilted and strong arms caught me before I hit the ground.

"Lyra—" His voice was rough, hoarse with fear. He pulled me from the pillar and into his chest. One hand cradled the back of my head as the other scooped my body off the obsidian. I felt the tremble in his body as he held me, like even he didn't quite believe what had just happened. He sat among the remaining mist, my skin and hair melding into the pale air.

I forced my eyes open.

Forced my head to lift.

Our gazes met, and in his eyes, I saw everything.

Awe.

Terror.

Hope.

He cupped my jaw with one hand, gently tilting my face up. In that singular touch I saw each word he hadn't said. I saw his father waiting for him when he returned from delivering the books. I saw as he made his each guard punish Cassian. The guards that now included Kaden. I watched as bruises formed and blood spilled. I watched a father smile at his beaten son, and I watched that son witnessing his father kneel.

Then, slowly, Cassian turned, his eyes trailing through the fog, seeking. I followed his gaze—

The crown.

It lay just inches away, half-lost in the mist still clinging to the jagged edges of the obsidian room. The gold was scratched faintly, the edges gleaming with torchlight and truth.

Cassian reached for it with a hand that trembled.

And then, he knelt.

Not to the King.

Not to his father.

To me.

He bowed his head, his chest rising and falling with breathless reverence. With a kind of solemnity that made the world still, he lifted the crown with both hands.

He met my eyes one more time.

And then, he placed it on my head.

The weight of it settled across my brow, heavy and cold and final.

The obsidian room seemed to exhale.

The court of Aurea fell to their knees one by one, like dominos. Nobles, guards, advisors. Each and every one of them knelt. They bowed because instinct told them what words could not.

This moment wasn't defined by bloodlines or coronation rites.

It wasn't born of ceremony or tradition.

This was a crowning born of fire and fear.

The reign of the Silver Flame.

EPILOGUE

I STOOD BEFORE THE MIRROR and barely recognized the girl staring back.

White silk clung to my body like a second skin, heavy with beading and pearls that caught the candlelight and scattered it across the walls like stars. My hair had been swept into soft, elegant waves, coiled and pinned with glimmering silver threads that shimmered against my pale curls. Silver mesh gloves covered my hands. The fabric was thin enough for me to push my powers through, but just thick enough to give me the slightest hint of comfort. Of control.

The night previous, they had washed me in a bath tinted an olive brown, and now, a slight stain brushed over every inch of my skin. I was no where near the bronzed golden of Cassian, but the contrast had lessened. I looked more like them, like an Aurean. My eyes were lined in the deepest black and looked too sharp. Too foreign. I looked regal.

I looked like a queen.

I should've felt proud. I should've stood taller, breathed deeper, felt the weight of the moment with something more than dread. A week had passed since the final trial, and tonight I was to be presented before the court, the continent, all of Aurea. I was no longer a region girl, no longer a hidden name or a whisper in the shadows. I was the beginning of something new, but all I could think about was him.

Cassian had vanished into court life, into whispered strategy meetings and long silences. He would go days at a time in his disappearances, leaving only to return exhausted and drained. A part of me wondered. The other enjoyed the bliss of ignorance.

I stared at the flames dancing in the hearth. Watched as they licked up only to die out and return to ash or air. I stood slowly, and walked over to my armoire, opening the bottom drawer and pulling out my dress made of pale, icy blue fabric. The dress I had once purchased in another life. I carried the dress, folded neatly and nicely, over to the fire. The heat soaked into my skin, ate away at the cold floor biting my feet. I didn't hesitate as I took the folded dress and tossed it gently into the flames. I watched as they swallowed the fabric, turning the blue into something almost red in color before sizzling to black. The dress dissolved in the ash of the hearth, lost in the heat of the fire.

I wasn't the girl who had worn that dress a month ago. I wasn't the horrified girl, sent to her death. I wasn't vulnerable, and I wasn't dangerous. I wasn't a curse or a fairy tale.

I was to be a queen. I was to be Cassian's.

The golden thread that bound us still pulsed between us, faint but alive. I clung to it like a lifeline, so I followed it.

I left the heat of the fire, the stench of burning fabric. I slipped out of my room as I tugged on my pearl-lined flats, the beaded hem of my gown whispering secrets across the stone floors. As I left, I passed Kaden, back at his post. With me. He was still empty. The cracks I had found were resealed, but I would never give up on him.

My heart pounded in time with the thread's soft pulse, golden and warm, tugging me forward with a steady rhythm. Not just to his chambers. No, it pulled me farther. Beyond them.

I passed the battle-scene tapestry that hung on his wall without thinking, but this time, it moved. Just slightly, as if brushed by a breath of wind that didn't exist. I hesitated, and I listened.

There, beneath the hush of stone and the crackle of torches, were voices. Faint, but unmistakable. My breath caught. With trembling fingers, I reached out and drew the tapestry aside, and the voices sprung to life.

Behind it was a narrow passage. A spiral stair, carved into ancient stone, wound downward into the dark.

The air shifted the moment I stepped through. It turned sharper, older. Laced with something more ancient than the stone.

I descended slowly, each step echoing like a heartbeat. The moss-slick walls brushed my bare arms. The deeper I went, the stronger the bond thrummed in my chest. He was here. I could feel him.

I didn't know what I expected at the bottom. A hidden room, maybe. But what I found was a corridor lit with torches. The flames shivered as I passed, and my gown whispered behind me like a ghost.

I heard it then. A voice.

Low. Commanding. It was hardened in a way I didn't recognize, but beneath the gravel and grit, I knew that warmth. That honeyed thread.

I moved toward it like a moth to flame, though my limbs had gone numb. My breath caught in my throat as I reached the edge of the doorway and peered into the chamber beyond.

He stood before a gathered crowd cloaked in shadow. Figures cloaked in deep gray and navy bordering black, their faces hidden beneath veils and masks. Cassian's back was straight, his presence undeniable. But his face. It was masked.

A silver mask, blank and metallic, covered every feature. Horns raised and curled like that of a ram on either side of his head, the metal sharpening to points at the end of the curved arcs. Only his voice gave him away. That, and the golden bond still tethered to my heart.

He raised his hands, and silence fell. "We've waited long enough," he said, his voice booming across the moss-covered stone. "Aurea rots under their rule. Valerieth starves while nobles toast to golden harvests and feasts made from dust. But not anymore." His words hit like arrows, swift and sharp. They weren't untrue. And still, something in me began to fray.

"We are ready," he continued, voice louder now. "The pieces are in place. The court is fractured. And now…"

He paused. And I felt it. That moment before the knife drops.

"…we have the Silver Flame. We have our weapon."

I didn't hear the cheers. Didn't hear the murmurs or the thrum of approval rising from the shadows. I heard one word.

Weapon.

The word split something inside me wide open. I wanted to scream. To throw something, to break something, but unfortunately for me, Cassian took care of that. My heart was shattered.

I remembered the night I'd nearly destroyed everything. I remembered how he held me, how he had whispered against my hair as I trembled in his arms.

You are my weapon.

It had sounded like comfort then, but now it sounded like a cage dressed in gold. My stomach twisted. The torches swam before my eyes.

He knew. Cassian had known. He had known who I was or what I was. He had known before me. He hadn't stumbled into my story.

He'd been writing it. Molding it. *Using it.*

I was never a person to him. I was a weapon for his rebellion. I looked at him now and didn't see the man who held my hand in the gardens or kissed me like I was the only thing real in the world.

He didn't love me.

He didn't care about me at all.

And he was a liar.

Cassian Vaelros was a liar.

ACKNOWLEDGEMENTS

I FIRSTLY WANT to praise God for the opportunities and the blessings I have been given. He is the way, the truth, and the life, and I cannot praise Him enough for the constant grace and mercy throughout this project. Without Him, none of this would be possible, and I pray that every reader this book touches comes to know and love Jesus.

I am immensely grateful to my parents and family for their constant love and support throughout this wild journey that is writing and publishing. When I first broke the news to my mom about writing and publishing this book, I think she was taken-aback to say the least. She has never left my side throughout this entire process, and I genuinely would not have any words on these pages without her. To my dad, thank you for reminding me of reality. It sounds harsh, but without him I would not have remembered the actualities of this world and how cruel people can be. He kept everything real for me, and in the process, built me into the author I stand as today.

To my sister for reading this book before anybody should have, thank you for being kind while also saving me from the millions of headaches that would have been rereading and editing my own work. You have always inspired me to chase any dreams without remorse, and I cannot put my gratitude for you into words. To my brother who made sure to keep me laughing, thank you for keeping this adventure fun and exciting. You will likely never read any of my books, or this for that matter, but your constant, and sometimes irritating, jokes have helped more than you could have ever known.

Thank you to Delaney and Meagan for reading my rewritten and still very much in progress manuscript. You can forever get review copies from me. For life.

And lastly, this wouldn't be an acknowledgment page if I didn't list all of the people I do not have page space to ramble on about. So, thank you to my entire family. Grandparents, aunts, uncles, cousins, and friends of all of those people. Thank you to my friends who heard about this crazy idea and jumped onto the train with me.

From the bottom of my heart, thank you, thank you, thank you.

Thank you Mia. Thank you Andrea. Thank you Logan.

THE
GILDED
CROWN

Book Two in the Argentum Series

Coming Soon

FIND ME ONLINE!

Instagram: @author.paigenicole

TikTok: @authorpaigenicole

Website: www.authorpaigenicole.com

ABOUT THE AUTHOR

PAIGE NICOLE is a self-published author and founder of Olive & Ark Press. She is working towards her Bachelors of Science in Mathematics Education, where the only thing imaginary is $\sqrt{-1}$. Eventually, Paige hopes to teach secondary mathematics along with being an author. When she's not writing, illustrating book covers, or crunching numbers, you can find Paige on her "runs" (she only jogs), swimming in the lake, online shopping, or with an iced coffee in her hand.